To Glen,

The Deception

Happy reading and
thank you for
inspiring

Marin Martinlac
December 2013

The Deception

Marina Martindale

Good Oak
Press, LLC

Good Oak Press, LLC
P.O. Box 12195
Tucson, Arizona 85732

Editor: Cynthia Roedig
Proofreader: Jean Young, Esq.
Cover Design: Good Oak Press, LLC
Cover Illustration: Wes Lowe
Typesetting: Good Oak Press, LLC

ISBN : 978-0983938439

Printed in the United States of America.

This book is a work of fiction. The characters, corporations, publications and small businesses depicted in this story are fictitious. Any and all real locations have been used fictitiously and without any intent to describe any real individuals who may be affiliated with those locations. Any resemblance to any actual persons, living or dead, is purely coincidental.

Acknowledgements

Special thanks to the team who helped me create *The Deception*. To my good friend, Geneva Jarrett, for letting me bounce my ideas off you, for critiquing the early draft, for coming along with me to the Sandra Day O'Connor Federal Court Building, and for sitting up with me until well after midnight to help me with final proofreading. Thanks also for sharing your expertise as a registered nurse and helping me with the nursing home and hospital scenes.

Thanks again to my friend and editor, Cynthia Roedig, for another outstanding job. Once again, some of your comments had me rolling on the floor. I'd also like to say a special thank you to my proofreader, Jean Young, Esq., for taking the time to work with me to insure that all my courtroom scenes were accurate, and for helping me shape my three fictitious attorneys; Steve, Reggie, and, most especially, Alex, into believable, three-dimensional people. And finally, a big thank you to Wes Lowe for the outstanding cover illustration. Once again, it was a pleasure working with you.

To Dennis

"Oh! what a tangled web we weave,
when first we practise to deceive!"
— Sir Walter Scott

❧One❧

CARRIE DANIELS CLOSED her eyes and took a deep breath as she tried to quell her growing anxiety. She heard the loud clicking sound of the big metal chain pulling her up higher and higher. Her breaths grew shorter and tighter as she opened her eyes. The last thing she saw before the first big drop was the stark, clear blue sky. She heard herself let out a loud scream as the roller coaster plunged and whipped along the track. The butterflies roiled in her stomach as she held tight while the car zoomed around another hairpin turn before taking one last, final plunge. As the ride slowed to a stop she reached up to pull a loose strand of her long, dark hair away from her face before leaning over to give Doug a kiss.

"Happy anniversary."

"I don't know why you insist on calling it that," he said as he climbed out and began walking away.

"Calling it what?" She climbed out, picking up her pace to catch up with him.

"Our anniversary. Anniversaries are supposed to commemorate a specific date. Neither of us can recall the exact date anymore."

"I can to," she flirtatiously argued. "How could I forget our very first date? You took me to the opening day of the Arizona State Fair, and every year for the past ten years we've come back on opening day to celebrate."

1

This year, however, Doug didn't seem to feel like celebrating. He'd been acting strange for some time. Carrie kept asking him what was wrong but he kept brushing her off, claiming he had a heavier than usual workload at the office. She couldn't shake the nagging feeling that there was more to it. They walked in silence as they wandered into the carnival gaming area. Finally, she tapped him on the shoulder.

"Aren't you going to try to win a big teddy bear for me?"

He stopped and turned, rolling his eyes. "Carrie, you know these games are rigged."

"That never stopped you before. Every year you try to win the big teddy bear for me, so that makes it a tradition for us. And remember what you said to me the year before last? You said if you ever won it you'd propose to me."

"You know I never meant that literally."

"What's gotten into you, Doug? You've haven't been yourself for weeks and it's scaring me."

"I'm stressed out with work. You know that. And on top of that all I'm hearing out of you lately is that your biological clock is ticking. All these years and you've been telling me you weren't in any hurry for us to get married. Now all of a sudden, you're in a big rush."

"Well, if you recall, we celebrated my thirtieth birthday last month. I've finally come to realize I can't wait another ten or fifteen years to start a family. I want to have a baby, Doug, and I want to have it with you." Carrie noticed some of the people walking by were giving them strange looks. "Look, this isn't the time or place, okay. Let's just try to enjoy what's left of the day. We'll talk more about it later."

She walked up to one of the games, opened her purse and handed the man a twenty-dollar bill. He gave her some large plastic rings, which she began to toss. Much to her surprise, a few landed around the pegs. Once she finished the game operator presented her with a fluffy white teddy bear.

"Well," she said, beaming, "it may not have been the big bear, but at least I won something."

"Carrie, would you mind taking a seat?" Doug pointed to a nearby bench. "We need to have a little talk."

Her heart dropped like a ball of lead. Nothing good was ever said after those words were spoken. She sat down on the bench. As Doug sat next to her, he let out a sigh.

"Carrie, I want you to know that the last ten years have

2

been really great, and for a long time I really thought you were the one."

"What are you saying, Doug?"

He let out another sigh, glancing around the midway before turning his gaze back to her.

"It's like I just told you. Back in college, when we first met, I really, truly thought you were the one. I figured someday, you know, when the time was right, we'd take it to next level and get married, but lately things have changed."

"Look, Doug, I know things haven't exactly gone the way we planned." A hint of desperation wavered in her voice. "We didn't expect my mother to have a stroke and end up in a nursing home. We didn't expect for her insurance to run out, and that I'd have to deplete my life savings in order to pay her medical bills, but things are going to get better, I know it. I know it's been a strain on you having to pick up the slack, but my photography business is starting to pick up. It really is. I've landed two new clients in the past month. If you'll just be patient with me and hang on for a little while longer, I know I'll be able to start paying more of the bills. Things are going to get better soon, just wait and see."

"That's not it." He paused for a moment, squeezing his lips tightly together. "Carrie, the reason why I brought you here today is because I wanted us to go full circle."

"What does that mean?"

He let out another sigh. "It means, Carrie, that this is goodbye." He paused another moment, allowing it to sink in. "I want you to know that the past ten years have been some of the happiest of my life, but now the time has come for me to move on."

"Have I done something wrong, Doug?"

The tears were rolling down her cheeks, as he took her by the hand.

"No, Carrie, you haven't done anything wrong. You've been great. It's me." He paused and took another deep breath. "I've met someone else."

"What!" She snatched her hand back, as she began to recoil.

"A few months ago the company hired a new receptionist. Her name is Jennifer Logan. She's twenty-five, she's cute and she's single, and I've been attracted to her since the very first time I saw her."

"So what am I? Chopped liver? I've never allowed myself to get fat and lazy, nor have I ever taken you for granted."

"I know that, Carrie. You're still a beautiful woman. You've hardly changed since the first day I saw you, and don't think I haven't noticed other men looking at you."

"I've never encouraged it, Doug. I've never so much as flirted with another man."

"I know you haven't. You've always treated me right and I've never had to worry about you cheating on me. Please understand that I tried, very hard, to ignore my feelings for Jennifer. I really did. But over time, as I got to know her better, I just haven't been able to stop myself."

She did some mental calculations, while he was talking.

"Wait a second… it was right after the Fourth of July when you were suddenly having to work longer hours, wasn't it?"

"You're right. I haven't exactly been honest with you. I've felt bad about it, so I guess it's time to come clean. I wasn't working late. I was out with Jennifer."

"Doing what? Taking her to dinner? Going to the movies with her?"

He nodded.

"And what else were you doing with her, Doug? We're you sleeping with her too?"

"At first, no. I honestly thought she and I could just be friends. I really believed that if I gave it a chance to get it out of my system my feelings for her would change, but they didn't. You remember when I went up to Flagstaff last month for that weekend training seminar?"

She nodded, as she could no longer hold back and began weeping openly.

"I lied to you, Carrie. There was no seminar that weekend. Jennifer and I went up there for a romantic getaway. Yes, we paid for separate rooms, just in case you called the hotel, but we only used my room. I don't know how else to say it. I'm head-over-heels in love with her. I guess the reason why I never asked you to marry me after all these years is because deep down something was holding me back, but I don't feel that way with Jennifer. When I'm with her, everything just feels right, you know. I'm so sorry, Carrie. I never meant to hurt you."

She reached into her purse for a tissue. She continued to weep, unaware of the looks people were giving her as they passed by.

"Well, thank you very much, Doug." The sarcasm was heavy in her voice. "Not only have you cheated on me, you've added insult to injury by dumping me at a place that holds special memories for me."

"Now, Carrie, that's not what I meant to—"

"Shut up, Doug! Please don't insult my intelligence by trying to deny it. You brought me here, thinking you could do your dirty work and I wouldn't cause a scene. Well, guess what? You thought wrong."

"Carrie, let me take you home, okay."

"Home? Did you just say 'home?' Now that's ironic, isn't it? Because, as of right now, I don't have a home."

"Carrie, look, I know—"

"Didn't I just tell you to shut up, Doug?" She looked him squarely in the eye. "We both know full well that the only reason we bought the house in your name was because of my mother's creditors, so I guess I'm out of luck, huh?"

Doug remained silent.

"So I'll tell you what I'm going to do. I'm going to walk away from you, right now. I'm going to call a cab, and then I'm going back to your house to pack. Once I have all my things out I'll leave my key on the kitchen counter. After that, you'll never see or hear from me again. I just need ask one little favor."

"What's that?"

"Tonight I want you to spend the night with your whore, because I don't want you coming back until after I've left."

"Okay." There was a tentative tone in Doug's voice.

"Oh, don't worry. I won't be begging you to come back. Would you like to know why?" She leaned over to whisper in his ear. "It's because I don't put up with liars and cheaters, and that's what you are, Doug. You're a liar and a cheater, and I can't believe I was such a poor judge of character. You really had me fooled."

"All right, I probably deserve that, but what about you? Do you have a place to stay?"

"Does it matter?"

She stood and began to walk away. He got up and began to follow her.

"Carrie, wait!"

She stopped and spun around. "Leave me alone, Doug! You stop following me, right now, or else I'm calling the cops. Got it?"

He froze in his tracks. He watched her approach a young couple pushing a baby stroller. She stopped to talk to them for a moment before handing the stuffed bear to the baby. He heard them shouting thank you to her as she walked away. She soon disappeared into the crowd. He sat back down on the bench and watched the people going by. A short time later his phone rang. Jennifer was calling.

"So, did you finally dump her?"

"Yes."

"Good. I just got here. I'm waiting for you in front of the Ferris Wheel."

Doug returned home the following afternoon. By then, all of Carrie's belongings were gone. He found her key on the kitchen counter.

❧Two❧

CARRIE WAS AWAKENED BY the sound of her cell phone ringing. She rolled over and scooped it up from the floor.

"Hello." Her voice sounded groggy.

"So what the heck is going on with you?" asked the woman on the other end of the line.

"Louise?"

"Yes, Sweetness, it's Louise. Karl and I ran into Steve and Allison last night at Hernando's. Allison said Doug dumped you at the state fair, and that for the past few weeks you've been camping out in your photography studio, even though they've offered you their guest room. So what the hell happened?"

"I got dumped. Doug found himself some bimbo who he's decided he's in love with. I really didn't have a choice. I had to move out."

"What about the house?"

"It's deeded solely in Doug's name, but even if I were to make a claim on it, my mother's creditors would end up with the money."

"So why haven't you found an apartment?"

"I've been looking, Louise. The problem is they all want to collect some hefty deposits up front, along with the first month's rent. Unfortunately, because of Mama, I just don't have the cash to do it. Once I pay off my monthly expenses, the rest has to go to help pay her bills. Nursing homes aren't cheap, you know."

"I know that, but you need to find a decent place to live. Your studio isn't in the best part of town, and you're probably violating some city code by staying there. Not to mention the fact that Christmas is only three weeks away. I'll bet you don't even have a tree."

"Actually, all things considered, I'm doing just fine." Carrie tried to sound upbeat. "Yes, I'm renting warehouse space in an industrial area, and no, I won't be putting up a Christmas tree this year, but you needn't worry. I'm okay, really. The tent city jail is nearby so there's plenty of police and sheriff's deputies around. My break room has a mini kitchen, and I'm sleeping on an air mattress in the back room where it's surprisingly quiet. And back when I signed my lease I had the landlord put in a shower for the models to use. So you see, I'm okay. I have all the amenities I need to live comfortably. It's not like I'm living in a cardboard box underneath a bridge."

"I understand," said Louise. "However, the reason I'm calling is because I think I may have a solution for you, that is, if you don't mind doing another modeling gig."

"I haven't done a modeling job in years. You know that. Besides, I've just turned thirty. In the world of print modeling, I'm ancient."

"It's not a print modeling job. I need an art model. I've just picked up a private commission. Some well-to-do couple in Berkeley just bought themselves a big house. Apparently, they're serious practitioners of tantric yoga, or some such thing, and they want a serious of black and white photos of a female nude, with some curves on her, to display in their new home. You'd be perfect for the job."

Carrie let out a sigh. She desperately needed the extra cash, but she wasn't sure if this would be the best way to get it.

"I've done some nude work, Louise, but I was always behind the camera, not in front of it. All the photos were done for advertisements. Even though the models were nude, you didn't see anyone's privates."

"I understand if you feel a little shy about doing this, Sweetness, but you'd be working with me. They want something erotic so yes, they'll want to see all the goods in the photos, but

8

they won't know your name or anything else about you. You'll be completely anonymous and I promise you the photos will be tastefully done. It's fine art, not pornography."

"Who would see the photos?"

"They'd be for the client's personal, private use only. That's what's written in the contract. They can only be displayed in their home. The only people who would ever see them would be the couple themselves and whoever visits them. They're not allowed to publish them anywhere, not even on their personal blogs or websites."

Carrie let out a sigh as she thought it over. "How much does it pay?"

"Enough to put you into a decent apartment in a good neighborhood. It should cover all the deposits plus your first month's rent."

"All right. So when and where do you want to do the shoot?"

"Next Saturday, at my home. Karl has an early-morning tee time and will be spending the entire day on the golf course. It'll be just you and me."

"What time?"

"It'll be a fairly long shoot, so let's have you here early, about eight o'clock in the morning. Bring a curling iron and some nice barrettes along with your makeup kit. We'll be doing some different hairstyles, so we'll have to spend some time working on your hair and makeup throughout the day. And do you by chance have a pair of strappy, opened-toed shoes? Preferably in black."

"Yes. They're black patent leather."

"They'd be perfect, so bring them along." The excitement was building in Louise's voice. "The shoes, barrettes, and some costume jewelry are the only things you'll be wearing. You'll also need bathrobe that you can slip on in between shoots."

Carrie still wasn't sure. Louise must have sensed it.

"Look, Carrie, you don't have to do this. I can call the agency and have them send another model. I just figured that right now you needed the money."

"I know, Louise, and you're right. If the city were to find out I'm living here, they'd probably fine the heck out of me before my landlord kicked me out on the street."

"Good. We'll have you living in a decent apartment before you know it. We might even be able to get you a Christmas tree too. But I need to let you know one other thing."

"What's that?"

"I have a show coming up at Hanson Sisters Fine Art in February. I'd like to include five prints from our shoot as a series of hand-signed limited editions. They'd be sold with the same restrictions as the ones going to the couple in Berkeley. You'd remain anonymous, and the photos cannot be published or displayed anywhere in public, except of course for the gallery, but that would be the only time."

Carrie let out a sigh. There had to be a better way for her to get into an apartment. She glanced at the calendar hanging on the wall. It was the first week of December, the time of year when business normally slowed down. This year would certainly be no exception and things wouldn't start to pick up again until late January. If she didn't act now, she'd be living in her studio until March or April, and the longer she stayed, the greater the chances of someone finding out and reporting her to the city. She let out another sigh, knowing she had no other choice.

"Okay, Louise, I'm your girl. I'll be there, Saturday morning, eight o'clock."

"Good. You really won't regret this, Carrie. You'll be proud of these photos, I guarantee it. I'll email a contract and release form for you to sign. Make some copies for yourself and bring them with you on Saturday."

Carrie couldn't shake the bad feeling she started getting after she ended the call. She thought it over and realized she was probably just nervous. She'd never been photographed in the nude before, and the idea of total strangers looking at her naked body made her feel uneasy. Then again, she'd be doing it for Louise, and she owed her success to Louise's hard work. She looked at the clock. It was time to get up. She had work to do and she'd be better off focusing her thoughts on the nice apartment she'd soon be living in.

⚭Three⚮

CARRIE PULLED INTO Louise's driveway at exactly eight o'clock Saturday morning. She shut down the engine and hesitated for a moment before grabbing her duffle bag. She stepped out of her car and slowly approached the front door. She seriously considered turning around and leaving before mustering up the courage to ring the doorbell. She was soon greeted by Louise's smiling face.

"Come on in, Sweetness." She gave Carrie a big hug as she stepped across the threshold. "You're right on time. Would you like a cup of coffee?"

"No, thanks. I'm nervous enough as it is."

"I understand. I'll grab a cup for me, and then we can get started."

Carrie followed her to the kitchen. Walking behind her, she couldn't get over how little Louise had changed over the years. Neither her looks nor her attitude fit the image of a woman in her mid-fifties. Louise still had smooth skin and a shapely figure. There wasn't so much as a hint of gray in her curly red hair, and she had the stamina of a woman half her age. As soon as she finished pouring her coffee, she grabbed her mug and motioned for Carrie to follow her down the hallway to a small room that had been made into a dressing room.

"Okay my dear." She pulled out the little chair in front of the vanity. "Let's get your curling iron plugged in. I'll step out in a minute, and when I do you'll need to take all your clothes off and put your bathrobe on. My studio is in the next room and I'll be setting up the lights. I'll come back in a few minutes to help with your hair and makeup."

As soon as she left, Carrie nervously undressed and got into her bathrobe. Louise soon returned and grabbed the curling iron, saying that for the first shoot she'd pull Carrie's hair back into a loose ponytail, with some wispy, curly locks dangling around her face. Louise thought that particular hairstyle would show off her oval-shaped face and deep-set blue eyes. She quickly went to work preparing her for the shoot.

"You really were born to be a model, you know that," she said as she brushed some bright red lip-gloss onto Carrie's lips. "You may be thirty years old now, but you're still drop-dead gorgeous, and you're going to be beautiful even when you get to be my age. Doug was an absolute fool to let you go. Now, take a look at yourself in the mirror."

Louise stepped aside while Carrie studied her reflection. She had to admit she still looked pretty, at least on the outside. But ever since her break-up with Doug, she'd felt less than desirable on the inside.

"Now I need you to put on those sexy shoes of yours and I'll be back in a flash. I have a surprise for you." She rushed out, returning a minute later with a wooden box. "I found this the other day at a craft fair. It's all handmade and one-of-a-kind, and when we're done you can take it home with you. Think of it as an early Christmas present from me to you."

Carrie thanked her as she eagerly opened the box. Inside was a collection of beautiful handmade costume jewelry. There were necklaces, bracelets and earrings of all different colors, shapes and styles. They carefully went through and inspected each piece as they decided which ones she would wear.

"Let's start with this." Louise set a matching black-beaded necklace, bracelet and earrings down on the vanity. "I think they'll go nicely with your shoes. We'll use some of the other stuff later on. I'm going back into the studio. Come in as soon as you're ready and we'll get started."

Carrie put on the jewelry as Louise stepped away. When

she was ready, she took a final look in the mirror. She let out sigh and slowly walked into the photo studio. Louise had the lights set up in front of a gray, textured screen that was pulled out for several feet onto the floor. She pointed to the spot she'd marked.

"Okay, we've got a lot of work to do, so let's get rolling. We'll start with a few warm-up shots. Take your robe off and go stand over there."

Carrie's hands were trembling as she untied her robe. She slowly removed it and set it aside. Walking to the mark, she suddenly felt as if she were naked to the world. It was more than a little scary.

"You look tense and you don't need to be. You're a beautiful woman, Carrie. Everything about you is beautiful and perfect and you have nothing whatsoever to be ashamed of. The Victorian Age is over. It's high time we women stopped feeling so self-conscious about our bodies and learned how to love and accept ourselves, exactly as we are."

She told her to turn sideways, bend down and grab her ankles.

"That's good. Now, turn your head toward me, look into the camera, and smile."

Since nothing was really showing from that position, Carrie quickly began to relax. Before long her smile began to look genuine.

"That's my girl." Louise took a few more shots. "Now, I need you lie down on the floor, facing me, with one leg in front of the other."

Carrie immediately lay down on her side, placing her top leg out in front.

"Good. Now prop yourself up on your forearm, just like you're doing now, and rest your other arm on your hip."

As Carrie put herself into the pose, she felt the cool air on her naked breasts. She looked down, realizing they were now fully exposed. She started to tense up.

"Are you okay?"

"I don't know. I'm sorry, Louise. I really thought that I could do this. Now I'm not so sure."

"Wait right there." She quickly stepped out, returning a moment later with a glass of white wine. "I was saving this for later, but I think a few sips right now might help you to relax."

Carrie sat up and took the glass while Louise popped a CD into a player. The soothing sounds of a Beethoven symphony filled the room. She raised the glass to take a whiff of the wonderful aroma. It was a fine chardonnay, her favorite wine. She took a sip, savoring it in her mouth for as long as she could before she swallowed. She drank more of it.

"Not too much," said Louise, as she took the nearly empty glass back. "I want you relaxed, not loopy. Now, close your eyes, breathe in deep, and just listen to the music for a little while."

Carrie closed her eyes. She soon began feeling the effect of the wine as her back and shoulder muscles started to unwind. She resumed the pose, and Louise began to take the photos.

"There you go, that's my girl. Now look up at me and smile. There, that's perfect. I need you to move your front leg out a little more toward me. There you go. Perfect. Now, turn your head and look this way. Follow my finger with your eyes. Good."

Now that Carrie had finally lososened up things were starting to go more smoothly.

"Let's take a short break. I want to redo your hair and touch up your makeup. Then I want you to put on some different jewelry."

"Can I see?" asked Carrie, slipping her robe back on.

Louise handed the camera over and waited while Carrie scrolled though the shots.

"Oh my." Her face turned red. It was a bit of a shock seeing herself bare breasted, but the photos were tastefully shot. "They sort of look like Renaissance paintings, don't they? Too bad there's no man at home to appreciate them."

"Give it some time, Carrie. You're still young. There are plenty of men out there."

She handed back the camera and headed off to the dressing room where Louise restyled her hair and touched up her makeup. This time she wanted Carrie's hair to be long and flowing. After selecting different jewelry, she went to set up the lighting in another room. She returned a short time later and led her into the guest bedroom. Inside was a queen-sized four-poster bed, with the coverlet turned down.

"I'm going start by taking some shots of that beautiful backside of yours, so I want you to go stand by the foot of the bed. Grab hold of the bedpost with your right hand, with your back to me. Then, when I say, ready, turn your head and look over your left shoulder."

Carrie removed her robe and walked to the bedpost, turning her head back and smiling as Louise clicked away on her camera.

"You know, I just don't understand why women get so uptight about their rear ends," said Louise. "A nice, round, curvy bottom is a beautiful sight to behold. Now, keep holding on to the bedpost and turn towards me, just enough so I can see the side of your breast. There you go. That's perfect. Now, turn your head back, look toward me, and smile."

After she finished, she told Carrie to climb up on the bed.

"Don't worry about your shoes. I'm not concerned about the bedding. I just want you to look good. Now, I want you to go over to the corner at the foot of the bed."

Carrie began crawling toward the corner. She was trying to keep her shoes from touching the bedding, so her movements were a little awkward. She giggled as she crawled.

"Let's see if I can do this without falling on my fanny. You know, Louise, that wine is really starting to kick in."

"I'm glad you're finally starting to relax. This really isn't that different from the shoots we did all those years ago. Now, turn to face me and balance yourself on your knees. No, not like that."

Carrie started giggling again.

"Come on, work with me, Carrie."

"Sorry, Louise. For a moment there I was recalling the good old days, and how I sometimes used to horse around, just to see what you would do."

"I remember it well, and you have no idea all how many times I was seriously tempted to bend you over my knee and paddle your butt."

"But you didn't."

"No, I didn't, but that's only because you were the best child model I ever worked with. Now let's get back to work, young lady. I want you to face me and raise yourself up on your knees, into a kneeling position. Yes, just like that. Now, I need you to hold onto the bedpost with your left hand. That's right. Turn your head and the top part of your body toward your right and look up toward the ceiling. That's good. Now, lean back just a little and raise your right hand up to your forehead, like you're brushing the sweat off your brow. There, you've got it. That's perfect. Hold it right there."

"But Louise, this is full frontal nudity." Carrie was starting to feel uncomfortable again.

"You have a beautiful body, Carrie. Trust me, this pose is sexy and classy."

Carrie took a deep breath. Holding the pose, she thought

about the times back in history when women were told to lie back and think of England. As soon as Louise was finished, she told her to lie down on the bed, facing the camera as she was positioned into a more sexually suggestive pose. Laying there, fully exposed, she realized she'd just sold her virtue. The only thing left for her to do now was to put on her best face, act like a professional, and do whatever it took in order to get the job finished as quickly as possible. Her only consolation was the fact that once it was over she'd no longer be homeless.

"Carrie, hello? Did you not hear me? I said go have a seat in that leather chair."

"Oh, sorry."

She walked over to the leather chair in the corner of the room, where Louise photographed her in several more erotic poses, none of which held anything back from the camera. She felt as if her body was no longer her own. Even the most intimate part of her was now being put on display as Louise instructed her to lean back into the chair and spread her knees as far apart as she could. She could feel more of the effects of the wine. It all felt like a strange, surreal dream.

"I don't know what's gotten into you all of a sudden," remarked Louise, "but you've finally relaxed. Keep it up. You're on a roll."

As soon as she finished, she announced that it was time to break for lunch. Carrie slipped back into her robe, suddenly realizing that she was starving. At least it would be a day when she'd get to have a decent meal. She took her seat at the kitchen table.

"Well, Louise, it's certainly been an interesting morning working with you. I guess by now there's isn't any part of me that you haven't had a good, close look at."

"Indeed I have." She poured Carrie another glass of wine. "For awhile there I was worried that you were really a man in drag. Now I know for certain that you're not."

Carrie's face turned red at her attempt at humor, while Louise hoped that whatever had happened to finally put Carrie's mind at ease would remain for the rest of the day. They had several more sessions to go, and having to stop for her occasional bouts of discomfort had taken up precious time. She watched as Carrie eagerly ate her chicken salad and drank more wine. Hopefully her good appetite was another sign she had calmed down and would be easier to work with.

"As soon as we finish our lunch I want to photograph you taking a bubble bath. Later on I'll be taking some shots of you outside, by the pool. The sun should be at just the right angle in a couple hours."

"What was that?"

"Don't worry," assured Louise. "There's a block wall, and our patio was designed for maximum privacy. I'll only put you in those areas where no one else can see you. After that we'll be all done and you can jump into the hot tub if you'd like. By then, you'll have earned it."

"Thanks. Those photos may look sexy, but most of the poses you've put me in so far sure didn't feel very sexy. My back is starting to ache a little. I'm looking forward to the hot tub."

Louise offered to get some aspirin, but Carrie refused. Once lunch was over they headed back to the dressing room. Louise decided to put Carrie's hair up, again leaving some loose strands around her face, which she touched up with the curling iron. She also redid her makeup.

"Put these on." She pulled a pair of long, dangly earrings out of the wooden box. "This time you won't need any other jewelry. And take your shoes off."

As soon as Carrie was ready, Louise led her into the master bathroom where she turned on the faucet to draw a bubble bath in the large, garden bathtub. As the tub was filling, she adjusted the blinds and moved the light reflectors around.

"This is the time of day when the sunlight comes directly through the windows and it makes for some interesting light and shadows."

Once she was satisfied with the lighting, and the tub was filled to the right amount, she had Carrie step into the water.

"Jeez!" she exclaimed as she tried to settle in the tub. "The water's a little on the cool side, Louise. You know, I'd forgotten just how unglamorous the world of modeling can actually be."

"You're right, so quit being such a wimp. I didn't want the water to be too warm, because I don't want your face to sweat. Besides, it's making your nipples hard, which is what the client wants. Now, if you'll just cooperate with me, young lady, I'll get you out of there as quickly as I can."

Once again, Carrie followed Louise's instructions as she leaned back into the tub. The cool water, however, made the time pass much too slowly. It seemed like forever before Louise told her stand up and place a few clumps of the foamy bubbles around her hips and stomach. As they slowly ran down her body, she explained she was doing her own interpretation of Botticelli's famous painting, *The Birth of Venus*. Carrie was greatly relieved when Louise finally announced they were finished and handed her a towel. Dried off, they headed back into the dressing room for yet another hairstyle change, and then it was time to go out to the pool. The afternoon sun was making some interesting shadows. Carrie stood by, trying to warm herself in her robe, as Louise set up the light reflectors and laid a beach towel down on the deck at the edge of the pool.

"Okay. As soon as you're ready, I need you to come lie down on the towel."

Carrie removed her robe. The outside air was a little chilly, but the warmth of the sun on her skin felt soothing. She felt a tremendous sense of relief knowing it would be their final session. She prayed that after today she'd never have to pose in the nude again.

"I'm proud of you, Sweetness," said Louise. "You got the hang of this and it's really not so bad. Now turn on your side, facing me and prop your head on your elbow. Move your other arm back so it's resting on your hip and bend your top leg, pointing your knee up toward the sky. There you go. Now, look at me and smile."

Louise took a number of shots of Carrie next to the pool and just like before, each pose became more sexually explicit. Finally, she said she was finished, but Carrie's sense of relief quickly faded as Louise moved the light reflectors and told her to step into the shallow end of the pool. At least this time the water felt pleasantly warm. Louise mentioned it was a heated pool and told her to stay at the pool steps. Just like before, many of the poses she was positioned in were very erotic.

"Okay, my dear, that was the last one," she announced as she put the lens cap back on her camera. "Now I'll go turn on the bubbles and you can relax in the hot tub."

Carrie let out a big sigh of relief as she eagerly stepped out of the pool and jumped into the hot tub. Louise soon appeared with a fresh glass of wine. It had been a long day, and Carrie's back, shoulders and legs were all feeling tired and sore. It felt good to finally unwind in the hot, swirling water. Trying to relax, she decided it would be best to not ever think about who would see the photos. Throughout the day Louise had reassured her she would remain anonymous and that anonymity would go both ways.

"I guess I shouldn't allow myself get too comfortable in here." She paused to take a sip of her wine. "I need to head back to my studio soon. You're right, Louise. It's not in the nicest neighborhood, and I try to avoid going in and out after dark."

"Then why don't you stay here tonight, in the guest bed? You drank quite a bit of wine over the course of the day and I don't think you should be driving right now. Besides, you've got your makeup with you, and since you hardly wore your clothes they'll still be fresh and clean tomorrow. I've got some steaks in the fridge that we can cook out here on the grill, and Karl's only known you since you were ten. He's not going to feel uncomfortable with you hanging out in your bathrobe. If he should come home while we're still out here, I'll make sure that he steps inside whenever you decide to get out of the hot tub."

"Thanks for the offer, Louise. I brought my toothbrush, but I don't have a nightgown."

"And I'm afraid that I don't have one to lend you." Now Louise was blushing. "Karl and I sleep in the buff, so you may as well do like we do. There are plenty of extra blankets in the guest room closet, if you need them, so you'll be warm enough."

"Thanks, Louise. I appreciate it. I've been hungry for some real food for weeks now. I've been living on canned soup and TV dinners ever since Doug..." Her smile quickly faded as her voice trailed off and her eyes began to well up with tears.

"I know, Sweetness, I know. It's hard, but you're going to make it through this. You're much too beautiful for other men not to notice you and I'm going to prove it to you. Tonight, after dinner, we'll park Karl in front of the TV while we hang out in my office. The client wants eight photos. Together we'll pick out the best of the best, not only for my client, but for my show at Hanson Sisters too. Sound like a plan to you?"

Carrie felt a tremendous sense of relief. She'd have an opportunity to at least try to keep the most suggestive photos out of Louise's show.

"It does. Thank you."

"Don't thank me yet. I'm thinking that tomorrow morning, after breakfast, we'll go out and find you an apartment. One you can move into right away. I don't want you camping out in your studio anymore."

As soon as the dinner dishes were washed, Carrie followed Louise into her office. She pulled up a chair and waited as Louise downloaded all the photos onto her computer. She felt mixed emotions as she watched her weed through them. On one hand, all of them were esthetically pleasing. They showed off the curves and shapes of her body within the context of interesting lighting and shadow effects. On the other hand, many of the poses were very sexual, blurring the line between fine art and soft pornography. Yet somehow Louise had managed to make even the most explicit photos look tasteful.

"My goodness, Louise, I don't know what to say."

"I know today made you feel uncomfortable, Carrie, but you handled yourself like the pro you are. And you're still the most beautiful model I know, regardless of your age."

They turned their attention back the photos. It took some time for Louise to decide on the eight that would go to the client, and the ones she finally selected were the most sexually charged of the bunch. Once again she had to assure Carrie that those particular photos would never be published or displayed anywhere in public. She then asked for her input on selecting five photos to be included in the Hanson Sisters show. It was well after midnight by the time they'd made their final choices, but at least those five were less explicit than the eight that would go to the client. After they finished, Carrie said goodnight and headed off to the guestroom. She took off her robe and crashed into her bed. Within minutes she'd fallen into a deep, exhausted sleep.

⪼Four⪻

CARRIE STAYED OVER FOR breakfast the following morning. When they were finished, Louise handed her a check and walked her to her car. She immediately headed out to search for a suitable apartment and by midafternoon she'd found the perfect place. It was a furnished one-bedroom in a nicely landscaped, well-maintained complex in a nice part of town. It was also an end unit on the second floor, giving her less noise and more privacy. She signed a year lease and wrote a check for her deposits plus two months rent. The apartment would be ready the following Wednesday.

Carrie spent that Wednesday packing and moving her belongings. Settling in her new home, she decided the time had come for her to resume a more normal life. She gave Allison a call to invite her and Steve to dinner on Saturday night.

Carrie Daniels met Allison Santiago on their first day of high school. Carrie was sitting alone in the cafeteria, when Allison sat down across the table from her and introduced herself. They soon became best friends, and after high school both attended Arizona State University. Allison was now teaching English at a high school in the nearby town of Chandler.

"Merry Christmas," greeted Allison as Carrie opened the front door. "And something sure smells good in here."

21

"That would be my famous roasted chicken, with all the fixings."

As Carrie invited her friends inside, she noticed Allison was carrying the box for a small, pre-lighted Christmas tree. "Allie, you shouldn't have. I wasn't going to do Christmas this year."

"Yeah, that's what we figured, so that's why we brought it." She looked around for a place to put it. "I know you've had a difficult year, but it's still Christmas and I don't want my best friend becoming Ms. Scrooge."

She set the little tree on the end table next to the sofa and took off her coat. The bright-red sweater revealed underneath hugged her svelte figure. Steve handed her a box of ornaments and she began to decorate it while Carrie got a towel to use as a tree skirt. It was soon ready to be plugged in. Everyone cheered as the lights came on.

"I really don't know how to thank you." Carrie hugged her friends. "It's the most thoughtful thing anyone's done for me in a long, long time."

Dinner was soon ready to be served. Carrie asked her guests to take their seats, and joked about her mismatched tableware, explaining that with her limited means she had to purchase all her kitchen items at a thrift store.

"It's all very unique. However, if a dish gets dropped, or a spoon accidentally winds up in the garbage disposal, it's no big deal. I don't have to worry about finding a matching replacement. I just go back to the thrift store and get whatever they have."

Allison looked at Steve. "Now I know what to get her for Christmas. Dishes and flatware."

"No, you don't have to do that. I now have a decent roof over my head. That's enough of a Christmas present for me this year."

"I'm relieved you found this place too," said Allison, as she spooned some mashed potatoes onto her plate. "So how were you able to come up with the funds to move in here?"

"Louise called me. It was the morning after you and Steve ran into her and Karl at Hernando's. She got me a modeling gig. That's how I was able to do it."

"What was the modeling job?" asked Steve.

"Well, it was a different sort of gig."

"How so?" asked Allison.

"It wasn't for a print ad."

"Okay, then what was it?"

"It was an art modeling job for Louise. Some rich couple

in California hired her to take some photos to display in their home. She needed a model and I needed the money, so I told her I'd do it."

"What kind of photos?" asked Steve.

"Black and white prints. Of a female model."

"Nude?" asked Allison.

Carrie quickly picked up her glass and started drinking. Allison noticed her face was turning red.

"Nude," she said, answering her own question. "Carrie, you need to be careful about doing things like that."

"It's for Louise, Allie. I know her. She's on the up and up. She said the photos would be for the client's personal use only, and that they couldn't be published anywhere."

"I understand. I'm just saying be careful, that's all. So when's the shoot?"

"It's already been done. It was a week ago today, at Louise's house."

"Did you sign a release?" asked Steve.

"Yes."

"May I have a look at it? If you don't mind."

"Sure."

Steve was an attorney who also considered Carrie a friend. He waited while she stepped away to retrieve the paperwork. Once she brought it back to the table, he carefully looked it over. She watched his hand sweeping through his thick brown hair as he read. His looks reminded her of a model she'd recently photographed for an athletic shoe store ad.

"Well, it does appear to be on the up and up, and you're right. You're to remain completely anonymous and the photos can't be published anywhere. The only person who can display them in public is Louise Dickenson herself, and she retains all rights."

"That's pretty much standard business practice," explained Carrie. "She took the photos, so she owns the rights. I use similar release forms myself. I know Louise. She would only use them for legitimate purposes, like her portfolio. She's also including five of them in her show at Hanson Sisters Fine Art in February, but she assured me they'd be sold with the same restrictions as those on the Berkeley couple. The buyers can't publish them or display them anywhere in public."

"Well, that's all fine and good, but just remember, she does retain all the rights. You signed away your rights to your images in the model release form." Both women noticed his eyebrows furrowing. "There is, however, one little glitch, hidden away in the fine print, that does concern me."

"What's that?"

"She can sell the rights to photos to a third party, anytime, at her discretion. Hopefully, this won't come back to haunt you someday."

"What do you mean?"

"For instance," he explained, "let's say Louise had an unexpected financial calamity. I'm not saying she would, but it happened to you, so anything's possible, especially in this economy. She could, if she had to, sell the rights to photos to someone else."

"But wouldn't whoever she sold them to have to honor the agreement she made with me?"

"That's not specifically spelled out, however, it certainly could be construed to be within the intent of the agreement she made with you. Problem is, there's always some attorney out there who can sniff out any loophole in a contract and try to manipulate it to his client's advantage. We have a guy in our office who specializes in that very thing."

"What Steve is trying to say," explained Allison, "is that we want you to be careful. Yes, we understand you're in a bad position right now, but please, be aware when doing side jobs like this. Awhile back one of my coworkers had a sister in Los Angeles who was trying to get into showbiz. She was down on her luck and going through some hard times, kind of like you are, so she decided to do a photo shoot for *Gentry Magazine*."

"But isn't that supposed to be a somewhat mainstream publication?"

"It is, but here's what happened to my friend's sister. They did a fairly extensive shoot, but only published one photo. A couple years later her sister started getting guest shots on some prime-time television shows, so *Gentry Magazine* decided to do a feature on her and published more of the photos. After that, the only offers her sister got were for porn films."

"I see."

"I don't think Louise herself would ever intentionally harm you, but like Steve just said, if she ever decided to sell the rights to someone else, then it's entirely possible that the photos could end up in the wrong hands someday. That's the problem with those releases they make you sign. You give up all your rights."

"I know that," said Carrie, "but I trust Louise. I was eight years old when I first started working with her. That was back when I was doing those Mercer's Market ads."

"Mercer's Markets?" asked Steve.

"It was an Arizona supermarket chain," explained Allison. "They were bought out by another company years ago, but back when I was a kid, Carrie was their little spokesperson."

"Yep," said Carrie. "At the end of all their television commercials I'd pop up on the screen and do their jingle. I'd look into the camera and say, 'My mommy shops at Mercer's Markets. You're mommy should shop here too.' You'd also hear a sound bite of my voice, with the same jingle, at the end of all their radio ads."

"And there'd be a picture of Carrie, will their jingle underneath it, in all their newspaper and magazine ads," added Allison. "Louise is the one who shot all the photos for print advertisements. For a time there, Carrie was quite the little celebrity."

"Whose stardom ended at the ripe old age of twelve. By then I was getting too old for their pitch line and Old Man Mercer passed away. His sons were more interested in being real estate developers, so Mercer's Markets was sold to a national chain and my career as a child model was over, which was fine by me. I'd had enough of being in front of the camera. I wanted some semblance of a normal childhood."

"I'll bet you made good money while you were at it," said Steve.

"I did, and my mother invested it wisely. By the time I turned eighteen, I was able to pay for my own college education, and for a long time after that I was sitting pretty. Then Mama had a stroke. She ended up in a nursing home and I ended up in the poorhouse after her insurance ran out."

"What about your dad?"

"Your guess is as good as mine, Steve. He walked out when I was five. He hasn't been seen or heard from since."

Carrie noticed everyone's plate was empty so she got up to clear the table. They made small talk over dessert and before long it was time for Steve and Allison to leave. They lived across town so it would take some time for them to get home in all the holiday traffic. She helped Allison with her coat.

"You know, Carrie, I'm sure in this instance there won't be any problem with those photos. Louise will make sure they don't fall into the wrong hands, and that whoever buys any of them knows there are strings attached. But in the future, just be careful, okay?"

❧Five❧

BY THE TIME CARRIE arrived at Hanson Sisters Fine Art, Louise's show was well underway. It took some time for her to find Louise in the crowd. She finally spotted her standing near the bar.

"There's my Sweetness." Louise walked up to Carrie and hugged her. "Come, let me introduce you to these two folks."

Louise made the introductions as Carrie graciously said hello and shook their hands. The man then pointed to something on the wall at the opposite side of the room.

"You know, Louise, I think my wife and I have made our decision on which of the prints to buy."

"Really? Which one?"

"One of the female nude. The one of her lying next to the swimming pool."

"Good choice," said Louise with a smile.

Carrie stood by, nonplussed, as the couple stepped away. At least they hadn't recognized her. Louise turned back to her.

"Well, thank you, Sweetness. You must be my good luck charm. Can I get you anything to drink?"

"Just a club soda, thanks."

26

Louise turned to the bartender and ordered Carrie's drink. While he was pouring it, she mentioned she'd had a much bigger turn out than she'd expected. Many of the people who had come were old business associates whom she hadn't seen in years.

"It's been like old home week," she said as she sipped her cocktail, "and hopefully they'll spend lots of money while they're here."

Before Carrie could reply someone else approached Louise and started talking. After a brief introduction, she took her drink and excused herself. She walked around the room. The walls were lined with black and white and color photos, all hand numbered, signed and beautifully framed. Louise had presented a good variety of subject matter. Her show included urban street scenes, landmarks, and breathtaking panoramic landscapes taken all over the state of Arizona. She'd even thrown in a series of humorous photos featuring her cat. The ones attracting the most attention, however, were the five nudes.

Carrie worked her way toward that part of the gallery. She took her time, stopping here and there to chat with people and exchanging business cards with potential clients. She made a mental note to sign the guest book before she left. Artist openings could be a good place for her to network. She eventually arrived at the display of her images. The five photos they'd selected had all been printed in black and white, emphasizing the contrast between the light and shadows. She checked the hand-written numbers on the lower corners of the prints. Louise was offering each as a limited edition of fifty. Along with the one of her by the swimming pool was the one of her standing in the bathtub with foamy bubbles running down her body. The other three had been taken in the guest bedroom; one of her backside, along with the one of her kneeling on the bed, looking up toward the ceiling. The last one was the most sexually suggestive. She was leaning back in the leather chair and the lighting illuminated her breasts and lower torso. She was positioned with her knees spread apart, her head turned sideways and her eyes closed, making it appear as if she were napping. There was a small crowd admiring the photos. Carrie remained off to the side so she could listen in on their conversations. Much to her relief, all the comments she overheard about the photos were favorable. Everyone was either remarking about the use of the light and shadows, or about how well Louise had incorporated all the elements in the scenes to complement the shapes of Carrie's body. A few even mentioned how pretty the model was.

"Well, look who's here." She heard a woman's voice behind her. "I see you've returned to the scene of the crime."

"Steve! Allie!" Carrie greeted her friends with hugs and kisses.

"So these must be the notorious photos." Allison paused for a moment while she looked them over. "My, my, my. You weren't kidding when you said they were provocative."

One of the men admiring the photos turned around. "Well, hello there, Allison. I thought I recognized your voice."

"Scott! Fancy meeting you here." The two shook hands and Allison made the introductions. "This is Scott Andrews. He's one of the other volunteers for the children's reading program at the library. Scott, this is Steve Hudson, my significant other, and this is Carrie Daniels. She's been my best friend since high school."

The two men shook hands before Scott turned to Carrie. She noticed that he was quite handsome. He was tall, with salt-and-pepper hair and a pair of gold-rimmed glasses. As his eyes met hers a puzzled expression came across his face. He looked back and forth at Carrie and the photos.

"Yes, it's me," she finally admitted and blushed. "I was the model."

"Well, I don't know what to say." He shook Carrie's hand once again. "I've never met a nude model before."

"Carrie and Louise go way back," explained Allison. "Carrie's a photographer as well. In fact, Louise was her mentor. So when Louise needed a model, Carrie decided to return the favor. You know, professional courtesy and all that. Carrie really doesn't make her living by posing nude for photos. It was just a one-time thing."

"Well, you'd never know it by looking at them." Scott returned his gaze to the display. "The camera obviously loves you, and you look very natural."

"Thank you," replied Carrie. "I was once a child model so I'm quite used to working in front of the camera. That's also how I met Louise, but that was some twenty years ago." She went on to explain that her early work as a model was what got her interested in photography, and she talked about how Louise had helped her get her career started. Scott seemed to be very interested in everything she had to say.

"So, what's your story, Scott?"

"I'm a software developer. I work for Morton-Evans."

"That big defense contractor?"

"Among other things. They make other products too. I'm involved with writing some of their educational software; the programs that schools use to help teach kids the basics. You know, reading, writing and arithmetic."

"Is that why you volunteer at the public library?"

"Yes. Helping to teach youngsters how to read helps create the best reading software. So, do you have any kids, Carrie?"

"No, I'm afraid not." Her smile faded from her face. "I'd love to have them, but so far it hasn't happened. I've just ended a very long-term relationship."

"I'm sorry to hear that."

As Carrie and Scott continued their conversation, Steve and Allison decided to step away. Both were pleased to see that Carrie had taken an apparent liking to Scott. When the time came for the show to end, they were still talking. Steve and Allison came back to say goodnight. Once they left Carrie decided to call it a night as well.

"It was nice meeting you, Carrie." Scott extended his hand once again. "If it's okay with you, I'd like to take you to dinner sometime. That is, if you think you're ready to start dating again."

"I'd be honored to have dinner with you, anytime." She handed him one of her business cards.

"All right, then I'll call you, sometime soon. In the meantime, I'm going to buy one of your photos."

"Which one?"

"Hmm... I'm not really sure." He looked them over again. "You really are a beautiful woman, Carrie. It's hard for me to decide. I'm really torn between the one of you kneeling on the bed, and the one of you seated in the chair."

"Why not get both?"

He thought it over for a minute. "I guess I could."

They shook hands once more as Scott stepped away to complete his purchase.

"I'll call you, Carrie, soon."

"I look forward to it."

As soon as he left, Carrie went to look for Louise. She soon found her, once again standing near the bar.

"Goodnight, Louise," she said as she gave her a hug.

"Goodnight, Sweetness. I'm so glad you came. Sorry I wasn't able to spend that much time with you, but I noticed you were spending a lot of time talking to a nice-looking man. Who is he?"

"A friend of Allison's. He seemed like a nice guy."

"Did he ask for your phone number?"

"He sure did." Carrie's face was beaming.

"Good job, Sweetness, I'm proud of you. See, I told you that other men would find you attractive."

"I know. So, I guess we'll have to wait and see if he calls me or not."

"If he does, he does, and go out and have some fun. If not, it's no big deal. There are plenty of other fish in the sea. Just remember, the first one after a big break up is never a keeper. Enjoy it for what it is, but don't get too attached. Okay?"

"I won't, Louise. It's going to be awhile before I'm completely over Doug, but it feels nice knowing another man finds me attractive."

"That's my girl."

Carrie exited the gallery and got into her car. Waiting for the engine to warm up, she sent a text message to Allison.

"Is Scott by chance single?"

By the time she returned to her apartment Allison had replied. "He's single. Known him for years. He's never once mentioned a wife."

❧Six❧

SCOTT PULLED INTO THE driveway, pressed the remote, and waited as the garage door slowly rolled up. He was about to step on the accelerator, when he noticed the bicycle in his path. Annoyed, he let out a loud sigh as he threw the car into park and stepped into the garage. Bicycle moved, he got back in his car and pulled into his space. He shut down the engine and pressed the remote again. Once the garage door closed, he came into the house.

"Damn it, doesn't anyone know how to leave a light on around here? Someone could trip and fall over who knows what in the dark."

He felt along the wall for the switch, flicked the light on and went into the kitchen, where he spotted three large pizza boxes stacked on the counter. All were still warm, and each still had several slices of pizza remaining. The bottom box held his favorite—pineapple, ham and bacon. He reached into one of the cabinets for a plate.

"Hey, Dad."

"Hey there, Ben. So, how was school today?"

"Okay, I guess."

"Just okay, huh?"

The boy shrugged.

"So, how's Mom?"

"Okay, I guess," repeated Ben. "She says she's feeling better, and that by tomorrow she should be up and about."

"Until you or your sister bring home the next bug that's making the rounds at school."

Ben stood and watched while his dad fixed himself something to drink. "So how come you're home so late?"

"I stopped by an artist's opening tonight at one of our favorite galleries and I bought a couple of black and white photos."

"Where are they? Can I see 'em?"

"Later, son." Scott took his seat at the table. "They're still at the gallery, being framed. Meantime, your dad has had a long, hectic day, and he needs to kick back and take a breather. So where's your sister?"

"Upstairs. She says she's doing her homework, but she's probably hanging out on Facebook. So where are you going to hang the pictures, once you get 'em? It's not like we have tons of wall space left, you know. I swear, our house is turning into one big art gallery."

"Your mother and I are art collectors, Ben. And who knows, maybe someday we can sell off some of our collection to pay for your college education."

"Gee, Dad, why don't you let a guy get through the fourth grade first." Ben reached for a slice of the pepperoni pizza and began to walk away.

"Where are you going?"

"To watch some TV, if that's okay."

"As long as it's Disney Channel or Nick at Night."

"I know, Dad."

Ben disappeared. Scott listened to the sounds from the television set in the family room while he enjoyed his pizza. Finished, he put his plate in the dishwasher and headed upstairs. He walked down the hallway, softly tapping on one of the doors before opening it.

"Hey, Sarah. What's up?"

"Hi, Dad. I'm busy doing my homework."

"No Facebook," Scott bluntly announced.

"But Dad." He heard the whine in her voice.

"Don't 'but Dad' me. You know the rules, and don't think for one minute that just because you're fifteen now I can't spank you. No Facebook for you young lady until you're homework is finished. Period. That means all of your homework, too. And yes, I will be going over your Facebook wall later on tonight, just like I do every night."

Sarah began to grumble, but Scott stood his ground until she exited Facebook and opened the files with her homework assignments.

"I'll be back to check on you later, and I'd better not be catching you on Facebook."

He closed her door and headed down the hallway, walking into the master bedroom. "So how are you feeling?"

Maggie Andrews had been bedridden with a bad cold for the past three days. He could see that the color had finally returned to her face, but her nose was still bright red. Her fair complexion and short blonde hair made it even more noticeable.

"I think I'm slowly returning to the land of the living." The sound of her voice revealed that she was still heavily congested. "So how was the show at Hanson Sisters? Was it as good as the last one?"

"It sure was, and I bought two new pieces to add to our collection of nudes."

"Really?"

"Yes," He motioned to the photos of a blonde nude on one of the walls. "This time the model is a brunette, a really pretty one too, and the photos are nicely done. They have to be framed. They should be ready day after tomorrow."

"I see. So where do you think we should put them?"

"How 'bout right here." He pointed to the wall directly above Maggie's head. "Over the bed is perfect. We can find a spot somewhere downstairs for the painting that's there now."

"All right. I should be up and about in the next couple days, so I'll pick them up and hang them over our bed."

✌Seven✌

CARRIE HEARD THE BEEP from her cell phone. She picked it up off the coffee table and smiled. It was a text message from Scott, asking if she was busy that day.

"Not too busy for you," she replied.

It was a Saturday morning. She'd just returned from doing her laundry and had no place special to go. Her phone beeped again. This time Scott wanted to know if he could stop by.

"Of course," she replied. She gave him her address and took her phone with her as she headed off to change her clothes. Scott soon replied to let her know he'd be there in about an hour. Exactly one hour later she heard a knock at her door.

"Come on in, Scott. It's good seeing you again."

"Likewise, although I now have those two photos of you hanging on the wall over my bed. You're the last thing I see before I go to sleep at night, and the first thing I see when I get up in the morning."

"I see." His comment, while well meaning, still made her feel a little ill at ease.

"So," he asked, "what plans have you made for today?"

"None so far, I'm afraid."

"In that case, what would you say to taking a little drive and perhaps going hiking at Lake Pleasant?"

"I'd love it." Her eyes lit up as she spoke. "I'll go get my camera."

He waited patiently as she grabbed a sweater and loaded up her backpack. A few minutes later he led her to a late-model, bright-red Chevy sedan in the visitor's parking lot.

"Nice wheels," she said as he opened the passenger door for her.

"Thanks."

He waited for her to settle in and fasten her seatbelt, then he slipped behind the wheel and they headed out.

"So, how have you been?"

"I've been good," she replied, "and I'm trying to keep busy. I'm in a feast or famine business. Last fall I was really swamped, but for the past couple of weeks it's been slow, so I'm doing some marketing. It looks like I'll have some new jobs coming my way in the next week or two."

"Good to hear. I always seem to be busy. I have to work long hours and put in a lot of overtime. As much as I'd like to be able to spend time with you, Carrie, you need to understand, upfront, that I'm just not going to be that available. But I'll still try to see you as often as I can."

"No worries. I sometimes have to work long hours myself and I'm not looking for anything serious right now. Remember, I just got out of a long-term relationship, and to be honest, I'm really enjoying having some time on my own."

They stopped for lunch, sharing a large order of fries with their burgers. Scott managed to brush his hand against hers a few times as she reached for a fry. He tried to make it look unintentional, but Carrie knew better. She gave him a wink in return. She enjoyed flirting with him. As soon as they arrived at Lake Pleasant they hit the hiking trails. Along the way she stopped to photograph the desert, the lake, and the mountains. They finally stopped to rest at a spot with a scenic view, where they would remain for the next few hours.

Scott continued to be fascinated by Carrie's stories of being a child model and local celebrity. He was surprised to hear that her childhood wasn't as happy, or as glamorous, as it appeared. While other girls her age played sports, took dance lessons, or just hung out with their friends, Carrie spent long hours in makeup chairs preparing for TV commercials or photo shoots and working under hot lights in dusty, draft-filled rooms. She made good grades at school, but she found herself rejected by her peers. The other children, particularly the other girls, were jealous, making her a social outcast. She described how painful it felt to be shunned and ridiculed by her classmates. She became a loner, with her only real friend being a boy named Alex. Allison would come along later, but by the time she finished high school, Alex and Allison remained her only real friends. Alex ended up going to college back east and they drifted apart once Doug came along. Even as an adult, however, Carrie remained a loner. Doug, Allison and Louise were still the only people she really knew.

Scott wrapped his arm around her and she leaned against him as she talked. Afterwards he silently held her while they watched a spectacular sunset. The clouds turned pink and red as the sky turned orange, purple, and finally, a deep indigo blue. Carrie captured the images of it on her camera. It was nearly dark by the time they made their way back to Scott's car. He drove around some of the back roads, eventually pulling over and parking in a secluded area. A full moon illuminated the night sky, creating stunning silhouettes of rocky hilltops dotted with saguaro cactus. He reached down and reclined his seat back, saying that he wanted to kick back and relax for a little while. They'd been enjoying the view for sometime when he finally broke the silence.

"Carrie, if you could describe yourself in one word, what would it be?"

"Well, I'll have to think about it for awhile."

Scott patiently waited for her response.

"Whole. That would be the word. I'm becoming whole. Last fall, when my ex first dumped me, I felt like I was broken and I didn't think I could ever be fixed. Now that some time has passed, and I'm learning how to live my life on my own terms, I'm beginning to feel whole, like I'm becoming a whole new person. So, what about you, Scott? What one word would you use to describe yourself?"

"Adventurous." He reached over to grasp her hand. "Safe and predictable bores me. I much prefer to live on the edge, in the spur of the moment, in the here and now."

He turned to face her, and as he looked into her eyes, he leaned forward and kissed her. It was a soft gentle kiss. When it was over, he began to slowly run his fingers through her hair.

"Carrie, I'm not going to make any promises about the two of us living happily ever after someday, but I want you to know something. I think you're an amazing woman. I also want you to know that I'm willing to take things as far as I can, for as long as I can. The only thing is, with my crazy workload, I just don't know how often I'll be able to see you. Please understand that most of the time it will be just like today. We'll have to do things at the last minute, and on the spur of the moment. But I can promise you this—it'll always be an adventure."

"I understand, Scott. Like I said before, I'm not ready for any kind of a commitment, from you or from anyone else. So let's just enjoy the here and now."

He kissed her again. This time his tongue went into her mouth as he slowly inched his hand down toward her breasts.

"Carrie, I'm not going to make love to you tonight, but I need to know something. Are you using any kind of birth control?"

"Yes, I use the rings."

He kissed her again. This time he reached down and began gently stroking her breasts. He could feel her body tensing up. He stopped and began caressing her face.

"It's been a long time since a man's touched you, hasn't it?"

She knew she was allowing herself to get too involved with him too quickly. Then she recalled Louise's comment about the first one after a break up never being a keeper.

"Yes." She looked into his eyes. "It's been a very long time since a man has touched me."

"That's what I thought. You know, you're much too beautiful of a woman to be all alone in the world. You need someone who'll appreciate you. I'd like to be that someone, if you'll have me."

As he began kissing her again, he started to unbutton her blouse. Once again, Carrie began to tense up.

"I don't know about this, Scott."

"It's okay. I know you're still getting over your last relationship, but it will be all right, I promise. I'm not going to do anything to hurt you."

He began to kiss her again. The next thing she knew her blouse was completely unbuttoned and his hands were reaching inside her bra.

"You've been without a man for far too long," he whispered as his fingers gently caressed her nipple. "Just relax and let me touch you." He kissed her again as he reached back and unhooked her bra. He pushed it away and began licking and sucking her breasts. It was all happening much too fast. "You're beautiful, Carrie, so incredibly beautiful."

He kept kissing her and stroking her. She liked the feeling of being desired and her resistance waned. Against her better judgment, she allowed him to take off her blouse and bra. Topless, Scott began to kiss and stroke her even more passionately. Soon he was unzipping her jeans and reaching inside her panties.

"I still don't know about this, Scott."

"It's all right, Carrie. Like I said, I'm not going to make love to you tonight, but I would enjoy giving you a massage. Just relax and enjoy it."

He reached over and pulled the lever to recline her seat. Seatback down, he began kissing her again as gently caressed her legs and slowly pulled her jeans and panties off. She closed her eyes as he viewed her naked body.

"Those photos don't do you justice. You're even more incredible in person."

She felt his hand gently stroking her across her hips, down her thighs and, finally, between her legs. As his fingers began working their magic she felt a warm, wonderful sensation. She moaned with pleasure as she spread her knees apart and opened herself up to him.

"There you go." He gently kissed her on the cheek as he whispered in her ear. "Just let me touch you and make you feel good. And you can make as much noise as you want, Carrie. There's no one else around and I want you to enjoy yourself."

He leaned over to kiss and lick her breasts as his fingers kept working. Carrie's pleasure grew and her moans became louder. The more she moaned, the stronger and more intense his touch became, creating even more pleasure for her. She arched her back and cried out, louder and louder. She let out a yell when she finally climaxed. Scott's lips covered hers as her body slowly began to relax.

"So, how was it, baby girl?"

For the moment, Carrie was unable to respond. She was lost in the afterglow. He reached over and gently brushed her on the cheek. He unbuttoned his shirt and began kissing her again. Suddenly, his cell phone started to ring.

"Aw nuts," he said in frustration as he checked his caller ID. "Sorry, Carrie. I'm going to have to take this call. It's an overseas client."

She gave his hand a quick squeeze as he stepped out of the car. He took a few steps away, trying to regain his composure before answering.

"Yeah, Maggie. What is it now?"

"Oh, nothing." There was a distinct whine in her voice that grated on his nerves. "It's just that it's getting kind of lonely around here. Sarah's spending the night tonight at Dana's, and I've just put Ben to bed."

"I see. Well, the guys are getting ready to play some poker. I was going to stay and play a few rounds."

"All right, Scott. So exactly when do you plan on coming home?"

The whine in her voice turned into a pout. He knew if he stayed out too long he'd come home to yet another ugly confrontation. He looked back at his car before letting out a frustrated sigh. Carrie certainly wasn't on the prowl, so the odds were she wasn't going anywhere soon. Next time, however, he'd be sure to leave his cell phone at home, in a spot where Maggie could easily find it. That would put a stop to her interruptions and she'd buy his explanation that he simply forgot it.

"Okay, okay. Dave is getting ready to light the grill. I'll have a bite of dinner and play a few rounds after that. Then I'll head home. I should be there in another couple hours or so." He disconnected his phone and walked back to the car.

"I'm sorry, honey," he said as he opened the door and slipped back into the driver's seat. "My client is having a real meltdown. I'm going to have to head back to the office and put the fire out."

"It's okay, Scott."

He watched as she tucked her blouse back into her jeans. The way she swayed her hips as she readjusted her clothing excited him. He'd just finished his appetizer and he looked forward to the main course. As she settled back into her seat, she pulled her hairbrush from her backpack and began brushing her hair. It was long, shiny and incredibly sexy. He yearned to feel the touch of her silky locks brushing against his skin. Sadly, it would have to wait until another time. He let out another sigh as he raised the driver's seat back up and fired up the engine. They stopped for a quick bite of dinner at another fast-food place on the way back. Arriving at her apartment complex, Scott walked her to her front door.

"I've had one of the best days I've had in a long time, Carrie. I promise I'll come see you again, real soon. I just don't know when that will be."

He gave her another long, lingering kiss before they finally said goodnight. He waited until she was safely inside before walking back to his car. When he arrived home, he found Maggie upstairs in bed, watching an old black and white movie on TV.

"Hi, honey. Did you have a good time with your buddies?"

"Sure did."

Scott was still aroused and he needed some relief. He sat down on the bed and began kissing Maggie.

"My goodness," she said, when she finally came up for air. "I don't know what's gotten into you, but if spending the day hanging out with your buddies does this to you then by all means, I think you should do it more often."

Undressed, he grabbed the remote and turned off the television before pulling up Maggie's nightgown. She reached for the lamp on the nightstand.

"No, leave the lights on."

Maggie started to giggle. The sound of her laughter irritated him. He dispensed with the foreplay so he could relieve himself as quickly as possible. He climbed on top of her and as he entered her he looked up at the nude photos of Carrie, hanging over the bed. Tending to his needs with Maggie, he kept his eyes on the photos and imagined he was with the nymph with the long, dark hair.

❧Eight❧

THE ALL TOO FAMILIAR feeling of dread filled Carrie once again as she entered the parking lot and pulled into a space. She scooped up the bouquet of flowers, stepped out of her car, and headed toward the front door. The signage over the entrance read, "Sierra Arroyo Long-Term Care," but she knew full well what it really was. It was a house of death. It was a place where worn-out, broken-down people came to die. She muttered Dante to herself as she stepped into the lobby to sign in at the front desk.

"Abandon all hope, all yea who enter here."

"Good morning, Carrie," greeted the receptionist.

"Good morning, Heather."

"Mr. Greene would like to talk to you."

Carrie let out a sigh. "I have a check. Is he in his office?"

"Yes, it's down the hall."

"I know where it is."

She walked down the hallway leading to the administrative offices and tapped on his door. He looked up and smiled, inviting her in and motioning to her to take a seat.

"I know what you're going to ask, and yes, I have a check for you." She opened up her purse and handed it to him. "I know it won't cover everything, but it's the best I can do for you this month. You have to understand. Ever since Doug and I split up, I just don't have the funds I had before. I'm now having to pay rent on an apartment."

"I'm aware of that, Carrie," he replied. "Look, I admire your spirit and your determination to take care of your mother, but you're fighting an uphill battle. The cost of her care is going up faster than you can keep up with it. It's time for you to make her a ward of the state."

"I can't do that."

"I understand if you're worried about the quality of her care, but I can assure you that nothing will change. She'll continue to receive the best care we can possibly give her."

"You don't understand. I don't take handouts. That's the one thing that she taught me never to do. She's my mother. I have a responsibility to her. She took care of me, and now it's my turn."

"I get that," he replied, "but you're taking on a debt that you may never be able to repay. It's like I just told you a minute ago. The cost of her care is going up while your ability to pay is going down. Carrie, I can only do so much. The bean counters at the corporate office don't care about your circumstances. They only see the red ink, and even though you're writing us a check each and every month, you're still falling behind. There'll be a time, probably sooner than you think, when they'll turn her account over to collections. At that point, you won't have much of a choice."

"I'm doing the best I can, Mr. Greene."

"I know you are, but please, just think about it, okay? Whenever you're ready, let me know and I'll help you with the paperwork."

She thanked him before leaving his office and headed to her mother's room.

"Good morning, Carrie," said Hilda as she came in. Hilda had a kind heart. She also looked as old as most of the patients she cared for.

"Good morning, Hilda. How's she doing today?"

"About the same. Take a look for yourself." She turned to her patient. "Linda, you have a visitor. Look who's here?"

"Hi Mama. I brought you some pretty flowers today." Carrie set them down on the small table next to her mother's bed.

Linda Daniels was only in her mid-fifties. Like Louise, her

skin was still smooth and she had very little gray in her long brown hair, but that was where the similarities ended. The stroke she'd suffered left her brain damaged and the right half of her body was permanently paralyzed. In the three years since the dreadful night it happened, her condition had remained virtually unchanged.

"Would you like for me to brush your hair for you, Mama?" asked Carrie. "Then when I'm done, I can braid it. A little braid down the side would sure make you look pretty."

Linda's eyes followed Carrie as she found her mother's hairbrush and began brushing her hair. Once she finished, she picked up a lock and started braiding it. As she worked she wondered how much, if anything, her mother could still comprehend.

"So, how's the rest of your life going, Carrie?" asked Hilda. "Did you get moved into that new apartment yet?"

"Sure did. I've been there since December."

"Good. I was worried about you being camped out in your office. It's not in the best part of town, you know."

"I know, but I kept my doors locked and I didn't venture out after dark."

Hilda looked at Carrie more closely. "Are you all right? You look a little upset about something."

Carrie finished the braid and looked for a rubber band. Hilda found one and handed it to her.

"It's Mr. Greene," she replied. "I just got called into his office, and I felt like a schoolgirl being sent to the principal. I'm doing the best I can, but he feels that it's time to make Mama a ward of the state."

"Well, I certainly can't tell you what to do, but I will say that if you were my daughter I'd want you to be living your life and putting some money away for your own future. You need to think about having a family yourself someday."

"Yeah, like that's going to happen. I'm thirty years old and my boyfriend just dumped me."

"Oh, listen to yourself. You're young, you're beautiful, and there's some man out there who's going to want you. You still have plenty of time to have a family."

Linda started making grunting, babbling noises. Hilda turned to check on her.

"See? You're mother agrees with me. We both know what's best for her, don't we, Linda?"

"I understand what you're saying, Hilda, but the one thing my mother taught me was to never ever to take a handout. Not from anyone. I guess we Daniels women are destined to be working poor. I've already come to terms with the fact that I'll probably never get to live in a fancy house or drive an expensive car, but I can still have a roof over my head, even if I have to camp out in my photography studio, and I'm still able to eat, even if I only get to have peanut butter and jelly sandwiches. At least I won't be starving."

Linda started becoming agitated and Carrie was unable to calm her down. Hilda finally had to have one of the nurses come in and give her a shot. Once she'd finally settled back down, Hilda left to tend to other patients. Carrie took a seat next to her mother's bed.

"It's all right, Mama." She reached over and took her mother's hand. "I'm sure I'll figure out something and it'll all turn out okay in the end. I promise."

She held her mother's hand until she fell asleep. When she finally appeared to be resting comfortably, Carrie got up and quietly left the room.

᪣Nine᪣

L OUISE'S SHOW AT Hanson Sisters Fine Art was a smashing success and the critics raved about her work. Carrie received some benefit as well. A few of the people she met on opening night were Louise's former clients, and in need of a commercial photographer. At long last, her photography business was getting a much-needed boost.

Having more clients meant working longer hours and occasional Saturdays. This particular Saturday would be four weeks to the day that Scott had taken her hiking at Lake Pleasant. They had started emailing one another, and a few times she'd been taken aback by the explicitness in some of his messages. He'd also invited her to dinner a couple times, but on both occasions he canceled at the last minute. It was always the same excuse—an emergency at the office. Carrie was glad she hadn't expected too much from him or the relationship. Scott was either a total workaholic, or perhaps he had another girlfriend. The latter was a possibility she'd not considered before.

She let out a sigh as she went back to work. She needed focus on setting up the lights and getting her subject matter ready. She was photographing auto parts. While hardly a glamour job, she was charging the client a handsome fee, which would go a long way toward paying some of her bills. She'd just finished shooting her photos when she heard her cell phone beeping. It was a text message from Scott.

"Busy today?"

"Yes," she replied.

"How busy?"

"Busy, busy."

Her phone began to ring.

"I hope you're not mad at me," said the voice on the other end.

"No, I'm not. Seriously, Scott, I really am in my studio. Business has picked up lately so now I'm working Saturdays too. You of all people should understand."

"I do, but you have to eat sometime and I still want to take you to dinner. When do you think you'll be done?"

"Let's see..." She glanced at her watch. "If all goes well, I should be home by five o'clock."

"Then why don't I pick you up at six? And wear something nice. The place I have in mind this time is a little fancier than a fast-food joint."

"You got it. Six o'clock it is. See you then"

She ended the call and went back to work. By the time she arrived home, she was beat. She debated whether she should bother getting ready. Scott had already disappointed her twice. If he canceled their plans this time, she'd take her cue and move on. She headed off to the shower, and it was only a couple of minutes past six when she heard the knock on the door. She looked through the peephole and smiled. This time he arrived, right on time. He greeted her with a long, passionate kiss.

"I don't know about you, but I'm starving." He gave her another long, passionate kiss.

"Me too."

She grabbed her purse and as they headed out to his car he mentioned the restaurant they were going to was across town.

"Isn't that kind of out of the way?"

"Maybe," he replied, "but we'll make tonight an adventure."

Over dinner Carrie discussed her new projects. While it was apparent that she loved her job and was excited about her work, Scott really wasn't listening that closely to what she had to say. He was much more interested in the low-cut, little black dress she had on. He kept seeing images in his mind of her dropping some of her food down her front and him having to lick it off. Finishing the main course, the waitress asked if they wanted dessert. He ordered a slice of chocolate cake, asking her to bring it in a to-go box.

"Why don't we have dessert at your place? We can take our shoes off, get more comfortable, and maybe listen to some music."

"Sounds like a plan to me," she replied. "It's been a long day. I'm ready kick back and relax for awhile."

They made small talk on the way back to her apartment. Once inside, she set the cake down on the kitchen counter.

"I'll be right back. I want to take my shoes off before we have dessert. Go ahead and make yourself at home."

Carrie headed off to her bedroom. Scott followed right behind her.

"Scott, what are you doing?"

"Making myself at home."

She heard the flirtatious tone in his voice. She laughed as she sat down on the edge of the bed. He sat down next to her.

"Okay, okay," she said with a smile. "Just give me a minute. I can only stand wearing high heels for so long." She reached down to unbuckle the shoes.

"I recognize those. You wore them in the photos, didn't you?"

"Yep." She took off the shoes and tossed them aside.

"You know, they're incredibly sexy shoes, and they really turn me on."

He began kissing her, his tongue probing her mouth. He reached back to unzip her dress. He stroked her breasts as he slowly pulled the top part of her dress down. He began kissing her again, this time reaching back and unhooking her bra. Kissing her breasts, he pulled off her bra and tossed it aside with the shoes. He smiled, and gently eased her down across the bed. He looked into her eyes, stroking the side of her face.

"You know, Carrie, every night, before I go to sleep, I look at those photos of you, wearing nothing but those shoes, and I get hungry for you. You look delicious. So, if you don't mind, I think I'll skip the cake and have you for dessert instead."

He removed his shoes and trousers before pulling off her dress and tossing it next to her shoes. He smiled in delight at the sight of her low-cut, black-lace panties. He was licking and sucking on her breasts again while he unbuttoned his shirt. He tossed it aside and knelt down on the floor in front of her, running his fingers back and forth across her panties.

"Scott, what are you doing?"

He stroked her panties once more before pulling them off and removing his briefs. Placing his hands on both of her knees, he spread her legs as far apart as they would go. He stopped for a moment to gaze into her, and then Carrie began to feel his soft, gentle caresses between her legs. Her heart began to pound. She'd been a virgin when she met Doug. This would be her first time making love to another man. She moaned in pleasure at his touch. She felt one of his fingers probing into her. As Scott began exploring deep inside, something he touched gave her an intense surge of pleasure that made her gasp and jump.

"Did that feel good, baby girl? There's more where that came from. You really are a beautiful woman, Carrie. In fact, you look good enough to eat."

He kissed the inside of her thighs. Her moans grew louder as she felt him licking her between her legs. Her body began writhing uncontrollably. She'd never experienced anything so intense before. Scott kept massaging her, inside and out, with his finger and his tongue. Her moans grew louder as she continued to writhe.

"Yes, Scott," she groaned, "yes, yes, yes."

Just as she was about to climax he stopped licking her and removed his finger. He quickly thrust himself into her. She wrapped her arms and legs tightly around him as she pushed and rubbed herself against him as hard as she could, crying out in her ecstasy. Her pitch reached a crescendo as she climaxed, again and again and again. Once she'd finally exhausted herself it would be his turn. She kept her arms and legs tightly wrapped around him. He thrust himself back and forth as hard as he could until she felt him pulsating deep inside her. Reaching his release, he slowly collapsed onto the floor in a state of blissful exhaustion, resting his head on the inside of her thigh. Neither one moved or spoke for several minutes. Finally, he opened his eyes. He noticed her legs were still wide open. He leaned forward, gently kissing her before climbing up to lay down across the bed next her. He began running his fingers through her hair as he whispered in her ear.

"Carrie, you were incredible."

She began wondering what she'd gotten herself into. She knew their relationship wouldn't be long-term, but she also knew it was going much too fast. She looked into his eyes. He smiled back and gently kissed her again. He'd been upfront from the beginning. It would be a fling, nothing more. Perhaps his intention was to get the most out of it in whatever time they'd have together. Once it was over, she hoped she'd ready to move on to a more lasting relationship. She let out a sigh as she sat up.

"I need to take a shower, and then we'll have dessert."

"Darling, don't you know? You are the dessert."

"Would you like to spend the night, Scott? It's getting late, so what would you say to staying over and having breakfast together?"

"I wish I could, but I can't." He began to stroke the side of her face. "Believe it or not, I have to be at the office early tomorrow morning for phone conference with a foreign client. But we'll definitely be getting together again, soon."

Once he was dressed, he stopped to give her long, passionate goodnight kiss before heading off to his car. Arriving home, he was happy to find Maggie out like a light in front of the television set in the family room. He left her where she was as he silently headed upstairs to check on the kids. Afterwards, he got ready for bed, relieved that Maggie still hadn't come upstairs. He hoped she'd stay where she was for the rest of the night. Before climbing into bed he stopped to admire the nude photos of Carrie.

"Wow. Not only did I get to have a really great piece of ass, I get to have keepsake mementos to remember it by. It doesn't get any better than this."

❧Ten❦

"I'VE FALLEN HEAD over heals in lust. Deep, dirty, carnal, lust."

Carrie was spending the afternoon at the mall with Allison. They'd just sat down at a table in the food court and were trying to decide what to have for lunch.

"Okay," said Allison, "I was about to suggest the hot dog place, but after hearing that I think maybe the chicken teriyaki bowls would be a whole lot safer. Does that sound good to you?"

Carrie nodded, waiting at their table while Allison went to get their food. She returned a few minutes later, setting the tray down and taking her seat.

"All right, so who's the lucky guy? Anyone I know?"

"Yep," said Carrie as Allison handed a rice bowl to her. "Your friend, Scott Andrews."

"I see. That's what I figured you'd say. I seem to recall you mentioning that you'd gone out with him once or twice, but I didn't realize it had gotten, well…" Allison wasn't quite sure how to finish her sentence.

"I know. All I can say is he's a wild man, Allie. He may come across as this quiet, conservative guy, but there's a whole 'nother side to him. He's nothing like Doug was. Doug took his

50

time, and then, when things got… intimate, Doug did it in a kind, gentle, and loving way. With Scott, it's more like a 'wham bam thank you ma'am.' He's a really fast mover. We went all the way to third base on our first date."

"Wow." An astonished Allison paused for a moment to take it all in. "I've known Scott for years, and he never struck me as the aggressive type. He was always more the quiet type, but then again, they say you need to watch out for the quiet ones. He's not forcing you into doing anything you don't want to do, is he?"

"No, not really. It's just that it happened so fast. We both agreed that it wouldn't be any kind of long-term thing, but still, he moved like lightening. I guess I threw caution to the wind."

Allison was concerned. Carrie was still emotionally vulnerable and she didn't want her being taken advantage of.

"Okay, so tell me, once you're done, does he stay the rest of the night with you?"

"So far he hasn't," replied Carrie. "On our second date, after we'd finished, you know, I asked him to spend the night, but he said he couldn't. He said he had to be at the office early the next morning, even though it was a Sunday. He mentioned something about an overseas client."

"What about your third date?"

"That hasn't happened yet. And that's the other funny thing. We had our first date, then he canceled the next two at the last minute, so I didn't get to see him again for almost a month. We finally had our second date two weeks ago. We were keeping in touch by email, but I haven't heard from him in awhile, and I've not sent him an email since the morning after our second date."

"What's keeping him so busy?"

"Work. He works long hours. Apparently, he's on call, or something. It seems he's always getting called into the office for one emergency or another."

"I see." Carrie heard the skepticism in Allison's voice. "So tell me, where did you guys go on the first two dates?"

"We went hiking at Lake Pleasant on our first date, and on the second, he took me to this really nice restaurant on the far west side of town. It was near the Arizona Cardinals stadium."

"Really? That's odd," said Allison.

"How so?"

"Do you know where Scott lives, Carrie?"

"No. I've never asked. Come to think of it, I don't think he's ever told me where he lives."

"Mesa," replied Allison, matter-of-factly. "Scott lives in Mesa. I've never been to his house, but I know it's only a half-mile or so from where Steve and I live. So why would a guy who lives on the far east end of town only be taking you to places on the far west side?"

"He says he likes adventure."

"Did he now? You know, Carrie, I think it may be time for you to move on."

"I thought he was your friend."

"No." Allison, shook her head. "He's really more of an acquaintance. I only know him from the library. I know he enjoys working with kids, so I just assumed he was a decent guy, but now I'm thinking he may not be the best boyfriend material for you after all. I'm starting to get a really bad feeling about this. You've had your post-Doug fling. Now I'd like to see you with someone who genuinely cares for you, instead of someone who's only interested in using you for sex."

"But I don't know if I'm ready for another serious relationship."

"Just saying."

Allison decided to steer the conversation to a safer topic, but the bad feeling she was getting about Scott continued to gnaw at her for the rest of the day. That night, after she went to bed, she had trouble falling asleep. She woke up in the middle of the night, anxiously tossing and turning.

"Okay," a half-awake Steve finally mumbled. "What's up?"

"It's Carrie. I'm really worried about her."

"How come?"

"For the past few weeks she's been seeing Scott, but something just isn't adding up."

"Like what?"

Allison let out a sigh. "First of all, he's much too aggressive with her sexually. Then he cancels most of their dates at the last minute. He keeps telling her it's an emergency at the office, which is a crock. He writes the software they use in the elementary schools. He's not the guy Morton-Evans would call whenever they have an emergency. Then, when he finally does take her out, it's someplace way on the other side of town."

"He's married."

"What?"

"He's married," repeated Steve with a yawn. "I get these guys in my office all the time. They have to change their will or family trust because they got caught having an affair, so now the wife has filed for divorce. Sometimes they'll talk to me about their mistresses. Some of them even like to brag about how they tricked them into thinking they weren't married. They did all the things that Scott's doing, like canceling dates at the last minute, or taking them out on the other side of town. They figure there's less chance of accidentally bumping into someone they know. Carrie needs to dump the guy, fast, before his wife finds out about her."

Steve rolled over and went back to sleep. Allison stayed awake. She finally got up and wandered into the living room, taking a seat on the sofa. Steve came looking for her about an hour later.

"What's wrong?" He sat down next to her.

"This is all my fault, Steve."

"How so?"

"That night, when Carrie first met Scott, she asked me if he was single. I told her yes he was, and that he was a decent guy too. She trusted me, and now I've thrown her under the bus. So what does that make me?"

"I was at the gallery that night too." He wrapped his arms around her and pulled her in close. "I thought he was single as well. Some of these guys are really, really good liars so it's not your fault, Allie. Scott lied to you, just like he's lying to her. What you need to do, right now, is come back to bed and get some sleep. Then tomorrow you'll need to call her and have a long, serious talk with her. After that it's up to her. If she decides she wants to stay with him, fine, but from that point on anything that happens won't be your fault."

Steve kissed her on the forehead and led her back into their bedroom. Once she settled back in bed she somehow managed to go back to sleep. The following morning, after breakfast, she picked up her cell phone and went out to the patio. She made herself comfortable on the chaise lounge and punched in Carrie's number.

"Hey, Allie."

"Morning Carrie. You sound kind of tired this morning."

"Yeah. I didn't sleep very well last night."

"Me neither. I was up half the night worrying about you. Steve and I talked it over. We're both getting a really bad feeling about you and Scott."

"I know," agreed Carrie. "I've been thinking about it too. I'm pretty sure he has another girlfriend. I think he was only seeing me whenever he was on the outs with her. I think the reason why I haven't heard from him lately is because they're working out whatever it is they need to work out, and I guess I'm okay with it. Just to be fair, he said from the get-go it wouldn't be anything permanent. I guess I just went along to boost my own ego."

Allison decided to not to mention she and Steve suspected it was probably a wife and not a girlfriend. Carrie, however, seemed to have the situation under control and she appeared to be handling it well. There was no reason to upset her any further.

"So, what do you plan on doing about it?"

"Not much. Like I said yesterday, I sent him an email after our last date, and I'd decided to not contact him again until I hear back. So now, if he does respond, I'll just say, 'Hey thanks, it was fun, but now it's time for me to move on and have a good life.' However, my gut tells me I probably won't be hearing from him."

"I'm really sorry about the way it all worked out. I really thought that he was a decent guy. I had no idea that he had another girlfriend. You know if I'd known—"

"Don't even go there, Allie. We both thought he was single and unattached. It's not your fault so I'm not putting any of this you. Besides, Louise told me that night the first one after a big break up is never a keeper, and to enjoy it for what it is."

"And it looks like she was right," agreed Allison. "But you know, I'm also getting a feeling that the next one who comes along really is going to be a keeper. I think he'll even be the one."

"We'll see, anyway, no harm done with Scott. He'll just be a fond memory."

"And a twinkle in your eye," added Allison and they both had a good laugh.

❧Eleven❧

MAGGIE ANDREWS' FAVORITE hour of day was in the morning, right after Scott went to work and the kids left for school. It was her special time to pour herself a second cup of coffee, go into the den, turn on her computer and read her email. She'd just settled in front of her screen to retrieve her email when something went wrong. Her computer suddenly crashed. She tried rebooting it, but she kept getting error messages. She picked up the phone to call Scott. After punching a few buttons to reach his extension, she was relieved to hear his voice when he picked up. She hated landing in his voice mailbox. He rarely returned her calls.

"Scott, I'm so sorry, but something's wrong with my computer and for some weird reason I can't seem to get it to reboot. Can you fix it for me?"

Scott bit his tongue, reminding himself that it would all be over soon. Until that time, he needed to act as normal as possible.

"Sure, Maggie, no problem. I've been telling you for months that you were overdue for an update, so now I guess the time has come. I'll work on it as soon as I get home."

"Thanks, sweetie. Meantime, can I borrow your laptop? I just need to read my email."

"Of course."

Maggie hung up and went over to the Mac sitting on the other desk. She booted it up and entered Scott's password. After she finished reading her email her curiosity got the better of her. Their seventeenth wedding anniversary was coming up and she wondered what Scott might have picked out for her. She clicked on the history tab in the browser menu to see what she could find out. What she found was that Scott had a second email account, one that she knew nothing about. She clicked on the link. When the login page loaded, she tried Scott's password. It worked. She was in. She noticed all the messages in the inbox had come from a single sender, someone named Carrie Daniels. The message that grabbed her attention the most was the last one. The words, "About Last Night," appeared in the subject line. Maggie anxiously clicked on the link and began to read the message.

"I'm still recovering from last night and it's a night I'll always remember. Let's just say I've never experienced anything quite like it before, but next time please stay and spend the rest of the night with me, okay?"

Maggie's stomach coiled into a knot. A choking sob welled up her throat. Tears flowed down her face as she let loose and sobbed like a child. She cried, uncontrollably, for several minutes before finally reaching for a tissue. Once she began to calm down she decided she'd better find out who this Carrie Daniels was. She read all of the email, both in the inbox and in the sent folder, and as she did, she began to piece the puzzle together. Scott met Carrie Daniels at Louise Dickenson's show at Hanson Sisters. They'd gone out twice and Scott had been having sex with her. However, Carrie seemed to have disappeared sometime after their second date, or had she? Perhaps they'd just stopped emailing. Maggie knew that if she wanted to save her marriage, and her comfortable lifestyle, she'd better find out more about Carrie, and fast.

"Okay, Maggie. So what's your plan?"

She copied the domain name in Carrie's email address and pasted it into the browser address bar. The Carrie Daniels Photography website immediately loaded. So, Carrie was also a photographer. Her attending Louise Dickenson's show at Hanson Sisters made sense. Maggie clicked on the About Us page and what she saw nearly made her fall out of her chair. There was a full-color headshot of Ms. Carrie Daniels and she was a strikingly beautiful woman. Reading the bio, she discovered that Carrie had once been the Mercer's Markets girl.

"I remember those ads, and you were certainly an annoying little bitch, weren't you? Your mommy may have shopped at Mercer's Markets, but your mommy sure as hell didn't teach you any manners now did she? I guess she never told you that having sex with another woman's husband isn't very nice."

As Maggie studied Carrie's face more closely something else suddenly occurred to her.

"What the hell?"

She raced upstairs to the master bedroom. Hanging on the wall, right above her bed, was Carrie Daniels in the flesh. She'd been in Scott's line of sight every time they'd made love. No wonder Scott had been more amorous than usual lately.

"Son of a bitch!"

Maggie let out a loud shriek as she ripped one of the photos off the wall and hurled it across the room as hard as she could. She heard the gratifying sound of the shattering glass as the photo crashed onto ceramic tile floor.

"You bitch! You whore! You belong in the centerfold of *Gentry Magazine* and not on my bedroom wall! You're nothing but slut, a cheap little trollop and a—" She abruptly stopped her rant in the middle of her sentence. The wheels were beginning to turn in her head. Her face lit up as it slowly began to dawn on her. "My God, Maggie, you're brilliant. It's the perfect plan."

She yanked opened the bottom drawer of Scott's nightstand and began rifling through the contents. She soon found what she was searching for. She pulled out the latest issue of *Gentry Magazine* and flipped through the pages until she found it. Every month *Gentry Magazine* invited readers to submit nude photos for its amateur photo contest, and they would publish the best of the best in each issue, with handsome cash prizes to boot.

She set the magazine aside and walked up to the spot where the photo had landed. She carefully picked it up. The glass was completely shattered, the frame was dented and scratched, but the undamaged full-frontal view of a bare-naked Carrie Daniels, kneeling on top of a four-poster bed, was beautifully shot. It would undoubtedly be the winner. She turned it over. As expected, Louise Dickenson's copyright notice and usage restrictions were adhered to the back of the frame.

"Sorry, Louise, but we're going to have to make an exception just this one time."

She got a broom and swept up the broken glass before taking the other photo off the wall. She carried both downstairs and set them on the kitchen table. She got a screwdriver and disassembled each frame, carefully removing the photos and taking them out of their mats.

She brought the photos into the den and placed one onto the scanner. It was slightly larger than the scanner bed, which meant she'd have to do some minor photo editing. As soon she finished, she scanned the other before taking them back to the kitchen and placing them back in their mats. The one frame, however, was damaged beyond repair and would have to be replaced. She let out a sigh as she took both frames to the garage and dropped them into the garbage can. When she returned, she placed the photos in a large shopping bag and headed off to the nearest arts and crafts superstore.

* * *

"May I help you?"

The pimple-faced young man behind the framing counter didn't look a day over sixteen. Maggie pulled the photos out of the bag.

"I accidentally dropped one of these this morning and broke its frame. They're a matching set. Can you put them into new frames for me?"

"Of course—wow!" He'd been caught off guard by the subject matter. The look on his face revealed that he was probably experiencing some sort of sexual fantasy. "These are great. The artist did a fantastic job. So who's the model?"

"I have no idea. I'm just upset that I broke one of the frames. How long will it take to reframe them?"

"Not that long. Since they're already matted I can have them ready for you by this time tomorrow. You just need to pick out a frame."

Maggie took her time, carefully selecting the perfect frame. She let out a little gasp when he totaled up her order. She was glad she'd stopped at the bank to get some extra cash on her way over.

"Name?"

"What?"

"Name," he repeated, "so we'll know who you are when you pick them up."

"Oh, right. Daniels. Carrie Daniels. And I'll be paying cash."

"Okay, Ms. Daniels." He handed her the pink copy of the invoice. "They'll be ready for pick up by one o'clock tomorrow afternoon."

Maggie thanked him as he counted back her change. A smile of satisfaction broke out across her face as she rushed back to her car. She stopped for a burger on the way home, and once she arrived she went straight to Scott's computer. The clock was ticking and she had a number of things left to do before Ben and Sarah came home from school. She quickly opened a new email account and immediately composed an email to Carrie Daniels.

"Dear Ms. Daniels, my name is Kendra Clarke and I'm in the fifth grade. I'm doing a report for school about you being the Mercer's Markets girl. If it's not too much trouble, could you tell me a little something about what it was like and would you mind emailing me an autographed picture? Thanks."

She quickly hit the send button. Her next step was to do some minor photo cropping. Once that task was complete, she looked up *Gentry Magazine* on Google. After a few clicks on their website, she had the instructions on how to submit a photo for the monthly amateur contest. She carefully reviewed them before downloading the release form. She filled it out using Carrie Daniels' name, along with the mailing address and telephone number posted on her website. The form also required an email address so that the magazine could send a confirmation notice once the materials had been received.

"Whoops. We wouldn't want to spoil the surprise, now would we Carrie? So I guess I'll have to give them Kendra's email address. That way I can stay on top of things and still keep you in the dark. By the time you find out what's happened, it'll be too late, but don't you worry. I'll make sure you get credited as the model in the photos. That way the entire world can see you for the tramp you really are."

While Maggie waited for the release form to come out of the printer, she decided to check the email. Sure enough, Kendra had received a reply, with a photo file attached.

"So, Carrie, I want to thank you for helping this sweet little fifth-grader with her homework." There was a venomous tone to Maggie's voice. "Of course, what you don't realize is that you've just dug your own grave. Hope you rot in it, bitch!"

Maggie printed out the photo and carefully studied Carrie's

signature. She practiced copying it a few times on a piece of scratch paper. She checked the clock. Ben would be home in less than thirty minutes so she'd have to hurry. She practiced a few more times before copying Carrie's signature onto the release form and placing it into the scanner. Ten minutes later all of the necessary files had been scanned, attached, and emailed to the magazine. The deed was done and not a moment too soon.

Maggie quickly gathered up the photo, release form and scratch paper. She took it to the family room, placed it in the fireplace, lit a match, and watched in delight as all the incriminating evidence turned black and crumbled into ashes. She returned to Scott's computer to delete her files and clear the browser history.

"Mission accomplished." She triumphantly shut the computer down. "A few months from now, Ms. Carrie Daniels, when you least expect it, your entire world will implode. But hey, with any luck, you'll get to keep the prize money."

❧Twelve❧

MAGGIE WAS BUSY preparing dinner when Scott arrived home. She put on her best poker face, greeting him with her customary kiss and asking him about his day.

"The usual," he replied. "I'll go in and start working on your computer. And the next time I tell you to do an update, Maggie, just do it, okay."

"Okay, okay. You don't need to be such a grouch about it. And by the way, I accidentally knocked one of the photos off the wall over our bed this morning while I was making it up. The glass broke and the frame got damaged. I'm so sorry. I feel really bad about it."

"Great."

"Now don't go getting upset," she said, trying to shrug it off. "The photo itself is okay, so I took it over to Taylor's Hobby and Crafts. They're reframing it and it'll be ready tomorrow afternoon, good as new."

"Why didn't you take it back to Hanson Sisters?"

"What?"

"I said, 'Why didn't you take it back to Hanson Sisters?' They probably could have replaced the frame, and it would have been a much better one at that. These are limited edition prints,

Maggie. They deserve something better than a cheap, hobby-shop frame. In all the years I've been trying to teach you about collecting art, have you not learned anything?"

"Sorry, Scott, I didn't even think of that."

"That's your problem, Maggie. You don't think. You don't have a brain in your head."

"So what's that supposed to mean?"

Scott let out a sigh. "It means, that instead of being able to relax and enjoy my evening, I get to spend it working on your computer because you refused to do the updates I told you to do months ago. What about the other photo?"

"I took it to Taylor's too. Did you think I wasn't smart enough to have them in matching frames? Heaven forbid your precious photos should be less than perfect. They'll be back up on the wall by the time you get home tomorrow night. If you don't like the frames I picked out, then you can take them back to Hanson Sisters yourself."

At least Scott was buying her story.

"Call me when dinner's ready," he said as he made his exit.

Maggie turned her attention back to the meal she was preparing. She couldn't wait to see the look on Scott's face when he found out exactly what she'd done to his mistress. Maybe then he'd finally learn to respect her.

"Yeah, we'll see who's stupid then," she mumbled to herself.

Scott headed into the den. He glanced at his watch as he took a seat in front of her computer. Thirty-six hours. It would all be over in another thirty-six hours.

* * *

"Are you sure this is what you want, Scott?"

He was standing in his supervisor's office. He'd just submitted his letter of resignation, effective immediately

"Yes, Howard, I'm sure. I'm really sorry to give you such short notice, but the firm in Kansas City wants me to start right away, and I need to head home to start packing. Don't worry. I've already brought John and Marcia up to speed on all the projects I'm working on. They'll take over where I've left off."

"You know, Scott, I wish you'd spoken up if you were that unhappy here. Maybe we could have worked something out."

"Thanks, Howard, however, this has nothing to do with

Morton-Evans. It's me. My home life has been less than happy for some time now, so my wife and I have decided to go our separate ways. I need to make a fresh start someplace else."

"I understand. Good luck, Scott, and don't be a stranger."

The two men shook hands before Scott left Howard's office. He went back to his cubicle and threw his personal belongings into a box, saying a quick goodbye to his coworkers before rushing out the door. It was Maggie's day to volunteer at Ben's school and he wanted to be sure he was on the road before the last class let out.

He raced home, parking in the driveway and popping the trunk open. He quickly gathered up the pieces of new luggage he'd stashed away, taking it inside to the master bedroom. He began hastily packing his clothes and other personal items. As he zipped up the last bag he looked at the wall over the bed. At least Maggie had picked out some halfway decent replacement frames. He took down the two photos of Carrie. They'd be something for him to remember her by. He brought them downstairs, along with all his bags, and quickly loaded his car. He came back for his laptop. He'd have to stop at the first out-of-town hotspot he could find to email the kids. He smiled to himself as he slipped the computer into its case. His only regret was that he wouldn't be there to see the shocked look on Maggie's face when she was served with the divorce papers. No doubt it would be priceless. He set the computer case down at the foot of the staircase and made one last trip up to the master bedroom. He deposited his house keys and garage door opener on the dresser. Coming back down, he stopped to look around the family room one last time.

"Well, Maggie, thanks for everything—not. It was fun, for about the first six months, and then you became a total bore. No wonder you had to get yourself knocked-up in order to keep your hooks in me. But as of today, my dear, it's all over, and I'm going to fight for custody of the kids too. I'll be damned if I'm going to sit back and let you turn them into a pair of snot-nosed, annoying whiners like you."

He picked up his laptop and opened the front door, carefully turning the bottom lock behind him. His fully loaded car was waiting. He tossed his laptop into the passenger seat, slipped behind the wheel, fired up the engine and drove away. For the first time in nearly seventeen years, he could savor the sweet taste of freedom. It was exhilarating. He would enjoy every moment of it. As he merged onto the freeway he began debating with himself. His route would take him past her exit, and he knew her studio was close by.

"Oh well, what the hell."

He took the exit and soon found the industrial park. There was an empty parking space in front of the suite with the words, "Carrie Daniels Photography," painted on the front door. Upon entering, he stepped into a small reception area with poster-sized samples of her work proudly displayed on the walls. He hadn't realized just how talented of a photographer she really was. He rang the bell on top of the counter and heard her voice calling out that she'd be right there. She appeared a moment later, obviously surprised to see him.

"Well hello, Scott." Her voice sounded somewhat tentative. "I guess it's been awhile. How have you been?"

"I've been well, Carrie. How 'bout you?"

"The same."

There was an awkward moment of silence before Scott spoke up.

"I know it probably appears to you like I've fallen off the face of the earth, but there was a reason for it. Shortly after our last date my old girlfriend contacted me. I hadn't heard from her in a long, long time."

"Yeah, I figured you had another girlfriend, but it's okay. There were never any strings attached."

"Thank you for understanding. However, Nancy was more than just another girlfriend. She's the love of my life. Unfortunately, at the time I first met her, she was married to someone else. She didn't think the time was right to leave her husband, so she ended it. Then one day out of the blue, she called me at work. She said she'd moved to Kansas City and she's now happily divorced. I'm on my way there right now. I just wanted to stop by to tell you goodbye."

"Thanks, Scott, I appreciate it. You came into my life at a time when my self-esteem desperately needed a boost, and now I'm back on track. I never expected anything more from you than what it was, and I'm genuinely happy for you. Take care and good luck."

"You too." He extended his hand, giving hers a final squeeze. "Goodbye, Carrie. Like I said to you before, you're an amazing woman. Some guy will be very, very lucky to have you."

Scott left the building. Both were happy, and relieved, that it had ended amicably.

❧Thirteen❧

EVEN THOUGH CARRIE had lived in Phoenix for most of her life, she never quite got used to the intense, stifling heat of the Valley summers. Even at ten o'clock at night it was likely to be over one-hundred degrees outside. Steve and Allison, however, seemed to take it in stride. This year they were hosting a Fourth of July dinner party at their home, with most of the festivities taking place in, and around, their backyard swimming pool.

"To you, from Allie," said Carrie as she presented Steve with a platter of hamburger patties and hot dogs. He thanked her and loaded them onto the grill. On her way back to the kitchen, she overheard a bit of a conversation between two of Steve's coworkers.

"Too bad Alex couldn't make it tonight."

"Yeah. He's a lot smarter than the rest of us. He's spending the holiday on some beach in San Diego."

Alex. Just hearing the name brought back memories of her long-lost other best friend. Over the years Carrie had deeply regretted losing touch with Alex. She often wondered whatever became of him. No doubt he was probably married by now, and he had a family as well. Wherever he was, she hoped he was happy. She wandered back into the kitchen.

"Penny for your thoughts," said Allison.

"Huh?"

"You look like you're a million miles away, girlfriend."

"Oh, sorry." Carrie set the empty platter into the sink. "I just overheard a couple of the guys from Steve's office talking about someone named Alex. It got me to wondering whatever became of our Alex."

"Alex Montoya?"

Carried nodded.

"Good question. I have no idea. I've wondered about him from time to time myself, although he was more your friend than mine. But he spoke Castillian Spanish…"

"What's that?"

"His dialect," replied Allison. "Don't you remember? His father's family came over from Spain, so they spoke a different kind of Spanish. It would be like you talking to an Englishman."

"You're right, Allie. There's nothing sexier than a guy who speaks with a foreign accent, so admit it. You did have a crush on Alex."

"No, I did not," said Allison with a smile. "I just said I liked his accent."

"Sure you did."

After a good laugh Allison decided to change the subject.

"You know, I really don't know a lot of Steve's coworkers either, and I certainly don't recall ever meeting one named Alex. Since we work in different parts of town, I'm rarely near his office during business hours, and this is the first time we've invited any of them to our home in a good two or three years."

"I see. And I've also noticed that you've had a happy glow about you all evening. What's going on?"

"Nothing," she said, coyly.

"Allie?"

She opened the refrigerator door and grabbed a beer. "Would you like something to drink, Carrie? I've got sodas, beer, wine…"

"I'll have a glass of white wine, thanks."

She pulled a plastic cup from the stack and poured some wine for Carrie.

"Let's go join the others," she said as she handed her the glass.

Carrie kicked her shoes off and followed her outside. She found an empty spot at the edge of the pool where she sat down and dangled her feet in the water. Sipping the wine, her mind kept wondering back to Alex. Steve soon announced that dinner was ready to be served. As Carrie ate her burger she made small talk with the other guests, but her mind kept wandering back to Alex. She thought about looking him up on Facebook or Google when she got home, but then again, if he was married, an online reunion might not be such a good idea. Steve's voice interrupted her thoughts.

"Ladies and gentlemen, if we could have your attention for just a couple of minutes, Allison and I have an announcement we'd like to make."

Allison walked up and stood next to Steve. Carrie noticed her left hand was concealed in the pocket of her sundress. Steve wrapped his arm around her waist.

"We've invited all of you here tonight, because we have some news that we would like to share."

"You're pregnant," shouted one of the guests. Allison blushed and giggled as she shook her head.

"Not yet, although we are working on it," replied Steve, "but since you brought it up... Allie and I have been living together for four years now, and we really are getting to be like an old married couple, but in a good way. We've decided that we're ready to start a family."

"Here, here," shouted one man.

"I can help you out with that," shouted another.

"We don't need your help, Stan, but thank you for asking," replied Steve. "Where were we? Oh yeah. Anyway, Allison and I have decided that maybe before we do the baby thing, we should do the marriage thing, so I've asked this lady to marry me, and she said yes. Welcome everyone, to our engagement party."

A chorus of hoots, hollers and cheers broke out as everyone gathered round to congratulate the happy couple. Allison pulled her hand from her pocket, revealing her flashy diamond engagement ring. Carrie ran up to congratulate her friend.

"Oh Allie, I'm so happy for you. So when's the wedding?"

"This fall, after the weather cools off, probably sometime in late October. We haven't decided on the exact date yet, but we have decided that the wedding it will be fairly small. Just family and close friends, and I want you to be my maid of honor."

"Oh wow, Allie, I'm honored, I really am, but I can't. I just don't have the money for the dress."

"It's okay, Carrie. I thought about that too. Since you'll be my only attendant, we have some leeway. We can go to a regular department store and pick out a nice party dress. One that isn't overly expensive, and that you could wear later on to a holiday party."

Carrie appreciated the sentiment, but with Doug, and now Scott, out of the picture, she no longer had much of a social life. She didn't anticipate being invited to very many parties, before or after the holiday season.

The party began to wind down. All of the guests congratulated Steve and Allison as they left. Carrie stayed to help with cleanup before saying goodnight. Steve and Allison walked her to her car, each giving her a long, lingering hug while she congratulated them again. She felt mixed emotions, driving back to her apartment. On one hand, she was sincerely happy for Steve and Allison. Their wedding was long overdue. But on the other hand, their engagement was a bittersweet reminder of everything she no longer had. It had been nearly nine months since she and Doug had gone their separate ways. In hindsight, she'd come to realize she'd wasted the best years of her life on him. As she parked her car and headed up the stairwell to her apartment she began to consider the possibility that she could very well end up alone for the rest of her life.

☙Fourteen☙

CARRIE SLAMMED THE phone down in disgust. It was the third crank call she'd received that morning. The calls had all come to her office number, posted on her website. She wondered if her website had somehow been hacked. She called her webmaster, asking him to investigate. He called back a short time later, saying that other than heavier than usual traffic that morning everything appeared to be normal. In the interim, she'd received yet another obscene phone call, so they decided to take her phone number off the website. Within an hour the harassing calls had stopped.

Carrie tried to pull herself together and go back to work. The calls were disturbing and she was having a hard time concentrating. She heard the bell at her front counter. She stepped into the reception area to find Marcy, her letter carrier.

"Good morning, Marcy. How was your Fourth of July?"

"Nice and quiet." She placed the mail on the counter. "I have something you need to sign for."

Carrie signed the form and Marcy handed her a large, thick envelope. The sender was GMH Publications, Inc., from Los Angeles. She didn't recognize the name. More than likely it was a prospective client. Marcy said goodbye as Carrie took the mail back to her desk and opened it. Inside the big envelope was a check, payable to her, for five thousand dollars. Attached to the check was a personally signed letter from Caleb Wyman, publisher of *Gentry Magazine*, congratulating her for winning the photo contest in their latest issue.

"What on earth? I never entered any photo contest. Not for anyone, and most certainly not for you."

She reached back into the envelope and pulled out the remaining contents. It was the latest issue of *Gentry Magazine*. As she thumbed through the pages something familiar caught her eye and she heard herself shrieking. Inside the pages were two of the nude photos Louise Dickenson had shot of her. One was of her kneeling on top of the four-poster bed, the other of her reclining in the leather chair.

"What the hell!"

She looked at the captions. Both photos were titled as self-portraits, and she was identified as both the model and the photographer.

Tears ran down her face as she stared at the photos. Her entire body was shaking and she was in state of total shock. Louise had assured her that she would remain anonymous and that no one buying any of the prints would ever know her name. The only buyer who knew her identity was Scott, but what reason would he have for doing this? She'd had no contact with him since the day he'd dropped by her office to tell her goodbye, and he certainly didn't appear to be angry or resentful.

Carrie picked up the letter. Wyman's address and phone number were printed on the letterhead. Her hands were still shaking as she dialed the number.

"Stay calm, Carrie," she told herself as she took a deep breath and waited for someone to answer. After punching a few buttons, a live person came on the line.

"Yes, hello." She fought to keep the tremble in her voice down. "This is Carrie Daniels. I'm calling about the pictures of me, in this month's issue."

"Yes, congratulations Carrie. Those photos were exceptionally well done. We've never seen anything this classy in our contest before. You've certainly raised the bar."

"Thank you, but I need to ask a favor. I can't find my release form. Would you mind emailing a copy to me?"

"Certainly. Let me pull up the file on my computer."

Moments later she read off an email address, asking if it was correct. Carrie didn't recognize it.

"Can you send it to this email address instead?"

She gave her the correct address and quickly ended the call. Ten minutes later she'd received the email, with an attachment, which she immediately downloaded and printed.

"Oh my God."

She looked it over. It had been filled out with her name, business address and office telephone number, but with an unknown email address. She let out a gasp as she looked at the signature. It had been forged. She sat in stunned disbelief, unsure of what to do until it finally occurred to her to call Steve. She was about to reach for the phone, when it started to ring. She quickly answered.

"What the hell do you think you're doing?" Louise Dickenson's voice had an accusing tone she'd never heard before.

"I was about to ask you the same thing," she tersely replied.

"Oh don't act so innocent with me." Carrie heard the anger in Louise's voice. "What reason would I have for entering *Gentry Magazine's* photo contest? Don't you think that if I were to publish any of my photos I'd want to be credited as the photographer? Sorry, Carrie, the jig is up. You'll have to find another way to pay your mother's medical bills, and you might want to get yourself a lawyer while you're at it. My attorney just got off the phone with *Gentry Magazine*. We know you're the one who submitted the photos, and we know they mailed a check to your office. This is copyright infringement and plagiarism, Carrie. Did you really think I wouldn't find out about it? Karl subscribes to *Gentry Magazine*, you stupid little bitch, so you can imagine our surprise at what we found in our mailbox today. You, of all people, should have certainly known better, but don't you worry about that. I'm going to teach you a lesson you'll never forget. By the time I'm through with you, you'll not only be out of business, you really will be living in that cardboard box underneath the bridge."

"Louise, I didn't do this. Someone set me up!"

"Yeah, right. You know, you must really think that I'm pretty damn stupid. Well, I've got news for you, Sweetness. You just picked a fight with the wrong person. Trust me, I'm someone you never, ever want to have for an enemy. My attorney will be in touch. From here on out you'll be talking to him, not me."

Louise slammed the phone down in Carrie's ear. Carrie burst into tears and cried for several minutes. Once she finally calmed down, she stepped out to get a bottle of water and lock her front door before coming back to her desk. She took a deep breath and placed a call to Allison. She fought back the tears, when she heard her friend's voice.

"Allie, thank goodness. I was afraid I'd get your voicemail."

"Carrie, what's wrong?" She heard the despair in her friend's voice.

"Everything. Allie, I have an emergency. I have to talk to Steve, right away. I need his work number."

"Here you go." Allison read the number off. "Carrie, what happened?"

"I can't talk right now, Allie, but I'll call you tonight. I promise."

She ended the call and quickly dialed Steve's number. She was connected to his secretary, who informed her that he'd stepped out.

"But you don't understand, it's an emergency. I have to talk to him, right now."

"And I just told you, he should be back in about fifteen minutes. If you'll just give me your name and number I'll give him the message."

Carrie quickly gave the woman her name and number, repeating again that it was an urgent matter. She hung up the phone and waited. It seemed like an eternity before her phone finally rang.

"Carrie, this is Steve. What's up?"

"Someone's out to ruin me." She quickly filled him in on the details.

"Holy crap! Carrie, I want you to listen to me closely and do everything I tell you to do. First, I want you to call your webmaster. Tell him to take your website down, immediately. Then I want you to gather up everything that was in that envelope, along with the release form, and take it with you. I want you to go straight home. As soon as you get there, I want you to call the police and have them send an officer over to take a report. Keep you door locked and don't open it unless it's me, or Allie, or the police. And don't answer your phone, unless you know who's calling."

"Steve, you're scaring me."

"Carrie, you have an enemy out there. Someone's gone to a great deal of trouble to set you up. Right now we don't know who it is and what else they're capable of."

Carrie shuddered. She was genuinely frightened.

"What about Louise? She's made it abundantly clear that she's going to sue me for breach of contract, copyright infringement, plagiarism, and who knows what else."

"We can help you with that. There's a guy in our office who specializes in this sort of thing. He has an excellent track record so you'll be in the best of hands. He's in court today and tomorrow, but if you'll hold on for a moment I'll go talk to his secretary and find out how soon we can get you in to see him."

Steve put her on hold. While she waited, she took a few more deep breaths and tried to calm her nerves. In a minute, he was back on the line.

"Alex has an opening at three o'clock on Thursday. I've already scheduled it for you and I'll make sure I'm there too. Do you need the address?"

"Yes."

Steve gave her the address and she looked it up on Google. At least his office was close to her apartment.

"I'll see you on Thursday, Carrie, and I'll fill Alex in before you get here. In the meantime, if you need anything, and I mean anything, you call me, or Allie, right away."

"I will, and thank you, Steve."

Carrie called her webmaster as soon as she hung up. Within minutes her website disappeared from the web. She gathered everything up in the envelope before setting the alarm, locking the door and quickly heading home.

◈Fifteen◈

CARRIE ARRIVED AT Steve's office a few minutes
early. She introduced herself to the receptionist and took
a seat in the waiting area. The office was beautifully decorated
with plush furnishings, confirming her fear that their services
would not come cheap. She set her satchel down and nervously
began flipping through one of the magazines laying on the coffee
table. Her ears perked up at the sound of a familiar voice.

"I have to make a quick phone call, Brenda. Is my three
o'clock here?"

"Yes, Alex."

"Good. Tell Steve I'll be ready in a couple minutes. We'll be
meeting in the conference room."

Carrie looked up, but whoever was talking to Brenda had
already left. She shrugged it off as nervousness. Her mind must
be playing tricks on her. She turned her attention back to the
magazine.

"Carrie?"

She looked up. "Hey, Steve."

"Are you all right? You look a little pale."

"I'm fine. As you can imagine, I've been under a lot of stress
and I haven't been sleeping very well."

"I understand. Are you ready?"

She nodded as she rose from her chair, picked up her satchel and followed him to the conference room.

"Alex, your three o'clock is here," he announced as he stepped inside.

Carrie abruptly stopped in the doorway. She couldn't believe who she was seeing. He'd filled out over the years, but she knew those distinctive gray eyes and curly blond hair. He was seated in one of the high-backed leather chairs surrounding the cherry wood conference table. A broad smile broke out across his face as he looked up from her file and recognized her.

"Well hey, Carrie-Anne."

"You remembered?"

"How could I forget our song?"

He walked up her and they embraced, lingering in each other's arms. Reluctantly, she stepped back and began to wipe her eyes with the back of her hand.

"I understand the two of you already know one another," said Steve as he handed her a tissue.

"Yes." Carrie dabbed her eyes as they took their seats. "Alex and I go all the way back to the fourth grade. I was the kid that everyone else hated because I was on TV, and Alex was the skinny, nerdy guy who took pity on me. He and Allie were my two best friends, but then we lost touch with one another about ten years ago. So, Alex, what have you been doing since then?"

"Going to college, going to law school, and coming to work here. And you?"

"Going to college, becoming a photographer, and most recently, watching my entire world go up in flames." The smile instantly faded from her face.

"Alex has gone over your file," explained Steve. "I've brought him up to speed on everything."

She looked at Alex. "So, you've seen them?"

He lifted up his folder, revealing the current issue of *Gentry Magazine* hidden underneath.

"Yes, I have."

Her face began turning red. "Alex, I need you to understand something. I'd been living with someone, long term, and during that time my mother had a stroke."

"I know. Steve told me about her insurance running out and you going broke trying to take care of her."

"That's right. So when Doug dumped me, I was literally left homeless. I was camped out in my office. Then Louise called and offered me that photo shoot. I was desperate. I needed the money so I could find a decent place to live. That was the only reason I agreed to do it. She promised me the photos would only go to serious art collectors and that I'd remain anonymous. I don't want you getting the wrong idea."

"I understand and I'm not judging you, but now we have to deal with the consequences. Steve tells me someone set you up, and Louise has threatened to take legal action against you."

"I'm afraid so." She reached into the satchel, removing Caleb Wyman's letter and the check, and handing them over to Alex. "This arrived at my office two days ago. I swear, on everything that is holy, that I never, ever, entered their photo contest. When I came across those two photos of me, along with my name identifying me as the model, I totally freaked out."

"I understand. So what did you do after that?"

"As soon as I calmed down, I called Mr. Wyman's office, and when whoever she was answered, I told her I'd lost my copy of the release form, and could she email me another. She asked me to verify the email address they had on file. Alex, it wasn't my email address. It was one I'd never heard of."

"Did you tell her that?"

"No," she replied. "I didn't want to tip my hand. I simply said it wasn't correct and I gave her my real email address. They sent me the release form a few minutes later. As soon as it arrived I printed it out."

She reached into the satchel again, handing the release form to Alex.

"Look closely at the signature."

She reached into her purse, retrieved a pen and asked for a piece of scratch paper. As soon as Steve handed it to her she signed her name on it and handed it to Alex.

"Now that's my signature."

Alex studied the two side by side. "It's not that good of a forgery. Whoever did this may have thought they were being smart, but it's the work of an amateur. We'll turn this over to our handwriting expert."

"Then this arrived in my apartment mailbox this morning." She handed Alex a business-sized envelope. It bore the logo of another law firm.

"It's from Louise Dickenson's attorney," Alex said to Steve as he opened the letter. "No surprise here. He's letting her know they intend to file a case against her. I'll get a letter off to him in the morning, along with a copy of the release form, and let them know it's a forgery. Hopefully, they'll back off."

"What happens if they don't? When Louise called me, I tried to tell her I'd been set up, but she wouldn't listen to me. She intends to destroy me. She's got a vindictive side to her I've never seen before."

"We're going to take care of you," replied Alex. "Carrie-Anne, you're not alone here. We know that you didn't do anything wrong, and we're here to help you. We're also going to find out who did this to you. Identity theft and forgery are both state and federal crimes, and I'll do my best to see to it that whoever did this will end up serving some hard time."

"Okay." She took a deep breath. "I was afraid of this. So I need the two of you to understand something. It's about your fee."

"Carrie, listen, I—"

"Please, Steve, just hear me out. I wanted you to know that I've made arrangements to pay your fee."

"How? You're broke."

"Steve, listen to me, please. I did everything you told me to do after I got off the phone with you. I took down my website and went straight home. As soon as I got there I went to my laptop to check my email. Before my website went down a film company in California contacted me, so I gave them a call. I'm driving to Los Angeles next week to meet with them. They've offered me a significant sum of money, and once again, I'm desperate."

"What kind of film company, Carrie-Anne?"

"What kind do you think, Alex? It's an adult film company. They've offered me enough to cover your retainer, as well as to pay down some of the balance of my mother's nursing home bill."

The two men looked at one another in stunned disbelief before Alex finally spoke up.

"Not on my watch."

"Look, Alex, I think we've already established the fact that I've fallen from grace, and now my photography business is, for all intents and purposes, shut down. I have bills to pay and no money coming in my door."

"No way." Alex held his ground. "I'm not going to sit back and allow my best friend to turn herself into a prostitute."

"Do you really think I want to do this? I don't have a choice."

"It's still a form of prostitution, Carrie-Anne. You're being paid to have sex with someone, whether it's a man, another woman, or maybe both at the same time. The only difference is that someone is filming you while you're lying on your back so that other people can watch it later on, and somehow that makes it all legal. I'll be damned if I'm going sit back and allow you to do that. You haven't signed a contract have you?"

"Not yet, but I have it with me."

"Let me see it."

Carrie sighed as she pulled it out of her satchel and handed it over. Alex looked it over before turning to Steve.

"I'll let them know, in no uncertain terms, that the deal's off." He placed it into her file. "Just so you understand, Carrie-Anne, even if you had signed this, I still would have tried to break it."

"You know, Alex, it's really easy to be virtuous when you have food in your stomach and a roof over your head, but right now I don't have that option. I just got another letter in the mail. The nursing home was threatening to turn my mother's account over to collections, so I had to use my grocery money get them off my back. Like Old Mother Hubbard, there's nothing in my cupboard."

The room began to spin around her. She grabbed the edge of the table, trying to steady herself as she began to sway in her chair.

"Carrie-Anne, are you all right?"

"I'm okay, I'm just really stressed out, that's all."

"When was the last time you had anything to eat?"

"The day before yesterday."

"What!" Alex looked at Steve.

"I'm on it." He raced out of the room.

"Where's he going?"

"To the break room to get you something to eat. Carrie-Anne, you're in way over your head. You can't handle this on your own anymore. I'm your friend, so please, let me help you."

Steve rushed back in with a couple of bananas, an apple, and a bottle of fruit juice. Carrie eagerly reached for one of the bananas and quickly began to peel it.

"Not too fast," warned Alex. "You don't want shock your system. But while you're eating, please listen to what Steve has to say."

"From time to time, Carrie, we take pro bono cases. Alex and I had a discussion about this before you got here. We can prove your signature was forged and your identity was stolen. If Louise is smart, she'll drop her vendetta against you and work with us to find out who the real culprit is. If not, and she decides to pursue you anyway, then she's a fool, because she can never win. So, if she forces the issue, we'll file a motion requesting that you be awarded attorney fees. If the judge agrees, then it will be on Louise's nickel, not yours."

"We need to find out who set you up," said Alex. "You said Louise promised you'd be anonymous, but obviously someone knows. Did you volunteer any information or tell anyone that the photos were of you?"

"The night at the gallery, when Louise's show opened, you were there, Steve." She looked at him as he nodded. "A friend of Allie's was also there. She introduced us. His name was Scott Andrews. We talked for some time, and he offered to take me to dinner. I ended up going out with him a couple of times."

"Did he know you were the one in the photos?"

"Yes. While I was talking to him, he recognized me as the model. He even bought two of the prints."

"Which two?"

"I can't remember."

"Are you still seeing him?"

"No. It was, for lack of a better description, a fling. I'd just ended a ten-year relationship and he told me upfront there would be no long-term commitment. It was what it was."

"Which one of you ended it?"

"Officially, he did," she replied. "Although it happened several weeks after I'd stopped contacting him. He stopped by my office one day out of the blue. Needless to say, I was surprised to see him there. He said he'd reconnected with his old girlfriend and he was leaving town to be with her. He seemed happy, so I wished him well. We shook hands and he left. I can't think of any reason why he'd want to do this to me."

"Carrie," said Steve, "I hate to have to tell you this, but from everything you've told Allie and me about your relationship, Scott fits the profile of a married man."

"What? No way! I sent Allie a text message before I left the gallery that night. I asked her if Scott was single. She said he was. I don't date married men."

"I know that, Carrie." Steve tried to calm her down. "That's what we all believed at the time. Unfortunately, it turns out that we didn't know him as well as we thought we did. By the time we figured out he was married, Allison said you'd already decided to move on, so we let it go. At that point, we saw no need to bring it up, and we didn't want to upset you."

"Damn. I thought I was a better judge of character than that."

"Don't go beating yourself up, Carrie-Anne," added Alex. "I have a hunch he's probably done this a time or two before."

"So what do we do now?"

"We have some paperwork for you to sign. Then, when you're done, I'm giving you a ride home. You can leave your car here overnight. After I drop you home, I'll go out and get you a decent dinner."

"And tomorrow I'll ask Allie to go over to your place," said Steve. "She'll help you pick up your car, and then she'll take you shopping so you can get your kitchen restocked. You can return the favor some other time."

"Guys, I appreciate this, I really do, but it's my problem. I'll handle it."

"How? By starving yourself and making porno films?" She heard the frustration building in Alex's voice. "I guess some things never change. You're just as stubborn as you ever were."

"Look, you're in no position to argue," added Steve. "We're you're friends, so let us help you."

Alex handed her the paperwork. She let out a loud sigh as she grudgingly began filling it out. As soon as she finished Steve gathered it up and said goodbye. She turned her attention back at Alex, who stared back at her.

"So, have you finished pouting yet? If not, I can wait."

He leaned back into his chair, putting his hands behind his head. They stared at one another until Carrie finally started laughing in spite of herself. Alex reached across the table and patted her hand.

"Okay, Carrie-Anne. If you're ready, I'll run you home. We have ten years of catching up to do."

❧Sixteen❧

ALEX DROPPED CARRIE OFF at her apartment and she changed into a t-shirt and a pair of shorts. She came back to the living room to lay down on the sofa. After going for two days without eating she felt light-headed and exhausted. That afternoon's meeting had zapped what strength she had left. She must have dozed off, because the next thing she knew she was waking up to sound of someone knocking on her door.

"I'm coming, I'm coming."

She opened the door to Alex's smiling face. He was carrying several grocery bags.

"Alex? What are you doing here?"

"Did you forget? I was going to bring you something to eat, remember?"

"Oh, right. Sorry, I'm not all here right now."

He stepped across the threshold, heading straight to the kitchen and setting the bags down on the counter. He glanced over and noticed she was laying down on the sofa. She looked tired and pale. He pulled a carton of orange juice out of one of the bags, poured her a glass, and brought it to her, along with an apple. She sat up to take a drink.

"You remember my mother's famous homemade macaroni and cheese, don't you?"

"Yeah. It was my favorite."

"Well, I make it just as good as she did. It got me through college, and law school, and it'll be just the thing for you."

"Thanks, Alex." She finished the juice and bit into the apple as he glanced around the room.

"Aha, I see, you've got one."

"What?"

"Your boom box has a slot for an iPod." He whipped out his iPhone. "Remember how my mother was always playing this for us when we were kids? It was our song."

He punched a few buttons and dropped his phone into the slot on the boom box. Moments later they heard The Hollies singing, "Carrie-Anne." Carrie laughed as he sang along and danced to the beat for a moment or two before returning to the kitchen to begin preparing dinner. As he was working he noticed her cupboards and refrigerator really were empty. The years had not been kind to Carrie. She'd enjoyed so much success in her youth. She was the last person he would have ever expected to end up this way. It was heartbreaking for him to see. He heard the sound of the kitchen timer going off. He took the boiling pasta off the stove and dumped it into the colander. As it drained he looked back at her. She appeared to be asleep on the sofa. He grabbed the juice carton and quickly refilled her glass.

"Alex?"

"Yes, Carrie-Anne?"

"I've missed you. A lot."

"Me too."

He returned to the kitchen, quickly dumping all the ingredients into a baking dish and topping it with breadcrumbs before popping it into the oven. He set the timer and came back in to join Carrie on the sofa. She sat up to make room for him, leaning her head on his shoulder as soon as he took his seat.

"Something's missing here." He glanced around the room. "You don't have a television set."

"No, I'm afraid not. I'm a pauper these days. I don't have the money for a TV set, so I download shows on my laptop."

"Yeah, but then there's no remote control. I'm a guy. How can I possibly live without a remote control?"

Carrie started to laugh. It felt good to have Alex back in her life. "So Alex, is there anyone waiting at home for you?"

"Not anymore. Like you, I seem to be in between relationships at the moment."

"I see. So what's your story? What have you been doing for the past ten years?"

"It's like I already told you, I went to college and then I went to law school."

"Where?"

"I went to law school down in Tucson, at the University of Arizona."

"I see. So did you meet anyone interesting while you were there?"

"You mean did I have any girlfriends?" He glanced at her as she nodded. "Yes, Carrie, I've had plenty of girlfriends. The first significant one was back in college, about the time we lost touch with one another. I met Mattie when you first started going out with Doug. I went out with her for about a year or so. Others came along after her. Some I kept around for awhile, others were just short-term flings, like you and Scott. For the most part, I've had a good time, but there was never anyone I wanted to make any kind of long-term commitment to. Except for one, sort of."

"What do you mean?"

"I got engaged a few years ago," he explained. "Her name was Casey. I met her at the U of A. She was an economics major. I was in love, or so I thought, but as the wedding date drew closer I kept having more and more second thoughts. Then one morning I woke up and realized I couldn't go through with it. It's hard to explain. It's like I loved her, as a person, but I was never truly in love with her. The passion just wasn't there, at least not for me. That's when I knew it would never work, so I called it off."

"What happened after that?"

"Well, she wasn't too happy with me, to say the least, so it didn't end very well. I heard through the grapevine that she married someone else, about a year or so ago."

"Have you met anyone since then?"

"Nah," he replied. "Certainly not anyone one worth mentioning. I'm much too busy being a workaholic lawyer. I go out here and there, but never anything serious. I think my parents have finally given up on me. They've pretty much written me off as a confirmed bachelor, but at least Mark got married."

"I'd forgotten about your little brother."

"He's not so little anymore. He's now about two inches taller than me. He's a structural engineer, working for a firm in San Diego. He's got a wife, a two-year old boy, and another little boy on the way. The baby's due in November. It's funny how the Montoyas always seem to have boys. I never had a sister, and neither did my father or grandfather, nor did any of my uncles have any daughters. And despite my apparent lack of a love life, for the past few years I've had a recurring dream off and on about a son I'll apparently have someday. I think he's still a ways off, but it'd be nice if somewhere along the line one of us had a girl. She'd be the family princess. So, how 'bout you?"

"You saw the photos, Alex. What else is there for you to know about me?"

"That's not what I meant."

"I know, and I'm sorry," she said, apologetically. "I'm just cranky these days. So, let's see... I got my degree in business administration, and I also took as many photography classes as I could. After I graduated, I went to work for one of those portrait studios. It wasn't a great job but it got my foot in the door. My mother's the one who first encouraged me to strike out on my own. So did Doug, later on. That was about the time he and I had decided to move in together. So I took their advice and set up shop. Louise was a big help too. I thought we'd be friends forever. Who knew, huh?"

"Carrie-Anne, can I tell you something?"

"What?"

"I've always had the ability to read people like books, even when I was a kid. I find it comes in really handy, especially when I'm in a courtroom. Most of the time I'm right on the money and Carrie-Anne, I'm telling you, right now, I never liked Louise."

"Really? Why not?"

"Because she's a self-centered narcissist. Sure, she comes across as very sincere and very charming, but when you listen, really closely, it's always all about Louise."

"What do you mean?"

"Well, I'll give you an example," he explained. "When she called you that day about that photo shoot, what did she say?"

"She said she was concerned about my living arrangements. Then she told me she'd just gotten a private commission, she needed a model, and it would pay enough to get me into an apartment."

"Bingo," exclaimed Alex.

"What do you mean?"

"Did she say, 'Carrie, why don't you stay with us until you get on your feet?' No. Did she say, 'Carrie, let me help you, and we'll work it out later?' No. It was, 'Carrie, so sorry you're down and out, but if you'll do me this one little favor you can get into an apartment.'"

"Good heavens, you're right." She sounded astonished. "When she first brought it up I was hesitant. Then she told me that if I didn't want to do it she'd find someone else. I knew, right then, that she wouldn't help me if I said no. And now that you bring it up, I honestly can't recall a time when Louise ever called me just to ask how I was doing. It was always to ask for a favor, usually her grunt work. She never did a thing for me without my having to do something for her first, but she always had a way of wording things that made you think she really cared. She'd also make you feel guilty if you said no."

"She's obviously a master manipulator, Carrie-Anne. She never was your friend. As unpleasant as this is all going to be for you, and please understand, you'll be in for a real roller-coaster ride, one good thing will come out of it. By the time this is over, you'll know who your friends really are."

They began to reminisce about old times and before long the timer went off. Alex went into the kitchen to pull the macaroni and cheese out of the oven. It was bubbling hot and crispy brown on the top. He filled two plates, grabbed some forks and napkins, and brought it back to the sofa. Carrie savored the cheesy flavor as she recalled the times his mother made her macaroni and cheese when they were children. She had two more helpings before Alex brought out some brownies for their dessert. By the time he finished cleaning up the kitchen, he noticed the color had finally returned to her face. It was time for him to say goodnight. He had to be in his office bright and early the following morning to begin work on her case.

"It's good having you back, Carrie-Anne," he said as he hugged her.

"You too. You know, it's funny, Alex. I've been thinking about you a lot lately. I've really missed you, and now here you are."

He kissed her on the forehead and gave her one more hug before he stepped out, reminding her to lock her door behind him.

⤙Seventeen⤚

ALLISON HELPED CARRIE bring the last of the grocery bags into the kitchen. They set them on the counter and Carrie began unloading them.

"I've got the receipt in my purse, Allie," said Carrie as she filled her empty cupboards with canned goods. "I'm going back to my office as soon as we're done. I have two projects that I need to finish. As soon as I get paid I'll pay you back."

"I've already told you, there's no rush. You've always been there for me over the years and now it's my turn. Remember, back in high school, how I was struggling with algebra, and you and Alex helped me. If it hadn't been for the two of you, I would have flunked."

"I remember, but that was more Alex than me. He was a whiz at math."

"And he's a pretty smart lawyer, too. Steve's mentioned him to me a few times over the years, and all this time I had no idea that his Alex was our Alex. It was surprise to me as well. So, what's he like these days?"

"The same. He's finally put on some weight so he's not bone-skinny and gawky like he used to be. In fact, he looks pretty darn good. Other than that, he's still our same old Alex. He's smart, he's funny, but nothing gets past him. Wish he'd been around last fall, back when Doug first dumped me. I wouldn't be in the mess I'm in now."

"You don't know that, Carrie. If I was down and out and had no place to turn I would have probably done Louise's photo shoot too. But somewhere along the line you've seriously pissed someone off and that's what has me scared."

"I know and I'm worried too, but worried or not, I have to go back to my office today. I have someone who's on a tight deadline. When Steve told me to shut my door and go home I sent an email blast to all my clients telling them I had an unexpected emergency. Now I'm starting to hear back from some of them. They need their photos and I need the work."

"I understand, but what if some sicko shows up at your door?"

"My website is still down," said Carrie. "If anyone looking at *Gentry Magazine* decides to do a Google search on me all they'll find is an under construction page, but at some point I have to get my website back up. I'm starting to worry that people might start thinking I'm out of business. I've had three cancelations so far this week. That's not good."

"No, it's not, but it might also be Louise's doing. You said she was going to ruin you. It's entirely possible that she's getting ahold of your clients and telling them to stop doing business with you."

"Then that's all the more reason for me to get back to work."

She began placing the frozen foods into the freezer. Just as she emptied the last grocery bag her phone rang. She checked the caller ID, quickly excusing herself as she stepped out of the kitchen and into the living room. Allison remained in the kitchen, although she could hear Carrie's end of the conversation. It sounded like there was some kind of a problem with her mother. She waited quietly until Carrie got off the phone.

"That was someone from the nursing home."

"Yeah, I gathered that," replied Allison. "Is there anything wrong?"

"They wanted to let me know that Mama's come down with a fever. Apparently she woke up with it this morning. They've put her on some antibiotics, but with her being in the condition she's in, her immune system just isn't that strong anymore. Even a cold can make her seriously ill, so now there'll be even more prescriptions to tack onto her bill."

"Carrie, I know you're heard this before, but it's time to make her a ward of the state. You're at the point now where you can no longer buy enough food for yourself. You did the best you could for her and I know she'd be really proud of you for everything you've done, but she's your mother. Trust me, she would never, ever, want to see you literally starving yourself in order to take care of her. In fact, if she knew that you'd gone without eating for two days, she'd be mad as hell at you."

Carrie let out a long sigh and remained silent for a few moments.

"You're right, Allison. I guess it's time, isn't it? Okay, I'll call Mr. Greene and set up a meeting with him. He said that when the time came he'd help me with the paperwork, but I still feel like I've failed her."

"You haven't failed her," assured Allison. "In fact, you've gone above and beyond the call of duty. Most people in your situation would have made her a ward of the state a long time ago, but you were willing to give up everything you had to take care of her. There's no greater love than that, but now it's time to start taking care of you. So let's start by going to lunch. Since I'm all ready in the neighborhood, I told Steve I'd meet him at twelve-thirty and Alex is joining us. I'm anxious to see him too. Why don't you come with us?"

"I would, Allie, but I have to get to the office. I need to get those projects finished, today if at all possible. I have to take care of my own clients."

"I understand. Just be careful, okay?"

"I will."

Carrie opened the refrigerator and grabbed the container with Alex's leftover macaroni and cheese. Packing it into a small cooler, she promised Allison she'd stop to take a lunch break. The two women headed out to the parking lot where Carrie said goodbye, thanking her friend once again before hopping in her car and heading to the studio. Once she arrived, she was relieved to find everything just as she'd left it. She set up her lights and started to work. She was well into the first shoot when she heard her cell phone going off. She checked the caller ID, relieved it wasn't the nursing home calling again.

"Carrie-Anne, how could you? After all I've done for you, you've turned around and stood me up."

"You're so full of it, Alex." She smiled at the sound of his laughter. "You know, if you'd actually called and invited me to lunch yourself, instead of just assuming that I'd come with Allie..."

"Okay, point taken, but I'm concerned about you being in your office alone. We still don't know who set you up, but they obviously know where you work. One of our other clients is a private security company. I'd like to talk to them about having someone guard you whenever you're there."

"Alex, I appreciate it, but if I don't have the funds to pay you then how can I afford to pay them?"

"We'll worry about that later. In the meantime, would you like to hear some good news?"

"You bet."

"I spent most of the morning on the phone with Caleb Wyman and his attorneys," he explained. "They're aware that you didn't enter their contest and that the signature on the release form is a forgery."

"Okay, so what do they plan on doing about it?"

"They're going pay Louise a handsome royalty. That's about all they can do. You are, of course, disqualified from the photo contest, and you won't be able to cash the check."

"I wasn't going to cash it."

"I know that," he said, "it's just standard business practice. I already told them you'd given the check to me and that we needed to keep it as evidence. They said they understood. What matters is that Louise will come out smelling like a rose. She'll collect a substantial sum of money and she'll get some free publicity to boot."

"Does that mean she won't sue me?"

"Hopefully not. It certainly minimizes her damages. Then we can focus on finding out who it was that did this to you and stop them before they can do anything else."

"Thank you, Alex."

"Don't thank me yet, we still have a long road ahead of us. But next time you get a lunch invite, don't stand me up, okay? It wasn't the same without you being there."

Carrie thanked him once again before ending the call. As soon as he hung up he picked up the message sitting on his desk. It was from Louise's attorney, Jack Collins, who called while he was out. He dialed the number and was immediately connected.

"Thanks for returning my call," said Collins. "I've received the letter you faxed me this morning and I've already spoken to my client about it."

"So what does she have to say? Is she willing to work with us to find out who really sent the photos to *Gentry Magazine*?"

"No, I'm afraid not. In fact, we've decided to follow through and file our claim against Ms. Daniels."

"May I remind you sir, that Mrs. Dickenson will be receiving a generous fee from the magazine as compensation for the unauthorized use of her photos. So may I ask the reason why she intends to pursue my client?"

"Certainly. It's our understanding that when Ms. Daniels called Mr. Wyman's office she told his secretary quote, 'I can't find my release form. Would you mind emailing a copy to me?' We're told that during that call she sounded very calm and collected. She never once came across as angry or upset. She even thanked Mr. Wyman's secretary, when she congratulated her on winning the contest."

"Yes," said Alex, "she admits making that call. She was trying to get a copy of the release form without raising suspicion. She needed to see the signature because she knew she hadn't signed it. She also tells me that the email address they had on file wasn't hers, and that she had to give them her correct address so she would receive their file."

"We understand that's her story. However, we're of the opinion that your client, possibly with the help of at least one other individual, has conspired to make it appear as if the photos were submitted without her knowledge. We believe that her partner either signed the release form, or that Ms. Daniels attempted to distort her own handwriting when she signed it. Either way, she did so that in the event she got caught, she could then turn around and claim that her signature was forged. Ms. Daniels is in dire financial straights. She needed the five-thousand dollars to help pay her mother's medical expenses. She didn't count on Mr. Dickenson being a subscriber to *Gentry Magazine*."

"This is a joke, right?"

"It's not a joke, Mr. Montoya. We're serious."

"In that case, I have to ask you if you've completely lost your mind. If that's the kind of fantasy world you and your client want to live in, go ahead. I have the five thousand dollar check my client received from *Gentry Magazine*. She freely turned it over to me. Are you also not aware that this is a criminal, as well as civil matter? Ms. Daniels has already filed a police report. She never had any intention of cashing that check, and we've also informed *Gentry Magazine* that she had no intention of ever cashing it. If you want to file your frivolous lawsuit, go ahead. We'll be defending her and we believe that once the court hears our side of the story, we'll prevail."

Alex ended the call and hung up the phone in disgust. Louise was going after Carrie out of pure spite. He wadded up the message and threw it at the little miniature basketball hoop attached to his wastepaper basket. He smiled as he made his shot. His mind flashed back to high school. He'd made the varsity basketball team his junior year, and even though Carrie was hardly a basketball fan, she nonetheless attended as many games as she could, just so she could cheer him on.

"And now, Alex, the ball is in your court. Whatever you do, don't let her down."

It was time to get back to work. He'd need to enlist the services of an old and trusted friend. He turned to his computer to look up the phone number. He quickly dialed, drumming his pencil on his desk while he waited for someone to pick up.

"Talk to me," said the gravely voice on the other end.

"Hey, George, Alex Montoya."

"Hey, Alex, long time, no hear. You ready to pay up on that bet yet?"

"Soon George, soon, but right now I have another favor to ask you."

"Okay, so who is she and what's she done?" George was direct and unapologetic as usual.

"She," said Alex, emphasizing the word, "is a woman by the name of Louise Dickenson. She's a photographer. Someone took some of her photos and gave them to a magazine to publish, without her knowledge or consent, and she thinks my client did it."

"So, did your client do it?"

"Do you think I'd be calling if she did? My client is an old and very dear friend. I've known her since the fourth grade. I looked out for her back then and I'm looking out for her now. Someone went to a great deal of trouble to set her up, George. They even forged her signature on a release form."

"That would be Betty's department."

"Yes, I know. Your better half is the best handwriting expert in the business and I'm going to need her help on this one too. In the meantime, I have to find out who did this. Not only is Louise Dickenson out to ruin my client's livelihood over something she didn't do, there's an unseen enemy out there stalking her, and

I don't know what else they're capable of doing. I don't want Carrie getting hurt."

"Sounds intriguing," said George. "I'd say your little friend's gotten someone's dander up."

"Well, not intentionally. She admits went out a few times with someone who she thought was single, and now it turns out he probably wasn't. My gut tells me that whoever sent those photos to the magazine is either the guy in question, or someone close to him."

"One of those, huh? So either the guy's ticked off because she got suspicious and dumped him, or the wife found out about it and is out to tar and feather her. Either way, someone's out to get her, and that's the kind of thing that can put your friend in an early grave if she's not careful. Tell you what. You let me know what day and time works best for you and I'll stop by your office to discuss my fee."

❧Eighteen❧

MAGGIE ANDREWS DISCREETLY slipped the copy of *Gentry Magazine* between the other books and magazines she was buying. She casually wandered around the bookstore shelves a few minutes longer before strolling up the cashier and placing her items on the counter. The gray-haired man standing behind the register looked like the grandfatherly type. His nametag identified him as the store manager.

"It's a gag gift for a friend," she said as he uncovered the magazine and scanned the barcode.

"No need to explain. Most of the time people tell me they buy it for the articles. You're lucky we still had a copy."

"Really. Why's that?"

"It's the middle of August. This time of year a lot of our customers are out of town beating the heat. Most of the time it sells out within a week or two. We rarely have any copies left by the time the next issue arrives."

"I see. So when is the next issue coming out?"

"In three days."

Maggie shrugged her shoulders and handed over her debit card. He bagged her purchases and thanked her as she headed out to the parking lot. Safely in her car, she fired up the engine, turned on the air conditioning, and pulled out the magazine.

Her face beamed with pride once she found what she was looking for. Louise's photos had indeed won that month's contest, and both had been published. Maggie had already suspected it when she discovered the Carrie Daniels Photography website had been replaced by an under construction page. She dropped the magazine back into the bag, put her car into gear, and exited the parking lot. At least she had one victory to celebrate.

She winced at the sight of the real estate sign in her front lawn as she pulled into her driveway and hit the remote to open the garage door. As she stepped inside the house, her mind wandered back to that awful night when her world suddenly turned upside down. Everything seemed normal when she arrived home from her volunteer day at Ben's school. She'd gone straight to the kitchen and started making dinner. The first sign of trouble was when she realized Scott was almost an hour late. Then Sarah burst into the kitchen, crying hysterically, screaming something about her father having just abandoned the entire family. Maggie rushed upstairs and discovered that Scott's clothes and personal belongings were gone. Ten minutes later there was a knock at the front door. A stranger waited on the other side. He handed her a paper, informing her that she'd been served. Scott called the following morning. He was somewhere in Colorado, en route to Kansas City. He said he was in love with a woman there named Nancy Edwards, and that he planned to marry Nancy once their divorce was final. Seventeen years of marriage went down the drain, leaving Maggie nowhere to go.

She let out a sigh as she stepped into the kitchen to mix herself a scotch and soda. She took her drink, along with her shopping bag, into the family room. She pulled the magazine out. Once again, a smile of satisfaction broke out across her face as she stared at the photos.

"Well, Carrie, I guess we both lost out on Scott, huh? Trust me, I'm going to get as much out of him as I possibly can before Nancy gets what's left. And as for you, you little tramp, you still had it coming. So if I'm going down, then by golly you're going down with me. And do you want to know something else, Carrie? I'm not quite finished with you yet. I still have a trick or two up my sleeve, just you wait and see."

Maggie tossed the magazine aside, picked up the remote and turned on the six o'clock news. Channel Seven had an anonymous tip line and they gave out the phone number during every news broadcast. She grabbed a pen and paper. A short time later her patience paid off. The anchorman announced the number and she quickly wrote it down. She reached for the remote to turn the volume down before picking up the phone and dialing the number. After a few rings she was greeted with a recorded message.

"Thank you for calling the Channel Seven tip line. At the sound of the beep please record your message. You may remain anonymous."

She waited for the beep.

"Yes, hello. Hey, you may find this interesting. Do any of you remember the Mercer's Market girl? She used to do TV commercials, here in Arizona, some twenty years ago. Anyway, my husband just got done reading this month's issue of *Gentry Magazine*, and there's a couple of nude photos of her in the magazine. Apparently, she's all grown up now, and she's in the photo contest section. Oh yeah, her name is Carrie Daniels. Anyway, he showed me the pictures. They're real eye-openers, if you know what I mean. You know, it's really shocking to see that innocent little girl from those old TV commercials displaying herself like a harlot. Makes you wonder what the world is coming to. Well, that's all I have to say. Thanks for listening. Bye."

Maggie let out a giggle as soon as she disconnected the call.

"Well, Carrie, what can I say? Just when you thought the scandal was dying down, I've added to another nail for your coffin."

She took another sip of her cocktail before picking up the remote to channel surf. She soon came across one of her favorite old movies, *The African Queen*. The movie had just started so she settled into her chair to watch. An hour later it was interrupted by a loud knock at the door. Maggie sat up straight with a jolt. She decided to ignore it. Whoever it was knocked again, this time much louder.

"FBI. Open up," shouted a man on the other side.

She ran to the door. As soon as she opened it, a forty-something man, with dark, thinning hair and a dark mustache, presented her with a badge.

"I'm looking for Scott Andrews."

"I'm sorry, my husband and I have separated. He no longer lives here."

"In that case, I'm sorry to bother you, ma'am, but I'll need to ask you a few questions. May I come in?"

"Certainly," she replied as she invited him inside. "Sorry

'bout all the mess. I'm usually pretty neat and tidy, but right now my kids are visiting their dad in Kansas City. While they've been gone, I just haven't been as motivated to keep up with the housework." She told him to take a seat on the sofa.

"Ma'am, my name is Ken O'Dell." He handed her his card. "I'm with the FBI, and I'm conducting an investigation. I promise to only take a few minutes of your time."

"All right."

"I understand you and your husband are art collectors."

"Yes, we are, or at least, we were," she replied. "As it turns out, that's about the only thing that he and I apparently had in common, besides the kids."

"I see. Mrs. Andrews, I'm told this past February, you and your husband purchased two limited edition photographs by Louise Dickenson, and they were purchased at Hanson Sisters Fine Art, in Scottsdale."

Maggie's heart skipped a beat. She put on her best face and tried to remain calm. "That sounds about right. I remember Scott going to an artist's opening at Hanson Sisters around that time. However, I was in bed with a cold that night so I wasn't able to go with him."

"I see. Did your husband make a purchase that night?"

"Yes sir, he did. He bought two black and white photographs, and yes, they were limited edition prints."

"What were they of?"

"A female nude," said Maggie. "We hung them upstairs, in the master bedroom, away from the kids. What's this about? Is there anything wrong with the photos?"

"No ma'am, not the photos themselves. May I see them?"

"I'm sorry, but I won't be able to show them to you. They're no longer in my possession."

"What happened to them?"

"My soon-to-be ex-husband took them with him to Kansas City. As I just told you, we're separated and in the process of getting a divorce."

"I sorry to hear that, Mrs. Andrews." O'Dell glanced around at the other art on the walls. "Did he take any other artwork with him?"

"No sir, just those two prints. Our attorneys are still hashing out who'll get which pieces in the final settlement. Is there something wrong with the photos? Were they counterfeit or something?"

"No ma'am, they're not counterfeit, however we are investigating a criminal case, but I'm afraid I'm not at liberty to discuss the details with you."

Maggie's blood turned to ice. She'd counted on Louise Dickenson going after Carrie for copyright infringement. That had been her plan from the beginning. It should have been a civil matter, but now the police were involved and that was something she hadn't anticipated. She'd have to very careful with her answers.

"Really? So what does this have to do with Scott? Has he done something illegal?"

"I'm afraid I can't discuss the details at this time, ma'am. However, would you mind telling me what the two prints looked like?"

"Well, I guess I could. Are you with the vice squad or something? These are fine-art photos. Are we in some sort of trouble for having them in our home because we have minor children?"

"No ma'am. Again, could you please describe the photos? We need to know which two of the prints that your husband purchased."

Maggie described the two photos as best she could. As she was talking she glanced around and noticed her copy of *Gentry Magazine* laying on the end table. There were other magazines on the table as well, and she'd set her drink, and the remote control, on top of it. She prayed he wouldn't notice it.

"So I'd still like to know what kind of proof you have that we've done anything wrong. I'm sure we're not the only people who purchased those two prints. I know both of the ones we had were sold in limited editions of fifty."

"I'm aware of that, ma'am. Now, I have one last question for you. Do you, or your husband, happen to know anyone by the name of Carrie Daniels?"

Once again, Maggie's heart skipped a beat. "Carrie Daniels?" She paused for a moment, pretending to be in deep thought. "I'm sorry, sir, but I'm afraid that name doesn't ring a bell for me. Who is she? Is there some reason why I should know her?"

"No ma'am, I guess there isn't. Thank you for your time. Is there anyway that we can contact your husband?"

"Yes, sir. He kept his old cell phone number, so it would be a local call."

As Maggie gave him Scott's phone number, she realized she'd just been given a golden opportunity. "You know, sir, I don't know if this would mean anything to you or not, but now that I think about it, Scott was acting kind of strange just before he left town. I mean he just wasn't himself. He was short-tempered and nervous. A few days later I came home and discovered he'd left. His clothes and personal items were gone, along with those two prints. We have many other pieces in our collection that are worth a lot more money. Funny how they were the only two that he took with him."

O'Dell thanked her again and she walked him to the door. She stood by and waited for him to leave. Once his car was out of sight she closed the door, snatched up the magazine and tossed it into the fireplace.

"Holy shit," she said in disgust as she lit a match and ignited one of the corners. "So, you just couldn't leave well enough alone, could you, Carrie? You had to go running to the authorities and now they're trying to figure out who really sent those photos to the magazine. You stupid little whore. You should have just kept your mouth shut and hung on to the prize money. You're nothing but a spoiled crybaby. Well, I can tell you one thing, Ms. Carrie Daniels, no one will ever find out it was me, especially since I just made that FBI agent think that Scott did it. So what do you think of me now? Hmm?"

She smiled once again as she watched the magazine burst into flames. Apparently O'Dell hadn't noticed it. Even if he had, it was gone for good now.

❧Nineteen❧

CARRIE WALKED INTO HER apartment and immediately set her camera on the dining table. She'd spent most of the afternoon working on a shoot in the hot August sun and she was anxious to jump into shower. She and Alex had plans for dinner that night and she looked forward to spending some time him. As she headed toward the bathroom, she heard a knock at the door. She checked her watch. Alex wasn't due for at least another hour. She looked through the peephole and smiled when she saw the tall, nicely dressed African-American woman standing outside. She opened the door.

"Hey, Billie, come on in. Anything new to report?"

Billie Hughes was a former model and one of the FBI agents assigned to her case. Her specialty was white-collar crimes, including identity theft and forgery. She greeted Carrie with a warm smile as she accepted the invitation and took her seat at the dining table. She reached into her purse for her notepad as Carrie sat down to join her.

"It turns out that there were two customers who purchased both of the prints that appeared in *Gentry Magazine*," she explained. "One is a retired art teacher who's only a part-year

Arizona resident. She took hers back to her other home in Minnesota, and she was driving back there the day the photos were uploaded. Her alibi checks out."

"Someone with her background would certainly know better too. So who was the other customer?"

"Your old friend, Scott Andrews."

"Damn. I was afraid of that. Billie, when I met the man I had no idea he was married. Later on I thought he had another girlfriend, but by then I was ready to move on. It was George McCormick, Alex's private investigator, who finally confirmed that Scott has a wife. Now I feel like a home wrecker."

"Well, you shouldn't," replied Billie, reassuringly. "Trust me, I see this kind of thing all the time in my line of work. There are a lot of good women out there who unknowingly get involved with married men, so don't go beating yourself up. These guys lie by omission and you're not a mind reader. Anyway, would you like to know what we've found out?"

"Yes, I would."

"The night before last, another agent went to the Andrews residence to talk to Scott. As soon as he arrived Maggie told him Scott was no longer living there."

"Like I didn't know that."

"I know, but we still have to check everything out. Here's the thing. Ken O'Dell, the other agent on your case, is convinced Maggie Andrews knows a whole lot more than she's letting on, especially since he noticed a copy of the current issue of *Gentry Magazine* sitting out on a table. So yesterday he returned to her home with a search warrant."

"I see. So then what happened?"

"At first she wasn't too happy, but then, in the blink of an eye, she suddenly decides to cooperate. In fact, O'Dell says she was being too helpful. She led them upstairs to the master bedroom and pointed out the spot on the wall where the photos had been hanging. He and some other agents searched the house, top to bottom, but the neither the photos, nor the magazine, were there. However, he noticed something else that was rather odd."

"Really? And what was that?"

"Ashes in the fireplace," said Billie. "It's the middle of August. No one uses their fireplace this time of year. It appeared as if someone had been burning a lot of paper, so they bagged it. Maggie acted nervous, but she maintained that the ashes had mysteriously appeared the same day Scott left town, and that she just hadn't gotten around to cleaning out the fireplace. They've taken the ashes to the lab to run some tests, however it will be some time before we get the results. Meantime, we're arranging to have someone in Kansas City talk to Scott. That's about all I can tell you at this point. The investigation is still ongoing. Oh, there is one other thing I keep forgetting to mention."

"What's that?"

"Hanson Sisters dropped Louise Dickenson," explained Billie. "Apparently, Louise called them the same day she called you. She also accused them of somehow being responsible for the photos ending up in *Gentry Magazine*, and she threatened to sue them as well. According to Cynthia Lindsey, the gallery owner, Louise was extremely belligerent and verbally abusive to her on the phone. She said Louise called her back a few days later and tried to apologize, but by then it was too late. Mrs. Lindsey had already contacted her attorney and told him to terminate Louise's contract. I've spoken to her on the phone a few times. She's a very nice woman who's been both professional and cooperative while we've been conducting this investigation. I just thought you might find it interesting."

"That's a shame. In spite of everything that's happened, Louise is still a brilliant photographer. Word of this is bound to leak out. If she keeps it up, I doubt another gallery will work with her."

Billie wrapped up her business. As soon as she left, Carrie headed to the shower. She'd just put on a fresh sundress when she heard a knock on her door. She looked through the peephole, expecting to see Alex, but it wasn't him. Instead, it was a man she'd never seen before.

"Who is it?"

"I'm looking for Carrie Daniels."

She cautiously opened the door and instantly heard Alex's approaching voice.

"Hey, Bruce, what's up?"

"The usual, Alex," he replied, turning his attention away from her.

"Have you got something for Ms. Daniels?"

"Yep."

"I can take it. I'm her attorney."

"Suit yourself."

He handed the piece of paper off to Alex and stepped away. Carrie closed the door as he came in.

"So what's this all about?"

"I have a hunch it's a love letter from Louise." He removed his sunglasses and dropped them into his pocket. "I've been keeping her attorney up-to-date with everything George is finding out, but she just won't listen to reason." He unfolded the paper and began reading it. "Criminy."

"What's wrong?"

"She's naming you, and Scott Andrews, as co-defendants in a copyright infringement claim."

"You're joking."

"I wish I were. Look, Carrie-Anne, I'm representing you and you alone. Scott will have to find his own council."

"Thanks, Alex. You know, I really thought I'd put that chapter of my life behind me. If I hadn't been such a whore none of this—"

Alex dropped the paper on the table and grabbed her by the shoulders. His eyes bore into hers. In all the years Carrie had known him, she'd never seen such a look of intense anger from him before.

"What did you just say?"

"Well, it's true, Alex."

Alex took a deep breath and chose his next words very carefully. "Caroline Lee Daniels, you listen to me, and you listen good. I don't ever want to hear you say that about yourself again. Do you hear me?"

"Well, I'm hardly the Virgin Mary, Alex."

"No one ever said you were, but you're hardly Hester Prynne either. Through no fault of your own, you ended up in a bad place, and while you were there a couple of predators came along and took advantage of your vulnerability. You are not, nor have you ever been, a whore."

"But Alex—"

"No buts." He pulled her in close and wrapped his arms around her. "You're my best friend, and friends don't let friends call themselves things like that, especially when it's not true. So you've made some bad choices. Big deal. Who among us hasn't made a mistake or two?" He held her for a moment to let it sink in. He began stroking the back of her head. "Carrie, I don't want you worrying about this, okay? I'm an attorney. It's my job to worry about this. Hell, I live for this stuff. It's like a game. Louise's lawyer and I will spend the next few months taking depositions, writing letters back and forth, and filing motions with the court. Eventually, they'll figure out they've got nothing and they'll try to disappear quietly into the night. That's when I let loose and kick their butts. I've rarely lost a case, Carrie-Anne, and I'm certainly not going to lose this one." He held her for a few moments longer. Deep down, he knew he was starting to become too emotionally attached. "Meantime, it's Friday night. Let's go grab a bite somewhere and try to enjoy the weekend, okay?"

Alex took her to a nearby steakhouse. It was noisy and crowded, but they were in no rush. They took a seat in the bar and had a drink while they waited for a table. Over dinner, Carrie brought him up to date on her mother.

"I saw her the day before yesterday. She's had a bad cold, but now she's finally doing better."

"Allie says you've decided to make her a ward of the state."

"Yes, I did. And you know what's funny, Alex? I thought I'd feel guilty about it, but I'm actually quite relieved. Mr. Greene made good on his promise and he helped me with the paperwork. Now that it's done, I feel as if someone's lifted an incredible weight off my shoulders. I can finally start thinking about upgrading my business, and maybe putting some money away while I'm at it. If only I didn't have this damn lawsuit staring me in the face."

"Don't go there, Carrie-Anne," he said with a wink. "It's after hours, so I'm not talking shop. So tell me, what would you say to going out and celebrating your new lease on life?"

"What do you have in mind?"

"I know of a resort, in the mountains outside of Tucson. It's called the Double-Diamond. It used to be a ranch at one time, and it's a beautiful place. The hotel was built during the Great Depression, so it's kind of a rustic art deco. You name it, they've got it; hiking trails, mountain biking, horseback riding, a pool and spa, and best of all, peace and quiet. They don't even have television sets in any of the guest rooms. The whole idea is to be able to unplug, unwind and get away from it all."

"I see. So when did you want to go there?"

"Soon," he replied. "You need a break, Carrie-Anne. A nice, quiet weekend at a desert spa, away from everyone and everything, would do you a world of good."

"I think you're right, and I'd like that. My birthday's coming up next month."

"Yes, I remember."

"It'd be a nice way to celebrate. By then, Mama should be completely over her bug."

The waiter came to take their plates. As they were talking, Alex noticed something on one of the big-screen television sets mounted in a corner. The ten o'clock news was on, and they were showing a clip of one of Carrie's old Mercer's Market's ads. It was followed by a shot of one of the nude photos of her in *Gentry Magazine*, with certain portions blurred out. Carrie noticed it too on one of the other screens.

"Oh my God."

"Calm down." He reached across the table to grasp her hand. "Don't do anything that might draw attention to yourself. No one is watching it. I've been concerned for some time that someone in the media would connect the dots, so we'll have to deal with it. I'll take care of the check, and then we're going to quietly leave. I'll take you home, and when we get there I want you to pack your bags. You can stay at my place for a few days. Don't worry, it's a big house. You can make yourself at home in the guestroom."

"Thanks for the invite, Alex, but I'll be okay."

"No, Carrie-Anne. Please, listen to me. There's litigation pending and I don't want you being hounded by reporters. You don't need that kind of publicity right now and it could jeopardize our case. Don't worry, this will all blow over in a few days. Until then, you'll be much safer at my place."

Alex took care of the bill and they left the restaurant. Fortunately, none of the other patrons recognized Carrie. Soon she was packed and they were back on the road. She was in her car, following Alex's white Camaro.

Alex lived in a well-to-do neighborhood in the mountains on the northeast side the city. The road to his house wound around a golf course and he soon turned onto another narrow, curvy road, leading to a house at the top of a hill. He pulled into the garage, while Carrie parked in the driveway.

"Here we are, home sweet home." He walked out to her car and took her suitcase out of the trunk. He noticed her eyes were as wide as saucers.

"Alex, I don't know what to say. I always knew you would do well, but this..."

"Looks can be deceiving, my dear," he said with a smile. "This house was in foreclosure. Let's just say I got a sweetheart deal. Come with me. I'll show you around."

She followed him inside. The house was beautifully furnished. It looked like something out of a home-decorating magazine. The living room had a wine-colored corner group sofa facing large picture windows that revealed a stunning view of the city lights below. He led her down the hallway and opened the door at the end. He waited as she stepped into a cozy, comfortable guest bedroom.

"The bathroom's at the first door on your left." He set her suitcase on the foot of the bed. "The master bedroom is off the other side of the living room, so if you want to stay up late and watch TV it's okay. You won't be disturbing me. Feel free to help yourself to whatever's in the kitchen."

"Alex, I don't know what to say, other than thank you."

"You're welcome." He gave her a hug and a quick kiss on the cheek. "Have a good night and I'll see you in the morning."

He stepped out and closed the door behind him, heading off to the master suite to get ready for bed. He turned on the television set and tried to relax, but he felt restless. He climbed into bed, grabbed the remote and began channel surfing, but he was unable to focus. He finally switched off the television and began fluffing his pillows around. Try as he may, he just couldn't make himself comfortable. He let out a sigh.

"Don't go there, Alex. It's forbidden fruit and you know it."

He somehow managed to fall asleep, only to wake up in the middle of the night. He glanced at the clock on the nightstand. It was a few minutes past three. After tossing and turning for another half hour he decided a glass of warm milk might help him get back to sleep. He climbed out of bed and quietly entered the living room.

"You too, huh?"

The unexpected sound of her voice in the darkness caught him off guard.

"Carrie-Anne?"

It took a moment for him to make her out in the darkness. She was laying on a section of the corner group. He noticed she'd brought a pillow and blanket with her.

"Sorry, Alex. I couldn't sleep, so I thought I'd come out here and watch the city lights for awhile. They're so beautiful. From here they almost look like some sort of magic fairyland."

"I couldn't sleep either. Must be one of those nights."

"Why don't you join me?" She pointed to the other section of the corner group.

"Don't mind if I do."

He went to fetch his pillow and a blanket. Once he returned, he made himself a bed on the other section. As he lay down he could feel the top of her head brushing against his. For some reason it made him feel calmer. As he relaxed, his mind's eye began seeing the images of their lives from when they were children. Before long he dozed off.

* * *

The morning sun woke Carrie. She slowly stirred, being careful not to disturb Alex. After she sat up she turned to watch him sleep. He looked so peaceful. She reached over and began to gently stroke his hair. He moaned softly at her touch. She looked at his face. He appeared to be content. She sat with him for a few minutes, lightly running her fingers through his hair, before she carefully got up and went into the kitchen.

❧Twenty❧

ALEX WAS DREAMING OF bacon and coffee. He opened his eyes to see the morning sun high in the sky, but he still smelled the scent of bacon and coffee. He got off the sofa and wandered into the kitchen. Carrie was there, frying bacon in a skillet.

"Morning, Alex." She smiled as she turned to face him. "There's fresh coffee brewing in the pot."

He poured himself a cup. As he took a sip, he turned to watch her. "What on earth do you have on?"

Carrie stopped to look down at her nightclothes. "It's a long, pink cotton nightshirt, Alex. What did you think it was?"

"I know that. Turn around. I want to see what's on the front."

She turned back to face him. A drawing of a laced-up corset was printed on the front of her nightshirt. She looked down again, realizing that was what he was talking about. She gave him another smile.

"So, I see you like my sexy lingerie. Allie gave this to me last year for my birthday. We both thought it was pretty funny."

He saw a vision in his mind's eye of her laced up in a real corset, and immediately chastised himself for thinking about her that way. She was a friend, not a lover.

Carrie returned to her cooking, announcing that she was making french toast for their breakfast. Over their meal he asked her if there was anything in particular she wanted to do that day.

"You know, Alex, I think I'm going to heed your advice and just unwind. I've brought a book with me. I'll probably spend the day just hanging out."

"Sounds like a plan. I'll head off to the gym in a little while. Then I can spend the rest of my weekend being a couch potato without feeling guilty."

"You? I figured a hot, eligible bachelor like you would be out somewhere playing golf or tennis, or doing sometime to attract the ladies."

Alex's ears perked up. Had Carrie just called him 'hot?' The well-worn t-shirt and sweatpants he had on were hardly sexy.

"Nah," he said with a smile. "This 'eligible bachelor,' as you put it, works hard for a living. By the time the weekends roll around, I'm usually beat. Besides, I did all that girl-chasing stuff when I was younger. I'm ready to settle down."

"I know what you mean. Unfortunately, Prince Charming—"

She was interrupted by the sound of her cell phone ringing. She excused herself as she stepped away from the table to answer it. Sierra Arroyo was calling, and the news wasn't good.

"You might want to come down here, as quickly as you can," said the nurse on the other end of the line.

"What happened?"

"Late last night your mother took a turn for the worse."

"I thought she was doing better."

"She was. Then last night she suddenly began to run a very high fever. She's developed a serious staph infection and she's not responding to the antibiotics. Her condition is deteriorating rapidly. I'm sorry to tell you this, Carrie, but we've called in hospice."

"What do you mean you've called in hospice?" She felt Alex's hand on her shoulder.

"We'll explain it all as soon as you get here."

"Thanks, I'm on my way." She quickly ended the call. "I have to go, Alex. There's some sort of a problem with my mother."

"I gathered that. Get dressed. I'll take you there."

"No. I appreciate the thought, but I have to do this alone."

"You're in no condition to drive over there, Carrie-Anne."

"I'll be okay." She stopped for a moment. "Alex, they told

me she has a staph infection and that they've called hospice. They don't think she's going to make it."

She suddenly burst into tears. Alex held her as she cried on his shoulder.

"Carrie, please let go with you. I knew her too."

"She's not the way you remember her, Alex. For the past three years, she's been a vegetable. She's no longer able to speak, half her body is completely paralyzed, and her mental capacity is very limited. I've never allowed anyone to see her like this. Not even Allison."

"Carrie-Anne, you can't go through this alone. We're your friends. We know her too and we're here to help you. We'd also like it, very much, if you'd give us a chance to tell her goodbye."

Carrie thought it over. Perhaps she was being unfair. "Okay, I guess maybe you're right. I'll let you and Allie see her, but first I need you to do a favor for me."

"Anything."

"Would you mind calling Allie? She has a key to my apartment. Tell her there's a storage box, with all of my important papers, on the top shelf of my closet. Inside that box is a folder with my mother's name on it. Would you ask her if she'd mind picking up that folder and bringing it with her?"

"Certainly."

As soon as Carrie stepped away, Alex grabbed his phone and called Allison.

"What's up?"

"It's not good, Allie." He quickly brought her up to date.

"Oh no," she responded in Spanish. "I knew this day would come, sooner or later."

It took Alex a moment to switch gears to reply to her in the same language. "I don't know if you caught the ten o'clock news last night, Allison, but there was a story about the Mercer's Market girl ending up in *Gentry Magazine*. I don't want any reporters bothering her, so I've brought her over to my place. She's staying in my guest room until this blows over."

"That's good, Alex. She doesn't need those vultures right now."

"My thoughts exactly. So we need to ask a favor, Allie."

"Sure, what is it?"

Alex relayed Carrie's request to go to her apartment and get her mother's papers.

"Sure, I'd be happy to. Where to you want me to bring them?"

"To the nursing home. I've talked to Carrie. She's decided to let us go in and spend some time with her mother. We both knew her."

"Thank you, Alex." There was a sound of relief in her voice. "I always loved her mother and I'd like to see her, one last time."

"Me too."

"Oh and Alex?"

"Yes, Allison."

"What has happened to that lovely accent of yours?"

"My grandfather passed away about seven years ago. He was the one who insisted we only speak Castillian Spanish whenever we were in his home. Nowadays, the firm has me come in and translate for clients from Mexico and Central America who aren't proficient in English. Apparently, I'm picking up their dialect."

Alex ended the call and quickly got ready to leave. Forty-five minutes later he escorted Carrie into the lobby at Sierra Arroyo. As they signed in Carrie quickly introduced him to the receptionist, explaining that two other friends were also on their way. She left him in the lobby, explaining that she wanted some time alone with her mother. He told her to take all the time she needed.

Carrie found Hilda in her mother's room along with a hospice worker named Maryanne. Linda was in a deep, sound sleep. Her face looked ashen and Carrie noticed her fingernails had a strange purplish hue.

"How long does she have?"

"Not long," replied Maryanne. "I'd say probably a few more hours."

"What if you're all wrong? She could still get better."

Hilda gently pulled Carrie off to the side. "Carrie, honey, she's fought the good fight, but she can't fight it any longer. She has no strength left. She's been trapped in a useless body for far too long. Now it's time to let her go so she can move on to someplace better." Carrie began weeping openly. Hilda wrapped her arms around her. "She loves you, Carrie and I know she's been worried about you. Even though she can't talk she's still been able to communicate with me, in her own way, mother-to-mother."

"Really? So what has she had to say?"

"She was relieved after you and Doug broke up. She thinks you could do better."

"She does?"

Hilda nodded.

"You know, Mama never disliked Doug, but she did mention once or twice that she didn't think we were the best match either. I guess that's one of the reasons why I held back on marrying him."

"Mothers know best," agreed Hilda. "Then, after you told her you'd reconnected with your friend, Alex, she seemed to be a lot happier. I can tell she really likes him."

"Yes, she always has. Alex and I were childhood friends. He spent a lot of time at our house over the years and my mother and Alex's mother used to take turns shuttling us around until we got our driver's licenses. Mama always talked about how much she adored him. She even used to say she hoped we'd get married someday, but then we ended up going to different colleges and we lost touch with one another."

"And now he's back," said Hilda.

"Yes, he is. Through a strange twist of fate, Alex Montoya is back in my life. He brought me here today, Hilda. I want to spend a little time alone with her, and then I'm going to let Alex come in and let him spend some time with her too. My other friend, Allison, wants to see her as well."

"I'm glad, Carrie. She may look like she's asleep, but trust me, she'll know they're here and I know she'll be happy to see them, especially Alex."

Carrie asked Hilda and Maryanne to step out of the room so she could have some time alone with her mother. An hour later she came into the lobby. Steve and Allison were there with Alex. All three came up and put their arms around her. Once again Carrie began weeping.

"I think we're ready for you to go and see her," she said once she regained her composure. "Allie, why don't you go first? Then when you're done, it'll be Alex's turn. After that the rest of us will go back in."

Allison nodded and Hilda came to escort her to Linda's room. Steve and Alex tried to get Carrie to eat something while they waited but she refused. Once Allison returned Alex left with Hilda.

"She looks almost normal," he said as he walked up to her bedside. "She's hardly aged a day since the last time I saw her. She's quite a bit thinner, and her hair's a lot longer, but other than that she looks much the same."

"I'll leave you two alone for awhile," said Hilda as she stepped away. "Feel free to talk to her. She can still hear you."

"Mrs. Daniels, it's me, Alex." As he took Linda's left hand, she immediately squeezed his. "I know, and it's good to see you too. It's kind of a long story of how I've come back into Carrie's life. I don't know how much she's told you, but I don't want you to worry about her, okay. I promise to take very good care of her."

Linda squeezed his hand again. Alex filled her in about going to law school, becoming a lawyer, and how happy he was to have finally found Carrie again.

"You know, Mrs. Daniels, I've thought a lot about Carrie over the years. She's the best friend I ever had, and I promise that I'm not going to lose her again. She and I will be best friends forever. You can count on it."

Linda gave his hand a final squeeze. They heard the sound of approaching footsteps. The door opened and Allison and Carrie came inside.

"Thanks, both of you, for coming," said Carrie. "It really means a lot to me. I'll call you later, Alex."

Alex and Allison looked at each other. "We're not leaving," said Alex as he pulled up two more chairs. "We're your friends. We're staying here with you."

Carrie let out a sigh. It was no use arguing. Deep down, she was pleased.

"So where's Steve?"

"He went out to get some sandwiches," replied Allison. "You have to eat sometime Carrie. We'll do our meal breaks in shifts so your mother won't be alone."

The three took their seats and as the hours passed they noticed Linda's breathing was becoming more and more labored. It was a few minutes past one o'clock the following morning, when she began to stir and slowly open her eyes.

"Mama?"

Linda looked at Steve, Allison, and then Carrie. When she finally looked at Alex, her eyes held his before darting back and forth between him and Carrie.

"Well, Alex, it's about time."

Her voice wasn't much more than a hoarse whisper, but she'd somehow managed to get the words out. Everyone sat in stunned disbelief as Linda closed her eyes and nodded off. They listened closely as she took three more deep breaths. The last one ended with a long exhale, and then the room was silent. No other breaths followed.

"Mama!" wailed Carrie as she rose from her chair. "Mama!"

Her friends surrounded her and all three hugged her at the same time. Carrie sobbed as the door opened. Some of the staff discreetly slipped into the room to confirm that Linda was indeed gone. They quietly left as Carrie's friends tried to comfort her. By then, all four were weeping.

"Carrie, is there anyone we need to call?" asked Allison, once she was able to compose herself.

"No." Carrie, shook her head. "Both of my grandparents are gone. Mama had an older brother, but he was killed in Vietnam. She and I never knew any of my grandmother's family, there was some sort of a rift, and my grandfather was an only child. I don't know if my father's alive or dead, nor do I care. It was always just Mama and me."

She started crying and once again her friends tried to comfort her. After she'd calmed down, Steve and Allison told her goodnight. Alex stepped out with them to give her some time alone with her mother. It was nearly two-thirty when he tapped on the door. A hearse had arrived to pick up her mother's body.

"No," said Carrie, shaking her head. "Tell them to leave."

"Carrie-Anne, it's time for me to take you home. You've been here nearly sixteen hours. You're exhausted, and so am I. You need to get some rest. I'll tell them to wait until after we're gone."

Alex stepped out, returning a short time later. They both said a final goodbye before he wrapped his arm around her and led her out of the building.

❧Twenty-One❧

WHEN CARRIE WOKE UP, it took her a moment to realize she was in Alex's guestroom. Her first thought was that it had all been a bad dream, but as she looked around the room she spotted the bag filled with her mother's meager possessions sitting on top of the dresser. It hadn't been a bad dream. Her mother really was gone. She rolled over to glance at the clock on the nightstand. It was going on eleven-thirty. The morning was nearly over. She climbed out of bed and reached into her suitcase for a t-shirt and a pair of shorts before heading off to the bathroom. Ten minutes later she emerged and headed to the kitchen for a cup of coffee.

"Morning, Carrie-Anne. How are you feeling?"

Alex was seated at the dining table in the small nook off the side of the kitchen. He was busy going through a thick folder, stacking and collating various papers. Carrie noticed he was wearing a pair of tortoise-shell glasses. They gave him a distinguished look, which she found intriguing.

"I'm okay, I guess." She poured herself a cup of coffee and took a seat across the table from him. "So where did you get those?"

"What?"

"The glasses. I like the way they look on you."

"Do you now? Well, thank you." So Carrie liked his look. "After putting in such a late night, I needed to take out my contacts for awhile."

"I see." She took a sip of her coffee. "So, when did you start wearing contacts?"

"About the time I finished law school." He shuffled more of the papers around. "Carrie-Anne, I hope you don't mind, but I've started going through your mother's folder."

"No, I don't mind at all. In fact, I was going to ask you to do that for me. I've only gone through parts of it so I have no idea what all is in there."

"That's what I thought. I've found a copy of her will." He handed it to her. "She intended to leave everything to you. At the time it was written she had a condominium, some stocks and bonds, and a savings account."

"All of which is long gone now. I tried to sell the condo, right after she had her stroke. Unfortunately, the real estate market had crashed. It was worth less than what she'd owed and the bank ended up foreclosing on it. Since then I've had to use up all her other assets to pay for her care."

"That's what I thought," said Alex as she handed it back to him.

"She had some jewelry that once belonged to her mother, but there was no documentation attached to any of it, so I put it in my safe deposit box. They're family heirlooms and I'll be damned if I'm going to let anyone take that away from me."

"It's okay Carrie-Anne. No one's going to rob you of your grandmother's jewelry."

"Thanks, Alex."

He presented her with another document. "She says her wish is to be cremated, but she's left it up to you to decide what to do with her ashes. If you like, I can call the funeral home and arrange the cremation for you."

"Thanks, Alex, I appreciate it." She took another sip of her coffee. "You know, I'm feeling so overwhelmed right now I can't think clearly."

He reached across the table and put his hand over hers. "That's what friends are for, Carrie-Anne. But I need to ask what you'd like to do with the ashes."

She took a few more sips of her coffee as she thought it over.

"Alex, do you remember back when we were kids, how every summer she'd take us camping up in the mountains?"

"How could I forget? Those camping trips are some of the happiest memories of my childhood."

"Mine too. So what do you think about driving up to Flagstaff next weekend and scattering her ashes out in the woods, where she always took us?"

"I think that would be perfect and I know she'd love it. Would you mind if Steve and Allison came along?"

"Not at all," she replied. "I want them to be there. I'll call Mr. Greene tomorrow. There are clergy people who volunteer at the nursing home. Mama wasn't much of a churchgoer, but she did believe, and I'd like to have someone give her a proper eulogy. I want Hilda to be there too. She was Mama's main caregiver and they shared a special bond."

"My parents would also like to come, if you wouldn't mind. They knew her too."

"Of course they can be there. Didn't you tell me they're living in Nevada now?"

"Yep. My father got transferred to Las Vegas shorty after Mark went off to college. They're in Boulder City, which means they're only a few hours' drive from Flagstaff. I'll let them know and we'll figure out a place where we can all rendezvous. My mother is also planning on calling you sometime later on today."

"She is? I'd like that." Carrie leaned back into her chair took a few more sips of coffee.

"Carrie-Anne, I know we asked you this last night, but is there anyone else you need to call? Perhaps some of your mother's friends?"

"No. Unfortunately, most of Mama's friends drifted away in the months following her stroke. The only one who stayed true to her was Bernie."

"Bernie?"

"Yes, Bernie Carson. He was a sous chef at the restaurant where they both worked. They had this… relationship, if you know what I mean."

"You mean they were lovers."

"Yes," she admitted. "Mama met Bernie about the time we finished high school, but please, don't get the wrong idea. It wasn't any kind of fling. They truly were in love, but they never got around to getting married. I think Mama was a little gun-shy about marriage, you know, because of my father. Anyway,

Bernie was never the same after Mama had her stroke. He died of a heart attack about a year later."

"I'm sorry to hear that."

"Me too, but I have a really strong feeling that wherever they are, they're together. True love never dies." Carrie took a few more sips of her coffee. "Somewhere in that stack of papers, Alex, there should be a life insurance policy. I don't know that much about it, or even when Mama took it out, but I kept up on the premiums so that when the time came she could have a decent burial."

Alex quickly sifted through the remaining papers in the folder. He found it at the very bottom of the stack. He started reading through it, and as he did his face lit up.

"Carrie-Anne, do you have any idea what this is?"

"Yes, it's to cover her final expenses."

"No," he said, gleefully, "it's a whole lot more than that. She bought this twenty-five years ago, and it's a whole-life policy."

"Which means I would have been about five when she took it out. Makes sense. That would have been about the time my father left us."

"Yes, that make sense, and did you know this policy has a fifty-thousand dollar face value?" He paused for a moment. It was apparent that she didn't fully comprehend the significance of what he was saying. "Carrie-Anne, assuming there weren't any loans taken out against the policy, this means you can finally get your life back."

"You're kidding."

"I kid you not."

He got out of his chair and walked to where she was sitting. She felt his hair brushing against her cheek as he bent down to show her the paperwork. She liked the way it felt. Alex showed her the policy. She couldn't believe what she was seeing. It really would give her the means to finally start investing in her own future.

"Alex, I don't know what say. I've been living like a pauper for so long that I don't even know what to think. I can't imagine what it would be like just to have matching dishes." She paused for a minute. "I guess maybe I should start thinking about paying you."

"Would you please knock that off?" There was a sound of mock despair in his voice. "As I've all ready told you, sooner or later, and with any luck, Louise will be taking care of that.

Meantime I'll give the policy to Steve. He'll be more than happy to take care of the claim for you."

There was something else he needed to show her.

"Carrie-Anne, I've found some information in here about your father. Would you like to know more about him?"

"He abandoned me, Alex. What else is there for me to know about him? I was his daughter. What the hell did I ever do to him to deserve it?"

"Nothing, Carrie-Anne. You didn't do anything wrong, and he didn't exactly abandon you."

"So what does that mean?"

"It means there's a whole lot more to the story than what you've been told. Would you like to hear it?"

"Sure, why not?" She got up to refill her coffee cup. "I'm all ears, and I'm sure he has a really dandy excuse."

She poured her coffee and returned to her seat as Alex grabbed a small pile of papers.

"His name was Kevin Earl Daniels. He and your mother would have been married thirty-two years this past June." He showed her the marriage license.

"I know they were married, but as I've mentioned before, it wasn't a happy marriage. What vague memories I have were of him and my mother, constantly fighting. That was back when we were living in Montana."

"I'm not surprised. Carrie, your father had a cocaine problem. He got busted when you were five years old. The police reports and court documents are right here, if you want to see them."

Carrie sat silently for a moment as she took it in. "All right. So, if he got busted, then why didn't he keep in contact with me? He was still my father. He could have written to me from jail."

"I'm afraid it's not that simple. From what I'm able to piece together, he checked into a rehab facility right after his arraignment, and he was there for several weeks. After they released him, he was living with a woman named Penelope Daniels."

"That's my Grandma Nell," explained Carrie. "She was my father's mother."

"I see. Anyway, according to the court records, he continued to be treated as an outpatient, and he apparently went back to school. This was the same time your mother filed for divorce. I've found some of those records as well."

"Okay, so he went into rehab, and from rehab he went to

Grandma Nell's. So why didn't he ever call me, or write me a letter, or come visit me?"

"I can't answer that. All I can tell you is six months later his case went to court, and his decision to go into treatment must have impressed the judge. He got probation and a deferred jail sentence. According to the records, the judge was going to dismiss the jail time once his probation was up, provided he stayed in treatment and didn't violate any of the terms."

"I see," she said, "but drug bust, rehab, whatever, I was still his daughter, and he still abandoned me."

Alex let out a sigh and shuffled more papers. "There's more to the story, I'm sorry to say. According to this police report, he was taking night classes at the university. One night, after his class had let out, he was in a parking lot, apparently getting into his car, when someone jumped him from behind and stabbed him. These are old records and a number of pages appear to be missing. What I can tell you is it happened about the same time you and your mother came to Phoenix." He waited for Carrie to take it all in. "Carrie-Anne, there's a lot that we may simply never know, and I'm sure your mother must have had her reasons for not telling you. Or maybe she meant to tell you, someday, but she never got the chance. If you want, I can ask George to investigate it further for you. I just didn't want you to keep thinking that your father simply got up one morning and decided to walk out on you."

"No, that's okay," she said. "He had a drug problem, and later on he was killed. That's all I need to know. Thank you, Alex, for sharing this. I really do appreciate it."

She leaned against him and gave him a squeeze. He liked the feeling of her body next to his.

"There's one more thing about your father that you might want to know." He handed her a photograph. "This is what he looked like. As you can see, he's wearing a tuxedo, so I'm guessing this was probably taken the day he and your mother were married. You look just like him, Carrie-Anne."

Carrie looked at the photo. Her father was a strikingly handsome man and the resemblance was uncanny. She had his dark hair, deep-set blue eyes, and similar facial features. As she studied it, Alex stood up, saying that he wanted to give her some time alone. He quietly slipped out of the room.

❧Twenty-Two❧

ALEX REACHED ACROSS his desk to grab his ringing phone. "Yes, Brenda?"

"You have a call on line three Alex, from a Scott Andrews."

Alex was taken aback. "Scott Andrews?"

"Affirmative."

He let out a sigh and gritted his teeth. There were, on rare occasions, those moments when he hated his job, and this was going to be one of them. The idea of having to speak to Carrie's ex-lover grated on him. Hopefully, Scott was calling to let him know who his attorney was and he'd only have to stay on the line long enough to get the information. He let out another sigh as he thanked Brenda and connected the call. He picked up a pencil and started drumming it on his desk.

"Hello, Mr. Montoya. My name is Scott Andrews. As you no doubt already know, I'm the other defendant in Louise Dickenson's copyright infringement claim, and I understand you're Carrie's lawyer."

"That's right, Mr. Andrews. What can I do for you?"

"Well, as soon as I was served, I contacted my attorney in Phoenix; the one handling my divorce. Unfortunately, she tells me her specialty is family law and she can't help me. So, I made some inquires and found out you're representing Carrie. Since you're already on the case, I thought I'd ask if you'd mind representing me as well."

"Sorry, Mr. Andrews, but I'm not able to oblige you. However, I'm sure your divorce attorney knows someone to refer you to. If not, the state bar association can help you."

"I understand." Alex heard the disappointment in Scott's voice. "Anyway, just so you know, I subscribe to *Gentry Magazine*. I recognized those photos as soon as I saw them, but I swear, I had nothing to do this."

"Mr. Andrews, please, don't say anything else. Just have your attorney contact me as soon as he or she comes on board."

"I'll do that Alex, but before you go, can I just say something off the record, between you and me?"

"I'd prefer that you didn't. In fact, I would advise you, sir, to not say anything to me. Please understand I'm representing Ms. Daniels and Ms. Daniels only. Anything you say to me would not fall under the guise of attorney-client privilege. I'm also an officer of the court. If you were to admit any kind of wrongdoing to me, I'd be obligated to report it."

"I understand, sir," said Scott. "I'm just letting you know that I intend to cooperate fully with you and with the FBI. I know there's a criminal investigation going on as well, and I want to assure you that I've done nothing wrong."

"I appreciate that, Mr. Andrews, but I'd prefer that—"

"I know, you're not my attorney, but I just wanted you to understand something else as well. I don't know what Carrie may or may not have told you about me, but I just want to set the record straight. I wasn't exactly honest with her when I first met her. I didn't tell her that I was married."

Alex held his tongue. With any luck, Scott was about to hang himself.

"Anyway that night at the art gallery she mentioned she'd just ended a long-term relationship. I could tell the wounds hadn't fully healed yet, so I figured she'd be really... easy, if you know what I mean. So there I was, talking to her and looking at those nude photos of her at the same time and hey, who wouldn't want a piece of that?"

Alex felt the pencil in his hand snap in two. He wanted nothing more in that moment than to be able to call Scott a son of a bitch. Professional decorum, however, wouldn't allow it. He had to grit his teeth and remain calm.

"So what's your point, Andrews?"

"My point is that I was a real heel for what I did to her. I have a fifteen-year-old daughter. If some guy did to her what I did to Carrie, I'd take my shotgun and hunt him down. He'd be worth going to jail for. I'm just saying that I'm really, truly sorry for what I did. I can't prove it, but I'm absolutely certain my soon-to-be ex-wife is the one behind all of this, so I guess it's my fault Carrie's in the mess she's in now."

"Have you told the authorities this?"

"Yes sir, I have. Like I just told you, I have every intention of cooperating fully. I'm now working for an Internet security company. I could lose my job because of this. I'm also fighting for custody of my two kids. I have every reason in the world to want to clear my name, as soon as possible. Meantime, would you please tell Carrie I'm really, truly sorry all this happened. I should have never gotten involved with her in the first place."

Alex couldn't have agreed more. "Just have your attorney call me. Okay, Mr. Andrews?"

He slammed down the phone as he ended the call. "Yeah, and I'd like to get my shotgun and hunt you down as well, you worthless son of a bitch!"

"Whoa," exclaimed Steve as he stepped into Alex's door. "So what's gotten you all riled up?"

"Your friend, Scott Andrews."

"Hey, don't look at me. He was merely an acquaintance of Allison's and he's not even that anymore. So what's he done to get you all fired up?"

"He called to ask me if I'd represent him along with Carrie."

"And?"

"I turned him down, naturally," replied Alex. "So while I'm trying to end the call the stupid bastard gets diarrhea of the month. He's telling me about looking at those nude photos of Carrie, and then he makes some wise-assed crack about, 'well, who wouldn't want a piece of that?' And all I wanted to do in that moment was to put the son of a bitch out of his misery. Of course, now he says he's sorry and he knows he did her wrong. He's sorry my ass! The only thing he's sorry about is that he got caught. Lying bastard."

"Hey buddy, chill. You're beginning to sound like a jealous lover. You need to calm down, okay?"

"Sorry, Steve. She just lost her mother, so I'm feeling very protective of her."

"Is that all?"

"She's my best friend. Always has been."

"Okay, Alex." Steve wanted to change the subject. "I just need to get that copy of her mother's life insurance policy, and I'll take care of any other details the need to be attended to."

"Oh, right." Alex reached over and handed him the paperwork. "Anyway, I'm sorry you had to witness my rant. I guess I needed to vent."

"It's okay, but you need to take it easy. She may be your best friend outside the office, but whenever you're here, she's your client. Got it?"

"Got it."

Steve quickly made his exit as Alex thanked him for helping Carrie. Once he left, Alex looked up another number and dialed his phone.

"Hey, Billie, Alex Montoya. I'm not sure, but I may have some new information for you on the Daniels case."

"Really? So, what have you got?"

Alex quickly relayed the information that Scott Andrews gave him.

"He swears he's innocent, Billie, but now I'm absolutely certain that the person who did this is either Scott or Maggie Andrews."

"Well, Alex, if you ever get tired of being an attorney, you can come work for us at the FBI. We've finally identified the computer that uploaded the files to *Gentry Magazine* through its IP address. That computer belongs to Scott Andrews. The Kansas City field office is taking it into evidence."

"But it's only circumstantial. All he has to say is someone else was using it."

"O'Dell is convinced that Maggie is the real culprit," said Billie, "but right now we don't have enough on her to bring her in for questioning. We'll know more once we get Scott's computer and the lab results come back on the fireplace ashes. In the meantime, I'll keep you posted, okay?"

"Sounds good, Billie, and I'll let you if I find out anything new on my end."

❧Twenty-Three❧

THE SCENIC MOUNTAINS of northern Arizona have a special beauty all their own during the late summer months. The goldenrod is in bloom and there's a hint of the coming fall in the air. The last Saturday of August would be the day to bid farewell to Linda Daniels. Alex and Carrie were riding with Steve and Allison in the backseat of Steve's Explorer. Carrie held the container with her mother's ashes in her lap. She was unusually quiet and subdued and her friends decided it would be best to leave her with her thoughts. They arrived in Flagstaff at a few minutes past one o'clock, pulling into the parking lot of the restaurant where they planned to meet the others. Alex noticed his father's car in the parking lot as Steve searched for a space. He found one close by.

"I feel kind of funny leaving Mama all alone in the car like this," said Carrie as she stepped out.

"It's okay, Carrie-Anne." Alex walked up behind her and wrapped his arm around her shoulder. "Her spirit really isn't in that box you know. She's someplace else, probably looking down on us and having a good laugh."

He kept his arm around her shoulder and guided her toward the front door. As they entered the building they quickly spotted his parents, who stood from the table to greet them.

"Alex didn't tell us that you'd become such a beautiful woman, Carrie," said his father as he greeted her with a hug.

"The last time we saw her she was sixteen years old," added his mother as she looked at the others. "Carrie is about three months older than Alex, which meant she got her driver's license before he did. They were going to a movie that night so she came by the house to pick him up."

"And after she drove for about a block I asked her to pull over so I could drive," Alex quickly added. Both of his parents gave him a surprised look. "What? I had my learner's permit. She was a licensed driver. It was legal, more or less, and I wasn't about to be chauffeured."

"So, Alex, you were thinking like a lawyer, even back then," said his father with a smile.

"You know, Alex was our shy child," said his mother to the others.

"Mom!" Alex tried to cut her off.

"No really, he was."

"Was he now?" said Steve. "Tell me more."

Alex's father spoke up. "Now don't embarrass the boy, Catherine."

"I'm not embarrassing him, Armando."

"Mom!"

"No really." Catherine ignored her son's protests as he began groaning in the background. "Mark was our outgoing son. He was the popular boy at school and he was always hanging out with his friends. Alex was our quiet child. I mean he wasn't disliked, but he was prettsy shy, so he kept to himself."

"Mom."

"Alex always had his nose stuck in a book. Then one day Mrs. Tyler, his fourth-grade teacher, teamed him up with Carrie for a classroom assignment and that's how they became friends. Here she was, the girl in those TV commercials, and the next thing we knew she and her mother were bringing him along to watch while they were filming them. You know, I think Alex's being around all those television people was a good thing. It finally got him out of his shell."

Carrie watched the door while Alex's mother was talking. It opened, and she recognized Hilda and another man as they stepped inside. She quickly waved; motioning for them to come to their table.

"Saved by the bell," muttered Alex under his breath.

Carrie introduced Hilda, who in turn introduced Reverend Fletcher, who would be conducting the memorial service. As they sat down, the conversation took a more somber tone. Everyone began to reminisce, sharing personal stories of Linda while Hilda talked about caring for her at the nursing home. After the meal was over they headed out to the parking lot. The reverend, and Alex's parents, would follow Steve.

"Looks like some clouds are building up," Steve remarked as they settled back into his Explorer.

"Yep," agreed Alex. "It's the time of year for afternoon thunderstorms. We should have enough time, though."

"Where to?" Steve asked Carrie as he started up the engine.

"I'm not exactly sure. Mama never had any place in particular staked out. We'd just get in the car and head north. Once we got here she'd meander down one of the back roads through the forest until we happened upon a spot we all liked."

Steve exited the parking lot and made his way out of the city limits. A half-hour later they were heading down a Forest Service road when something caught Carrie's eye.

"Steve, can you slow down?"

"Sure. Is everything okay back there?"

"I'm good. It's just that some of this is starting to look familiar to me. I think maybe we've been here once before, haven't we, Alex?"

"Maybe, now that you mention it."

After driving for another quarter-mile Carrie asked Steve to pull over. He shut down the engine and glanced in the rearview mirror. The other two cars were pulling up behind him.

"It's somewhere back there." Carrie was pointing out the window. "It's a little bit of a hike, but not too far. It's just on the other side of that clump of trees." She stepped outside and was reaching for her mother's ashes, when Alex walked up behind her.

"Let me take them for you, Carrie-Anne. We have a ways to walk and they're a little too heavy for you to carry by yourself."

He scooped up the container while she led the others into the woods. After a short hike, she entered a small clearing and stopped. It was a beautiful spot. Golden wildflowers were mixed in with the grass.

"This is it. I think Mama's final resting place should be right here."

Everyone formed a circle and the reverend began his eulogy. He began by reading a few Bible verses, then he spoke of Linda's dedication to her friends, her coworkers and, most especially, to her daughter. He mentioned her desire for Carrie to have a better life than the one she'd had. He spoke of her friend, Bernie Carson, as he recalled the times when he consoled Bernie after Linda's stroke. He concluded by saying while both Linda's and Bernie's deaths were indeed untimely, their souls were now together in Heaven, where one day they all would be eternally reunited. As he led the group into a final prayer the sun went behind a cloud and a breeze began to blow.

"Amen," said everyone in unison.

"Are you ready, Carrie?" he asked.

She suddenly felt hesitant. She looked at Alex, not sure what to do.

"Come on, Carrie-Anne. It's time to tell her goodbye."

He took her by the hand, leading her a short distance away from the others. He stopped to open the container. He tilted it slightly forward, allowing the contents to slowly escape. They were quickly caught in the breeze, which scattered them across the grass, blending them into the wildflowers. As the last of the ashes trickled out Carrie began to weep.

"She's finally free now, Carrie-Anne." He took her in his arms and kissed the top of her head. "But there will always be a part of her that will live on in you." He held her for a few moments.

"Alex, could you do me a big favor?"

"Anything."

"Would you go thank everyone for coming? And then would you mind waiting in the car with Steve and Allie? I need a few minutes alone."

"I understand." He gave her one last hug and a kiss on the cheek. "Take all the time you need."

He stepped away quietly and relayed Carrie's words of appreciation before everyone headed back to their cars. He walked his parents to their vehicle, telling them goodbye and thanking them once again for coming. He stood by the side of the road, waving goodbye as they drove away. As he walked back to the Explorer, he heard the distant sound of thunder. The clouds were thick and heavy and the sky was turning dark.

"Looks like it's getting ready to rain," he said as he hopped into the backseat.

"Is she okay?" asked Allison.

"She's fine, Allie. She just needed a few minutes alone."

As the minutes passed a smattering raindrops began to appear on the windshield.

"I wonder if I should go get her."

"You just said she's fine," Steve reminded him. "I have a hunch she'll be along in a couple of minutes."

A few more minutes passed, and then the rain began falling in earnest. A bright flash of lightening streaked across the sky, followed by a loud clap of thunder.

"That's it," declared Alex. "I don't care if I have to drag her back here by the hair."

He jumped out of the Explorer and ran toward the clearing. He soon found Carrie, working her way toward him. He ran up and put his arm around her, trying to shelter her from the pelting rain. As they jumped into the backseat of the suv, Alex noticed she was soaking wet.

"Sorry, guys," she said as she reached for her seatbelt. "I guess I just lost track of the time."

"You're shivering," observed Alex, "and you're soaked to the bone. We don't need you catching cold. I've got a sweatshirt for you to put on." He reached behind the seat and handed it to her.

"I have a blanket in the back as well," added Allison. "It's got some of Lucy's fur on it, but other than that it should be clean."

"Don't worry Allie, I happen to love your dog," replied Carrie as Alex reached for the blanket and began covering her up. She noticed he was soaking wet too. "You may as huddle up underneath this with me. That way you won't catch cold either. We can keep each other warm and dry off together."

Alex eagerly accepted her invitation. Once they got back into town Steve took them through a fast food drive-thru to get hot coffee for the two of them and soft drinks for Allison and himself. Before long they were back on the Interstate, bound for Phoenix. Steve glanced into the rearview mirror. Alex and Carrie had dozed off in each other's arms, but by the time they reached Phoenix both were wide-awake and dry. He dropped them off at Alex's door. Everyone said goodnight as Carrie once again thanked them for coming. Steve waited until they were safely inside before he pointed the Explorer toward home. As they headed down the road, he let out a loud sigh.

"Is something wrong, Steve?"

"I'm afraid so."

"What is it?"

"Alex and Carrie. C'mon, you saw it. They've become much too emotionally attached to one another."

"They go way back," she reminded him.

"No, there's more to it than that. He's fallen for her. Hard. Really, really hard."

"Is that such a bad thing?"

"In itself, no. They're two of my favorite people and under normal circumstances I'd be happy for both of them, but their situation isn't normal. He's representing her in a civil case and he's losing his objectivity."

"Are you sure?"

"Yes," he replied, matter-of-factly. "A few days ago I walked into Alex's office. He'd just happened to have gotten off the phone with our old buddy, Scott Andrews. Apparently Scott had made some crack about his prior involvement with Carrie and Alex went into a screaming rage. I've never known him to ever do anything like that before. It was like listening to a jealous lover. That's what has me worried."

"How so?"

"Alex has always been unflappable. That's why he has such a good track record. He stays calm and collected, just like a lion stalking its prey, while he waits patiently for the other side to make a mistake, and then he goes for the kill. He's always been able to do that because he never allows himself to become emotionally wrapped up. But now he's crossed that line, and even though it appears to be an open and shut case, this time he could, very easily, be the one who makes a mistake. If that happens, he could lose, and this is the one case, Allie, the one case that he can't afford to lose."

"Damn," she said. "You can't let that happen, Steve. It could destroy both of them."

"I know that, so I'm going to have to keep close watch on him and I'm going try to persuade him to bring Reggie on board."

"Who's he?"

"He is a she. Regina Peters. Remember, she was at our engagement party? I introduced the two of you."

"Oh, right," recalled Allison. "I think I remember her now. She was tall, thin, forty-something, with a dark-brown pageboy."

"That's Reggie. She's one of the senior partners in the firm. She mentored Alex when he first came on board so he respects her. She also specializes in civil cases. If push comes to shove, Alex may have to step aside and let Reggie take over."

❧Twenty-Four❧

CARRIE RETURNED TO her apartment the following afternoon. Alex's prediction had been accurate. There was some flack in the local media for a few days after the story broke of the Mercer's Market girl showing up in the pages of *Gentry Magazine*. It had since faded into obscurity, being replaced by newer headlines, and Carrie didn't want to wear out her welcome. She gave Alex a long, lingering goodbye before getting into her car and heading home, but by the time she turned off his street and onto the main road she was starting to miss him. Alex spent the rest of the day moping around his empty house, missing her as well.

The following weekend was the Labor Day holiday. Allison wanted to take advantage of all the sales to do some wedding shopping and she decided to take Carrie along. The time had come to find a bridesmaid's dress.

Their first stop was the bridal shop. Allison had picked out a traditional white satin gown, trimmed with lace and pearls, with a chapel-length train. She had an appointment that morning for another fitting. Both women marveled after she put on the gown and looked in the full-length mirror. Her dress had a Victorian look with its high collar, tight-fitting bodice, and long lace sleeves. Completing the outfit was a fingertip length veil with a pearl-trimmed headband.

"Allie, you're a beautiful, blushing bride, and I can't help it. I'm jealous."

"Don't worry, your day will come," she replied.

"I wish I had your confidence, but I'm afraid my Prince Charming was abducted by someone named Jennifer Logan."

"Whoever said Doug was your Prince Charming? What about you and Alex?"

"We're just friends, Allie."

"Is that all?"

"Okay, so we're best friends, but that's all it is. That's all it'll ever be."

Carrie was obviously in denial so Allison decided not to force the issue. Whatever was meant to happen would happen, when the time was right. She only hoped that time wouldn't come until after Carrie's lawsuit with Louise was settled. In the meantime, she decided to change the subject.

"Did I mention that my family and I are about to come to blows over my wedding?"

"What? No way. What's going on?"

"My parents, and my grandparents, are what you'd call old school," she explained. "They want me to have a traditional Catholic wedding, just like my two younger sisters had. I'm already on thin ice with them because Steve and I have been living together for the past four years. On top of that, I'm marrying a man from a Protestant background with no intentions of converting. So, we've decided to have our wedding at a different church and that's not going over too well with some of my family."

"What a shame. You know, I recall Alex once telling me the story of a similar thing happening to his parents. His mother was not only Protestant, she'd also been married and divorced."

"I didn't know that."

"Not that many people do," said Carrie. "She'd been married, briefly, when she was very young. Obviously, the marriage didn't work out and there were no children, but I guess when she and Alex's father decided to marry there was a big ruckus over it. They ended up getting married at her family's church, and Alex's dad decided to leave the Catholic Church. You know, the whole thing is just wrong. You should be able to marry the person you love and not be hassled over it."

"You just did it again, Carrie."

"Did what?"

"You just brought up Alex's name. Again. That's the fourth time you've done that this morning."

"I have not."

"Yes, you have."

Before Carrie could respond the alterations lady arrived to check Allison's gown. After a close inspection they determined it was ready and Allison made arrangements to have it delivered the day before her wedding. Next, they headed to the mall. It was time to look for a bridesmaid's dress for Carrie. They didn't find anything they liked at the first two department stores. They were now in the third, and so far they were coming up empty. Allison was nearly at her wits' end. If they didn't find the right dress soon, they'd have to return to the bridal shop.

"I think I've found something," exclaimed Carrie as she pulled out a dress from one of the racks. "Take a look at this. It's my size, and it's even on sale."

She brought it to Allison for a closer look. The dress was royal blue chiffon. It too had a slightly Victorian look with a tight-fitting bodice similar to the one on Allison's wedding gown. It was low-cut, with three-quarter length sleeves and a double-layered skirt. Carrie placed the dress in front of her so they could check the length. It came down to her mid calf.

"Now that one I like," said Allison.

"Me too. It's pretty, it's feminine, and it's kind of sexy too. Can I try it on?"

Allison ran her fingers up and down the bodice to get a feel for the fabric.

"Yeah, you can try it on, but you know what? It'd probably look better if you had a bustier underneath. Let's run down to the lingerie department and see what we can find before you try it on."

Carrie handed the dress to a salesclerk, asking her to put it on hold. They took the escalator down and soon found a lacy-beige bustier in Carrie's size. They were just about to complete their purchase when something else caught her eye.

"I absolutely, positively have to have that."

Allison followed her gaze. Carrie had spotted a beautiful white negligee set. She went to take a closer look. The flowing, sleeveless nightgown was low-cut and very sexy. It was topped with a low-cut, lace-trimmed sheer peignoir with ruffled sleeves.

"It's been far too long, Allie, since I've had anything as pretty as this." The gown felt soft and silky as she caressed it.

"Most of the time I sleep in raggedy old t-shirts. I still have the pink nightshirt you gave me last year for my birthday, but even it's starting to get a little threadbare, although Alex thought it was pretty funny."

"What was that?"

"I wore it while I as staying at his place. He brought me there to hide out from the media, remember? It was on the up and up. I told you, I stayed in the guestroom."

"Humph. That's makes the fifth time that you've brought Alex up."

"Allie, please." Carrie rolled her eyes. "You don't know how good it feels just to be able to buy new clothes again, and I'm going to get this negligee set. It doesn't matter if anyone else ever gets to see me in it or not. I'll still wear it and I'll still enjoy having it."

Carrie took the nightgown off the rack and made her purchases. Afterwards, they headed back up the escalator. She was anxious to try on the dress. Allison browsed while she waited.

"Look at this," Carrie exclaimed as she stepped out of the fitting room.

"Oh my gosh. Carrie, it's perfect. It's like this dress was made just for you. You look absolutely stunning in it, and the color even matches your eyes. There is one little problem, though."

"What's that?"

"You might upstage the bride." Both women started to laugh. "Do you have a pair of shoes to go with it?"

"Not any more. I used to have a pair of strappy, open-toed, black patent leather high-heels, but I threw them out."

"Why?"

Carrie let out a sigh. "Because I had them on when I did that stupid photo shoot, and then I wore them on my second, and final, date with Scott Andrews. They were tainted. Every time I saw them in my closet it brought back bad memories. Nothing good has ever come from that photo shoot, Allie. Doing it will always be one of the biggest regrets of my life."

"Well, that's not entirely true," argued Allison. "One good thing came of it."

"What's that?"

"Alex came back into our lives."

"Aha! Now you just dropped his name."

"So I did," replied Allison with a smile. "Now if you'll just head back into the fitting room and change we can get out of this place and go grab a bite to eat. I don't know about you, but I'm starving."

"What about the food court?"

"Not today. Let's go someplace else, away from the mall."

"What about the shoes?"

"There's a big discount shoe store, not too far from here, where you'll get a much better deal. We'll head over there after lunch."

As Carrie headed back to the fitting room, Allison decided to take a closer look at something that was bothering her. She thought she'd seen someone casually following them around the mall, and she'd just spotted that someone again. The person tailing them was a middle-aged woman with short blonde hair, and Allison noticed she'd been watching Carrie very intently. Both she and Steve had been concerned for her safety ever since the photos had appeared in *Gentry Magazine*. They became even more worried when the story broke on the local news. She turned to face the woman, giving her a strong look. A startled expression suddenly appeared on the other woman's face. She looked like a child who'd just been caught with a hand in the cookie jar. Allison took a few steps toward her, but as she did the other woman turned on her heel and quickly walked away. Allison hoped she'd scared her off. Carrie arrived a few minutes later with the blue dress in a plastic hanging bag.

"Ready?"

"Yeah," replied Allison. "Let's get out of here. I know the perfect spot for lunch."

As they headed back into to mall, Allison once again spotted the blonde-haired woman. She was still watching Carrie, this time keeping more of a distance. Allison quickly wove her way through the crowd, saying she was starving and wanted to beat the lunchtime rush. As they headed out to the parking lot, she let out a tiny sigh of relief. She'd successfully managed to ditch their stalker. They quickly got into her car and drove away.

❧Twenty-Five❧

THE *GENTRY MAGAZINE* controversy damaged Carrie's photography business and she needed to find new clientele. Now that the next issue was on the stands, she hoped to be able to put the episode behind her, as least as far as business was concerned. Her website was back up and she'd added new items to her professional portfolio. She'd just finished emailing a prospective client, when she heard her cell phone beeping. It was a text message from Alex, reminding her about their meeting in his office at four o'clock that afternoon to discuss her case. She glanced at the clock. She'd been so wrapped up with work she'd completely lost track of the time. It was nearly three-thirty and Alex's office was across town. At least there wasn't anything on her desk that couldn't wait until the following day. She sent a quick reply.

"On my way."

She grabbed her purse and headed out the door. The traffic on the freeway was heavier than usual, causing her to arrive ten minutes late. The receptionist quickly ushered her into the conference room. Alex was waiting, along with Steve and two other men.

"Sorry I'm late. My bad."

"Don't worry about it," replied Alex with a smile. "We have some new information about your case, so as soon as you take a seat we can get started."

As Carrie took a chair Alex introduced her to the others. They were George McCormick, Alex's private investigator, and Jonathan Fields, an Internet and computer expert.

"You seem familiar to me. Have we met before?" asked Carrie as she shook Jonathan's hand. He appeared to be in his fifties, but he was still quite handsome. His dark hair had a touch of gray, and his wire-rimmed glasses gave him a distinguished look.

"I can't say we have. I guess I must have one of those common faces."

"I guess so," agreed Carrie as she acknowledged the others.

"As you know, I brought George onboard to investigate your case," said Alex, "and Jonathan has been working with George."

"Jonathan owns a computer networking business in Tucson," explained George. "As far as I'm concerned, he's the best damn computer and Internet forensics expert in the entire state of Arizona. He's been working diligently on your case and we want to let you know what we've found."

Jonathan began by explaining that each computer has a unique IP address, and that there were ways to track all of that computer's activities on the Internet.

"We already know the computer that uploaded the photos to *Gentry Magazine* belongs to Scott Andrews, and I've tracked down everything that computer did on the Internet for the entire day. I have the report with me." He pulled some papers out of his folder, explaining that Scott's computer had first been used to access Maggie Andrews' email account, then it went to another email account, this one belonging to Scott. "It appears to be an email account he used exclusively for contacting you, Carrie."

"I see." Her face began to turn red. "So tell me, were you able to actually read any of the email?"

"Yes, I was, and, I did. Scott Andrews used this account to, shall we say, describe in great detail his feelings of lust for your client, Alex. However, Carrie conducted herself like a lady. She never responded to any of his racier messages—"

"Because I immediately deleted them," she interjected. "Look, you two need to understand something. I'd been in a ten-year relationship that had just ended rather unexpectedly. Then Scott came along. I had no idea he was married, and I wasn't thinking clearly at the time I got involved with him."

"They know that, Carrie," said Alex, "and they understand that Scott took advantage of you. You don't need to explain yourself. Please continue, Jonathan."

"There was one email in particular that Carrie initiated, and in it she does refer to the intimate nature of their relationship. To her credit though, she wrote it in a very tactful, discreet way. If it should end up being read a courtroom, I doubt the jury would hold it against her."

"Great," said Carrie, sarcastically. "That was supposed to be a private email. Will it be presented in court?"

"Not if I can help it," said Alex.

"It appears that for the most part Scott used this email account to arrange dates with Carrie, most of which he ended up cancelling," continued Jonathan. "And I also see that she ceased contact with him shortly after their second date. In fact, her last contact was the email I just mentioned."

"So, what would have happened had Maggie Andrews accessed this email account?" asked Alex.

"She would have been able the piece together all the details of her husband's affair with Ms. Daniels. She would have learned how and where they first met, and that they'd gone out twice. And you know, Alex, that's what I found to be a little odd. This account had been inactive for several weeks, yet that morning someone opened each and every email, both in the inbox, and in the sent folder. What we don't know, of course, is who was on the computer at the time."

"What time would that have been?"

"The first email was opened just before ten o'clock that morning, the last around ten forty-five. The details are all in my report."

"Thank you, Jonathan." Alex turned to George. "You've told me that Scott Andrews can prove that he was in his office that morning."

"That's what the Kansas City FBI report says. I know Maggie Andrews is the one who did this. I'd stake my reputation on it. I just don't have a smoking gun right now. You'd think the FBI agents here would have the evidence they need to bring her in for questioning. I know they've got their own computer forensics guys working on this too. Meantime, Jonathan has more."

Jonathan went on to explain that after the last email was read the computer was directed to the Carrie Daniels Photography website.

"Someone was definitely taking an interest in you, Carrie. After that, there was no on-line activity on that computer for the next few hours. It resumed later that afternoon, shortly after two o'clock, when someone created a brand new Yahoo account and immediately sent you an email. The sender claimed to be a fifth-grader named Kendra Clarke, who wanted to know about you being the Mercer's Market girl."

"Wait a minute, that rings a bell. As I recall, she also wanted me to email her an autographed photo."

"So, did you?" asked George.

"Yes."

"And I have a copy of the photo," added Jonathan as he took it out of the folder and handed it to Alex, who in turn showed it to George.

"Aw jeez," said George, rolling his eyes. "Well, at least we now know how Maggie got ahold of your signature so she could copy it. So, Jonathan, do we know who created the email account?"

"Unfortunately, I can't determine if it was Scott or Maggie. I can only identify the computer. The name used to create the fake Yahoo profile was, of course, Kendra Clarke. But what I can tell you is I've identified Carrie's computer responding to the email."

"That would have been my office computer," said Carrie. "My office is in southwest Phoenix, and no one besides me has access to it."

"And her office is many miles away from the Andrews' home," added Alex, "which means she has an alibi. So how long between the time she sent the reply, and when the photos were uploaded to *Gentry Magazine?*"

"I'm getting to that," replied Jonathan. "Right after the email was sent to Carrie, someone did a Google search for *Gentry Magazine*, and that's when the release form, and the instructions for the photo contest, were downloaded from their website."

"Good to know," said Alex, "but again, how long was it from the time Scott's computer received Carrie's email, with the signed photo attached, to the time the files were uploaded to the magazine?"

"Exactly twenty-three minutes, and Kendra Clarke's email account was also used to send the files. Carrie wouldn't have had enough time to leave her office and get to Scott's computer in Mesa in twenty-three minutes. I think that we can now safely debunk Mrs. Dickenson's claim that Carrie tried to disguise her own signature on the release form. Her signature was most definitely forged."

"That would also explain why I didn't recognize the email address *Gentry Magazine* had on file for me," said Carrie. "So tell me, does this prove that Maggie Andrews is the person who did this to me?"

"Unfortunately, no," said George. "Scott Andrews has no alibi for the time when the photos were uploaded. According to the Kansas City FBI report, Scott left his office around one fifteen that afternoon, claiming he had a dental appointment. He now admits he lied to his supervisor, and that he went to purchase some luggage instead. He said he was getting ready to leave town and he didn't want anyone knowing of his plans. Problem is, he claims he paid cash for the luggage, so there's no credit card record. He also says he no longer has his receipt. We're trying to find some store security camera footage to back up his story, but so far we haven't been able to locate any. It's been several months since Scott left town, and they typically don't keep the footage that long. What this means is that as of right now we can't prove whether it was Scott or Maggie who uploaded the photos. All we know is the sender was someone in the Andrews home."

As George was talking, Allison entered the room. Steve motioned for her to take a seat.

"We have some additional information," he said, "which is why I've asked my fiancée, Allison Santiago, to join us. She and Carrie are old friends, and something unusual happened this past Saturday, while they were at the mall."

"What's this about, Allie?" asked Carrie

"I didn't say anything at the time, because I didn't want to frighten you, but while we were shopping for your bridesmaid's dress we were being followed."

"What! By whom?"

"It was a woman," explained Allison. "I started noticing her shortly after we arrived. At first I thought she was just another shopper, but then, when we went into the next store, I noticed that she was there too. The same thing happened when we went into the third store. That's when I knew something was up, so I started watching her more closely."

"What did she look like?" asked George.

"Middle-aged, Caucasian, average height and weight, with short blonde hair."

"That matches Maggie Andrews' description."

"Oh my God," exclaimed Carrie.

"So, where was this?" asked George.

"Desert Caliente Mall."

"Which is within a mile of the Andrews' home. Please continue, Ms. Santiago."

"While Carrie was in the fitting room, I decided to approach the woman and—"

"You did what?" exclaimed Steve.

"You shouldn't have done that," said George, firmly. "She could have had a weapon on her."

"Which means you could have gotten Carrie, and yourself, killed," said Steve.

"Oh my God. I'm so sorry, I didn't even think of that. All I was trying to do was to find out what she wanted, but as soon as I took a few steps toward her she took off. I noticed that she had a really guilty look on her face too."

"You were lucky," said George. "So what happened after that?"

"Carrie came out and I told her it was time to go to lunch."

"So that's why you were so anxious to rush out of there. Allie, why didn't you tell me?"

"Because I didn't want to frighten you. You've been through a lot, and your mother just passed away."

"Really?" said Jonathan. "I'm sorry to hear of your loss."

"Thank you, Jonathan." Carrie turned back to her friend. "I'm not angry with you Allie, but if anything like that should ever happen again, please let me know, okay?"

"Okay, and I'm sorry, Carrie."

"Did you see the woman again?" asked George.

"Yes. As Carrie and I were leaving the mall I noticed her watching us again, so I wove our way through the crowd toward the exit. Thankfully, I didn't see her once we reached the parking lot."

"At the risk of butting in," said Jonathan, "I have to ask if any of you are doing anything to protect her. I have some experience dealing with cyber-stalkers in my line of work, and stalkers of any kind can be very dangerous. This woman's gone to a lot of trouble to set Carrie up, and she knows where she works. That has me concerned."

"Me too," said Alex. "And I'll be discussing the matter with my client, in private, once were done here."

"I have to agree with Jonathan," added George. "I was a

homicide detective in Pittsburg for over twenty years. I worked a hell of a lot of cases that started out just like this one. Maggie Andrews found out about you, Carrie, and as soon as she did she put in a lot of time and effort setting you up. Then, two days later, her husband ditches her for yet another woman in Kansas City. We all know the old adage about Hell having no fury like a woman scorned, and believe me, Maggie Andrews is a woman scorned. The woman Scott left her for is halfway across the country and Maggie probably doesn't know that much about her, but she knows all about you. She knows who you are, what you look like, and where you work. So guess which of the other women she's going to vent her anger on? First, she was hiding behind a computer screen, but now she's starting to get bolder. I know how you ladies are about going to sales at the mall, so it may be a coincidence that she was there, but my point is that once she recognized you, she didn't hesitate for a second to start scoping you out, which means she may not be finished with you yet."

"But as I've already told you, I didn't know that Scott was married. Believe me, had I known I would have never gotten involved with him. The reason why I stopped communicating with him was because I was beginning to suspect he had another girlfriend. I never meant to cause her any harm and I deeply regret whatever pain I may have caused her. Isn't there some way I could make her understand?"

"Probably not" said George, "and just so you know, Jonathan and I aren't judging you. But what's done is done, kiddo, and I doubt Maggie would care if you knew he was married or not. As far as she's concerned, you're the other woman and now you're going to pay."

"My God, does this never end? Do I have to keep paying for this for the rest of my life?"

Allison reached over and tried to calm Carrie down. "This is my fault, Carrie. I'm the one who told you Scott was single."

"No," said Jonathan, shaking his head. "This is Scott Andrews' fault. I've read all the emails. The son of a bitch lied to her."

The meeting concluded. Jonathan handed Carrie one of his business cards, saying he'd call her soon to make an appointment to inspect her office computer.

"My office, now," said Alex to Carrie after she hugged Allison goodbye. She quickly followed him into his office.

"Close the door."

She quickly closed the door behind her.

"Are you all right, Alex?"

"No, I'm not. In fact, I'm about to have a total meltdown."

"What's wrong? Are you mad at me or something?"

"No." He took a deep breath. "I'm not angry with you. I'm just scared out of my wits right now for you. George is right, Carrie. This is the kind of thing that gets people killed. That woman is out for blood—your blood."

"I know that, Alex. How do you think I feel?"

"Look Carrie-Anne, until Maggie Andrews is safely behind bars we're going to have to make some changes, and we're going to have to make them fast."

"Like what?"

"For starters, I don't want you staying in your apartment anymore."

"But Alex, I've never published my home address anywhere."

"Didn't you tell me that Scott Andrews picked you up at your apartment the two times you went out with him?"

"Yes, he did," replied Carrie.

"Then Maggie may already have your home address. Even if she doesn't, she could get that information fairly easily."

"Oh my God."

"I think that for the time being you're better off in my guestroom, and don't argue with me. As soon as we're done, I'm going with you to your apartment to help you pack."

"All right, Alex."

"Okay, one problem solved, and now for the next. Your office."

"Alex, I have to get back to work," explained Carrie. "My business has suffered enough already. If I don't get things back on track soon, I'll be out of business and back to being poor."

"I understand, but you need to understand this; Maggie Andrews already knows where you work. You're in there by yourself most of the time and I know you keep your front door open during business hours. What's to stop her from walking through your door one day and simply blowing you away?"

"Oh my God," she replied. "So what am I supposed to do?"

"For starters, I want you to have those armed security guards, like I suggested to you before. I also think you should consider changing your business name and moving to another location."

"That's easier said than done, Alex. I've signed a multi-year lease. I can't just move out."

"Didn't you tell me that you're starting to outgrow your office space?"

"I think I did."

"There you go," he said, matter-of-factly. "Let me have a look at your lease, and I'll see if I can negotiate something for you. But in the meantime, I don't want you going back there without the security guards, nor do I want you going any place else alone."

"But Alex—"

"Damn it, Carrie! Would you please, for once, just do as I say and not argue with me? Are you not getting this? I'm not trying to run your life, okay. What I'm trying to do is keep you from getting hurt—or worse. You're the best friend I've ever had. Do you have any idea, any idea at all, of what my life would be like if anything were to happen to you? I don't think I could handle it."

"I'm sorry, Alex."

"Don't be sorry, dammit. Just do what I say, please."

"Okay." She wrapped her arms around him. "I didn't mean to upset you. I'm scared too. I just didn't want to let it show, because I didn't want to worry you."

"I'm okay, Carrie-Anne. I'm your friend, and sometimes worrying comes with the territory."

"Don't worry, Alex. Nothing's going to happen to me, I promise."

They held one another in silence, while Alex pulled himself together. A few moments later he spoke up. "It's quitting time. Let's head out and get you packed."

⁊Twenty-Six⋘

"I SURE HOPE I'M NOT IMPOSING." Alex had just deposited Carrie's bags in the guest room.

"Again, will you knock it off, please?" At least he had a smile. "You're not imposing. Truth be known, I kind of like having you around. It gets lonely sometimes rattling around this big house all by myself. Sometimes I wonder why I even bought the place."

"You said you got a good deal."

"Yeah, I suppose. I figured if it would be a good place to raise a family someday, but so far…"

"I understand completely," she replied. "But at least you don't have a biological clock that's ticking. You could wait another twenty years and still have kids. Me? I turn thirty-one on Saturday. It's not like I have all the time in the world. Maybe I'm just not meant to have a family."

"Oh, come on. You hardly fit the image of a lonely old spinster, and you can still have kids well into your thirties, maybe even your early forties. But since you've dropped your not-so-subtle hint I may as well let you know that no, I didn't forget your birthday. In fact, I have something really special planned."

"Really? Like what?"

"You'll just have to wait to find out."

"Oh, come on, you mean you're not going to give me a hint."

"Nope."

"Aw, c'mon, Alex." Her voice was somewhat flirtatious. "Not even just a little teeny-weeny hint?"

"Okay, one little hint. Road trip."

"Really? So, I have to know what to pack..."

"Nice try, but all I'm saying is road trip. No further information will be divulged at this time." He turned to leave. "Meantime, it's been one hell of a day. I'm going to go do a few laps around the pool. Feel free to join me, if you'd like."

"I don't have a suit."

Alex's face turned red. It took him a moment to find his voice.

"Well, then, you might want to pick one up. You'll need it this weekend. In the meantime, I suppose you could go skinny dipping."

Now Carrie's face turned red.

"I think I'll pass, for now, if that's okay. I'll just change into a pair of shorts, grab a glass of wine, and hang out on a chaise lounge in the shade. Meantime, you just dropped another little hint. So, we're going somewhere where I'll need a swimsuit. Where oh where could that possibly be?"

"You know, Carrie-Anne, one attorney in the house is quite enough, thank you, and I'm not telling you anything else. I'll be out by the pool."

Alex stepped out and Carrie changed into her shorts. He was all ready in the pool by the time she got her wine and took her seat on the patio. The house sat on a good-sized lot, and he'd once mentioned that if he ever did have a family he'd have the backyard redone. The desert landscaping would be replaced with trees and grass for his kids to play in. As she looked around the yard and imagined his future children, she felt an unexpected tinge of jealousy. Who might their mother might be? She took a sip of wine as she watched him swimming laps across the pool. He'd turned into a handsome man, with a successful career and a beautiful home to boot. He most certainly wouldn't remain a bachelor forever. Some lucky woman was bound to find him. The day she'd have to step aside for her would be a sad one indeed. She was starting to realize she'd allowed herself to become much too emotionally attached. She let out a sigh and took another sip of her wine.

* * *

Carrie hopped into the passenger seat of the white Camaro, while Alex loaded their bags into the trunk. She waited as he climbed behind the wheel and fired up the engine.

"So are you going to tell me where we're going now?"

"Nope." He backed the car out of the garage and they headed down the roadway. "It's a surprise, remember."

"Well, it can't be that far away if we're leaving town during the Friday evening rush hour."

"Maybe, maybe not. We might have to drive all night to get there."

Carrie kept asking questions, but Alex remained tight-lipped. They made their way to the freeway and then to the Interstate where he took the eastbound ramp, heading toward Tucson.

"I knew it! You're taking me to that resort near Tucson that you told me about. What was it called? Oh yeah, I remember. The Double-Diamond."

"Maybe, maybe not," he replied with a grin. "You'll just have to find out, won't you?"

They stopped at a diner in one of the little towns between Phoenix and Tucson shortly after sundown. Carrie kept asking questions, but Alex remained tight-lipped over their meal. Before long they were back on the highway. They were getting close to Tucson when he exited the freeway and took a road heading toward the mountains.

"Aha! We're going to the Double-Diamond, aren't we?"

"Maybe, maybe not," he replied with a smile. "This could be a back road to someplace else. You never know."

Carrie laughed as she relaxed in her seat. After driving for another half hour they came around a bend and she finally saw the welcome sign.

"Back road my Aunt Fanny." She leaned over and kissed him on the cheek.

The Double-Diamond was a huge resort, surrounded by tennis courts, a pool and spa, a riding stable and hiking trails. The main building resembled a mission-style adobe mansion. As they pulled up to the entrance a bellhop appeared to unload their luggage. Carrie marveled at the lobby as they stepped inside. The spacious room was wood-trimmed art deco furnished with southwestern decor. It was rustic yet elegant at the same time. She took a seat on one of the sofas, waiting patiently while Alex checked in and got their room keys.

"Ready?" He handed her a key and walked her toward the elevator. "I got adjoining rooms, and mine even has a Jacuzzi. We'll hop in as soon as our bags arrive, and I'll have room service send up a bottle of wine."

"Alex, you shouldn't have."

"Hey, it's my treat. It's my best friend's birthday, and she was living in the poorhouse for far too long. Now it's time for you to relax and enjoy a weekend of pampering. We'll get up early tomorrow morning and do a short hike, before it gets too hot. After that I've arranged for you to get a full treatment at the spa."

"Alex, I don't know what to say."

"It's your birthday. I want it to be special."

The elevator arrived and they headed up to their rooms. Carrie couldn't believe her eyes when she opened her door. She had a small suite, with two king-sized beds and a huge garden bathtub. There was also a balcony with a spectacular view of the mountains. She knocked on the door that connected her suite to Alex's.

"Oh my." He unlocked his side and she stepped in.

His suite indeed had a hot tub. It too had a view of the mountains, along with mini refrigerator and wet bar. There was also a balcony, right next to hers.

"With a room like this, you really don't need to go out, but where do you sleep?"

"Over here."

He led her around a divider, revealing a beautifully furnished sleeping area with two king-sized beds. She was completely memorized.

"This place is so amazing it doesn't even seem real. You know, it's been eleven months since I ended up homeless. Now I can't believe I'm actually in a place like this. I must be dreaming. I'm afraid someone's going to pinch me and wake me up."

"Well, believe it, Carrie-Anne." He wrapped his arms around her and looked into her eyes. "This isn't dream. It's real. From this day on, your life is going to be better, I promise."

He was about to give in to his instincts and kiss her when they heard a knock at the door. Their bags had arrived and Carrie returned to her room to change. After Alex tipped the bellhop, he chastised himself.

"Are you out of your mind, Montoya? You're still her attorney, and she's still your client."

He let out a sigh as he changed into his swim trunks. He'd barely gotten his bathrobe on when room service delivered the wine. He uncorked the bottle, stopping to savor the distinctive bouquet of a perfectly aged cabernet sauvignon. He filled the two glasses, setting them next to the hot tub as he switched on the jets. He'd just settled into the water when he looked up to see Carrie entering the room, clad in a blue and purple Hawaiian print bikini. For a moment, he was speechless.

"Can I join you?"

"Come on in, birthday girl."

He handed her a glass of wine once she'd settled in the water.

"This feels like Heaven," she said, "especially when you consider that my life has been more like Hell lately. The last time I was in a Jacuzzi was at Louise's house. It was right after we'd finished that damn photo shoot. It was early December and she had me out by the pool, wearing nothing but a pair of earrings. It felt like my buns really were freezing off."

An interesting visual began popping into his head. Once again, he had to silently chastise himself.

"I remember back when we were kids, and you'd take me along on some of the photo shoots you did for Mercer's Markets. It always amazed me just how unglamorous of a job it really was."

"You got that right. The only good thing that came of it was that I was able to pay for college, but it sure wrecked my childhood. How different my life might have been if I could have just been a typical, average kid. But, I can promise you one thing. If I ever am lucky enough to have kids, they won't be child models or go into any other kind of showbiz until they're eighteen."

She took a few sips of wine and leaned her head on Alex's shoulder. He wrapped his arm around her and held her close. It wasn't long before she became so relaxed that she started dozing off.

"Hey, sleepyhead." Alex gave her a gentle shake. "Why don't we call it a night? It's getting late and tomorrow morning I'll be knocking on your door, bright and early."

"Sorry, Alex," she said, yawning. "I guess between and wine and the hot tub I should sleep well tonight."

They climbed out of the hot tub. Carrie grabbed a towel and gave Alex a goodnight kiss on the cheek. He stood by and watched as she headed back toward her room. She turned to say one last goodnight before closing the door behind her.

"Damn it, Carrie. Why did you have to buy that swimsuit? And why do you have to look so damn good in it?"

He headed off to shower, but once he went bed he couldn't make himself comfortable. As he tossed and turned, he realized the time had come to stop denying his feelings. Somehow, he'd become careless and he'd allowed himself to fall hopelessly in love with his best friend.

❧Twenty-Seven❧

T HE SUN WAS BARELY UP when Alex knocked on
Carrie's door. She looked positively radiant when she
opened it. She was already dressed and had her hair swept back
into a ponytail.

"Rise and shine, birthday girl."

"I'm ready. I just need to put my camera in my backpack."

A minute later they were waiting for the elevator. They
decided to postpone breakfast, stopping just long enough to grab
a couple bottles of water before heading out. The hot Arizona sun
would soon be bearing down on them, and they wanted to get
in as much of a hike as they could before that happened. Carrie
stopped a few times along the trail to snap photos, saying that
she also enjoyed art photography, and that one day she hoped to
be able to get some of her work into an art gallery. Two hours
later, the sun turned up the heat. It was time to head back to the
hotel for breakfast.

"So, what will you be doing while I'm at the spa?" she asked,
taking her seat in the dining room.

"Taking a nap. I didn't sleep very well last night."

"Sorry to hear that. Is everything okay?"

"I'm fine. Sometimes I have trouble sleeping in a strange bed. How 'bout you?"

"I slept like a baby," she confessed as she picked up her coffee cup. "The wine and the hot tub sure did the trick."

After breakfast they returned to their rooms and Carrie got ready for the spa. She wanted to tell Alex goodbye before she left. She stepped into his suite and called his name. When he didn't respond right away, she went inside to look for him. She found him asleep on top of one of the beds. She took the blanket off the other bed and wrapped him up in it, giving him a light kiss on the cheek. He smiled and moaned softly. She gently stroked his head before she stepped out.

The next few hours would be heavenly. She would be getting the works—a body scrub, body wrap and a facial, followed by a Swedish massage. For a brief time, she felt as if she hadn't a care in the world, and by the time she returned to her suite she felt invigorated. She noticed the door between their suites was still open. She went to look for Alex, but he'd apparently stepped out. She ordered a sandwich from room service, but by the time she'd finished he still hadn't returned. She finally decided to help herself to the hot tub. She leaned back and closed her eyes, basking in the hot, flowing jets.

"Caught ya!"

She let out a shriek while Alex doubled over in laughter.

"Oh now that's just fine." Her cheeks turned pink as she tried to stifle her own laughter. "I oughta pull you in here, clothes and all."

"Now, now, Carrie-Anne. I had to go out to get you a birthday present. Then, when I returned, I felt like Papa Bear, only this time Goldilocks has helped herself to my hot tub instead of eating my porridge."

"I'm not Goldilocks," she replied, flirtatiously.

"You're not?"

"Nope." Her tone was still flirtatious. "She was a blonde. I'm a brunette. Also you would be Baby Bear, not Papa Bear, being as she ate Baby Bear's porridge, not Papa Bear's. Papa Bear's porridge was too hot, so there. How do you like me now?"

Alex started laughing again. "You know, Carrie-Anne, you should have gone to law school. You have a real knack for arguing a case."

Laughing, she thought about the good rapport they had, and how she could let go and truly be herself. She'd never felt that way with anyone before, not even Doug.

"Seriously, Alex, you didn't have to go out and buy me a present. Just being here with you, away from all of life's troubles, is enough of a present for me."

"You've had it too hard for too long, Carrie-Anne. It's time for you to enjoy some of the nicer things in life."

"Well, in that case, when do I get to open it?"

"Later. Tonight I'm taking you dancing."

"Dancing?"

"Yes, dancing," he replied. "Tonight there'll be a band and dancing by the pool terrace. That ought to be the perfect way to celebrate your birthday. In the meantime, would you like to have some company?"

"You bet. Come on in, Baby Bear."

Alex changed into his swim trunks and joined her in the hot tub. Once again, he had to fight the urge to kiss her. Before long she excused herself, explaining that she wanted to take a short nap before getting ready for dinner.

* * *

It was nearly sundown when he knocked on Carrie's door.

"Whoa," he exclaimed as she opened it. "Where did you get that?"

"Do you like it?"

"It's gorgeous. I don't think I've ever seen you this beautiful before."

"Thanks, Alex, but please, whatever you do, don't tell Steve that you saw me in this dress. Allie would have a fit if she knew I was wearing her maid of honor dress before the wedding."

"Your secret's safe with me. Attorney-client privilege, you know, and I have the perfect thing to go with it." He handed her a small, gold-foil gift box with a matching gold ribbon and bow. "Happy birthday, Carrie-Anne."

"Oh my," she exclaimed as she opened the box. "Alex, I don't know what to say. It's the most beautiful thing anyone's ever given me."

Her hands were trembling as she removed the pendant from its box. The stone glimmered in the light as the gold chain dangled through her fingers. There was also a matching pair of earrings.

"Sapphire is your birthstone, and I wanted to get something that would match the color of your eyes."

"It's absolutely stunning. Can you help me put it on?"

"Of course."

She walked up to the mirror, pulling her hair aside as he came up behind her. He breathed in the sweet scent of her perfume as he put the pendant around her neck and hooked the clasp. It was intoxicating. He put his hands on top of her shoulders for a moment as he gazed at their reflection. They made a great couple and the pose would have made the perfect portrait. He stepped back and watched as she put the earrings on. Carrie marveled as she stepped back to look at her reflection. He'd given her the perfect accessories for her dress.

"Thank you, Alex, so much." She turned to kiss him on the cheek. "No one's ever given me such a wonderful gift before. You have no idea what this means."

"You're my best friend." He kissed her forehead. "Making you happy makes me happy."

He escorted her to the elevator and took her down to the main dining room. After a candlelit dinner, it was time to head out to the pool terrace. Candles floated and bobbed on the gently undulating water, tiki torches flared brightly around the lawn, and the trees were lit with soft white lights that shined like the stars above. The band began to play "Unchained Melody" and he asked her to dance. He escorted her onto the terrace and she looked up into his eyes. He finally gave in and kissed her. It was a soft passionate kiss. He could tell she felt their passion too.

"Alex, I'm so sorry." She laid her head on his shoulder. "I guess I must have gotten carried away in the moment. I didn't mean to be so forward."

He let out a sigh. Carrie was still in denial. "It's okay, Carrie-Anne. You have nothing to apologize for. What's a kiss between two good friends?"

They stayed and danced, stopping for an occasional glass of champagne. Neither wanted the night to end. Both felt a little sad when the band played their encore and said goodnight. Alex escorted her back to their rooms. It was nearly midnight, and they'd have to get ready to leave the following morning. He walked her to her door.

"Thank you again, Alex, for everything. It was the best birthday ever."

"You're welcome, Carrie-Anne."

She gave him a long hug goodnight and he waited until she was safely inside before heading to his own room. As soon as he closed the door behind him he let out a long sigh. Once again, he felt restless and he wasn't looking forward to another long, sleepless night. He changed into his sweatpants and after turning down his bed he went to get his phone. He'd downloaded a few new books into his e-reader app. Perhaps reading in bed might help him unwind. He picked it up, only to discover the battery was nearly dead. He let out another frustrated sigh as he went to get his charger. He searched everywhere for it but it wasn't in his bag. He realized he must have forgotten to pack it. He knew Carrie had the same phone that he had. Hopefully, she'd remembered her charger. He walked up to the door between their rooms and noticed her light shining underneath. At least she was still awake. He tapped on the door.

"Carrie-Anne?"

"What is it?"

"Can I borrow your phone charger?"

"Sure," she replied as she opened the door.

As Alex stepped into the room, he froze in his tracks. Carrie had on the most incredible white negligee he'd ever seen. He stood mesmerized, while he watched her pull her charger from her suitcase.

"Here you go."

Somehow things got awkward as she handed it to him and it fell to the floor. Both reached down to grab it and their hands accidentally touched. As his hand covered hers there was no denying the pulse of electricity that sizzled between them. Their eyes met and they left the charger on the floor. It was no longer important. Their eyes remained locked. He took her in his arms and kissed her passionately. This time she wasn't resisting. The time had come for her to stop denying her feelings. He swooped her up and carried her back to his room, laying her down on top the bed. He looked into her eyes once again.

"Are you sure, Carrie-Anne?"

She nodded as she took his hand and gave it a squeeze. He gently laid down next to her and began kissing her again. This time his tongue went into her mouth as she held him tight. He began stroking the side of her face, her hair, her shoulders, and then down her side. Her negligee felt soft and satiny smooth. His gently rubbed his hands across her hips before slowly and carefully inching his way up toward her breasts. Her nipples responded to his light, gentle strokes as she softly moaned. Her breasts felt soft and supple in his hands as he began to gently caress them. He stopped for a moment to remove his sweatpants. Tossing them aside, he began kissing and stroking her again, while she began massaging his back. He reached down and began rubbing her thigh, slowly pulling up her nightgown. As he pulled it off, her body was revealed to him. He marveled at the sight of her. The photos he'd seen of her were nowhere close to the real thing. He began kissing her again, this time with a passion he'd never experienced before. He felt her hands running through his hair, rubbing his back, butt and thighs, and then she began intimately caressing him, giving him an intense pleasure that made him shiver and moan as he began to kiss her breasts. She moaned with pleasure again as his hands reached further down. She opened her legs, allowing him to gently massage her. As soon as she was ready, he slowly and carefully entered her. She wrapped her legs tightly around him. He kissed her breasts and she stroked his hair, back and butt while they danced their dance. Their moans grew more intense as they kissed and held each other tight. As she began to climax he felt his own body hitting new heights until he thought he'd touched the sky. He felt her arms squeezing him tight as he slowly came back down to earth. Afterwards they stayed in each other's arms, lovingly caressing one another until both fell into a blissful, exhausted sleep.

❧Twenty-Eight❧

BILLIE TOOK HER SEAT at her desk and started going through the Daniels file. The lab results from the fireplace ashes were in. They'd managed to partially reconstruct several items, including the signed release form, an autographed photo of Carrie Daniels, and a piece of paper that someone had used to practice copying her signature. A copy of *Gentry Magazine*, with the published photos, had also been recovered. Many of the magazine's interior pages were scorched around the edges, but otherwise intact. As she reviewed the rest of the file, her supervisor approached her desk.

"Morning Billie. How's your Saturday?"

"So far, so good. How 'bout you?"

"Not bad so far, and I see you've got it."

"Indeed. Interesting reading."

"It's time to call Kansas City and have them pick up Scott Andrews."

"But Ken is convinced his wife, Maggie, is the forger," argued Billie.

"And we certainly haven't ruled out the possibility of collusion between Scott and Maggie, so we'll continue investigating her. We know she was using Scott's computer that morning, and we know she paid for her lunch at The Cattle Rustlers at one forty-nine that afternoon. We also know that Scott left his office around one-fifteen, and at that hour of the day it, would have only taken him about ten minutes to get home. He was getting ready to leave town. We think he came home early that day to take care of some last-minute business. Maggie has steadfastly maintained that she returned home around two o'clock and that when she arrived, she found Scott in the den in front of his laptop. Scott has no other alibi for the time when the signature was forged and the files were uploaded, and his laptop was used for the upload."

"What about finding any security camera footage from the luggage shop?"

"It doesn't exist. Turns out their security cameras weren't working that day. In the meantime, he lied to his supervisor about having to leave early for a dental appointment. He also took the two photos of Ms. Daniels with him when left town."

Billie was still unconvinced. "Maggie doesn't have an alibi either and she has the perfect motive—revenge."

"I know she doesn't have an alibi for the time the files were uploaded, however, her story's always been consistent. Scott, on the other hand, lied to his supervisor. He also lied to Ms. Daniels about a whole lot of other things when he was seeing her. So, how much would you like to bet he's lying when he says he didn't know anything about this? He's a jilted lover, Billie. Ms. Daniels abruptly stopped communicating with him several weeks before he left town, so he decided to get even with her. Let's get the ball rolling on this. I want him picked up today so we can begin the extradition process on Monday. Let him spend some time in a holding cell. Maybe that'll motivate him to tell the truth."

* * *

Scott looked up from the lawn mower to see a white SUV pulling up in front of the house. Two men, wearing jackets identifying them as FBI agents, exited the vehicle and started walking up the driveway. As they approached, they produced their badges, and Scott shut down the mower.

"Can I help you, gentlemen?"

"Are you Scott Andrews?"

"Yes, I'm Scott. So what's this about?"

"Sir, I'm placing you are under arrest for identity theft and forgery."

"What!"

One of the agents pulled out his handcuffs, telling him to raise his hands in the air while the other patted him down and read him his Miranda rights. As they were handcuffing him, a woman came running out of the house.

"What the hell is going on here?"

"Ma'am if you would please go back inside," barked one of the agents.

"I will not. This is my house, you're on my property, and this man is my fiancé."

"Ma'am, I warning you for the last time, go back inside the house."

"It's okay, Nancy." Scott tried to reassure her. "This is Maggie's doing. She set me up. Are you people taking me back to Phoenix?"

"Eventually."

"Nancy, I need you to call my attorney. Hillary Johansen. Her card is on my desk."

"But Scott—"

"Just do it, Nancy, please," he shouted as the agents herded him back to the white suv. "I love you. It'll be okay, I promise."

They shoved Scott into the backseat and quickly sped away. As soon as they arrived at the field office, he was taken into a small room where he spent the next hour being grilled. He steadfastly maintained his story that his wife called his office that morning, asking to borrow his laptop, and that he had no knowledge of anyone's signature being forged on any kind of document. He finally leaned back in his chair. Folding his arms across his chest, he informed them that he was through talking and he wanted his attorney.

"Okay, Mr. Andrews," said the agent, "you can call your attorney, but before you do, I have one last question for you."

"All right, I'm listening."

"How long do you want to sit in a holding cell?"

"I don't." Scott's voice was firm. "I've already told you. I've done nothing wrong. This is my ex-wife's doing. You've arrested the wrong person."

"So you say, but that'll be up to a jury to decide. In the meantime, you have an important decision to make. You can fight extradition to Arizona, and maybe spend the next thirty to ninety days sitting in a holding cell, or you can cooperate with us and waive extradition. If you do that, we'll send you to Phoenix on the next available flight."

"What happens then?"

"After they book you, you'll get to see a judge. If you're able to post bond, you'll be free to go."

"I see. So, how soon can you get me there?"

"I take it you want to waive extradition."

"Absolutely," replied Scott. "I want to post bond and get this cleared up as quickly as possible."

"All right. Let me see what I can do."

Scott was turned over for booking. He was led to another room to be fingerprinted and have his mug shots taken. Afterwards, he was returned to the interrogation room, where he waited for nearly three hours until another agent and a deputy U.S. Marshal entered. The deputy was carrying a small duffle bag.

"You just got lucky," he said. "We managed to get you on a flight to Phoenix that leaves this evening."

"Don't I get to pack first?"

"Sorry, but I'm sure the folks in Phoenix will be more than happy to provide you with a toothbrush and a change of clothes."

"Don't I at least get a phone call before we go?"

"Look, you're the one who wanted to waive extradition, so now we have a plane to catch. You can make your phone call once we get to Phoenix."

Once again, Scott was handcuffed and placed in the back of an SUV.

It was a long, uncomfortable and unpleasant flight. It was after ten o'clock by the time the plane finally touched down on the runway at Sky Harbor International Airport. Scott was immediately escorted off and handed over to two waiting FBI agents.

"He's all yours."

"Thanks for bringing him in."

"No problem. He didn't make any trouble on the flight."

Scott was taken out of the terminal and loaded into the back of yet another SUV.

"You're not taking me to jail, are you?"

"Gee, how did you know?" joked one of the agents. "I told you, Chris, these computer guys are really smart."

"Yeah, they're real small all right—until they decide to steal their girlfriend's identity and forge her signature."

"Look, I didn't steal anyone's identity, and I didn't forge anyone's signature," argued Scott. "I was told I'd see a judge as soon as I got here. So, when can I make my phone call? I need to call my attorney and I need someone to come and bail me out."

"Look buddy, it's Saturday night. You won't be seeing judge until sometime on Monday. So for now, why don't you just sit back, relax, and enjoy our free hospitality."

Scott let out a sigh. He was trapped in a nightmare he couldn't wake up from. They arrived at the jail and once again he was taken into another small room for questioning. The door opened and a thirty-something blonde woman entered, taking her seat across the table from him.

"Finally, a friendly face."

"Hello there, Scott. My name is Deputy U.S. Marshall Diane Hall, and I'll be taking care of your booking. After we're finished, Billie Hughes, with the Phoenix FBI office, wants to talk with you."

She handed Scott over to two male deputies. Once again, he was taken away be photographed and fingerprinted. When they finished he was escorted into another room.

"Okay," said one of the deputies. "I want you to slowly and carefully remove each item of your clothing, one at a time, and hand it over so we can inspect it."

"Why?"

"It's routine, sir. Take off the shirt, then your shorts, and your shoes and socks."

Scott did as he was told. When he was done, he was standing in his underwear.

"Did you not hear me, buddy? Remove your drawers and hand them over."

"What? Then I'll be standing here naked."

"That's why we call it a strip search."

Scott removed his underwear and handed it over. As he stood naked, one of the deputies looked inside his mouth, ears, and armpits before looking down to closely inspect his genitals.

"Don't you dare touch me!" Scott felt both embarrassed and humiliated.

"I'm not going to touch you, however, you're going to lift it up so I can have a look underneath."

Scott had no choice but to comply. It was a horrible experience. Once the deputy was finally finished the other picked up a flashlight.

"All right, spread your legs, bend over and grab your ankles. You'll remain in that position until I tell you that you can move."

"What! Are you kidding me? Why are you doing this? I've been accused of a non-violent crime."

"Sorry, it's routine. You're going into the general jail population. We have to search you for contraband."

Scott bent over. For the first time in his life, he knew the feeling of being violated. It was the most humiliating experience of his life and the deputy seemed to be taking an unusually long time. When they finally finished, they led him to a shower. They watched him while he showered, and handed him an orange jail suit with a pair of open-toed rubber shoes when he was done. As soon as he was dressed, he was taken to an interview room, where Billie Hughes was waiting. As he took his seat, she opened her folder, removed a photo, and pushed it across the table toward him.

"My name is Agent Hughes. Do you know who this woman is?"

"Yes. Her name is Carrie Daniels."

"So, you know her."

"Yes, I used to know her."

"How do you know her?"

"I had a relationship with her."

"What kind of a relationship did you have with Ms. Daniels?"

"I had sex with her, okay," admitted Scott. "And she was a really great piece of ass, too."

"So I take it you weren't exactly in love with her?"

"Nope. I admit my intentions toward Ms. Daniels were far less than honorable. I met her last February at Louise Dickenson's opening at an art gallery in Scottsdale. She'd posed nude for some of Ms. Dickenson's photos. I saw the goods and she said something about having recently broken up with her boyfriend. I figured her guard was down and I was determined to have her, so I pretended like I was a nice guy who was interested in getting to know her better. It worked like a charm. I got to hump her brains out."

"So, did Ms. Daniels know that you were married?"

"Are you kidding?" Scott rolled his eyes as he was speaking. "I wasn't about to tell her something like that. I could tell, that in spite of her showing off the merchandise for Louise's camera, she had some scruples. She wasn't the type who'd hang out with a married guy, so I lied to her. Big deal. She's over the age of eighteen and I wasn't aware that adultery was a jailable offense in this state."

"It's not," said Billie, "however, identity theft and forgery are. So tell me, Mr. Andrews, how many times did you see Ms. Daniels?"

"Twice. I wanted to take her out a third time, make it a trifecta, if you know what I mean, but then she stopped emailing me. That was also about the time I heard from Nancy."

"Nancy?"

"My fiancée, in Kansas City," explained Scott. "The one you all hassled today, because she wanted to know why you were harassing me, on her property."

"I see," said Billie. "So, before Nancy came along, you were seeing Ms. Daniels, and then you said she'd suddenly stopped emailing you. How did that make you feel, Scott?"

"Disappointed, but then, like I said, I heard from Nancy. We'd had a prior relationship that didn't work out and I didn't expect to hear from her again. As soon as I found out she was free and available, it was no contest. I decided to leave my wife, and Carrie, and go to Kansas City to be with Nancy. She's the only woman I've ever truly loved. I was happy too, until you people came along and grabbed me and started accusing me of a crime I didn't commit. Just so you know, the truth will come out, and when it does, I'm going to sue all of you for false arrest."

"Whatever," said Billie with a shrug. "So, you say you were disappointed when Carrie stopped responding to your emails. Did that make you angry? Were you angry enough to want to get even with her?"

"What? No! Are you kidding? Like I just said, Carrie was a really great piece of ass, but no, I certainly didn't wish her any harm. By the time Nancy came back on the scene, I'd already conquered Carrie so I was ready to move on."

"I see, so if you'd already conquered Carrie, as you say, then why did you take the two photos of her with you to Kansas City?"

"I guess I wanted a souvenir, a memento. The photos were limited edition prints. They have a certain value to an art collector, although they'd been taken out of their original frames."

"What was that?"

"Maggie, the stupid bitch. Two days before I left town I come home from work and Maggie tells me she'd accidentally knocked one of the prints of Carrie off the wall while she was making up the bed that morning."

"Making the bed?"

"Yeah," said Scott. "We had them hanging on our bedroom wall, right over the bed. Then the stupid cow goes and knocks one of them off while she's making the bed. She said it broke the frame."

"So what did she do after that?"

"She told me that she took them to some arts and crafts store to get them reframed."

"Both of them?"

"Yeah. We'd bought them as a matching set, and she said she wanted them in matching replacement frames."

"When was this?"

"Two days before I left town."

"Do you know what store?"

"I think she said Taylor's Arts and Crafts, but I'm not sure. When I got home, she told me that she'd accidentally broken one of the frames, so they were being reframed and she'd pick them up the next day. When I got home from work the following night, both of the photos, in their new frames, were back up on the wall."

Billie jotted down the information. Scott watched her as she wrote. His patience was beginning to wear thin.

"Look, are we done here? I want to call my lawyer. I'm not saying anything more until I get my lawyer."

"Okay Scott," said Billie, "you can call your attorney, but I doubt if he or she would be answering the phone this late on a Saturday night. Besides, you're not being arraigned until sometime on Monday, so why don't you just make yourself comfortable until then?"

Billie stepped away while Scott was taken to a holding cell. Monday would be an eternity away.

❧Twenty-Nine❧

CARRIE AWOKE TO THE sound of her ringing phone. It sounded somewhere far away. Fully awake, she remembered it was in her room, and she was in Alex's suite. She started to get up, but as she stirred she felt an arm reaching over, pulling her back into the bed.

"No," whispered Alex as he wrapped his arm around her. "Don't answer it. Let it go to voicemail."

She snuggled close to him. "So how'd you sleep?"

"Like a rock. I was exhausted. You wore me out." He paused for a moment before asking the inevitable question. "So, how are you feeling this morning, Carrie-Anne? Are you all right with this?"

"Yes, I think I am. How 'bout you?"

"I'm good. No, I'm better than good. I'm fantastic. But can I tell you something?"

"Of course."

"Carrie-Anne, what has happened between us didn't just happen on the spur of the moment. It's been a long time coming. Probably longer than you know."

"What do you mean?"

"This goes way back," he said. "My feelings for you were beginning to change about the time we getting ready to graduate from high school. Did you know that?"

"No."

"Then I won that scholarship to Cornell. Remember how I was going to turn it down?"

"And I told you you'd be nuts if you did. It was a golden opportunity for you, Alex. I wasn't about to let you throw it away."

"I know, and in hindsight you were absolutely right. I wouldn't be where I am today if I'd turned it down, so I decided the next four years would be a test. I'd keep in touch, and if you were still available by the time we finished college, I'd take it as a sign and we'd go from there."

"Alex, I had no idea." Carrie stroked the back of his hand. "I wish you'd said something to me. You were my best friend too, although it was starting to become a little more than that for me as well, but I blew it off as a teenage crush. Then you faded away, right after I met what's his name. But as the years went by, I always regretted that we'd lost touch with one another."

"I didn't exactly fade away. At the time, we were thousands of miles apart. You'd met some other guy and I'd met someone else too. I figured we weren't meant to be after all, so I cut you loose. Did I regret it? You'd better believe I did. Then, after Casey, I let myself drift. I debated with myself, many times, about trying to find you, but by then, so many years had passed that I figured you had to be married."

"I had no idea, Alex, but would you believe me if I told you I almost looked you up this past Fourth of July?"

"You're kidding."

"No, I'm not. For some strange reason you'd really been on my mind. Then, when I was at Steve and Allie's party, I overheard someone mention the name Alex. Of course I had no idea that they were talking about you, but after hearing the name, you were all I thought about for the rest of the evening. I was going to look you up on Google when I got home, but then I changed my mind. I thought it over again and I too assumed that you were probably married."

"Dang," he said. "You know, I'd planned on going to that party, but then my brother called me at the last minute, so I went to San Diego instead."

"It's okay, Alex. It was only a week later that my entire world turned upside down. Thank goodness you were there." She heard Alex let out a sigh. "Uh-oh. This is about my case, isn't it? Are we going to get into trouble over this?"

"Not exactly, but, since you've brought it up, I need to let you know that I'll have to recuse myself."

"Oh no. Alex, you're not going to be brought up on some sort of ethics charges, are you? Because if you are, then I'm a willing accomplice, and I'll swear to that in court if I have to."

"No, Carrie-Anne." He laugh as he began stroking her hair. "I'm not going to be disbarred or anything like that. In fact, I'm hoping that we can wrap up your case very soon. I've proven, conclusively, that your signature was forged and that you couldn't have possibly been in the room when the release was signed and the files were uploaded. I sent a detailed letter, along with a copy of Jonathan's report, to Louise's attorney late Friday afternoon. It's over. She doesn't have a case, at least not one against you. It's only a matter of time before she figures it out. I don't want you worrying about this anymore, Carrie-Anne. It's time for you to move forward."

She looked around for her negligee. She found it lying on the floor next to the bed. She grabbed it and put it on.

"Where are you going?"

"To freshen up and make some coffee. Don't worry, I'll be back."

She gave him a quick kiss before stepping away. Alex soon smelled the delicious aroma of fresh coffee brewing. He stepped away to freshen up as well. He'd just returned to bed when Carrie came back into the room.

"I've plugged your phone into my charger and the coffee's ready. Would you like a cup?"

"In a minute. Can you come over here? I need to ask you something."

"Sure, what is it?"

"This." He reached up, pulled her back down on the bed and began to kiss her passionately. The coffee was momentarily forgotten and once again Carrie's nightgown ended up on the floor.

* * *

"Are you sure we can't stay over for an extra day?" Carrie was stroking Alex's chest as they basked in the afterglow.

"That would be nice, wouldn't it? Unfortunately, duty calls. I have to be back in the office bright and early tomorrow morning."

"Yeah, me too I'm afraid. So when's check-out time?"

"Noon."

She looked at the clock on the nightstand. It was almost ten-thirty. She let out a sigh as she put her nightgown back on and brought the coffee back to their bed. As they were enjoying it, she heard her phone began ringing once again.

"Well, someone's certainly persistent," he said.

"Yeah, and I guess I'd better go find out who it is. It's probably the only way to get rid of 'em."

She headed back into her room and picked up her phone. Both calls had come from Billie Hughes' cell phone. She hit the call button and waited for Billie to answer.

"Hey, Billie, Carrie Daniels. I'm returning your call."

As she was speaking, Alex entered the room. She motioned for him to take a seat on one of the beds. As soon as he did, she sat down next to him and put her phone on speaker.

"I wanted to let you know we've made an arrest in your case," said Billie.

"Really. So did you finally get the goods on Maggie Andrews?"

"No, I'm afraid not. The person we arrested was Scott."

"Scott?" Carrie's voice sounded incredulous. "Why him? All the information we got from George McCormick points to Maggie, and last weekend Allison caught her following us around the mall."

"It wasn't my call, Carrie. However we decided to bring Scott in because it was his computer, he has no alibi, the two of you had a prior relationship, and he has a really bad habit of lying."

"Tell me about it."

"Anyway, he decided to waive extradition. He's in custody, here in Phoenix, and they'll arraign him sometime tomorrow. I just wanted to let you know."

"But what about Maggie? I'm no fan of Scott, but I know he's not the one who did this to me. It had to have been Maggie."

"That's what Ken O'Dell thinks too. He's still investigating her, so you may want to speak with him."

Carrie thanked her for calling and said goodbye.

"They've got the wrong person, Alex. I'd bet my life on it."

"I know, and all the evidence against him is still circumstantial. However, it's out of our hands."

"Will I have to testify?"

"I'd say it's a good possibility," he replied, "but I don't want you to be concerned about it right now. It could be six months to a year or more before he goes to trial, and between now and then he may decide to plea bargain his way out, assuming his case doesn't get tossed out first."

"But what if it doesn't? I don't want to be forced to take the stand and rehash a part of my life that I desperately want to forget."

He took her in his arms and kissed her on the forehead. "If you get subpoenaed, you'll have to testify. If that happens you just get on the stand and tell them the truth. I know it may seem scary, but I promise I'll be right there with you. You didn't do anything wrong, Carrie-Anne. You're not the one who's on trial. It's going to be all right."

The time had come for them to start packing. Both were sorry to leave, and both were unusually quiet on the drive back. It was midafternoon when the Camaro pulled into Alex's garage.

"I wonder if it's safe for me to return to my apartment," said Carrie, stepping inside the house.

"Nope," Alex replied definitively as he carried their bags inside and set them down in the living room. "That's all I thought about on the way back. As long as Maggie's walking around free she's still a threat to you. No doubt Scott will post bail, and as long as he's on bail, Maggie has the perfect scapegoat."

"Won't he go back to Kansas City?"

"Possibly, although I doubt his bail-bondsman will allow him to travel that far. I'd like to give Ken O'Dell a call. Have you got his number handy?"

Carrie nodded as Alex pulled out his phone and took a seat on the corner group. She gave him the number and he put the phone on speaker. Once they were connected Alex introduced himself.

"I know why you're calling, and I have a hunch we're on the same page," said O'Dell. "The good news is Scott just gave us the information we need to bring Maggie in questioning."

"What's that?"

"It seems that Maggie had a little accident the day the photos were uploaded. According to Scott, she accidentally knocked one of them off the wall and broke its frame. He says that when he got home that night both photos were out being reframed. He says they were back on the wall the following day. The day after that he took them with him to Kansas City."

"Which would have given her plenty of opportunity to scan them into his computer," observed Alex. "Have your forensics guys been able to determine when they were scanned?"

"Unfortunately, no. Whoever scanned them apparently deleted the files once they were done. Scott had a Mac, and it was configured to automatically delete files securely. Several months passed before we seized his computer. By then, whatever was left of the files had been completely written over, so we were unable to recover them."

"I see," said Alex. "So, have you brought her in yet?"

"No, not yet. It's Sunday, and I want to do this while the kids are at school. They've been through enough of an ordeal, and I don't want to put anymore stress on them than I have to."

"I understand."

"I'll pick her up first thing tomorrow morning, as soon as the kids leave, but unless she slips up and incriminates herself we won't be able to hold her. I have a hunch she'll spend her time pointing the finger at Scott. That's all she's done so far."

"I see." There was a tone of disappointment in Alex's voice.

"Don't worry, the investigation is still ongoing. We still think that she and Scott may have been working together."

"Well, at least that sounds encouraging," said Carrie after they wrapped up their call. "I'll feel a lot safer once they have the right person. Maybe then I can finally move on with my life."

She picked up her bag, not sure for the moment where she should take it.

"That way." Alex pointed toward the master suite. As she headed down the hallway, he picked up his bag and followed her.

"Oh good, you have a king-sized bed. So, which side do I take?"

"Whichever one you want, my dear."

"Okay Carrie, think… Aha! There it is."

"What?"

"The remote control." She pointed it out on the nightstand. "I know how you are about your remote control."

"I am not."

"You are too."

"Am not."

"Okay, then in that the case you won't mind if I do this."
She picked up the remote and began walking out of the room
with it.

"Oh no you don't."

"Gotcha!"

Carrie laughed as she started to play a game of keep away
with Alex. Every time he'd reach for the remote she'd toss it into
her other hand. He played along until she finally slipped in down
her front and tucked it into her bra.

"There you go. Now you can't get it. Ha, ha."

"Yeah, like it'd be safe from me down there. I'll show you
who's the keeper of the remote around here." He reached down
her front. His hand brushed against her breasts as he scooped it
out. "Hey, that felt nice. Can I do that again?"

"Nope." She plopped down on the bed, rolling over on her
back. "Move over, Montoya, I'm staking this claim for me. You
and your remote can go hang out on the other side."

"What remote?" He dropped it on the nightstand and
plopped down bed next to her. He started patting down her
chest and squeezing her breasts. "So, what else have you got
hidden down there? I may have to strip search you."

"Stop that," she said, laughing.

"No."

"Stop that."

"No."

"Alex Montoya, you're incorrigible, but you're still my best
friend."

"That I am, and me too."

❧Thirty❧

KEN O'DELL WAITED patiently in his suv. He, along with a female agent, had been staking out the Andrews home for the past thirty minutes. During that time, a car pulled into the driveway and honked. A teenage girl came out the front door, hopped in, and the car drove away. Finally, his patience paid off. The garage door rolled up and Maggie Andrews backed her silver Honda out. He noticed a young boy sitting in the passenger seat. He discreetly followed her, pulling off to the side of the road as she drove up to the front of the school. The passenger door opened and the boy jumped out, waving goodbye to his mother before running off to join his friends. As Maggie pulled back onto the street he began tailing her again. He became concerned when she got back to the main road and turned in the opposite direction from her home. He stayed behind her as she entered a supermarket parking lot. Once again, he patiently waited. Twenty-five minutes later she emerged from the store with a cartload of groceries. He watched from a safe distance while she loaded them into her trunk and got back into her car. She headed straight home as she exited the parking lot. He followed from a distance, again being careful to not alert her to his presence. By the time he got back to her house, the garage door was rolling shut. He glanced at his watch and looked at the other agent. They decided to give her some time to put the groceries away. There were children living in the home so there'd be no sense in allowing their perishables go to waste. Ten minutes later they stepped out of the vehicle and knocked on the front door.

"You again?" Maggie's greeting was less than pleasant. "Look, my husband's been arrested. He's sitting in jail somewhere in Phoenix, so why don't the two of you go bug him and leave me the hell alone? I've had enough of being harassed by you."

"I'm aware of that, ma'am," said O'Dell, "however, we need you to come to the field office and answer some questions."

"So am I being arrested too?"

"No, not at this time Mrs. Andrews. However, you're still a person of interest in this case, and we have a few more questions to ask you. It shouldn't take very long and you'll be free to go, once we're finished."

"And what happens if I refuse to cooperate?"

"I understand your concerns, ma'am, but trust me, it will be much better if you cooperate."

Maggie let out a sigh. With Scott in jail she was nearly home free. This wasn't the time to do anything that would raise suspicion.

"I'm sorry, sir. I guess I'm just having a bad morning. I spent the entire day yesterday trying to console my children. As you can imagine, they're quite distraught over their father being arrested."

"We understand, Mrs. Andrews," said the female agent. "I promise this won't take very long."

Maggie got her purse and headed out the door. Once they arrived, she was taken to a small room and told to take a seat. Billie Hughes soon joined them, and they began by asking her about the day the photos were uploaded to *Gentry Magazine*.

"We've been over this a dozen times now." There was a tone of exacerbation in Maggie's voice. "My computer crashed, so I called Scott and asked to borrow his laptop. He said it would be okay. After I finished reading my email I got curious. Our wedding anniversary was coming up. I wanted to find out what he was getting me so I looked at his browser history. That's when I discovered that he had another email account. Okay, I'll admit I shouldn't have done it, but I tried his password and it worked. That's when I found out he was having an affair. You're right. I stuck my nose in where it didn't belong and it wasn't a very nice thing for me to do. However, Scott had freely given his password to me and I was using his computer with his consent. The rest is a private matter between my husband and myself."

"I'm sure it must have been very painful to learn that he was being unfaithful to you," said Billie.

"Yes, it was. I sat there and cried my eyes out. I was heartbroken. I've been in love with Scott since I was nineteen, and I thought we had a happy marriage."

"Obviously, you thought wrong," countered O'Dell. "So, how did that make you feel? Did it make you angry? Were you angry enough to lash out? Perhaps lash out at your husband's mistress?"

"Of course I was angry, but my anger was directed toward Scott. This woman, Ms. Daniels, is a total stranger to me."

"So, what did you do after that?" asked Billie.

"I've already told you. I went out for a long walk."

"Where?"

"Our subdivision has a common area with a playground. I walked around there for awhile, and then I sat down on a bench. I don't know for how long. After that, I decided to go to The Cattle Rustler and console myself with a greasy burger and a hot fudge sundae."

"Mrs. Andrews, I'm afraid your husband is telling a very different story," said Billie. "According to him, that morning you accidentally knocked a photograph off the wall while you were making up the bed."

Maggie's blood turned to ice. Once again, she put on her best face and tried to remain calm.

"You know, I'd forgotten about that. That actually happened a few days before the morning I borrowed Scott's computer. He must be mistaken about the date."

"You're sure?" asked O'Dell.

"Of course I'm sure. Yes, I recall accidently knocking one of the photos off the wall. You remember, Agent O'Dell. I showed you where they'd been hanging; right over the bed. I wasn't paying attention that morning and I accidentally knocked one off the wall."

"What day did that happen?"

"I can't remember the exact day, sir. It's been months. But it wasn't the on same day I borrowed Scott's computer. That I do know."

"I'm sure you must have been very upset when that happened," said Billie. "I understand that you and your husband are both art collectors, and that it was a limited edition photo."

"Yes, we are. Or rather, we were. And you're right, it was a limited edition photograph."

"Did it get damaged?"

"The frame did, luckily the photo itself wasn't damaged."

"Did you know who the model in the photo was?" asked O'Dell.

"No. The title of the print was on the back of the frame, but I don't recall ever seeing the model's name. So who was she?"

"I think you all ready know who the model is, Mrs. Andrews," said O'Dell. "According to the computer forensics report, right after you read your husband's email you went to the website for Carrie Daniels Photography. Would you like to explain?"

Maggie felt a chill running down her spine. She'd deleted the browser history that day, along with all of the other files. Many months had passed since then. How could they have retraced her tracks? Surely all the deleted files would have been written over by now.

"I'm sorry, sir," said Maggie, apologetically. "You must understand it was a horrible day for me, and I'm sure I've blocked out many of the details of what happened. But now that you've brought it up, I vaguely recall going to that website, but I was so upset that I really don't remember it."

"According to our report, you spent a lot of time on the about us page of Ms. Daniel's website. There's a picture of her on that page."

"So what are you getting at, sir?"

"What I'm getting at, Mrs. Andrews, is that you've been lying to me." Maggie heard the anger in O'Dell's voice. "So, here's what really happened. You went to Carrie Daniels' website because you wanted to find out who your husband's mistress was."

"Okay, so maybe I did. Is that a crime?"

"No," said Billie. "Under the circumstances, it would have been perfectly understandable. If I'd just found out that my husband had been cheating on me, I'd want to know with whom."

"But stealing the other woman's identity and forging her signature is illegal, Mrs. Andrews, and it will get you a long prison term."

Maggie could feel herself starting to sweat. She had to remain calm.

"Look, I didn't steal anyone's identity, and I didn't forge anyone's signature. Scott did that, not me. Like I said, I went for a long walk, and then I went out to lunch. I didn't return until much later that day."

"I want the truth, Mrs. Andrews," demanded O'Dell. "You saw Carrie Daniels' picture on her website. You recognized her as the nude model in the photos so you got angry. I'll bet you were so angry that all you wanted to do at that moment was to rip those photos of her to shreds, but you couldn't do that because you didn't want your husband to know you'd found out about his cheating on you, so you broke the frame instead. Then, once you had the photo out of its frame, you decided to scan it into Scott's computer. It was the perfect plan, wasn't it, Maggie? You're an art collector. You know how copyrights work. You decided to set Carrie Daniels up so that Louise Dickenson would go after her for copyright infringement, and you'll be happy to know that your scheme worked. Mrs. Dickenson has indeed filed a copyright infringement claim against Ms. Daniels, along with your husband Scott. Only there's a problem. Carrie got a copy of the release, and as soon as she saw it she knew that someone had stolen her identity, and that her signature had been forged. That's against the law, Mrs. Andrews, so she called the police and reported it."

"That's quite a picture you've painted there, Agent O'Dell. Unfortunately, it's not quite accurate. Yes, I did break one of the frames. I've already told you it was an accident, and it happened a few days before I found out about the affair."

"Did you replace the frames?"

"Of course I did."

"Where did you get the new frames?" asked Billie.

"I can't recall right now. It been months, and since that time I've had other things on my mind. Like having my husband suddenly walk out on me for yet another woman. Like coming home and finding all of his belongings gone, because he decided skip out and move halfway across the country without so much as a goodbye. Like having to go through a painful divorce and having to deal with two children who are also trying to cope." The tears were streaming down Maggie's face as she reached for a tissue. "Are we done here? We'd better be, because I'm through talking to you. You've found your culprit and it's not me. It's my husband, Scott."

O'Dell motioned to Billie to step outside.

"She's guilty as hell," he said after he closed the door behind them. "She would have needed to take the photos out of the frames in order to scan them. If only I could prove she's the one who did it."

"I'm convinced she's involved as well, but we still don't have a smoking gun, and she's never going to admit to it."

"It's so damn frustrating that both of their handwriting comparisons were inconclusive. We couldn't determine if it was Scott or Maggie who forged the signature. We could only prove that it wasn't Ms. Daniels' handwriting."

"I'll run her home, Ken. With any luck she'll feel comfortable enough with me to slip up and say something."

O'Dell nodded stepped away while Billie went back into the interrogation room.

"Okay, Maggie, we're done. I'm going to take you home now."

"Thanks, I appreciate it. Like I said, I'm going through a bad divorce and I really don't need any additional stress right now."

"I understand, and I'm sorry you're having to go through this. We just needed some additional information, that's all. We want to make sure there's a conviction in this case, and we appreciate the fact that you've been helpful."

Maggie kept to herself on the drive back. The authorities were getting much too close to the truth. As Billie pulled up the curb she thanked her for the ride home. She walked through her front door and waited for Billie to drive away.

"All right, you stupid little bitch! Thanks to O'Dell, it's now confirmed. You're indeed responsible for bringing the FBI in, so thanks to you I just got hauled in and treated like a criminal. And for that little outrage, Carrie, you're going to have to pay. I've told you before and I'll tell you again. If I go down, you're going down with me."

Maggie needed to come up with another plan and she knew not to use a computer this time around. She'd learned the hard way that anything she did electronically would be too easy to trace. She picked up her keys and walked to the corner to pick up her mail. Perhaps some fresh air and sunshine might help her think.

"If it weren't for junk mail, I'd get no mail at all," she mused after she turned the key to open her mailbox. Along with a few bills, her box was crammed with flyers, coupons, and other unsolicited advertisements. She headed home and was about to drop it into the recycling can when, just like before, the perfect plan suddenly flashed across her mind.

"Of course. I see them doing this on TV all the time, and it's not that hard. And since it's low tech they won't be able to track me down."

She brought the junk mail back into the house and set it on the kitchen table. She reached into the cabinet underneath the sink and took out a pair of rubber gloves. She dropped them on the table and opened the junk drawer, rummaging through it until she found a glue stick and a pair of scissors. She set them on the table and put the gloves on before stepping into the den and opening the credenza. She carefully removed a sheet of paper from the center of the stack, along with a self-adhesive envelope. She brought both items back to the kitchen table and began cutting individual letters out of pieces of the junk mail, gluing a message onto the paper.

"This is fun. It's sort of like putting a puzzle together, and when I'm done I'll have the pleasure of torturing you, Carrie."

Satisfied with her message, she took the envelope back into the den and placed it into the printer. Her printer was a popular brand. No doubt thousands of other households had one just like it. She grabbed the phonebook and looked up Carrie Daniels Photography. As soon as she found it she removed her gloves, typed in the address and hit the print button. She closed the file without saving it, put the gloves back on, and took the envelope back to the kitchen. By then the glue on the message had set. She carefully folded the paper, stuffed it into the envelope, and pulled off the backing to seal it. She stepped back into the den, grabbed her roll of stamps from her desk drawer, and pulled one off the backing.

"Well now, I guess it's a good thing I got a job with a temp agency," she said as she stuck the stamp on the envelope. "They're sending me on an assignment in Phoenix the day after tomorrow, and I'll have to mail it while I'm there. Hope you enjoy your little surprise, Carrie. I made it special just for you."

❧Thirty-One❧

STEVE LOOKED UP when he heard the sound of someone tapping at his door.

"Hey, Alex. What's up?"

"I need to talk to you about something."

"Of course. Come on in."

Alex stepped inside, closed the door behind him, and pulled up a chair. He let out a sigh as he sat down.

"Are you all right, Alex? You look pretty serious."

"I'm afraid your boy wonder has turned himself into boy blunder."

Steve looked closer at Alex's face. "You've slept with her, haven't you?"

"Yeah."

"Well now, that explains the happy glow."

"Oh very funny." There was a hint of sarcasm in Alex's voice.

"Well, buddy, I can't say I'm surprised. I saw this coming the day we all drove up to Flagstaff for her mother's funeral. So, you know what happens next, don't you?"

"Yeah, I do. I'll have to recuse myself from her case."

"It's for the best for everyone involved, Alex. Even if you hadn't taken it to that level, I've been concerned about your objectivity ever since the day you flipped out after speaking to Scott Andrews on the phone. That's not like you. You never lose your cool. If something like that had happened in a courtroom—"

"It'll never see the inside of a courtroom, Steve. Louise doesn't have a case. She never did."

"I know she doesn't. Hopefully you're right and it'll never make it to court. However, our immediate concern is the here and now, which means we need to talk to Reggie."

Before Alex could respond, Steve picked up his phone and dialed Reggie's extension. As soon as she answered Steve asked her to come to his office. A minute later they heard a knock at the door. Steve opened it and she stepped inside, bringing a folder with her.

"So how's it going, guys?" She looked closely at Alex, while Steve motioned for her to take a seat. "Uh-oh, you've slept with her, haven't you?"

"Jeez! It is that obvious?"

"Yes," replied both at the same time.

"Your face is turning red too," added Reggie, "that's another giveaway."

"Great."

"Anyway, we need to sit down and have a little discussion about this. I take it that it was mutually consensual."

"Yes, it was."

"Good. The next question I have to ask is did you have a prior relationship with her?"

"I've known her since the fourth grade," said Alex. "And we stayed friends all the way through high school."

"So, did you ever date her?"

"We went out, as friends, when we were in high school. I even took her to the prom."

Reggie looked at Steve. "I think we can establish that a prior sexual relationship existed between them."

"Hey, I said I took her to the prom. I didn't say I nailed her."

"I understand," said Reggie. "However the point is a prior relationship existed between the two of you before she become your client, which means you're off the hook as far any possible ethics violation goes, but it's still problematic. At the moment, my concern is what's in Ms. Daniel's best interest. We still have a fiduciary responsibility to her, and as a senior partner of this firm, I have to be sure that everything is above board. That said, I'm now going to have to ask you to step aside and let another attorney take her case."

"I understand, Reggie. I've already told her I'd have to turn her case over to someone else and she's okay with it. In fact, she was more concerned about the possibility of some sort of disciplinary action being taken against me."

"That sounds like our Carrie, all right," commented Steve.

"You've kept track of all your billable hours, haven't you?" asked Reggie.

"Yes, I have. As you know, I took her case pro bono. My plan was to ask the court to order Louise Dickenson to cover the cost of her legal expenses."

"That's all well and good, but since that time an anonymous donor has come forward to pick up her tab."

"What? I hadn't heard about that," said Alex. "When did this happen?"

"A couple weeks ago," explained Reggie. "And no, I don't know who it is either, being as they've asked to remain anonymous. My guess is it's probably one, or both, of the Mercer brothers. She helped make their family rich, back in the day, so now they're returning the favor."

"Of course, that would make sense. Anyway, I have the invoices for George and Betty McCormick's services, and Jonathan Fields will sending me a bill."

"Good, then you'll need to talk to Joan as soon as we're done. In the meantime, Alex, I'll be the one who'll be handling her case from here on out, so you know she'll be in good hands. Steve's already given me some information, but I need to be brought up to speed, so let's head over to your office."

They told Steve goodbye as they left. Once they arrived at Alex's office he brought out the file and proceeded to over Carrie's case, step by step, explaining every detail.

"I've proven that she couldn't have been there when the release form was signed," he explained, "and I've forwarded the information on to Jack Collins. Carrie will be meeting with Jonathan Fields later on this week so he can run some tests on her laptop and her office computer, but it's just a formality. It's not if, but when, Louise drops her claim. I do have one other thing that I need to do for her, but it's a separate issue."

"What's that?"

"I need to change her business name and break her office lease. Our official excuse will be that she needs more space. However, we all know Maggie Andrews is the one who really did this, and now that she's starting to stalk Carrie, I'm very concerned about her safety. I've also arranged for her to have a security guard present whenever she's in her studio."

"I understand," said Reggie. "I'll let you handle name change, but I'll take care of the lease, if you don't mind, since there's always the remote possibility it could end up in litigation. Meantime, I'll contact her later on today to schedule a meeting. So, would you like to hear you some good news?"

"Of course."

"I've been talking to a prospective client, and I've scheduled a meeting for you later this week. You really are the best attorney for them, Alex, and they're looking forward to meeting with you. Think of it as a swap for the Daniels case."

Reggie handed Alex her folder, explaining that it was a family business partnership gone sour, and now one partner was suing his brother-in-law for breach of contract. It was a complex case involving a company with a net worth of several million dollars. Alex's face lit up as she went over the details.

"It's right up my alley, Reggie, and it'll go on for years. There's nothing quite like the feeling of having a little job security, especially on a day when I feel like I've been taken out behind the woodshed."

"Oh come on, Montoya," she said with a smile. "Trust me, you'd know it if I ever took you out behind the woodshed. You're human, Alex, and we've all noticed the change in you since she came on the scene. You're much happier now. Your life seems to have more of a purpose, and in the bigger scheme of things, a happy attorney is more productive and a bigger asset to this firm. Now you can move forward without the complication of representing her. In the meantime, I hear she's a really good lady and I look forward to working with her."

Reggie was about to take her leave when Alex's phone rang. Louise's attorney was calling.

"Hang on, Reggie. With any luck, we'll be able to put this one to bed right now."

Alex greeted Collins, asking him to please wait while he put his phone on speaker. He then introduced Reggie.

"Mr. Montoya has had an unusually heavy caseload lately," she explained, "so he's delegating some of his work to other attorneys and he's asked me to take over the Daniels case. I've read the report he just sent you. The time has come for your client to drop her claim against Ms. Daniels. Her signature was most definitely forged and we can also prove that it would have been impossible for her to have been in the Andrews home at the time the files were uploaded."

"I've read the report too," replied Collins, "and I've also sent a copy on to my client. To be honest Ms. Peters, I agree. It's time to focus our attention solely on Mr. Andrews, especially considering that he was just arrested for identity theft and forgery. I've advised my client accordingly. Unfortunately, Louise just doesn't see it that way."

Alex started to speak up, but Reggie quickly cut him off.

"So what's her reasoning?"

They could hear Collins letting out a sigh. "Louise is convinced that there was some sort of prior agreement made between your client and Scott Andrews to enter the photo contest. She keeps bringing up the fact that she observed them having a very long conversation in front of the photos that night at Hanson Sisters."

"That's her proof?" asked Alex as Reggie shot him a strong look. "That's the same night Allison Santiago first introduced Scott to Carrie. So why would she plan such a scheme with someone she'd just met?"

"Off the record, your guess is as good as mine. But Louise keeps bringing up the fact that the prize check was made out to Carrie, and that she needed the money to help pay her mother's medical expenses, so there you have it. In the meantime, we're getting ready to start taking depositions."

"Just let me say something," whispered Alex. Reggie nodded.

"Look, Jack, before I go, I just want to make one final comment. Louise Dickenson and Carrie Daniels have a long history together. Louise owes much of her success to the work Carrie did for her as a child model, and Carrie owes much of her success as a commercial photographer to Louise for having mentored her. These two ladies were friends for many, many years. Unfortunately, their friendship is now irretrievably broken. That said, I think it would be best for all concerned if they could both walk away from this thing without hating one another. I think the best way to make sure that happens would be for your client to drop her vendetta against Ms. Daniels, the sooner the better."

"I understand what you're saying, Alex, and I've had the same concern. I'll keep talking to Louise, but I'm not making any promises. She's a stubborn woman and she's not the kind of person who likes to admit when she's wrong."

Collins ended the call.

"Damn it." Alex switched off the speaker. "What do I have to do to convince the bitch? Hit her over the head with a shovel?"

"No. You take Carrie to dinner and keep her mind off things, while I hit Louise over the head with a shovel. You're officially done here, Alex. It's my baby now, but I'll keep you in the loop, okay? You go worry about the Gillespie case, the one I just handed you. I need George McCormick's contact information, and then I'm going to subpoena all of Carrie's phone records so I can prove, once and for all, that there was no contact whatsoever between her and Scott Andrews in the weeks prior to the photos being uploaded. So for now, my friend, you need to be patient. If all else fails, I'll file a motion for summary judgment. By then it will be so airtight that the judge will have no other option but to rule in our favor."

❧Thirty-Two❧

"THAT'S PERFECT, you two. Hold it right there."
Carrie clicked away on her camera. She was doing a shoot for a motorcycle ad with two models posed in front of the bike.

"Okay, Carlos, I need you to stand over there, right next to Tina, and put your arm around her shoulder and yes, that's it. Perfect."

She was about to take her next shot when the security guard knocked at the door.

"Sorry to interrupt, Ms. Daniels, but someone named Jonathan Fields is here. He says he has an appointment with you."

"Thanks. Have him take a seat in the reception area. Tell him I'm finishing up a shoot and I'll be there in a few minutes."

The guard stepped away and Carrie took her shots.

"Okay guys, that's a wrap, for now. I have to take back the leather jackets and there's a shower in the restroom if either of you want to use it."

"We're good." Tina sat down in a nearby chair to remove her boots and change into a pair of sandals. Once they'd gathered up their gear they followed Carrie to her office to sign their paperwork before she escorted them to the front door. Jonathan was patiently waiting in the reception area.

"Sorry to keep you waiting, Jonathan."

"It's quite all right." He stood and picked up his case. "In fact, I've been admiring your work. You're very talented."

"Thank you. Once upon a time Louise Dickenson was my mentor and she taught me everything I know. Who knew that someday we'd end up as adversaries?"

As she led him into her office she mentioned that she'd brought in her laptop.

"You'll need to examine it too. That way I can prove, beyond any reasonable doubt, that I had no contact whatsoever with Scott Andrews for several weeks prior to those photos being uploaded, and that I had no knowledge of any diabolical plot to infringe upon Louise's copyright."

"I understand, and believe me, I'm here to help you."

He opened his case and began to take out his equipment. Carrie excused herself, explaining that she'd be in the next room cleaning up her studio. She returned a short time later to find him still hard at work.

"So, how's it going?"

"So far, so good. I don't see anything that Louise could possibly use against you."

"That's because it doesn't exist," she said, gleefully.

"I know that, and while I've never doubted your innocence I've wondered one thing."

"What's that?"

"Well, this may be none of my business, but I've wondered what it was that could have possibly happened to you to put you in this mess in the first place."

"Short story long, it all began a few years ago when my mother had a stroke that should have killed her. But, thanks to modern medicine, they managed to keep her alive, although she was more or less a vegetable."

She went on to explain that once her mother's insurance ran out she was left penniless, then homeless, once Doug dumped her.

"I was camped out here, in the back room, for about two months, and it wasn't if, but when, I got caught by my landlord. So when Louise called and offered me that damn photo shoot, I didn't have a choice. It was either sell my virtue and have a roof over my head or live out on the streets, so I had to sell my virtue. Doing that shoot was one of the most unpleasant experiences of my entire life. I honestly felt as if I were being raped by the camera. All I wanted to do was get it over with, as quickly as possible, so I could put it behind me and not have to ever think about it again. Who knew I'd have to live with the unintended consequences for the rest of my life."

"What a horrible position for anyone to find themselves in, and how awful that someone would use it to exploit you in such an ugly way. So what about Alex, your attorney friend?"

"Alex and I go back to our childhoods," she explained, "but then we lost touch with one another for a number of years. This all happened before we reconnected. The real irony is that if I hadn't done the photo shoot, and if I hadn't gotten involved with Scott Andrews, Alex and I probably would have never reconnected. I guess it just goes to prove that every dark cloud really does have a silver lining."

"I suppose, but what about the rest of your family? Didn't any of your siblings try to help you out?"

"No, I'm an only child."

"I see. So what about your father?"

"Dead and buried."

"Really? I'm sorry to hear that."

"I'm not," she replied, coolly. Jonathan appeared to be taken aback by her attitude. "One day he simply vanished from my life, never to be seen or heard from again. I was only five years old when it happened and my mother rarely spoke of him after that. Once I got older I figured out that he must not have given a damn so I quit asking about him. Mama passed away a few weeks ago. After she was gone, Alex went through her papers and found some old court records. Turns out my father got busted for drugs so my mother divorced him. He was killed about a year or so later. Stabbed to death in a parking lot. Case closed and mystery solved."

"So you would have been what, about six when that happened?"

"Yep. After he and my mother separated he could have called me, or written to me, but he never bothered. Apparently, I wasn't worth his time."

"I see." Jonathan let out a sigh. "Carrie, I hope you'll take what I'm about to say in the spirit in which it's intended, and that is to please not judge the man so harshly. Cocaine was all the rage at the time this would have happened. Eric Clapton even recorded a song about its evils. It's a bad, bad drug. It's highly addictive and it destroys people's lives. I should know, because it nearly destroyed mine."

"You're joking."

"I wish I were." Jonathan looked her squarely in the eye. "I'm a recovering cocaine addict, Carrie, and I'll be a recovering addict for the rest of my life. I guess that means we both have our demons that we have to live with. I was a young man when it happened and I didn't think I had a problem until the day I got busted, because I was in complete denial. Going to jail was a life-changing experience for me, because that's what finally woke me up. Luckily for me, my story has a much happier ending. I went into a drug treatment program and I started taking computer-programming courses. I discovered a talent I never knew I had, and once my sentence was up I never looked back. I came to Tucson so I could have a fresh start. That's when I started up my computer business. I got in at the right time and I've done very well, although I have to admit there were times when having money was a real challenge to my recovery. Later on I met a beautiful lady, who I ended up marrying. She's been my inspiration to stay clean and sober, as is our sixteen-year-old son."

"Really?"

"Yes, indeed," he replied, beaming. "Danny plans to go to Arizona State, when he finishes high school. He wants to study business administration and take as many golf classes as he possibly can. His dream is to play golf professionally someday, but even if that doesn't happen, he says most business deals are made on the golf course and I suspect he's probably right."

"Well, he's made a good choice for college. Arizona State is my alma mater."

Jonathan finished running his tests on Carrie's office computer and started working on her laptop. The guard stepped in a few minutes later with her mail. Carrie took a seat at her desk and started opening it. Moments later she let out a blood-curdling scream. Jonathan quickly turned around to find her shaking and whimpering. He saw a cryptic note, made from hand-cut letters, on top of her desk. It read, "I'm not finished with you yet, bitch. Bang. Bang. You're dead."

The security guard burst into the room.

"Call nine-one-one," barked Jonathan. "Now!"

The guard pulled out his cell phone and quickly summoned the police. Jonathan reached over and took Carrie by the shoulders, gently raising her from her seat.

"Come with me, Carrie. I'm taking you to the restroom so you can wash your hands. We don't know if there's strychnine, or arsenic, or some other poison on that paper."

"What?"

She seemed dazed and confused as he wrapped his arm around her shoulder and led her away. He quickly found the bathroom and walked her up to the sink. He turned on the faucet, once again telling her to thoroughly wash her hands. She was in a mild state of shock, so he had to help her through the process. Once she finished drying her hands, he led her back to her office, pulling her chair away from the desk before sitting her back into it. He heard the sound of approaching sirens and quickly grabbed his phone, placing a call to George.

"We've just had another incident with Carrie Daniels. I need you to come down to her office, as soon as you can."

"What's wrong?"

"She just got a death threat in the mail. I'll fill you in as soon as you get here."

"On my way," said George, "but I may have to make a stop first."

"What for?"

"Alex Montoya, her attorney. Has anyone called him yet?"

"No. I don't have his number, and she's gone into shock."

"In that case, I'll call him and let him know. Just hang on 'til I get there."

"I'm not going anywhere. In fact, the police have just arrived."

He disconnected the call as two uniformed officers rushed into the room. He pointed to the note. One of the officers tried talking to Carrie, but she still seemed dazed and confused.

"I'm working with a private investigator on her civil case," explained Jonathan to the other officer. "You should have a file on her. In fact, there was an arrest made in her case this past weekend."

"What's her name?"

"Daniels. Carrie Daniels."

As the officer radioed his dispatcher for more information, the paramedics arrived. Jonathan stayed with her as they began to check her vital signs. She appeared to be coming out of her fog, but as she did her body began shaking even harder. She started crying and babbling, asking over and over why anyone would want to do this to her. Jonathan handed her a tissue and tried to comfort her as best he could so the paramedics could do their job. The guard soon opened the door. This time Billie Hughes entered.

"Billie!"

Carrie stood and pushed her way past the paramedics to embrace her friend. She began sobbing in Billie's arms.

"Calm down," said Billie. "It'll be all right."

"It came in the mail," explained Jonathan. "She was seated at her desk, opening her mail, when I heard her scream."

Billie led her back to her chair. As the paramedics went back to work, she stepped over to the desk to take a closer look at the note. Jonathan stayed with Carrie, once again trying to comfort her.

"It has a Phoenix postmark," explained one of the police officers. "And naturally, there's no return address."

"Bag it," said Billie. "We'll have to turn it over to the Postal Inspector."

"How much you wanna bet the perp was wearing gloves and they won't find any prints?"

"It's still worth a shot, Johnson."

Billie pulled out her phone. Scott Andrews would have to be brought in for questioning. As she was talking, George and Alex entered the room. Alex stepped past the others, making a beeline toward Carrie. She stood from her chair as they wrapped their arms around each other and she began crying again. For the moment both seemed oblivious to the others in the room.

"Scott Andrews didn't do this. My money's on his estranged wife, Maggie," George told Billie as she disconnected her call.

"Really?" She turned to the Phoenix police officer. "Johnson, what's the date on the postmark?"

"It was mailed yesterday."

"You're sure about that?"

"It's right here." He pointed it out as she took a closer look.

"Well what do you know? I guess you're right, George. According to my sources, Scott was arraigned late Monday afternoon. As soon as he posted bond, he left town with his sister, who lives in Payson, and he's been up there ever since."

"Which means he has an alibi. You've got the wrong guy, sister."

"Not according to my supervisor. This could also be the work of someone else who wants to start trouble. For all we know it could even be Louise Dickenson herself."

"So what the hell happened?" asked Alex.

"Someone mailed her a death threat." As Jonathan filled him in on the details, Alex walked over to the desk to take a closer look.

"Son of a bitch! And did I just hear someone say that Scott Andrews has an alibi?"

"Yes, you did," said Billie.

"Hey, guys," said Carrie, "I appreciate everything you're doing here, I really do, but I have to agree. Scott isn't the one who's doing this. It's Maggie. I've paid my penance for whatever sins I've committed. I just wish you all would go do whatever it is that you have to do in order to get the witch locked up and kept as far away from me as possible. This has gone on far too long and I've had enough."

Alex stayed with Carrie while Billie and the two police officers gathered the evidence. They left once Billie finished questioning Jonathan and the security guard.

"She's not showing any signs of being poisoned," said one of the paramedics. "You did the right thing, sir, when you took her in to wash her hands."

"I was just being cautious," replied Jonathan.

The paramedics wanted to take Carrie to the hospital so she could be more thoroughly checked out, but she refused.

"Are you sure?" asked Alex.

"Yes, I'm fine. I'm just a little shaken, that's all."

"Okay then," said the other paramedic, "but if you should start feeling ill get to an emergency room right away."

"I'll keep close watch on her," said Alex, "and thank you again."

After the paramedics left, George waited with Alex and Carrie while Jonathan finished testing Carrie's laptop.

"That's it," he finally said. "I'm all done."

"Did you find anything?" asked George.

"Not a thing. The lady's telling the truth, not that I ever doubted her. She had no contact with Scott Andrews. Not by email, instant messaging, social media, or even by letter for several weeks prior to the photos being uploaded to the magazine. I'll send you my report as soon as it's ready."

"Thank you, Jonathan." Alex extended his hand. "And thank you for taking care of her until I got here."

"My pleasure." He began packing his gear, but before leaving he turned to say goodbye to Carrie.

"Thank you, Jonathan, for everything." She also extended her hand. "I really appreciate you being here for me today."

"Like I said, it was my pleasure, but could you do me one favor?"

"What's that?"

"It's about your father. Remember how I said for you to not judge him so harshly? I know, from my own experience, there would have been extenuating circumstances beyond his control. You need to let go of your anger toward him, for you own sake, and let him rest in peace."

After saying a final goodbye, Jonathan stepped out. George walked him to his car.

"Go ahead and send me your bill, Jonathan."

"Thanks, but this one's on the house. Hey, before I go, can I ask you something?"

"Sure. What is it?"

"Isn't he supposed to be her attorney? Because what I just saw in there sure didn't look like an attorney-client relationship."

"He was her attorney, but not anymore. He's taken himself off her case. They had a prior relationship that goes way back and apparently nature has taken its course. I've known Alex for years. He's a good guy and he'll do right by her. They deserve a long, happy life together, I just hope she lives long enough for that happen."

Jonathan shuddered. "What are you saying?"

"I was a homicide detective for years, and whenever I get a really bad feeling, like the one I'm getting now, it usually doesn't end well. Stay safe, my friend."

ᕗThirty-Threeᕲ

CARRIE LOCKED HER OFFICE door and Alex walked her to her car, slipping behind the wheel as she got into the passenger seat. She still felt too shaken to drive, although Alex was just as shook as she was. Both were silent as he merged the car onto the freeway.

"When does the nightmare end?" she finally asked.

"I don't know, Carrie-Anne. I'm starting to lose a bit of faith in the system myself."

"Really? So were does that leave me? I want my life back. I have a business to run and I'd like to be able to go home. I appreciate all you're doing for me, I honestly do, but I can't keep imposing on you like this."

"Don't be silly, Carrie-Anne. You're not imposing. Not one bit." For the first time that afternoon, Alex smiled. "It's a big house and you're still my best friend. You're welcome to stay as long as you like. Besides, I kind of enjoy being with you."

"Well, I would certainly hope so." Her tone sounded somewhat flirtatious. "And I enjoy being there, but it's still your home, Alex, not mine. You don't need to have me there twenty-four seven. Which, on a more serious note, brings up something that I need to talk to you about."

Alex suddenly felt a knot in his stomach. "What's up?"

"I'm doing a project for J. Duncan Advertising. They're one of the biggest agencies in town."

"I know who they are. They've done some work for us too."

"I see. So earlier today, before everything fell to pieces, I was shooting some photos for an ad campaign they're doing for a motorcycle company. They've also asked to me to do some work on location."

"Where?"

"All the way up the west coast. I'll be working with Carlos and Tina, the two models I had in my studio today. We start in San Diego and work our way up to Seattle. It's a big opportunity for me, Alex."

"I understand," he replied. "How long would you be gone?"

"Two weeks—longer if we have bad weather along the way. At first I wasn't sure about doing it with Allie's wedding coming up, but now, after what just happened, I know I made the right decision. I need a time out. I need to be someplace where I don't have to walk around in fear."

"I understand, Carrie-Anne." He let out a sigh. "On one hand, I'll miss you like crazy, but on the other hand, I'll feel relieved knowing you'll be safely out of Maggie's reach. With any luck, they'll nab her while you're gone. When are you leaving?"

"A week from Sunday, which means I should be back around the first of October, and the wedding isn't until the last weekend of the month."

There was another reason why Carrie took the job. As much as she cared for Alex, a part of her was still unsure about another serious relationship. She needed a chance to sort out her feelings. Alex was quiet for the rest of the drive. To him, two weeks sounded like an eternity. They soon pulled into his office parking lot.

"Do you have a few minutes?"

"Sure," she replied. "What's up?"

"I know you have an appointment to meet with Reggie next week. However, before I left, she mentioned she had some time this afternoon, if you feel like talking."

"Of course."

Alex escorted her inside the building and accompanied her to Reggie's office. After making the proper introductions, Reggie told her to take a seat.

"Are you alright?" she asked as Carrie took her chair.

"I'm not sure. I don't think I've ever felt so scared in my life."

"It was bad, Reggie." Alex pulled up the chair next to Carrie's. "Her life's definitely been threatened, but it turns out Scott Andrews has an alibi for the day the letter was mailed."

"I see," said Reggie, "and speaking of the man, would you like know who his attorney is?"

"Of course."

"Fredrick Carlton Lancaster."

"Really." Alex sounded astonished. "Then Scott Andrews must have made good money while he was with Morton-Evans."

"Who is this guy?" asked Carrie.

"Fredrick Carlton Lancaster, or Freddie, as he likes to call himself, is Phoenix's answer to the O.J. Simpson dream team," explained Alex. "The guy's a shrew. If I were a criminal defense attorney, he's who I'd aspire to be. He's been around for a good thirty years, and rumor has it that all that time he's never once had a client get convicted. It's a safe bet that not only will all the charges against Scott be dropped, he'll conduct his own investigation as well. If there's even the slightest hint of any wrongdoing on the FBI's part, Lancaster will undoubtedly turn around and file a civil suit against them for wrongful arrest. If that should happen, Scott Andrews will end up being a very rich man. So what about our mutual case?"

"That's what I wanted to talk to you about," said Reggie. "Freddie called me this morning to let me know that as of now he's representing Scott in the civil case as well. Louise doesn't stand a chance. Meantime, Carrie, I'm getting copies of all your phone records. They should help prove that you and Scott didn't know one another before Allison introduced you that night at Hanson Sisters, and that you had no contact whatsoever for several weeks prior to the files being uploaded."

"Jonathan Fields got the same information today from my computers. He said he'll send you a report as soon as it's ready. So what happens next?"

"You're done," said Reggie with a smile. "All that's left for me to do is file a motion for summary judgment, which I'll be doing as soon as I get all the reports and I take depositions from George and Betty McCormick, and Jonathan Fields. Don't worry, the judge should rule in our favor. Please keep in mind, however, that it will take several weeks for me to get all my documentation, and that once the motion is filed it, may take some time to get a hearing date."

"I see," said Carrie. "So what's a summary judgment?"

"In layman's terms, a summary judgment means we're asking the judge to dismiss Louise's claim against you before the case before it goes to trial, because there is no issue to be resolved, by either a judge or a jury. So there you have it."

"I know you're also going to ask the court to order Louise to pay my legal expenses, but as I mentioned to Alex on the way over here, I've just picked up a project that's going to pay very well, so I'd like to start taking care of your bill. There's no guarantee the judge will order her to pay, or that she'd comply if he did. But after what I went through with my mother's nursing home, I'd like to be debt free."

"Don't worry about it, Carrie," said Reggie. "It's all ready been taken care of. You have a guardian angel. An anonymous donor has come forward to pick up your tab."

"What? I don't understand. Who would do that, unless it was you?" She looked at Alex with a smile.

"Don't look at me, I was working pro bono, remember? I was just as surprised as you are. Reggie and I think it's the Mercer brothers."

Carrie shook her head. "No, it wouldn't be them. Neither one of them were particularly close to their dad and I hardly knew them. In fact, I can only recall meeting them one time. We were filming one of the last TV commercials that I ever did, and for some reason they decided to come and watch. Both of them were rude and condescending. They wouldn't even shake my hand when we were introduced. I could see it in their eyes. As far as they were concerned, I was beneath them. I could see their father coming forward to help me, if he were still alive, but not the two boys."

"Well, then, I suppose it could be Mrs. Mercer," said Reggie. "So far as I know she's still around. The point is, Carrie, you have a friend out there, but the donor has stipulated that he or she remain anonymous. It's a gift. Take it for what it is and let's focus on finding out who really did this to you."

"I'm on it," said Alex. "I talked to George before we left Carrie's office. He's going to pull out all the stops to prove it was Maggie."

"Good to know, and speaking of your office, Carrie, I've also contacted your landlord. I told them you needed more space, and it turns out they have a small office building, less than a mile from here, that's completely vacant. You'll have a little more square footage in a better location to boot. They're willing to transfer your current lease over, so you need to call them to make arrangements."

"Thank you, Reggie," she said. "I'll get on it first thing tomorrow morning. Meantime I'm renaming my business L.J. Reed Photography, in honor of my mother. Her maiden name was Linda Joyce Reed. Alex is working on that."

"And I've all ready sent in the paperwork."

"Then it sounds like we're good to go," concluded Carrie. "So, if you all don't mind, I'd really like to go home now. I've had one hell of a day. Thank you again, Reggie, for everything you've done for me." The two women shook hands and Alex walked Carrie back to her car.

"Are you going to be okay until I get home?"

"I'll be fine. I'll see you then."

Alex kissed her goodbye before she got into her car and headed back to his house.

❧Thirty-Four❧

CARRIE CALLED HER landlord the following morning and looked at his vacant office building. It had plenty of space to accommodate her growing business and she loved the location. It was close to her apartment and a five-minute drive away from Alex's office. She took him to see it that evening. He too was pleased. The following week she signed the paperwork and made arrangements for a contractor to renovate the interior. If all went according to plan, her new studio would be ready by the end of October.

J. Duncan Advertising made the final arrangements for the location shoot and Carrie soon received her itinerary. It would take two weeks and she and the two models would travel by rented minivan. It would be a scenic, but busy journey, with photo sessions scheduled each day in a different coastal town. They'd have the weekend off in San Francisco and would finish up the following weekend in Seattle.

Carrie picked up the van on Saturday and Alex looked like a sad puppy as he helped her load it. He took her out to dinner that night, and when they got home they experienced one of their most intense lovemaking sessions ever. Both were unusually quiet the next morning. As soon as breakfast was over it would be time for Carrie to leave. Alex walked her out to the van.

"You're sure you've got everything?"

"Yes, Alex, I'm sure."

"They checked out the van and you've got a full tank of gas."

"Yes, Alex." She gave him a smile. "The van is good to go."

"You've got your camera, and all your bags, and you've got something to drink."

"Right here."

She opened the driver's side door, and as she put her water bottle into the console, she suddenly realized that saying goodbye to Alex was harder than she thought. She felt herself fighting back tears. He wrapped his arms around her and they held one another close before he finally broke the silence.

"I'm proud of you, Carrie-Anne. This is a big feather in your cap."

"I know."

"I just wish you weren't going to be gone for so long."

"It's only two weeks." Except now two weeks seemed like a very long time to her as well. She felt a tear rolling down her cheek. "I'll call you the minute we get there, I promise. I've left you a copy of my itinerary, and I'll text and email you everyday."

"Me too." Alex's voice sounded strained. "Like I said before, Carrie-Anne, I don't want you to worry about anything while you're gone. Not about Scott, or Maggie or your case. We'll all pray that by the time you return they'll have Maggie locked up and this whole nightmare will finally be over."

He gave her a long, lingering goodbye kiss. Once it was over, she returned the kiss before climbing into the van. He stood by as she programed the GPS device. They had one final kiss before he closed the van door. Carrie fastened her seat belt and rolled down the window.

"Call me as soon as you get to San Diego."

"I will."

"And by the way, I have a surprise for you once you get there."

"You do? What is it?"

"Now if I told you it would spoil the surprise. Drive safe, Carrie-Anne. You're still my best friend."

He watched as she started up the engine and began to drive away. She looked into the rearview mirror, watching him wave goodbye as she headed down the hill. She suddenly felt a deep pang of loneliness shoot through her body. It too was unexpected.

She stopped to pick up Carlos and Tina before heading west on the Interstate. As the hours passed they began sharing their stories. Both were part-time college students doing modeling work to help finance their educations. They reminded Carrie of her own youth and she began to see them as kindred spirits when she described her time as a child model.

The drive to San Diego passed quickly. By midafternoon they entered the city and were in awe of the spectacular view of the bay. The GPS guided them to their motel and Carlos helped unload their bags. Carrie followed him as he carried her bag into her room, thanking him as he stepped out. Her room may not have been as plush as her suite at the Double-Diamond Resort, but the accommodations were clean and comfortable.

She opened a window, taking in the cool ocean air before grabbing her phone. She plopped down on the bed and called Alex. He was relieved to hear she'd arrived safely and she realized she missed him more than she thought. After ending the call, she grabbed the remote and turned on the TV. She surfed until she found a news channel. A short time later she heard a knock on the door. She looked through the peephole, expecting to see Carlos or Tina. Instead it was a young couple with a small child. The woman was also very pregnant. She cautiously opened the door.

"Hey, there, Carrie Daniels. Long time no see," said the man.

"Of course," she replied, not wanting to tip her hand. He looked somewhat familiar, although she couldn't quite place him.

"What, you don't remember me?" He turned to the woman. "She doesn't remember me. She doesn't have a clue."

As he turned back to face Carrie, she noticed his features were similar to his brother's. However he was taller, with a stockier build, and his wavy hair was dark brown.

"Mark? Mark Montoya?"

"That would be me." He gave her a quick hug.

"My gosh, you're all grown up. You were a sophomore in high school the last time I saw you. You were starting to get tall, but you were a lot thinner." She invited them in and Mark introduced her to his wife, Olivia. "And who is this?" She knelt down to see the young boy at eye level. His looks reminded her of his uncle.

"That's Jacob," Mark proudly announced. "He's two and a half."

"Hi, Jacob." She gently stroked the top of his head. At first the child seemed a little unsure, then he smiled and hugged her. She looked up at Mark.

"Do you mind?"

"Not at all."

Carrie picked the boy up and started talking to him. It was obvious that she loved children and had strong maternal instincts. Mark asked if she had any plans for dinner.

"Not yet. My two models mentioned something about eating in. They both need to be well-rested for tomorrow morning, so it looks like I'm free and available, although I can't make it a late night either. We have to be up before dawn. We start right after sunrise."

"Not a problem," said Olivia. "When you have a two-year-old, you don't do late nights."

"Yep," agreed Mark. "Kids really change your life, but you get used to it after while."

They headed out to Mark's Jeep. Olivia offered to take the backseat with Jacob, but Carrie wouldn't hear of it. They took her to the San Diego Maritime Museum for a late afternoon stroll. She stopped to photograph the ships, including the famous Star of India. The USS Midway was docked nearby. The retired carrier had also been turned into a museum. She pointed out the big ship.

"That's where we'll be doing our shoot. The dealer will deliver the motorcycle at five o'clock tomorrow morning. We have to be out of there before nine, when the museum opens to the public. After that we head up to Venice Beach for our next shoot."

"Sounds like you're going to be busy," said Mark.

"Yep."

Carrie hoped the next two weeks would pass quickly. She was already missing Alex. They walked to a nearby seafood restaurant, getting a table by a window looking over the pier.

"Mark didn't hang around us that much," she explained to Olivia after they were seated. "He was the big man on campus and he had his own circle of friends. Alex and I did our own thing. The challenge was keeping Mark and his buddies out of our way."

"Everyone loved me. What else can I say?"

Mark went on the tell Carrie about going to college at Cal Poly in San Luis Obispo. Like his brother, he'd won a scholarship. He went to graduate school at USC where he met Olivia, who worked in one of the college libraries. They'd been married five years, and the new baby was due in six weeks. Their dinner soon arrived. Carrie offered to help Jacob with his meal.

"You have a real knack for kids," observed Olivia. "Do you have any at home?"

"Unfortunately no. I wasted ten years on a relationship with the wrong guy. Now I'm in my thirties. I'd really like to have a couple kids, but I'm not sure it'll happen."

"It'll happen," said Mark, matter-of-factly.

Carrie decided to change the subject, but once the meal was finished Jacob started getting fussy.

"Almost bedtime, huh?"

She put the child in her lap and tried to calm him down. Her efforts worked as he soon nodded off. When the time came to leave, she carried him back to the Jeep, somehow managing to get him into his car seat without waking him.

"I wish I could take him home with me," she said as she took the seat next to him.

"Trust me, there've been a few times when we needed a break," laughed Mark. "He has his moments."

"But he's a good kid, and I can tell the two of you are good parents."

"We try," said Olivia, "but it's not always easy. We'll see how we do once his little brother arrives. We were hoping for a girl this time, but we'll take another boy. Then that's it. We're not having any more."

They dropped Carrie off at her motel. She carefully got out of the Jeep, not wanting to disturb Jacob. Once again she thanked Mark and Olivia for the night out. They waited until she was safely in her room before Mark backed the Jeep out.

"Nice lady," said Olivia as they drove away. "I like her a lot better than Casey."

"Me too. I've known her since I was eight years old. She and Alex always were close. She was one of the few people who really understood him. Give it six months, maybe a year. She'll be my sister-in-law."

❧Thirty-Five❧

"**Y**OU AGAIN? Don't you have better ways to spend our taxpayer dollars?"

Once again, Ken O'Dell, along with another female agent, was at Maggie's door.

"I apologize for the inconvenience, Mrs. Andrews, but I'm going to have to take you back in for more questioning."

"What for?"

"We need to fingerprint you."

"What! I'm not going with you."

"Sorry, Mrs. Andrews," he said, firmly. "There's been another incident involving the Daniels case, and while you may not be a suspect, you're still a person of interest."

"Am I being arrested?"

"Not at this time, ma'am, but just like before, it would be best if you cooperated."

Maggie let out a sigh and picked up her purse. As usual, O'Dell was right. It had been several days since she'd mailed the letter to Carrie Daniels. No doubt she'd received it by now. Crybaby that Carrie was, she would have brought in the authorities again. But then, if all went according to plan, they'd pin the blame on Scott and put him back in jail. She smiled to herself as O'Dell led her to his vehicle. She cooperated fully once they arrived at the field office and as she wiped the ink off her fingers Billie came in to take her back into the interrogation room where O'Dell was waiting, along with someone with the Postal Inspector's office.

"We just have a few questions that we need to ask you," said Billie, "and then someone will take you home."

"Of course."

"Someone's mailed a death threat to Carrie Daniels." The Postal Inspector noted the date the letter was mailed as he explained that any crime involving the U.S. Mail fell under his jurisdiction. The FBI would be assisting him in his investigation. "So, Mrs. Andrews, can you tell me where you were the day this letter was mailed?"

"I can't quite recall, sir, although I was probably at home."

"Were you?" asked O'Dell. "According to our sources, you were working on an assignment for a temp agency in Phoenix that day."

"That's right. I'm so sorry. Yes, I'm working with a temp agency. Some days I'm working and others I'm not. Since I don't have a regular schedule it's sometimes hard for me to remember where I was any given day. Sorry for the confusion."

"Nice try, Mrs. Andrews, but you're not fooling us one bit," he said, firmly. "Someone mailed a death threat to Carrie Daniels, from Phoenix, the same day you were working in Phoenix."

"So what are you trying to say? Are you saying that I'm the one who wrote it? How many million people live in Phoenix? I'm sure Carrie Daniels has slept with more than one woman's husband. Why am I being singled out?"

"You're not being singled out, Mrs. Andrews," explained the Postal Inspector. "In fact, your husband was our prime suspect."

"Makes sense. So where is Scott? Is he back in jail?"

"Sorry to disappoint you, Maggie," said O'Dell, "but this time Scott has an airtight alibi."

Maggie's heart skipped a beat. She let out a tiny gasp while O'Dell was talking. She hoped he and the others hadn't heard it.

"You look surprised, Maggie. Is there anything you'd like to tell me?"

"Only that I'm through talking to you. I'm not saying anything else without my lawyer."

"Okay, Maggie," said Billie. "You're not under arrest at this time, and I'll be happy to take you home."

"Thank you, ma'am, I appreciate it. And just so you know, you won't find my fingerprints on whatever it is you think I've touched, because I've never mailed anything to Carrie Daniels. Maybe you should stop wasting your time harassing me and go look for the real suspect."

"That's what we're doing, ma'am," said the Postal Inspector.

"You know what, Maggie," said O'Dell, "before you were only facing forgery and identity theft charges. Now you're looking at mailing a threatening communication, and even more jail time."

"Scott's the one who stole her identity and forged her signature, not me, and I never mailed a letter to Ms. Daniels. Why would I? Scott left me for Nancy Edwards, not Carrie Daniels."

O'Dell leaned across the table. His eyes bore into hers.

"So you say, but we both know better, don't we, Maggie?"

"I've heard enough, O'Dell. You either charge me, right now, or you let me go."

"Get her out of here, Billie." Maggie could hear the tone of disgust in his voice. "Don't worry, Mrs. Andrews, we'll be seeing more of one another."

O'Dell stormed out of the room and quickly walked back to his cubicle.

Maggie remained silent during the ride home, offering only a brief thank you when Billie pulled up to the curb. She realized she'd overplayed her hand. Fortunately, she'd been careful handling the envelope the letter had been mailed in and she was positive she hadn't left any prints.

"Damn it," she muttered after she stepped inside. "So Carrie, it looks like I've made a teeny-weeny little mistake, but it's nothing I can't recover from. Next time I'll be more careful, and yes, Carrie, there will be a next time. You can count on it. You may have O'Dell fooled about your innocence, but not me. I'll bet you're even sleeping with O'Dell too. Enjoy your little reprieve while you can, because I'll be back when you least expect it."

❧Thirty-Six❧

THE WEATHER HAD cooperated so far and the all the photo shoots had gone well. Carrie and the two models had been working on a sunrise shoot near San Luis Obispo with a beautiful secluded beach in the background. She wanted to finish before the beach got too crowded.

"Okay, Tina, one more with your right hand on the handlebars and… that's it." She snapped the photos. "Now, one more, looking up at Carlos, there you go, and that's it. We're done."

Both models let out sighs of relief as they began to relax.

"What time is it?" asked Carlos.

Carrie glanced at her watch. "Eight-fifteen. Since we've finished a little ahead of schedule today, we can kick back and enjoy the beach for a little while. They won't be coming to pick up the motorcycle until nine."

Carlos decided to take a short walk to explore the beach while Tina went to the van to get her beach towel.

"Would you like to join me?"

"Sure, why not," replied Carrie.

After securing the motorcycle she grabbed her towel and joined Tina on the trail down to the beach. Tina soon found a desirable spot. She spread her towel on the sand, took off her top, and plopped down.

"It's a clothing optional beach," she explained, "and I want to get a tan without any lines. I've done nude work before, so it doesn't bother me."

"I know it's a clothing optional beach. That's why we did the shoot from a safe distance." Carrie took off her blouse, revealing her tank top underneath. She spread her towel on the sand and sat down next to Tina. "I've only done one nude modeling job. It was the biggest mistake of my life. It turned into a nightmare and I'm still dealing with the fallout."

"Really, what happened?"

Carrie filled her in on the whole story. Tina had an astonished look on her face while she listened.

"Good grief. It certainly sounds like the proverbial snowball rolling down the mountain, but at least you and your friend, Alex, were able to find one another and reconnect. Strange as this may sound, I think it may have happened for a reason. Maybe the two of you are meant to be together."

"Maybe, but surely there had to have been an easier way. And speaking of proverbial things, I can't help wondering if I've gone from the frying pan and into the fire."

"What do you mean?"

"After Doug and I split, and I was left homeless, I promised myself I'd never, ever allow anything like that to happen to me again."

"Understandable," said Tina.

"So now here I am, practically living with Alex, and I can't help it. I'm scared. What if it happens again?"

"Carrie, can I speak candidly with you?"

"Certainly."

"Okay. First of all, Alex isn't Doug, so you really shouldn't be comparing the two. Secondly, there are no guarantees in life. I should know."

"What do you mean?"

"I lost my husband two years ago," she explained. "He was on his way home from work and he was hit by an uninsured drunk driver running a red light. He was killed instantly."

"I'm so sorry, Tina. How awful for you."

"Thank you. However, the point I'm making is what I just

told you a minute ago. There are no guarantees in life. The only thing that's certain is death, so we need to make the best of it while we can. Nick was the love of my life, and looking back, I have no regrets. We didn't waste our time worrying about stupid, petty little things. We somehow managed to make the most out of what we had."

"So how are you coping?"

"I take it one day at a time. I have a daughter, Nicole, who's just turned three. My mother is taking care of her until I get back and I miss her terribly. She's the reason why I'm doing this job. I want to get my degree so I can get a better job and so she can have as good of a life as possible without having her father there to take care of her."

"Do you think you'll ever remarry?"

"Who knows," replied Tina with a shrug. "No one can ever take Nick's place and I'm not really looking, but I suppose anything's possible. What I'm trying to tell you, Carrie, is to stop being afraid. You and Alex already have a long history together and he sounds like an amazing guy. You're lucky to have found him again, even if it was under bizarre circumstances, so please, whatever you do, don't let the actions of some idiot from your past ruin your chance to be happy. If you love this man, and I can see that you do, then go for it. Let what's meant to happen, happen. It'd be a real shame if you were to lose out because you allowed your fears to get the better of you. You may never have another opportunity like this again."

Carrie noticed that someone had come to pick up the motorcycle. Tina slipped her top back on, grabbed her towel and they began hiking back to the van. Soon Carlos returned, and they were back on the road, heading north to San Francisco. They were scheduled for a sunset shoot in front of the Golden Gate Bridge. It, too, went smoothly. Once they finished, it was time to head to the hotel and a weekend off. Carrie got behind the wheel and programmed the GPS device.

"So what are your plans for tomorrow?"

"I'll be hanging out with friends here in the Bay area," said Carlos.

"And I'm spending the day in my room, curled up with my Kindle," added Tina. "I'm tired and I want to look good for the camera. I'll leave all the sight seeing and touristy stuff for another time. How 'bout you, Carrie?"

"I'm not sure yet."

"It's a beautiful place. If I were you, I'd grab my camera

and go take photos. You're incredibly talented. Go out and have some fun."

"Thanks, Tina. I was having the same thought."

As Carrie drove across the Golden Gate Bridge Tina's words from their earlier conversation echoed in her mind. She really was allowing her fears of the past to keep her from being truly happy with Alex. She hoped the following week would pass quickly. She was more anxious than ever to get the job finished so she could return home.

She spent the following day exploring the streets of San Francisco, taking photographs of Union Square, North Beach, Fisherman's Wharf, and the Ghirardelli Chocolate Factory. She stopped for a sandwich at a sidewalk café, and as she watched the people walking by, she suddenly felt envious of the mothers pushing their baby strollers. She watched young lovers walking by arm in arm, and she even noticed a few men who looked like Alex. She realized she'd missed him more than she'd expected, and she thought about Tina's words again. Finishing up her sandwich, she heard her phone ring. A smile spread across her face as she checked the caller ID.

"Hey, there, I was just thinking about you. You must have been reading my mind."

"I guess so," he replied. "I'm out by the pool. This house is so empty without you."

"I'm sorry, and I miss you too, Alex. I'm sitting at a sidewalk café wishing you were with me. San Francisco is a beautiful city, but it's a lonely place to be when you're on your own. But hey, a week from today we finish up and we'll start heading back that afternoon. Carlos and Tina are anxious to get home too."

"A week seems much too long. Do you have to drive the van back?"

"I'm afraid so," she replied. "That's what's in the contract."

"Tell you what, Carrie-Anne, let me have a look at it and I'll see what I can do."

"You got it. I'm ready to come home, the sooner, the better."

The second week flowed nearly as smoothly as the first, with only minor glitches, such as nosey tourists, or a motorcycle arriving late, marring the way. They arrived in Seattle Friday evening. The final shoot would take place early the following morning. Once it was finished, they would begin the trip home.

"Carrie, we need to talk to you about something," said Tina as they were checking into their hotel.

"What's up?"

"Carlos and I have decided not to ride back in the van with you." She turned to give Carlos a knowing look as she was talking. "We're both anxious to get home, so we've booked a flight for tomorrow afternoon."

Carrie let out a sigh. "I understand. I'm anxious to get home myself. I'm waiting for Alex to get back with me about leaving the van here so I can fly back with you."

For some strange reason, Alex had been dodging the question about leaving the van behind. Now Tina and Carlos were giving each other an odd look.

"No," Carlos quickly replied. "I mean, we already looked into it. The plane's full. Tina and I got the last two seats."

"Maybe I can catch a different flight, or fly standby."

"Sorry." Tina was shaking her head. "We already asked. All the flights are booked."

"All right, so what's up you two?"

"Nothing, Carrie." Carlos was trying to suppress a smile. "It's like we told you. Everything's booked. Tina and I were lucky to get the last two seats."

"Enjoy your trip home," added Tina, "and take lots of photos."

Carrie shook her head as she grabbed her room key and headed toward the elevator. She was tired, she wasn't in the mood to argue, and she certainly wasn't looking forward to a long drive all the way back to Arizona on her own. Once inside her room, she headed to the bathroom. She let out a shriek as soon as she opened the door. Someone was in the shower.

"Oh my God. I'm so sorry, Carrie-Anne." A startled Alex popped his head out from behind the shower curtain. "I didn't think you'd be here this soon. Are you okay?"

"I oughta smack your butt." She was clutching her chest and laughing at the same time. "You just scared the living hell out of me." She heard a knock at the door. Her bags had arrived. "Wait here."

"I'm not going anywhere at the moment."

She stepped away to take care of the bellman. As soon as he left, she stripped down and went back into the bathroom.

"Move over, Montoya." She stepped in and joined him in the shower. "So tell me, how did you end up here?"

"Reggie said I needed a vacation. Can you believe that?"

"Really? So when was the last time you took any time off?"

"Never. I've been with the firm ever since I finished law school. Other than an occasional day off here and there I've haven't had a real vacation since college. Then the other day Reggie reminded me that if I didn't use at least some of my vacation time soon I'd lose it, so here I am."

"I see. So tell me, Mr. Attorney, how did you manage get into my room?" There was a playful tone in Carrie's voice.

"You had your two models names and phone numbers listed on your itinerary as emergency contacts, so the other morning I called Tina and had a little chat with her. Nice lady. She said she and Carlos planned to fly back to Phoenix as soon as you were done, so she called the hotel and had them add my name to your reservation. I thought I'd surprise you. I just didn't expect you to show up this soon."

"Aha," said Carrie with a knowing grin, "so that explains why they were acting so strange when we were checking in. They were your co-conspirators."

"We plead guilty as charged, Your Honor. I decided to fly here and then we'd drive the van back together. I don't have to be back to the office for another week."

Carrie let out a sigh. "What a bummer we have to go home at all. This trip was just what I needed. It got me away from all my troubles. Now I'm finally feeling grounded and like myself again, but it'll all be waiting for me when I get back."

"Not all of it. I have some good news for you."

"Really? What is it?"

"Reggie's making progress and she's started taking depositions. She's got all your phone records and Jonathan Fields has sent her his report. We're in the home stretch. She'll soon be ready to file her motion with the court. After that, we wait for a hearing date."

"And how long will that take?"

"With any luck, not long. We also have to give Louise an opportunity to respond."

"What if she objects? I have a feeling she's going to fight this."

"She certainly has the right," said Alex, "but even if she does, it won't be that big of a deal. Reggie will present oral arguments to the judge. Her attorney can respond, but we can show proof that your identity was stolen and your signature was forged. You need to stop wasting your time and energy worrying about Louise. It's time to start thinking about the future."

"Thank you, Alex." She wrapped her arms around him. "You were always there for me when we were kids, and you're still here for me now. I'm so incredibly lucky to have found you again." It felt good to feel his wet skin next to hers.

"You're welcome, Carrie-Anne. And the feeling's mutual, you know. I'm lucky to have found you again too. I do love you, you know."

"Me too," she said with a kiss.

* * *

"Aw, come on, Carrie-Anne." There was a mock whine in Alex's voice. "I've never been to Seattle before. Let's make a night of it."

"But I'm much too comfy here." They were cuddled in the bed, enjoying the afterglow. "Are you sure you don't want to order room service?"

"I'm positive. We're in Seattle. Let's go do something we've never done before, like go see the Space Needle."

"All right, all right," she said with a smile. "I swear, at times you're like a little kid. So we'll go to the Space Needle."

"Yea," said Alex, in his best child-like voice.

"So what do you have to say for yourself now?"

"I say I love you, Carrie-Anne."

"I love you too, Alex."

The following morning Carrie let Alex sleep in while they went to do the last shoot. As soon as they finished, she dropped Carlos and Tina off at the airport and headed back to the hotel. She and Alex would spend the rest of the weekend in Seattle before heading back to Phoenix. They planned to take the same route along the Pacific coast. This time, however, the pace was more leisurely. They even spent a day with Mark and Olivia once they got to San Diego. The van finally pulled into Alex's driveway on Sunday night, and for the first time, Carrie didn't feel like a guest. It was now her home too.

҂Thirty-Seven҈

CARRIE MADE THE final adjustments on the bridal veil while Allison watched in the mirror. She nodded as soon as Carrie stepped back.

"This is it, Allie. Are you ready?"

"I guess I'm ready as I'll ever be, although I never thought I'd feel this anxious."

"It's just a little stage fright," said Carrie, reassuringly. "You'll be fine. This is your moment to shine. Steve's out there waiting for you."

Carrie followed her out the dressing room door and into the church foyer where her father was waiting. Much to Allison's relief, her family had finally come around and accepted the fact their oldest daughter was breaking tradition by marrying a Protestant. They realized her happiness was what mattered.

Carrie walked up the aisle, ahead of Allison and her father. Steve's face was beaming. He looked handsome in his tuxedo, while his cousin, serving as his best man, stood next to him. Carrie smiled and nodded at Alex as she passed by. He was seated next to his parents, who had come for the wedding. When Carrie reached the altar, she turned to face the bride, taking the bouquet from her as her father handed her off to Steve and stepped away.

As the ceremony began Carrie couldn't help but wonder about her own future with Alex. She had, for all intents and purposes, moved out of her apartment and into his home, but so far they'd not discussed any long-term commitment. Earlier that day Alex's father had tried to broach the subject. Both times she and Alex told him they would make those decisions when they felt the time was right. She had a nagging feeling, however, that they hadn't heard the last of it.

The ceremony ended with the traditional kissing of the bride before the minister formally introduced Mr. and Mrs. Steven Hudson to their guests. Carrie felt happy and relieved as the best man escorted her back down the aisle and out the sanctuary, where they quickly formed a receiving line to greet their guests. Once the photographer finished, the wedding party hopped into the waiting limousine and headed to the reception. As soon as they arrived, Carrie joined Alex and his parents at their table. While his parents were polite, she noticed they just didn't seem like themselves. She felt relieved when the time came for Allison to toss the bridal bouquet.

"Ready ladies?"

Three other women had joined Carrie, but Allison made note of where she was standing. She turned her back and tossed the bouquet in her direction. Carrie stepped forward. Much to her surprise, the flowers landed squarely in her hands. She smiled to the sound of everyone's applause. She turned to see a smile break out across Alex's face. He immediately walked up to give her a congratulatory kiss, and when the deejay began to play the next song, he asked her to dance.

"Is everything all right, Alex?" She tilted her head toward their table as they stepped onto the dance floor.

"It's fine. They're just trying to get used to the idea of us living together. My mother was quite fond of Casey. Apparently, she was harboring some far-flung hope that somehow she and I would get back together someday. She didn't realize until today that Casey's now married to someone else."

When the dance was over, she excused herself, explaining that she wanted to say hello to Reggie and would join them later. Alex returned to their table alone.

"Alejandro, we need to talk," announced his father.

"Gee, Dad, I can hardly wait." Alex pulled at his cuffs after he took his seat. "So what could possibly be the matter?"

His mother tried to soften the blow. "It's about your

relationship with Carrie. Please understand, son, your father and I both think the world of her and she's been a part of the family for years."

"I can hear the 'but' coming, so let's not mince words, Mother. What exactly has Carrie done that's upset you, besides the fact that she's not Casey?"

"This has nothing to do with Casey," said Armando. "This has to do with Carrie and her background."

"Oh wait, I think I see it coming." There was a hint of sarcasm in Alex's voice. "She's not from a moneyed family, so she's automatically disqualified from being a Montoya. Is that it?"

"Keep your voice down," hissed Catherine. "It's not about her family. Linda was a lovely woman whom I considered a friend as well. This has to do with our family traditions and values. You keep forgetting the fact that your father wasn't born here and that he still has the morals and standards of the old country."

"We're not in Spain, Mom. We're in America, and yes, we are different here. You're forgetting that I'm American born and I live my life the American way. Here in America, we're free to marry the people we love. Look at Steve and Allison. Her parents came to this country from Mexico, yet they consider themselves Americans. They managed to come to terms with the fact that their daughter fell in love with a man from a different culture and tradition then theirs, yet they've accepted Steve as a part of their family. Carrie and I grew up together. You've known and loved her for years. So why is it that now, when she's living under my roof, that all of a sudden she's not good enough?"

"We understand Carrie is still your friend," said Armando, "however, you lost touch with her for ten years, and during that time she changed. She's no longer the Carrie we used to know."

"And what exactly is that supposed to mean, Dad?"

"Come on, Alex. First, she posed nude for a photographer, and then she had an affair with a married man. Where I come from that's what a harlot does, not the woman my son's in love with. I'm sorry, Alex, but I don't want her for my daughter-in-law. Even if you do marry her, it will be without my blessing, because I'll never accept her. I don't mean to upset you, but that's the way I feel. You're still a young man. You have a lot to offer. There's no reason in the world why you can't find someone more suitable."

It was one of the rare moments in Alex's life when he

suddenly found himself at a loss for words. It took a moment to find his voice.

"Did I not explain this to you properly? I mean, what did you not get? First of all, the man in question led her to believe that he was single, and she ended the relationship once she realized things weren't adding up. As for the photo shoot... did I not tell you that she was homeless at the time, that she was going broke trying to pay off her mother's medical expenses, and her so-called friend swooped down on her like a bloody vulture to take advantage of her vulnerability? Do you not recall me saying that the day she showed up at my office she hadn't eaten for two whole days because she had no money for food? That she almost fainted, literally, at the conference table."

"I understand she was going through some hard times, but surely there had to be a better way. She has friends. She could have gone to some charity or women's shelter or somewhere to get help, but she didn't. Instead, she chose to make a whore out of herself."

For the first time in his life, Alex had to fight the urge to strike his father. He took a deep breath as he fought to keep control.

"I'm sorry you feel that way, Dad, but you're treading on dangerous ground. You're my father and I love you, but please, I'm begging you, don't ask me to choose between you and her. You won't like the choice I'll make."

"All right, son. You think you're in love with her, so I guess we'll have to let you get it out of your system, but don't you dare marry her. She won't be welcome in our home."

"You know, considering our own family history, I'm surprised at your attitude."

"Your mother may have been a divorced woman when I married her, son, but at least she'd been properly married to her first husband. Your mother was, and still is, a proper lady. She would never have her photograph taken in the buff."

"Well, Dad, as Carrie herself once told me, it's really easy to be virtuous when you have food in your stomach and a roof over your head. We'll have to continue this conversation at a later time." Alex stood from the table and grabbed Carrie's purse. "In the meantime, do you need directions back to your hotel?"

"We're fine, son," he replied.

"Where do you think you're going, Alex?"

"Away from here, Mom. Goodnight you two. It's been...

interesting, seeing you again. Have a safe trip home to Boulder City." He turned and walked away.

"Alex!"

"Let him go, Catherine. He thinks he's in love with her. He'll come to his senses, eventually."

"What if he doesn't? I don't want to wake up one morning and find myself cut off from my grandchildren."

"There won't be any grandchildren, Catherine, at least none with her."

"How do you know, Armando?"

Carrie looked up to see Alex approaching. He had a troubled look on his face.

"Is everything all right?"

"Not really." He handed off her purse. "Would you mind if we called it a night?"

"Of course not."

After saying a quick goodnight to Reggie and the bride and groom, they headed out to his car. Carrie noticed his hands were shaking as he turned the key in the ignition.

"What's wrong, Alex?"

"Trust me, you don't want to know."

"Yes, I do want to know. We don't keep secrets from one another, remember?"

Alex let out a long sigh. "It's my parents. My father, to be exact."

"So, what's the problem?"

"He was born in Spain. He didn't come to this country until he was ten. He's still what you would call, old world, in many ways."

"Meaning?"

"Meaning he has issues with your relationship with Scott and for doing that damn photo shoot for Louise."

"It's okay, Alex." Carrie tried to reassure him. "I can talk to him. Once I explain that I didn't know Scott was married, and the reason why I had to do the photo shoot, he'll understand."

"He already understands. It's all been explained to him, many times. He thinks, however, that you could have handled your homeless problem differently."

"Really? How so?"

"He thinks you should have gone to a woman's shelter, or something to that effect."

"I see. So what you're saying is that he thinks I'm a tramp, doesn't he?"

216

Alex didn't respond. He kept his eyes on the road. Carrie felt the tears welling up in her eyes.

"I'm sorry, Alex. The last thing I ever wanted to do was to come between you and your family, I still have a couple of months left on my apartment lease. Maybe I should move back in."

"What! Oh now that's just great. I just went to bat for you, and now you want to leave me?"

"No, Alex, that's not what I want at all. But I can't be the cause of trouble between you and your parents."

"Please, Carrie-Anne, just let me handle this, okay. I know them and I know what I'm doing. Every once in awhile my father has to pull this old world crap on me. It's unfortunate that both he and my mother thought Casey walked on water, and that no other woman can possibly take her place. Trust me, they'll get over it, eventually."

"And what if they don't."

"Then I guess they don't, and it'll be their choice. I'm not a kid anymore, Carrie-Anne. They're not going to tell me how to run my life."

"I understand. So what do we do in the meantime?"

"We live our lives and we let them live theirs."

Carrie was silent for a few minutes. Finally she spoke up.

"It can be very lonely when you don't have a family, Alex. Trust me. I know."

"I know you do, Carrie-Anne, and we still have family. Aren't you forgetting about my brother? He and his wife both loved you and Jacob keeps asking about you."

"He does?"

"Yes, he does," said Alex. "You have an amazing way of handling kids, Carrie-Anne, and when the time comes, you'll be a damn good mother to ours."

"Really?"

"Well, of course. I wouldn't have asked you to move in with me if I wasn't willing to make a long-term commitment. It's just that between your case, Steve and Allison's wedding, and you getting ready to relocate your business, we just haven't had much of a chance to sit down and discuss our future." He reached over and patted her hand. "In the meantime, if push comes to shove, Mark will be on our side. Mom and Dad did a similar number on him before he married Olivia, although I can't recall the reason anymore. That's how petty it was. It's just how they are. They're doting parents, both of them. No one is good enough for their sons."

"Except Casey."

"Except Casey, and that's probably because I wasn't really in love with her."

The Camaro soon turned onto Alex's street.

"Then I guess you must really love me, a lot."

"Yes, I do. You're it, Carrie-Anne. It's either you, or I spend my life alone."

❧Thirty-Eight❧

IN THE WEEKS FOLLOWING Steve and Allison's wedding, Alex and Carrie's lives fell into a comfortable routine. Carrie moved into her new photography studio and started up business as L. J. Reed Photography. It seemed to have the desired effect. Maggie Andrews' harassment appeared to be over and business was booming. She moved her remaining belongings out of her apartment and into Alex's home. It was now her home too. She and Alex had even redecorated some of the rooms.

Alex's birthday was in early December. He decided to celebrate by spending another weekend at the Double-Diamond Resort. This time they had a suite with a Jacuzzi, but without an adjoining room, and both spent an afternoon being revitalized in the spa.

He bought her a diamond engagement ring shortly after they returned. He planned on giving it to her for Christmas, but then he decided to wait. Reggie had followed through and filed the Motion for Summary Judgment. A hearing was scheduled for the first week of February. Alex wanted to celebrate the official end of her case by taking her to the finest restaurant in town and presenting the ring to her over dessert. However, as the hearing date drew near, he became more and more concerned. Carrie wasn't well and her symptoms appeared to be getting worse. The Saturday before the hearing she woke up sick again.

"I'm so sorry," she said as she returned to bed. "I really thought I'd be feeling better by now, but this stomach bug must be worse than I thought. It doesn't seem to matter what I take, it just won't clear up."

"This has been going on for about two weeks now, Carrie-Anne. I think we need to get you to a doctor. You're starting to look pale and you seem to tire easily."

"I know. First I thought it was the stomach flu. Then I thought it was a bad case of nerves over my hearing. Now I'm wondering with everything I've been through if it's an ulcer, because I'm starting to feel lousy all over. The hearing's on Tuesday. If I'm not feeling a whole lot better on Wednesday, then I'll know for sure that's what it is."

Alex let out a sigh. He already had his suspicions about what was wrong.

"Carrie-Anne, I'm thinking it could be something else entirely."

"Like what?"

"When was the last time you had your period? I've noticed it's been awhile."

"Don't even go there. I'm not pregnant. No way, no how."

"Well, actually, there is a way and a how, and we've sort of been doing a lot of it."

"Look, Alex, I would know if I was pregnant."

"Really? You're absolutely certain."

She let out a sigh. "I've been using the rings for years, but I ran out last fall and I'll admit I've been really busy since I moved into my new studio, so I haven't had a chance to get them refilled. I've been using my diaphragm. It's my backup birth control."

"And you've been using it for the past few months?"

"Religiously. I'm not pregnant, Alex. I've just been a little irregular since I ran out of rings and started using my diaphragm."

"Of course," he replied, "and denial's not a river in Egypt. They're not one hundred percent reliable, so humor me. If I'm wrong, I'm wrong. Either way, you need medical attention. It's just a matter of knowing which doctor we need to send you to."

He reached into his nightstand and handed her the home pregnancy test he'd stashed in the back of the drawer. He'd even wrapped a white ribbon around it.

"Aw jeez." She rolled her eyes as she snatched it away from him. "Nice touch with the ribbon, but since I'm not pregnant, I guess I'll just have to prove it to you. In fact, I'm so sure I'm not pregnant I'll even make a wager with you."

"Okay, let's hear it."

"Loser has to buy winner dinner tonight at Hernando's."

"Deal," said Alex as they shook on their bet. "Just be prepared to pay up."

"Fine."

She climbed out of bed and headed back to the bathroom. She returned a few minutes later. Her hand covered the result.

"Well?"

"I didn't look. I want you to you tell me."

"Okay, hand it over."

She looked away as she passed him the test strip. She waited for him to tell her the results. Several seconds passed, but Alex remained silent.

"Alex?"

He didn't respond. She turned back around. Alex sat staring at the test strip. His face was pale and he appeared to be in a mild state of shock.

"Alex, come on. You're scaring me."

He slowly looked up. He glanced back and forth a few times at her and at the test strip. The expression on his face was deadly serious.

"It's positive, Carrie-Anne." His voice sounded almost mechanical.

"No way. Here, let me see it."

Alex handed the test strip to her. It bore a plus sign.

"Holy crap." She slowly eased herself down on the bed and started doing some mental calculations. "Well, all right then. My best guess would be that I'm about nine weeks along. This would have happened while we were away celebrating your birthday. There was one morning when I forgot to put the diaphragm back in. I didn't realize it until after the fact, but I didn't think I was in the part of my cycle when I'd conceive. I'm so sorry, Alex. I guess I got sloppy. This is all my fault. If you don't want this baby, I'll understand."

"Come here," he said softly. After she laid down next to him, he pulled her in close.

"This isn't all your fault, Carrie-Anne. I seem to recall being there at the time."

"So, what do we do now?"

"For starters, you can buy me dinner tonight at Hernando's, and don't look at me like that. It was your idea to make a bet. I won and you lost."

"Fine."

"But before that, we need to decide which room to make into a nursery."

Carrie's face lit up. "You mean you want this baby?"

"Well, of course I want this baby." He leaned over and gave her a kiss. "We're in this together and this little person is a part of you and me. I admit I wasn't expecting this to happen quite so soon, but come on. We're both in our thirties. If we're going to do the baby thing, which it looks like we're going to be doing, then we need to do it now. You're clock is ticking, and I don't want to be one of those guys who ends up changing diapers in his fifties."

"But what about your family, Alex? They've made it quite clear that they'll never accept me. What happens if they won't accept this baby?"

"Honestly, Carrie-Anne, I'm not going to worry about them right now. This baby is far more important to me than whatever my parents may think. If they don't want anything to do with their grandchild, then it's their problem, not mine." He reached down and began rubbing her stomach. "Hey, little guy, it's your dad." He looked at Carrie with a startled expression on his face. "Wait a second… this means I'm a dad, doesn't it?"

"Yes, Alex, it does. You're a dad now."

He began kissing her passionately. As he ran his hand across her breast, he suddenly stopped. "Carrie-Anne, is it okay to be doing this?"

"Yes. I think we can do this until late in the pregnancy. Look at it this way… the damage is already done."

After they finished, Carrie got up to take a shower while Alex reached for his phone. He quickly pulled up his brother's number.

"Mark?"

"Hey, Alex, what's up?"

"Are you sitting down?"

"Yeah," said Mark. "What's wrong, Alex? More trouble with Mom and Dad?"

"No, nothing's wrong. Guess what? You're going to be an uncle."

"What?"

"You heard me, Mark. You're going to be an uncle."

"When?"

"We're not exactly sure yet," said Alex. "We think in about seven months."

"You're joking."

"No, I'm not joking. Carrie really is pregnant."

"Well then, congratulations. How long have you known this?"

"Honestly? Only for about the past hour or so. We just did one of those home tests. It came out positive."

"Good lord, Alex, you're still in shock. Wait a few hours, and then it will really hit you. You may even cry."

"I will not. Why? Did you cry?"

"I'm pleading the Fifth. Do Mom and Dad know?"

"Nope, and until Dad gets off his high horse, I don't plan on telling them a thing. Who knows if they'd try to use this as ammo to hurt Carrie, and she doesn't need the stress right now. We have a hearing on her court case coming up Tuesday afternoon. She's nervous enough already, and I'm suddenly finding myself feeling even more protective of her than I was before."

"Understood," said Mark. "Olivia and I send her our love, and congratulations again, Big Brother. There's nothing quite like being a dad. It can be the most trying, yet most rewarding thing you'll ever experience in your lifetime."

Alex heard the sound of a baby crying in the background.

"And speaking of which—"

"Dad!" Alex could hear Jacob's voice as he came running into the room. "Daddy! Austin just dropped a bomb!"

"Dropped a bomb?"

"It's a metaphor, Alex."

"Oh, right."

"Meantime, Mom's at the store and someone needs to have his diaper changed. Enjoy the next seven months while you can, Alex, because after that you'll life will never be the same. Be prepared for dirty diapers, round the clock feedings, teething and colic, but don't worry, they outgrow it—eventually. Brother, I love you, I'm proud of you, and Olivia and I will be there for you guys. Congratulations again. Gotta run, I'm being paged."

Mark quickly ended the call and Alex began to wonder what he'd gotten himself into.

Carrie made good on her bet that night and took Alex to dinner at Hernando's. They invited Steve and Allison to join them, and as soon as they were seated, Alex ordered a bottle of champagne and three glasses, while Carrie asked for a glass of mineral water.

"Still not feeling well?" asked Allison.

"Not really."

"What's up?" asked Steve.

"You'll find out soon enough," said Alex. A few minutes later the champagne was poured and he raised his glass.

"Steve, Allie, we'd like to thank you two for coming. Tonight we wanted to include our two closest friends as we celebrate our family, and welcome the newest Montoya."

"Here, here," said Steve as he and Allison raised their glasses. "So have you two set a date yet?"

"We're not exactly sure when the due date is," explained Alex. "We think in about seven months. We'll know for sure once Carrie sees a doctor."

"Come again? I'm a little confused here."

"Oh my God!" Allison nearly dropped her glass. "You two aren't talking about getting engaged. You're having a baby, aren't you?"

"That's right, Allie," said Carrie. "I'm pregnant."

There was a brief moment of stunned silence before Allison spoke up.

"I don't know what to say, other than congratulations." She reached across the table to give Carrie's hand a squeeze. "I just can't believe this. How long have you known?"

"Only since this morning. You know I haven't been feeling well lately. I thought it was nerves, or maybe even an ulcer, but Alex thought I might be pregnant, so we decided to try a home pregnancy test. It came out positive."

"Tell them the rest of the story, Carrie-Anne," said Alex. "You were so sure it was an ulcer that you made a bet and you lost. And because she lost the bet, dinner tonight is on my best friend."

"What?" exclaimed Steve. "Oh now that's just wrong in so many ways. You don't go and make the mother of your child buy dinner for your friends, Dude, even if she did lose a bet. Allie and I will treat you tonight."

"Thank you, Steve," said Carrie with a smile. "Looks like you got me off on a technicality. You know you're now one of my best friends too."

Steve and Allison were happy, yet sad, to hear the news of Carrie's pregnancy. They too were hoping for a baby, but so far it hadn't happened.

"These things really do happen when you're not trying," said Carrie. "Do what we did. Take a weekend off. Go someplace romantic, like the Double-Diamond Resort. It seemed to do the trick for us."

Alex raised his glass. "I'd like to propose another toast. Here's to Caroline Lee Daniels, my very best friend, my lifelong companion, and the mother of my children."

❧Thirty-Nine❧

THE PAST FEW MONTHS had been the most difficult
time of Scott's life. He was still in Payson, free on bond
while awaiting trial. His trial, however, would not start for at
least another six months, perhaps longer. In the meantime, he
lost his job in Kansas City and he'd nearly lost Nancy as well. His
bail bondsman would not allow him to travel to Kansas City to
visit, and Nancy's visits to Arizona were rare.

Scott was in limbo. He was living in a motel room and
working in the electronics department at a big-box retailer. The
position was hardly worthy of an experienced software engineer,
but until his name was cleared it was the best he could do. His
meager salary, however, barely covered his living expenses and
child support payments and his savings and brokerage accounts
were nearly depleted. Those funds had been used to pay his
attorney's retainer and Frederick Carlton Lancaster's services did
not come cheap. However if destitution, followed by years of
living in debt was the cost of his freedom, then it was a price he
was willing to pay. He now understood how Carrie Daniels must
have felt when she did the photo shoot for Louise Dickenson.

For the first time, he felt a genuine remorse over Carrie. He'd intentionally mislead her and had taken advantage of her, and his moment of lust had turned her world upside down along with his own. The hearing on the motion for summary judgment would be on Tuesday. He hoped his sworn testimony in his deposition—that he was in Phoenix, purchasing his luggage at the time the files were uploaded, would be enough to convince the judge he'd done nothing wrong.

At least he was finally free of Maggie. His divorce was final in December. In the end, Maggie got the house as well as half his pension and other assets, including their art collection. She'd also won custody of Sarah and Ben. He knew she was guilty of the forgery, but ever since he'd had an alibi for the day the letter was mailed to Carrie, she'd laid low. The FBI had kept the case open, but it was growing cold and would remain so until new evidence surfaced.

He'd just returned to his room after a typical workday, when he heard a loud knock at the door. Ever since his arrest, any loud, unexpected knocks at his door made he jump. He looked through the peephole to see a young man in a brown uniform.

"Who is it?"

"UPS."

He remembered Nancy mentioning something about sending more of his belongings back. He cautiously opened the door, and indeed a large parcel was being delivered. He thanked the driver as he signed for it and brought the box inside. He picked up a box cutter, carefully opening the carton. Inside was another piece of his luggage, and inside the luggage was more of his winter clothing. He unpacked the items and put them away. He was about to zip the empty bag shut when he noticed something odd. Sticking out from one of the pockets was the corner of a piece of paper. He pulled it out and looked it over. He couldn't believe his eyes. It was no ordinary piece of paper. It was the receipt for the luggage. It included the name and address of the store as well as date and time that the luggage was purchased. He heard himself laughing and crying at the same time. At long last, he had his alibi. The receipt would prove, conclusively, that he was miles away from his home at the time the files were uploaded. His hands were trembling as he grabbed his phone and placed a call to his lawyer. As usual, Freddie was unavailable, but his secretary instructed him to fax a copy as soon as possible. He stopped to dab his eyes with a tissue before picking it up and dashing to the motel office.

"Afternoon, Scott," greeted the heavy-set woman seated behind the desk.

"Afternoon, Jane."

"You seem pretty happy today."

"That's because I am. I just struck oil, Jane. I've got my ticket to freedom. I just need to use the fax machine."

"In the back." She motioned to the room behind her.

"Just charge it to my room," he said as he raced past her. "Oh, by the way, I need to make a few photocopies."

"Help yourself, and it's on the house, Scott. You really saved my rear end the other day when the computers crashed."

"All in a day's work, my sweet."

"Shameless flirt."

He emerged a few minutes later, photocopies in hand, stopping to give her a quick kiss on the cheek before flying out the door.

"Story of my life," she said, shaking her head. "I always end up with the love 'em and leave 'em types."

As soon as Scott returned to his room he grabbed his phone, this time placing a call to Ken O'Dell. He quickly introduced himself as soon as O'Dell answered.

"Of course I remember you, Scott."

"I've got it, O'Dell. I just found the receipt."

"What receipt?"

"The receipt from the luggage store. The one that proves, definitively, that I wasn't anywhere near my home at the time the files were uploaded to *Gentry Magazine*, which means there was only one person who could have done the deed."

"I see." O'Dell was grinning from ear to ear. "I'll need to take it into evidence, as soon as possible."

"Of course. I'll fax a copy to you as soon as we're done, but I'd like to deliver the original to you in person, if you don't mind."

"I understand. My shift was just about up, but this one's worth putting in a few hours of overtime. You understand that once I have that receipt, I'll be placing your wife under arrest."

"I understand, and make that my ex-wife." There was a triumphant tone in Scott's voice. "We also need to make arrangements for my children. The kids are supposed to be with me this weekend and I want Child Protective Services kept out. They have a father, and an aunt, to take care of them until my attorney can do whatever has to be done in order for me get full custody. In the meantime, they're not to be placed in a foster home."

"I see no reason why that can't be arranged, although they may need to stay with your sister until all the charges against you are dropped and you're officially cleared."

"I understand, however, I need for you to understand something as well." Scott's voice now sounded firm. "I'll be delivering the receipt to you in about two hours. As soon as I'm done, I'm going straight to my ex-wife's house to pick up my kids. Please, do not arrest her until after I've left. I don't want Ben and Sarah to see their mother being taken away in handcuffs."

"I understand, Scott. I'm a dad myself. I'll be waiting for your fax so I can get a warrant sworn out. It'll all be ready by the time you get here. Don't worry, I'll be there when she's arrested."

Scott ended the call and grabbed his things. After a quick stop to send the fax to O'Dell, he hopped into his car and headed to Phoenix. He was a free man once again.

* * *

Maggie kissed her children goodbye and told them to have a good weekend with their father. Before closing the door, she gave Scott a civil goodbye as well, but it was only for the kids' sake. With all that had happened, her love for Scott was dead. In its place was a burning hatred that seemed to grow stronger with each passing day.

"Rot in hell, you worthless son of a bitch," she said out loud as she closed the front door, "and enjoy your freedom while you still can. It won't last much longer."

Her plans had all fallen neatly into place. All she was waiting for was the next opportunity to make Carrie Daniels' even life more miserable. She'd have to quiz the kids, when they returned home Sunday night. With any luck, they'd reveal the next time Scott would be in the Phoenix area. She went to the kitchen to fix herself something to drink, and when she returned to the living room she picked up the remote and settled into her easy chair. She looked forward to a nice quiet weekend. She'd just made herself comfortable, when she heard a knock at the front door.

"Great," she muttered as she went to answer it. She paused for a moment to put on her best happy face, again for the kids' sakes. She took a deep breath and swung the door open. "Okay you guys, what'd you forget this time?" Her smile instantly faded as soon as she recognized who was standing there.

"You again? And I see you brought reinforcements." She motioned to Billie Hughes and the two men in FBI jackets standing with him. "So what the hell do you want this time, O'Dell?"

Billie stepped forward. Maggie noticed she had a pair of handcuffs.

"Maggie Andrews, I'm placing you under arrest for identity theft, forgery, and mailing a threatening communication."

"You've got to be kidding me. This is laughable. You've all ready got the right person under arrest—my ex-husband, Scott."

"Nice try lady, but it won't wash this time, said O'Dell. "Scott now has concrete proof that he was nowhere near your home at the time the files were uploaded. The jig is up Maggie, and now you're going to jail."

"I want my attorney." Her voice was defiant. "He'll have me out before you know it and then I'm going after you for false arrest."

"Whatever, Maggie."

Billie read her Miranda rights and placed the cuffs on her as the two other agents secured the house. Maggie was quickly loaded into the back of their SUV and taken to the field office. As soon as they arrived, she was taken back into the interrogation room. Just as before, she vehemently denied any wrongdoing, once again pointing the finger of blame at Scott.

"We now have proof that Scott was in Phoenix at the time the files were uploaded. So tell me, Maggie, exactly how is it that he could have been in two places at once?"

"What do you mean, you have the proof? I'm not saying another word without my attorney. Can I make a phone call?"

"Help yourself,"

One of the agents escorted her to a phone. She called the only attorney she knew; her divorce attorney. It was after five o'clock and she wasn't in, so Maggie left her a voice mail. As soon as she finished, she was handed over to Diane Hall, and two female Deputy U.S. Marshals.

"Where are we going?"

"To booking," she replied.

"I see. So you want to fingerprint me and take my photo. Can I go home after that?"

"Not until you see a judge."

"And when will that be?"

"Not for awhile. We have some procedures we need to follow first."

She was taken to a room for fingerprinting and to have her mug shot taken. Afterwards she was taken into another room and was ordered to remove each item of her clothing. Once she was stripped naked, she was told to bend over and spread her legs apart. Maggie started crying.

"Sorry, lady, but we have to do this for everyone. We have to make sure you're not smuggling a weapon or contraband."

"You don't understand. My husband was having an affair. I never had any intentions of actually harming her. I just wanted to teach her a lesson, that's all. Besides, what the hell kind of weapon would I have up there anyway?"

"You'd be surprised."

Once the strip search was over, she was taken to a shower, given an orange jail suit, and taken to a holding cell. As she curled up on her bunk, something deep within her psyche snapped, and she recalled the vow she once made to herself. If she went down, Carrie Daniels would go down with her, only now she no longer feared any repercussions or consequences. All that mattered was how she would make Carrie pay. After spending the weekend in jail, Maggie had a bond hearing early Monday morning. Once she made bail she took a cab home and when she arrived she immediately called Scott.

"You'll pay dearly for this," she coldly announced as soon as he answered.

"I don't think so. You tried to frame me for a crime I didn't commit. You're the one who'll end up paying."

"So where are the kids?"

"At school. I dropped them off this morning and I'm on the way to meet with my attorney. We have to start the process of getting all the charges against me dismissed, and then I want to talk to him about suing the FBI wrongful arrest."

"Whatever, Scott. You got everything you had coming to you, and then some. You're a liar and a cheater. You deserved all of it, and so did your little whore. My only regret is that I wasn't able to go after Nancy, but I sure as hell got the goods on Carrie. So, how do you like me now?"

"I don't like you at all," he replied. "I'll admit I was a real ass, and that I was wrong to cheat on you, but you had no right to drag Carrie through the mud like you did. I've told you this before. I lied to her, Maggie. I intentionally mislead her into thinking I was single and available. She's not a mind reader and none of this is her fault."

"Yeah right. Pity poor Carrie—not! The little trollop had it coming."

"When are you going to let it go, Maggie? I don't think you hate her because she had an affair with me. I think you hate her because she's everything you're not. She's beautiful, she's talented, she's successful and she even used to be a child star. On top of that, she has a good heart and she sure as hell didn't deserve to be used the way that I used her. Compared to her, you're just a frumpy, mean-spirited little housewife. That's what this vendetta is really about, isn't it?"

Maggie didn't respond. There was nothing for her to say.

"You know, in hindsight I should have divorced you years ago," continued Scott, "but I thought I was doing the right thing by staying with you until the kids were grown. This past weekend I had a long talk with Ben and Sarah. They know you've been arrested and they know you tried to frame me. Right now they're understandably angry with both of us, and they'll probably need some family counseling, but at least they now understand what kind of a person you really are and why I had to get away from you. They're staying with me tonight and then tomorrow afternoon, after the hearing, I'm taking them back to Payson with me. All three of us have agreed it would be best if they stayed with Aunt Lorraine for now."

"I didn't agree to this. So what time is this hearing and why wasn't I informed?"

"The hearing tomorrow isn't about the kids. It's about the copyright infringement case. Our attorneys have filed some sort of a motion to have it dismissed. Carrie can prove her identity was stolen and her signature was forged. And now I have proof that I was somewhere else at the time the files were uploaded to the magazine. I expect the entire case will be thrown out. But don't worry, Maggie, now that we can prove you're the one who uploaded the files, I'm sure Mrs. Dickenson will be more than happy to file a claim against you."

"Rot in Hell, Scott."

Maggie fumed as she disconnected the call. She had to think fast. She'd worked too hard for too long and she couldn't allow Carrie to walk away now. There was only one thing left for her to do, and if she played her cards right, she wouldn't get caught, at least not for this.

"If I told you once, Carrie, I told you a dozen times—if I go down, I'm taking you with me, and right now I have absolutely nothing to lose. So you'd better get ready, because tomorrow afternoon, as soon as your hearing's over, I'm sending you straight to Hell."

She grabbed a pencil and paper and starting making a list.

❧Forty❧

TUESDAY MORNING Carrie woke up sicker than usual. She rushed into the bathroom before the alarm stopped ringing. No doubt her morning sickness was compounded by the anxiety of the hearing that afternoon.

"I'm so sorry, Carrie-Anne." Alex watched her as she came out holding a cold washcloth to her face. "I'm the one who did this to you, and now I'm starting to feel guilty about it."

"It's okay, Alex." She eased herself back on the bed. "We're having a baby. There's nothing for you to feel guilty about. I'm just experiencing a few raging hormones, that's all. I'm going to the doctor next week and she'll probably give me something to take care of it. I'll be fine."

"I know. I just worry about you, that's all."

"I'm okay." She lay back down and placed the wet cloth across her forehead. "Just give me a few minutes and I'll be good as new. I promise."

Alex tried to shake off the foreboding feeling he felt building deep inside. He'd once again had the recurring dream he'd had from time to time ever since law school. In that dream, he was standing in a hospital room. A nurse was handing him a

234

newborn infant while everyone around him congratulated him on the birth of his son. Normally, it was a happy dream, but this time it was different. This time he'd called the baby Tyler, and as he looked into the child's face someone told him Tyler was not the baby he was expecting now. He would be his next child. He woke up in a cold sweat, fearing it was a bad omen and that Carrie would lose the baby. He looked down at her as he ran his hand up and down her shin.

"Feeling better?"

"Yeah. It's setting down so it's safe for you to go into the bathroom. As soon as you're done I'll start getting ready."

He bent down to give her a kiss before he headed off. He soon returned, relieved to find her feeling better. After he dressed, he went to the kitchen to make some coffee and toast. As he poured the water into the coffeemaker, he silently prayed that his dream was nothing more than just a dream, and that the day's court proceedings would have the outcome they all desired. Delores, the housekeeper, arrived while the coffee was brewing.

"Morning, Alex. How's Carrie feeling this morning?"

"The usual. I'm going to see if I can get her to eat some toast."

"She'll be fine. Morning sickness usually goes away after the third month."

"I sure hope so."

He poured himself a cup of coffee and took a seat at the table. Carrie arrived a few minutes later, wearing the gray conservative-looking dress she usually wore for her formal business presentations. She gave Delores a friendly greeting, but Alex noticed she still looked pale.

"Coffee?"

"No thanks." She opened the refrigerator door. "I'm going to see if I can hold down some orange juice."

As she took her seat at the breakfast table Alex went over the plan for the day.

"The hearing is set for one o'clock at the Sandra Day O'Conner Federal Courthouse. It's that fancy, modern, high-tech building downtown. I'll drive you there, so we'll rendezvous at my office at eleven. Reggie wants to have a short meeting before we leave and we'll have lunch, if you're up to eating."

"I should be fine by then."

"That's my girl." He reached over and patted her hand. "I can't imagine the hearing lasting more than thirty minutes.

Once we're done, we'll head back to the office, and then tonight, I'm taking you out for night on the town. This day's been a long time coming, Carrie-Anne."

Alex still planned to surprise her with her engagement ring that night. He dropped it into his coat pocket before heading off to work, giving her his usual goodbye kiss as he left.

After a light breakfast, Carrie went to her studio to catch up on paperwork before leaving for Alex's office. Reggie joined them for lunch at a nearby bistro to go over the last-minute details. Everything was in order and she assured her that she had nothing whatsoever to worry about. Before long it was time to leave for court. Carrie felt the knot tightening in her stomach as she climbed into the passenger seat of the Camaro.

"It's okay, Carrie-Anne," said Alex as they pulled out of the parking lot, "but I need to bring you up to date about something."

"What's that?"

"Apparently, Scott Andrews has found some sort of receipt which proves he was in Phoenix at the time the files were uploaded, so he's now able to prove his innocence."

"What about Maggie?"

"She spent the weekend in jail and she was arraigned yesterday. She's looking at serving some serious time."

"Finally." He could hear the relief in her voice. "I don't mean to sound mean or vindictive, but I'm glad. I want to see justice served, and I want to see her put away for as long as possible. I don't want her harming our child."

"I understand and I totally agree. And you're not being vindictive. You're a mother trying to protect her baby, although I'm still trying to get used to all of this."

Carrie leaned back into her seat and tried to relax for the rest of the ride downtown. Alex dropped her off in front of the courthouse. She walked across the plaza and spotted Reggie standing near the entrance. They would wait inside the atrium, while Alex parked the car, but as soon as they passed security, Carrie felt a sudden wave of nausea.

"Reggie, is there a ladies' room?"

Reggie heard the urgency in her voice. "Yes, that way."

She raced in the direction where Reggie had pointed, barely making it into the stall on time. When she finally came out, she found Reggie waiting at the sink.

"So, how far along are you?"

"I'm sorry."

"Come on, Carrie," she said with a smile. "You're not supposed to keep secrets from your attorney. I've had three kids, and with all of them I spent the first few weeks with my head in a commode. So how far along are you?"

"About nine weeks. I see the doctor next Wednesday."

"Good for you." She reached into her purse for a roll of mint candy and offered one to her. "Let's get you ready, and then I'm going to get Louise Dickenson off your back, once and for all."

They left the ladies' room and found an anxious Alex waiting in atrium.

"We're good, Dad," said Reggie. "She just had another little bout of morning sickness, but she's fine now. And congratulations."

"Thanks. We'll be making a formal announcement very soon."

He rang for an elevator. As soon as one arrived, they headed up to the courtroom. George McCormick was seated in the gallery, along with his wife, Betty, and Jonathan Fields. Carrie greeted Jonathan with a hug. Alex discreetly squeezed her hand as she and Reggie walked past him and took their places at the defendant's table. Scott and his attorney entered a few minutes later and joined them, while Louise and Jack Collins took their places at the plaintiff's table. A few minutes later court was called into session. All rose as the judge entered the room.

"Be seated," he said as the Clerk of Court called their case. Each side presented their arguments, and the judge asked several questions of council.

"It's going well," whispered Reggie to Carrie. "He's just making sure he has all the facts, and I can tell he's not happy with Louise."

The judge asked a few more questions before silently leaning back into his chair. After a long, tense moment of silence, he removed his glasses and began rubbing his temple.

"Ladies and gentlemen, after serious consideration, I grant summary judgment in favor of the defendants. I further consider the defendant's motion for attorney fees and court cost, and after further considering the evidence, I find that an award of attorney fees of twenty-five thousand dollars for Ms. Peters and fifteen thousand dollars for Mr. Lancaster is awarded. Ms. Peters, Mr. Lancaster, would you please present an order for my signature."

"Thank you, Your Honor," said Reggie. "My client and I are both very appreciative."

"My client and I thank you as well, Your Honor," added Freddie.

All were ordered to rise and the judge left the bench.

"That's it, Carrie-Anne." Alex leaned over and kissed her on the cheek as she stepped back into the gallery. "It's all over."

Jonathan shook her hand. "Congratulations, Carrie. I knew it was a bum rap. Now you can go on with your life."

"I couldn't have done it without you. Thank you so much again, for everything."

As she was speaking to Jonathan, she noticed a profoundly sad look in his eyes. She wondered what could be troubling him, but before she could ask, Alex began leading her away. As they waited for the elevator, another man approached Alex.

"Do you have a some time? I'd like to go over something with you regarding the Gillespie case, if you don't mind."

"Sure, Donald." Alex looked at Reggie. "Duty calls. Would you mind running her back to the office for me?"

"My pleasure."

The elevator doors opened. Reggie stepped inside and immediately turned her phone back on. Alex gave Carrie a quick goodbye kiss before she stepped in. Scott Andrews raised an eyebrow and smiled to himself as he walked in behind her. He felt relieved in knowing she'd apparently found someone else. George, Betty and Jonathan came in just before the doors closed.

"This way." Donald led Alex to a private room where they could talk.

The elevator doors opened on the ground floor. As Carrie stepped out, she looked around the glass atrium and noticed Louise and her attorney having a rather animated conversation off to the side. Judging by the body language, it wasn't a pleasant one. They were nearing the exit, when Reggie's phone rang. She stopped to check her caller ID.

"Wait a minute, it's one of my kids."

Carrie and Jonathan stopped and waited as she stepped aside to take the call. She soon disconnected and walked back up to them.

"Sorry guys, my son just took a tumble on the basketball court. They think he might have sprained an ankle. Would you mind running her back to my office, Jonathan?"

"It would be my pleasure. You go do what you have to do."

"Thanks." Reggie began to place another call.

"Thank you again, Reggie, for everything." Carrie extended her hand. "Hope your son will be okay."

"He's fine. Enjoy the next seven months while you can, Carrie, because once the baby gets here, your life will be just like mine."

"Please, don't remind me." As Reggie stepped away Carrie looked up at Jonathan. He had a surprised look on his face. "Are you all right?"

"Yes, yes I'm fine."

"I'm afraid my attorney just spilled the beans. Alex and I are expecting, we just haven't announced it yet."

"I see... Well, congratulations."

"Thank you. Are you sure you're all right, Jonathan? You look a little pale all of a sudden. Would you like to sit down for awhile?"

"No, Carrie, I'm fine. I've just had a very long day. Let's get you back to Alex's office."

He followed her out the door. As they stepped outside he noticed something odd in the trees in front of the plaza. One thing he'd learned after his brush with the law was to always be alert to his surroundings, and the woman standing next to one of the trees appeared to be out of place. She wore a pair of dark sunglasses and her long red hair was topped with a baseball cap. She was also wearing two overcoats and a pair of leather gloves. The February afternoon was cool, but not cold enough for anyone to be so heavily bundled up. Jonathan tried to hurry Carrie along as they headed toward the street. He glanced over his shoulder. The woman was staring intently at Carrie as she reached for something underneath the overcoats.

"Carrie!"

As he heard the popping sound he tried to shield her with his body. The bullet whizzed above their heads, striking the light pole in front of the building across the street. He heard people screaming in terror as he quickly positioned himself squarely between Carrie and the shooter. The gun went off again. This time he felt the searing pain of the second bullet tearing through his left side as he fell. Carrie let out a scream in agony as she too fell to the ground.

"No Maggie!" screamed Scott. She turned to face him and immediately fired. The bullet hit him in the chest. He collapsed onto the concrete plaza as a pool of blood began to form around him.

The sharp, searing pain took Carrie's breath away. She felt as if her left side was on fire. She reached down and felt something wet, just above her hip. She looked at her hand and discovered she was bleeding. She looked at Jonathan, lying on the concrete next to her. He, too, had been hit and she could see the blood. He was still conscious. He reached for her other hand and gave it a squeeze.

"Forgive me, Cara Mia, for failing you."

There was only one person who'd ever called her that name. Her mind instantly flashed back to long-forgotten memory. She was in the backyard at their house in Montana. Her father was pitching a big red rubber ball to her as she swung at it with a bat. "Come on, Cara Mia," he said as he gently tossed the ball. "You can do it. Just like I taught you." Suddenly, it all made sense. No wonder Jonathan kept telling her not to judge her father so harshly. As she looked into his eyes, she recalled her father's face.

"Oh—my—God!"

The look he gave her in return confirmed it. She squeezed his hand.

"You didn't fail me, Daddy, you really didn't. You just saved my life." She could hear the sound of the approaching sirens as she gave his hand another squeeze. "Just stay with me, okay. Now that I've found you I'm not going to lose you again."

❧Forty-One❧

LOUISE WAS CERTAIN she'd experienced worse days than the one she was having, but she couldn't remember when. She'd just lost her case. Then, to add insult to injury, she'd been ordered to pay all of their attorney fees and court costs. Karl was going to be furious with her. He, too, had been pressuring her for months to drop the case, but she'd steadfastly refused. She'd told Carrie on the phone that day she was going to teach her a lesson she'd never forget, and Louise was someone who never backed down. As soon as she stepped off the elevator she gave her attorney a piece of her mind. He, too, reminded her that he'd advised her, many times, to drop the case.

"You're supposed to be on my side."

"I am on your side, Louise. I've been telling you for months that your case was weak and you'd be better off waiting for the criminal investigation to wrap up. Now you finally know who really infringed on your work—Maggie Andrews. You're perfectly free to go after her. Hell, you may even win, but you'll have to find another attorney, because I'm done. My office will send you my final bill."

"Yeah, well you're fired anyway," she yelled as Collins walked away.

It took Louise a few moments to gather her wits. She let out a sigh as she headed toward the exit. As she stepped onto the plaza she heard a loud, popping sound, like the sound of a car backfiring. People starting screaming and running as another loud pop was heard. She looked in the direction it came from and saw a woman standing near the trees with a gun in her hand. She watched in horror as the woman turned and fired a shot at Scott Andrews, who immediately crumpled to the ground. People were running in panic, but Louise kept her eyes on the woman. After she fired at Scott, she carefully tucked the gun into her overcoat and began walking away.

Louise began her career as a newspaper photographer and her instincts immediately kicked in. She reached into her purse and powered up her smart phone as she began following her from a safe distance. The woman calmly walked to the back of the plaza, turned and headed to the street corner. From there, she turned and began walking south. Louise kept her distance behind her, stopping to occasionally snap a photo. One block later the woman turned to her left, crossing the street and heading east. As she was walking, she reached up and pulled off her baseball cap. Louise noticed the red hair coming off with it, revealing short blonde hair underneath. She kept her stride as she casually dropped the wig and cap into a trashcan. Louise kept snapping photos. She could hear sirens in the distance and she knew she'd have to call the police. She stopped for a moment to place the call. By the time she looked back up, the blonde woman was out of sight. Louise headed in the direction she'd last seen her walking. Her call connected, but to her dismay, she got a busy signal. She stopped momentarily and tried again. This time the call went through.

"Nine-one-one, what is your emergency?"

"There's been a shooting in front of the Sandra Day O'Conner building."

"Yes ma'am, we're aware of it. The police have already been summoned."

"Wait! Don't hang up," she shouted. "I saw the shooter. It's a woman. I've followed her down Fourth Avenue to Jackson Street. She was walking east on Jackson, when I lost sight of her. By the way, I saw her take off her baseball cap. She was wearing a red wig. Underneath she has short, blonde hair."

"Okay, ma'am. Please, don't follow her anymore. I'll pass the information on to the dispatcher. Thank you."

"Wait! Are you still there?"

The operator had already disconnected the call. She heard the sound of sirens coming from all directions. Police cars were beginning to swarm. She thought about going to the parking garage to get her car before the police blocked off the area, then it occurred to her—she might be able to sell the photos for a tidy profit. She kept walking. As she approached the Caesar Chavez Memorial Plaza she hit pay dirt. The woman suddenly stepped out from behind one of the marble slabs at the plaza entrance. This time she was wearing a different overcoat, with the one she had on before draped over her arm. Louise stepped back into the trees, once again reaching for her phone and discreetly snapping a few more photos. She thought about calling the police again, but there were a number of patrol cars already racing down the streets with their lights on and sirens blazing.

The woman began walking through the plaza, this time heading north. She casually dropped the overcoat into another trashcan. As soon as she reached Washington Street she turned, again heading east. Louise kept a safe distance, watching as she walked up to a small silver sedan parked in front of the old county courthouse. She reached into her pocket for her keys. A minute later she opened the driver's side door. Louise calmly approached her.

"What on earth do you suppose is going on?"

"I have no idea," she replied as she slipped behind the wheel. "Someone must have had a wreck, or something."

"I guess so."

Louise began to walk away. She turned to make a quick note of the car license plate number as she slowly headed toward the corner. As the car drove off, she stopped and reached into her purse for a piece of scrap paper, jotting down the license number along with the make and model of the car. Once again she called the police, and once again it took a few attempts before her call went through.

"Nine-one-one, what is your emergency?" This time it was a different operator.

"Yes, I called a few minutes ago. I've followed the female shooter from the Sandra Day O'Conner building and I've taken some photos of her. She was wearing a red wig, which she threw into a trashcan near Fourth Avenue and Jackson. She's middle aged, with short blonde hair, and she's now wearing a dark-brown overcoat with black pants. She's driving a late-model, silver Honda Civic."

"Where are you, ma'am?"

"I'm on Washington Street. I'm standing right in front of the old Maricopa County court building, and my name is Louise Dickenson."

"Ms. Dickenson, if you would please stay there, we'll send an officer to talk to you."

Louise stood by, and a short time later a patrol car pulled up. She approached the officer inside.

"Are you Louise Dickenson?"

"Yes sir, I'm Louise."

She immediately pulled out her phone and started showing him the photos.

"Where is the woman now?"

"I have no idea. She got into her car and drove away about five minutes ago. It was a late model Honda Civic. I wrote down the license plate number."

She handed him the paper. He immediately radioed the information to the dispatcher.

"Ma'am, if you'll hop into my car I need to take you down to the station so the detectives can interview you. We also need to download the photos."

"Of course."

As they headed to the station, Louise got curious.

"I saw her shoot a man named Scott Andrews. He and I had just made an appearance in front of the judge. Is he all right?"

"I'm not sure, ma'am. There were three people shot. I heard one is critical and not expected to make it."

"Who were the other two?"

"A man and a woman. I don't know their identities."

The car turned into the station and Louise was immediately escorted into a room where two FBI agents waited. She spent the next hour being interviewed.

"You did a very brave thing today," he said as someone returned her cell phone. "But please, don't ever attempt anything like this again. She's armed and dangerous, and she could have just as easily shot you as well. Meantime, we've copied your photos, and they're going to be extremely helpful with our investigation."

"It was my pleasure, however it's been a long day and I'm

ready to go home. I'm parked in a garage near the courthouse. Would one of you mind taking me there?"

"That might present a problem. Right now the police have the area around the courthouse cordoned off and the courthouse itself is in lockdown, along with several adjacent buildings. We're still looking for the shooter, so we can't allow anyone in the area until we're sure it's safe. You may as well make yourself comfortable, and as soon as we're able, we'll have someone take you to your car."

"Can I have someone pick me up here?"

"Of course. You can always come back and pick up your car later."

Louise called her husband. Forty-five minutes later Karl picked her up. They immediately drove to the nearest television station.

* * *

Maggie pulled into the parking lot by the movie theaters at Desert Caliente Mall. She congratulated herself, knowing she'd pulled it off perfectly. She'd stopped to buy a movie ticket for one of the early matinees and she went inside the theater to buy a soda, putting all the charges on her debit card. As soon as she took her seat in the auditorium, she shut down her phone. Once the previews started she walked out, got into her car and drove to downtown Phoenix. Mission accomplished. She'd returned to the theaters in Mesa in plenty of time. She waited patiently. As soon as people began exiting the theater, she turned her phone back on and stepped out of her car, heading inside the mall to do a little shopping. It wasn't if, but when, O'Dell showed up at her door. This time she'd have the perfect alibi.

❧Forty-Two❧

CARRIE HELD TIGHTLY TO her father's hand. He was going in an out of consciousness while she kept reassuring him he would be all right. A crowd surrounded them and some of the people were trying to help. She heard the sound of approaching sirens. To her relief, the paramedics had arrived. She noticed two of them racing toward someone else. She'd overheard people saying there was a third victim. Whoever it was, she hoped they would be all right. She looked up and saw another medic looking down at her.

"My father's been shot. He's a recovering cocaine addict. Please, be careful with him, and would someone please go find Alex, Alex Montoya. He's an attorney. He's inside the court building."

"Please, calm down, Miss. We're taking care of your father. My name is Eric and I'll be taking care of you. It looks like you've been hit on your side. Have you been hit anyplace else?"

"No, but my side feels like it's burning."

Eric checked her side. "It looks like you were grazed by the bullet. I know it really smarts, but it's a superficial injury. I doubt you'll even need stiches. Do you have any medical conditions that we need to know about?"

"Yes, I'm pregnant."

"How far along?"

"About nine weeks."

Carrie heard him shouting something to the other paramedics, along with the sound of the other stretcher rolling by. As Eric started to put an IV into her arm, she looked over and saw them loading another man into a waiting ambulance.

"Don't be scared, I'm really good at this. I'll try not to hurt you, I promise."

"What about my father? I want to ride in the ambulance with him."

"Sorry, there's only room for one, but we're taking him to the hospital right now. He'll be in the ambulance ahead of you."

"He's a recovering cocaine addict."

"We already know that. We'll be very careful with what we give him for pain. He's alive and at the moment his injuries don't appear to be life threatening."

They put her on a stretcher and loaded her into the ambulance. "What about Alex? Did anyone call Alex?"

"Please, Miss, calm down. We'll take care of that once we get you to hospital."

"Which hospital?"

"Sonoran Southwest. They have a Level-One trauma center. You and your father will be in the best of hands."

Carrie was silent for the rest of the ride. Soon they were unloading her and rushing her into the ER. She was quickly taken into a treatment room where a nurse began asking her questions.

"Where's Alex? Would someone please call Alex. He's my significant other."

"I'll call him right now, just give me his number."

Carrie gave her the number and the nurse dialed, but the call went straight to voice mail. After she left a message, Carrie gave her Steve's number, explaining that both he and Allison had her medical power of attorney. This time the nurse was able to get the call through.

"You're friend is on his way," she said as she hung up. "He says he'll call his wife and Alex. Don't worry, they're coming."

"What about my father? Jonathan Fields."

"They're working on him right now. You're his daughter? Correct?"

"I am."

"Would you mind signing his paperwork? He's heavily sedated right now."

"Of course."

While Carrie was busy signing the paperwork for her father and herself, Billie Hughes entered the room.

"Billie! I'm so glad you're here." Carrie reached out and Billie took her hand. "I don't understand what's happening. Why would anyone want to do this to me?"

"Calm down, it'll be alright. That's what we're trying to find out. Because this happened on federal property the FBI will be in charge of the investigation, so I've volunteered to come talk to you. I'll need to ask you some questions, and as soon as they bring you a gown I'm going to have to take your dress and your blazer."

"Why?"

"It's evidence." Billie reached over and stroked Carrie's hair. "Besides, they're ruined anyway. They're torn and they have some bloodstains."

Someone brought in a hospital gown and Billie carefully helped her out of the dress. She quickly sealed it into the evidence bag and helped Carrie into the gown. While she was interviewing her, the doctor came in. He introduced himself as Dr. Patrick Arnold.

"You're a very lucky young lady," he said as he examined her injury. "We'll have to clean out the wound and bandage you up. You'll be a little sore for a few days and it'll leave a scar, otherwise you'll be fine."

"That's good, but what about the baby?"

"That's our main concern right now. As soon as you're bandaged, we'll need to check your cervix to be sure you're not bleeding or dilating. If not, then it's a good sign, and we'll know how far you're along. I also want to do an ultrasound, just to be sure the baby's all right."

"You and me both. I'm not going to lose my baby, am I?"

"Not if I have anything to do with it." He reached down and touched her arm. "I've seen pregnant women go through far worse injuries than yours and still deliver healthy babies. However, we'll need to keep a close watch on you to make sure nothing happens, so after we're done here, you'll be admitted." He looked over at Billie. "Are you about done? We need to start treating her."

"I can come back later, and Carrie, congratulations."

"Thanks. Billie, would you please call Alex? He needs to know that I'm all right."

"Will do. I'll be back in a little while."

Billie stepped out and the doctor went to work. He confirmed that she was indeed about nine weeks along, and she let out a big sigh of relief as soon as he told her he saw no sign of a possible miscarriage. Afterwards, he stepped out, saying a technician would be coming later on to do the ultrasound. The nurse asked if she wanted anyone to be with her while it was being done.

"Yes," she said. "Please go get my friends."

Billie soon returned to the room, bringing Steve with her. He reached down and took her hand.

"I've called Allison. Her last class ends at three and after that she'll come straight to the hospital."

"Thanks, Steve. Where's Alex?"

"The court building's still in lockdown, so I sent him a text message and I left a message on his voice mail."

"Has he returned either message?"

"Not yet."

"Damn. He must have turned off his phone."

Billie continued interviewing Carrie, and about an hour later the technician came in with the ultrasound machine. She asked them to stay with her, but Steve felt out of place. She then asked if he would mind checking on Jonathan.

"What's this about him being your father? George McCormick is here and he says it's true, but he won't give me any details. He just said that Jonathan's family is on the way from Tucson and they'll explain it all when they get here."

"I'm just as surprised as you are. I've always felt a connection to him, but I had no idea we were related. He must be the one who paid my legal bill."

Steve stepped out. The technician squeezed the gel on Carrie's belly and started the ultrasound. Billie reached down and held her hand.

"There's the baby." The technician pointed it out on the screen. "The heartbeat appears to be normal, and I'll be taking some measurements." She took her time, pointing out the little fingers and toes.

"He looks like you," said Billie.

"No, he looks like Alex."

"You're a mama now, Baby Girl." Billie squeezed her hand. "So, how do you feel?"

"I'm not sure. I don't know how to describe it, really. It's a miracle. I'm so grateful the baby's okay."

"Okay and perfectly healthy," added the technician. "And you're right, you're in your ninth week. This little person, however, is completely unscathed. Probably slept through the whole thing. Oh, look at that. The baby's moving and stretching."

Carrie marveled as she watched her baby move. "Alex says his family always seems to have boys, but we've decided to wait until the baby's born. We want it to be a surprise."

The technician soon finished. "If you'll give me your email address, I'll send you a copy of the sonogram. Then you can show it to the father later on."

Carrie thanked her and gave her the email address. After she left, Carrie was taken upstairs to her room. Billie came along with her. Much to her relief, she was put in a private room. A police officer was standing outside the door.

"Jonathan Fields will be in the room next to yours," explained Billie, "that way the rest of the family will have easy access to both of you. However, you'll both be under police guard, so please let us know who to allow into your room."

"Good heavens, Billie. You're making it sound like I'm a prisoner here."

"No, you're not a prisoner, but until the shooter is apprehended, we have to keep the two of you safe. We also have to keep reporters, paparazzi, and other stalkers away from you. You need your privacy, Carrie, and trust me, in a high profile case like yours, people can and will show up to harass you."

Steve soon arrived, and this time Allison was with him. Billie took her leave, while they helped her settle in. Carrie tried to call Alex, but she too got his voice mail, so she sent him a text message. It was nearly four o'clock and she'd been at the hospital for a couple hours. Hopefully, he'd call back soon. She handed her keys over to Allison, asking her to go to the house and bring her an overnight bag.

* * *

Alex's impromptu conference took place in a small, windowless room in a quiet part of the court building. While they were talking they'd heard an alarm going off. Donald shrugged it off, saying he'd heard talk that they'd been having problems recently with false alarms. They had been discussing the Gillespie case for sometime before he finally looked at his watch.

"Guess what? It's almost four o'clock. We've been here over two hours and my phone is still turned off. I'd better call my office before they send a search party."

"Same here," said Donald. "I'll talk to my client and let him know what we discussed."

"Me too."

Alex put on his coat and powered up his phone. It beeped, letting him know he had voice mail and text messages. He would have to check them later. The two men walked to the elevator together, and both were surprised at what they saw when the doors opened on the ground floor. A large crowd had filled the atrium and yellow crime scene tape blocked the exits.

"Uh-oh, guess it wasn't a false alarm after all," said Donald. "Looks like they've locked down the building."

Alex looked around the atrium. He couldn't see Carrie anywhere, but he soon spotted Reggie, standing near the exit. As he got closer to her, he noticed she was with a small group of people gathered around someone's electronic tablet. He noticed she was crying, and the people standing near her, including Jack Collins, were trying to console her.

"Reggie? Are you all right?"

"Oh my God. Alex, where have you been?"

"I was upstairs talking to Donald Morrison about the Gillespie case. We just got done. Where's Carrie? What's going on?"

"Come with me. We need to talk." Reggie took him by the hand and led him back to the elevators.

"Reggie, what's wrong."

"I'll explain in a minute." She waited for an elevator. As soon as one arrived they stepped inside and headed back up. "Take me to wherever you were talking with Donald. It's obviously a private room."

"You're scaring the living hell out of me, Reggie. What's wrong? Where's Carrie?"

The elevator doors opened and Alex led her back to the room where he and Donald had their conference. Reggie closed the door behind her and told Alex to sit down as she fought back the tears.

"Alex, I took Carrie downstairs, just like you told me to do. We were near the door, when my phone rang. My oldest had a minor emergency, so I was going to pick him up. I asked

Jonathan if he'd mind giving her a ride back to the office. He said he would."

"I see. Go on."

Reggie was started crying again. She reached into her purse for another tissue, before pulling her tablet out of her briefcase.

"This is all my fault, Alex. I should have gone with her."

"What do you mean, Reggie?"

"Jonathan and Carrie had just left the building. I stayed behind to call Brenda to let her know that I wouldn't be back in the office, but before the call went through I heard this loud popping noise from outside. It was gunfire. Some woman out in the plaza had a gun, and she opened fire."

Alex's heart skipped a beat. He felt a chill running down his spine.

"My God. Reggie, where's Carrie?"

Reggie didn't respond. She began crying harder.

"Where's Carrie, Reggie?"

"She's gone, Alex."

"What do you mean, she's gone?"

"Carrie, Jonathan, and Scott Andrews were the three people who were shot. I saw it happen with my own eyes."

"No!" The color was draining from Alex's face.

"They rushed them all to Sonoran Southwest." She punched up a live Internet feed to Channel Seven on her tablet. "The news just broke the story a few minutes ago. They're saying Carrie didn't make it, Alex. I'm so sorry."

"What! No way! Let me see that."

Reggie handed her tablet to Alex. He stared at the screen in stunned disbelief. They were showing clips of Carrie's old Mercer's Market commercials. A minute later they showed the head shot from her website, with her name, and the years of her birth, and death, underneath.

"Alex?"

He didn't respond.

"Alex!"

"Go home, Reggie."

"Are you all right?"

"I said go home. Here's you tablet." He pushed it across the table toward her.

"Okay, Alex. I'll leave you alone for a little while. I'll come back and check on you later."

"Whatever, Reggie."

She headed to the door.

"Who's the shooter?" Alex's voice sounded mechanical.

"They think it's Maggie Andrews."

"Well, of course it's Maggie Andrews. Some fool was dumb enough to release the stupid bitch from jail, and I'll have that someone's ass before I'm through. I'm personally going to see to it the bitch gets the hot needle. Have they found her yet?"

"Not yet. That's why we're still in lockdown."

"Well, that's just great. So I'm being held hostage by the Keystone Cops."

Alex's phone went off. He thought about ignoring it, but the caller ID revealed it was his mother calling. He took the call as Reggie stepped out and closed the door behind her.

"Hey, Mom, what's happening?"

"Alex, we just heard about Carrie. It's on the news here. Your father and I are booking a flight to Phoenix that leaves Las Vegas in two hours. We'll be there as quick as we can."

"Thanks, Mom." Alex's voice was starting to break. "Hurry, I need you."

"We're on our way, son. We'll call you as soon as we land."

Alex's phone beeped. It was a warning that the battery was nearly drained.

"Mom, before you go… I don't think you knew this, but Carrie was pregnant. I've lost them both."

"Oh my God. I'm so sorry. Alex, if you need any—"

Her sentence abruptly ended. The battery on Alex's phone had just run out. He set it on the table, pushing it aside as he laid his head down and buried his face in his arms. He emerged from the room a half hour later.

Courthouses have rooms and corridors off limits to the public, but used by staff, police and attorneys. Alex headed down such a corridor, taking a service elevator to the underground parking facility where the Camaro was waiting. He climbed in, fired up the engine and made his exit. He soon found the road off blocked by two patrol cars. One of the officers approached as he stopped. Alex recognized him.

"Hey, Robert, how's it going?"

"Been a hell of a day, Alex, but I think they're about to wrap things up and let people out of the building."

"Found the shooter yet?"

"Not yet, but apparently they're getting close. As least they've cleared the area here."

"Hey, could you do me a favor and let me through? I've got a family emergency I need to take care of."

"Sure, Alex. Take care of yourself."

"You too."

Robert motioned for one of the officers to move a patrol car. Once it was out of the way Alex waved goodbye as he quickly drove off.

❧Forty-Four❧

ITT TOOK ALLISON OVER AN hour to go from the hospital to Alex and Carrie's house and back again. As soon as she returned, she accompanied her into the bathroom to help her change from the hospital gown into her pink nightshirt with the corset on the front.

"Have you heard from Alex yet?"

"No," Carrie replied. "Steve and I left a few more messages, but so far nothing. However, I did get some other good news while you were out. Jonathan Fields is out of surgery. They said he's doing fine and he's going to be okay. He's still in recovery, but they'll be bringing him to his room soon. Once he's awake, I want to see him. We have a lot to talk about."

"I'm sure you do, but for now let's get you back to bed."

As Carrie settled back into her bed, Steve turned on the television set. All of the local stations were doing extended live news coverage about the shootings, but all three were stunned at what they were seeing. The stations were retracting an earlier report that Carrie had died.

"What the hell? I wasn't even close to dying. How could they have put out a story like that?"

"I'm not sure," said Steve. "I know it's all about ratings, but that's no excuse. What if Alex heard the earlier report?"

All three looked at one another.

"Reggie!" exclaimed Steve. "I'm such an idiot at times. I completely forgot about Reggie."

"It's okay, Steve," said Carrie, "we've had other things on our minds. Reggie stayed behind when Jonathan and I went outside. Maybe she knows where Alex is."

Steve picked up his phone and placed a call to Reggie, who quickly answered.

"Reggie, are you alright? You sound strange."

"It's been a horrible day, Steve. We're still in lockdown, but they're finally getting ready to let us out. I have to go get Alex. I told him about Carrie and he's extremely distraught."

"Carrie's fine. The media got it wrong, Reggie."

"What do you mean they got it wrong? I saw the news report. She was killed."

"No, she wasn't. In fact, I've been with her at the hospital for the past three hours. We've been trying to reach Alex, but we keep getting his voice mail."

"Let me talk to her," said Carrie. Steve handed her his phone. "Reggie, it's me. I'm all right. I wasn't seriously hurt."

"Oh my God! You don't know how relieved I am to hear your voice. They were saying on TV that you were dead."

"I know, Reggie. Jonathan Fields stepped in front of the shooter and literally took the bullet for me. I was grazed on my left side, but I'm fine. The baby's fine too. They checked me out and there's no sign of any miscarriage. We're both all right, so where the hell is Alex?"

"Upstairs. He was in a private meeting with another attorney for over two hours, apparently he was unaware of the shooting. When he finally came down, I took him back up. We saw the news report on my tablet. We both thought you were dead. Alex didn't take it very well."

"Oh no! Reggie, please, you have to find him. Right now."

"Don't worry, I know where he is. It'll only take me a couple of minutes to get to him and I'll have him call you."

"I'll be waiting, and Reggie, thank you."

"Sounds like you found him," said Allison as Carrie disconnected the call.

"Yes, thank goodness. Reggie says he heard the report and now he thinks I'm dead. She's going to talk to him, but I'm so upset right now—"

"Calm down, Carrie. You're pregnant and you've just had another shock. Take it easy. It'll be all right."

"Sounds like you heard," said Dr. Arnold as he entered the room. "I'm not sure how this rumor about you dying got started. We think someone with a police scanner may have overheard that Scott Andrews' heart had stopped beating in the ambulance. They were able to revive him and he's still in surgery. We're holding a press conference at six o'clock. They want me to be there, but I need your consent to discuss your case."

"You can tell them I was grazed by a bullet, but please, don't tell them I'm pregnant."

"Understood. Someone will be bringing you some paperwork to sign."

"Thanks. By the way, how's my father?"

"He's doing quite well, actually. He should be in his room soon."

He checked her vitals and made some notes on her chart before rushing out. Steve's phone began to ring. While he was answering, George McCormick stepped into the room with a bouquet of flowers, which he presented to Carrie.

"George, these are beautiful, thank you." She set them next to her bed. He explained that the flowers were from both him and his wife.

"Betty had to go back to the office, but she sends her love. We'd barely left the building when the shooting started. We saw it all, and we stayed there with you and Jonathan until the ambulance arrived."

"Thank you both. I was in such a state of shock that I didn't even know you were there. George, did you know he's my father?"

"Yes, I know he is. I've known for sometime that Jonathan had a daughter from a prior marriage whom he'd lost contact with, but I didn't know you were she until very recently. It's been really hard on him, Carrie. He said he was going to tell you who he was that day at your office, but then, when you started telling him about your father, he changed his mind. He said you thought that he'd abandoned you, and you were still very bitter about it. He didn't think you'd accept him."

"I'm so sorry, George. I had no idea who he was. I thought my father's name was Kevin Earl Daniels, not Jonathan Fields."

"He legally changed his name from Kevin Daniels to Jonathan Fields. I don't know how much you know about him, but he got into some trouble when he was younger."

"Yes, I know," she replied. "My mother had some of the old records, but they're incomplete. I know he got into trouble over cocaine. I also know that sometime later on he was stabbed in a parking lot."

"That's correct. It happened because he'd gotten clean and he wasn't going back. So later on, when his former dealer got busted, he assumed your father had become an informant. That's why the dealer's brother stabbed him. After he recovered, and after his probation was up, his attorney helped him legally change his name and expunge his record. He'll have to tell you the rest of the story himself."

"I hate to interrupt," said Steve as he disconnected his phone, "but we've got a problem. That was Reggie on the phone. Alex is missing."

"What!"

"He's missing. Reggie went back up to the room where she left him, but he wasn't there. She's looked everywhere for him, but he's nowhere to be found."

"Oh my God," Carrie grabbed her phone and punched up Alex's number. "It's still going straight to voice mail." She left a message, assuring Alex that the news reports were wrong and she was okay. After she disconnected, she looked at George and Steve. The tears started rolling down her face. Steve filled George in on what had happened.

"It's okay," said George. "I'll find him. I know he's distraught, but I don't think he'd do anything to harm himself. Was there anyplace in particular where he might have gone? Perhaps someplace that had a special meaning for the two of you?"

"The Double-Diamond Resort. It's just outside Tucson."

"I know where it is, but it'll take me sometime to get there, especially when I'm fighting rush-hour traffic. Just let me call Betty and I'll head out."

Steve looked at Allison. She nodded her head.

"I'd like to go with you, if you don't mind," said Steve. "Alex and I are good friends. He trusts me."

After a hasty goodbye, Steve and George stepped out, nearly colliding in the doorway with a nurse who was coming in to check on Carrie.

"You're blood pressure's getting too high," she said as her removed the stethoscope from her ears. "You're to need to calm down."

"She's right," said Allie. "I'll be right here with you, I promise, but right now you need to relax."

The nurse stepped out. Carrie laid down, closed her eyes and tried to relax. A short time later an elderly woman cautiously entered the room. She was tall, slender and well dressed, and she was carrying a tattered shoebox. Allison approached her.

"Can I help you?"

"Yes. My name is Penelope Daniels. I'm Kevin's—I mean Jonathan's mother."

"You mean, you're Carrie's grandmother?"

"Yes, I'm her grandmother."

She walked up to Carrie's bedside. As she gazed down at her, she was overwhelmed with emotion. Allison quickly got her a tissue and helped her into a chair.

"The last time I saw her she was only five years old. She's grown into a beautiful woman."

Carrie opened her eyes and began focusing on the older woman. A look of recognition slowly crossed her face as she sat up.

"Grandma Nell? Is that really you?"

"Yes, Carrie. It's me."

Allison excused herself and stepped out as the two women embraced.

"I don't understand any of this," said Carrie. "One day Daddy was just gone and Mama wouldn't talk about it. As the years went by, she let me think that he'd walked out on us. Mama passed away last summer. When we went through her papers, we found out Daddy had a drug problem and that he'd been arrested, and that later on he was attacked in a parking lot. We thought he was dead. It's been over twenty-five years, Grandma Nell, so where were you?"

Penelope let out a sigh. "It's a long, complicated story, Carrie, and I guess the best place for me to start would be at the beginning, wouldn't it?"

"I would think so."

Penelope sat back down, reaching for another tissue and putting the shoebox in her lap before she took Carrie's hand.

"All right, from the beginning. You knew your parents met in college, didn't you?"

"Yes, that much I know."

"I see. Back then they were young and in love, and while Linda was a likeable girl, I knew from the start that she and Kevin really weren't suited for one another. Looking back, I should have stayed out of it and let it run it's course, but I didn't. I started meddling. I wanted Kevin to move on, but the more I interfered, the more I pushed him toward Linda. Finally, one day I overplayed my hand, so Kevin proposed to Linda, just to prove

259

to me that he was right and I was wrong. His strategy worked. From that day forward, I stayed out of it. I put on a brave face at the wedding, but I knew they were making a terrible mistake."

"It wasn't a very happy marriage, at least, what I'm able to recall. They were always fighting."

"You were born fifteen months later," explained Penelope. "It had to have been one of the happiest days of Kevin's life. From the moment you arrived, your father worshipped you, but those were difficult years. He was trying to support a family and work his way through college at the same time. He was under a lot of stress. He was putting in too many long hours and getting too little sleep. It was too much for him. Cocaine was like an epidemic back then, and peer pressure was a factor too. One day, he finally succumbed. He hid it for a long time, but it eventually caught up with him. Linda and I tried, unsuccessfully, to get him into a treatment program, but he refused. Typical addict, he didn't think he had a problem, so he tried to pin the blame on us. Then one day, the cops showed up. Kevin spent a few days in jail, and he decided to check himself into a rehab clinic once he posted bail. Unfortunately, by that time Linda had had enough. She refused to let him come home after he completed the inpatient program, so he moved back in with me while she filed for divorce."

"That I did know about," said Carrie. "And I know he was sentenced to probation."

"That's right. He'd never been in trouble before, and because he was in a treatment program, the judge deferred his jail sentence. He was doing really well. He was getting his life back, but Linda had the upper hand and she wouldn't allow him to see you. You have to understand that while he was on probation he had to be very, very careful. One phone call from her and he would have ended up in jail. He wasn't giving up though. He was going to wait for his probation to end and for the judge to dismiss his jail sentence, and then he was going to fight for visitation. Unfortunately, he was stabbed before his probation was up and as soon as Linda heard about it, she took you and fled the state. Later on, we found out the two of you were in Arizona, but Linda still wouldn't allow any of the family to have any contact with you. Not even me, or Aunt Shelly. It was agonizing."

"I'm so sorry, Grandma Nell. I had no idea. I was so young that I really can't recall much about it. I just remember coming home from school one day and Mama was loading the car. She said we were leaving and never coming back. She said my other grandparents had moved to Arizona and we were going to go live with them. All I know is once we left Montana, Mama wouldn't talk about Daddy."

"I suppose that in her own way, your mother thought she was protecting you," said Penelope. "After all, a lot of addicts end up going back on drugs. I can also understand her wanting to go back to her parents, but her actions hurt us deeply. A part of our family was missing and it left a really big hole."

"I'm so sorry, Grandma Nell. I didn't know. All I can tell you is I've spent most of my life believing that my father had abandoned me and that he didn't care. I know you're not supposed to speak badly of the dead, but at the moment I'm not very happy with my mother. I had a right to know the truth."

"I was angry with her too, for a long time, but as the years passed, Kevin and I both realized that we had to let it go. Kevin had to. It was part of his recovery. He was no longer himself once he got involved with drugs. His actions hurt her and they hurt you, and she'd made it very clear that she'd never allow him to have another opportunity to hurt you again. He had to move on, so he built a whole new life for himself. He found Julia and they had Danny, but even with a new family, you were still the missing piece of the puzzle. There was never a day that went by when your father didn't miss you terribly, especially on your birthday and over the holidays." She reached over and squeezed Carrie's hand. "But that's all in the past. What matters now is that we're a whole family again."

The nurse came back in to check on Carrie. Penelope waited patiently as she worked.

"Your blood pressure is much better, but you still need to relax and stay calm. Have they found your significant other yet?"

"Not yet. We think we know where he went, so my other friends have gone to look for him. I'll be okay, once they find him."

"All right, but until then, we're keeping a close watch on you."

The nurse stepped out and Carrie turned her attention back to her grandmother.

"I take it your significant other is a young attorney named Alex."

"That's right, Grandma. How did you know?"

"I know things," she said, with a smile. "Your father's kept his eye on you ever since George brought him in on your case. So, what's happened to Alex?"

"We've been trying to reach him all afternoon, but so far we've not had any luck. Then the media reported that I'd died. We know Alex heard it, and now he's disappeared. George, and our friend Steve, went to look for him."

"Then we'll all say a prayer that he'll be found soon, safe and sound. In the meantime, while we're waiting, I've brought you something."

Penelope handed her the shoebox. Carrie carefully took the lid off and discovered it was filled with envelopes.

"This belongs to your father," she explained. "It contains all of the letters he wrote to you after his arrest."

Carrie began looking through the envelopes. All were addressed to her, at a Montana address, and none had ever been opened. All were marked, "return to sender" in her mother's handwriting. She began to weep.

"It's okay, it's okay." Penelope tried to comfort her. "Now you finally know the truth. Your father never, ever abandoned you. You were taken away from him."

Penelope handed her a tissue and held her until she began to calm down.

"There's something else in there too. It's in the big manila envelope."

As soon as Carrie finished wiping her eyes, she took it out of the box and looked inside. It was stuffed with folded pieces of paper. She carefully took them out and began unfolding them. They were her old newspaper and magazine ads from Mercer's Markets.

"Good heavens. It looks like he has every print ad I ever did."

"You know, it was sort of a mixed blessing," said Penelope. "On one hand, your father never approved of you being a child model. But then again, he often used to say that if it wasn't for Mercer's Markets, he wouldn't have been able to see you at all."

Penelope sat quietly in her chair as Carrie looked through the ads. She finally let out a sigh and began to put them back in the envelope. She then placed the envelope back in the box.

"Thank you, Grandma, for showing this to me. It means a lot." She handed the box back to Penelope.

"Like you said, you have a right to know the truth. You've spent far too many years believing in a misconception." Penelope rose from her chair and gave her a hug and a kiss on the cheek. "So for now, I think I'd better take my leave. You need to get some rest and I need to check on your father. We're right next door, if you need us."

"Grandma Nell, before you go, I have one other question."

"What is it?"

"What else do you know about me?"

"I know all of it," she explained. "I know you were homeless and destitute, and that you were taken advantage of by a so-called friend. I don't know if you remember, but I dabbled in art when I was younger and I've even taken a few life-drawing classes myself. There's nothing wrong with being an art model, but I've seen the photos. I personally think that she went way beyond the boundaries and exploited you."

"You don't think I'm a slut because of it?"

"Good heavens, no. Like I said, I know all about it. We've all been following your case and we understand what happened. I guess we'll always feel some guilt because we weren't there to help you when you so desperately needed it. I just wish there was some way you could go after the witch, even though I know you can't. But they say, what comes around goes around, so we'll have to see what happens. In the meantime, Carrie, we all still love you, very much. No one is judging you for doing what you had to do in a horrible situation."

"Thank you, Grandma Nell. That's good to know. So is my father awake yet?"

"Not yet, but we'll let you know as soon as he is." She stooped to give her a final kiss on the cheek. "Welcome home, Carrie."

She left the shoebox behind as she stepped out of the room.

❧Forty-Five❧

GEORGE SWITCHED ON his police scanner as he merged onto the Interstate and headed toward Tucson. The rush-hour traffic seemed heavier than normal, adding to their sense of urgency.

"We know he left the courthouse sometime between four and five," he said. "If he's bound for Tucson, like Carrie says, then he shouldn't be that far ahead of us, assuming he hasn't come to his senses and turned back."

"Somehow I doubt that," replied Steve. "I just hope he hasn't gone off the road somewhere. I want this to end well."

"So far I'm not hearing anything on the scanner about any accidents between here and Tucson, so no news is good news. I'm more concerned about us arriving and him not being there."

"From what I understand, it's a very special place for both of them. She even said that's where their baby was conceived. If it was me, and Heaven forbid, something happened to Allie, I'd probably be drawn to the place where we'd shared our most special memories."

George's car crawled along the crowded sections of the freeway. Precious time slipped by before the traffic began to speed up. Once they were finally out of the city, he hit the accelerator and sped along the Interstate, weaving in and out of traffic at nearly ninety miles per hour. Steve was in for a white-knuckle ride.

"Relax. I used to be a cop, remember? We're trained in high-speed driving."

Steve leaned back in the passenger seat and listened to the scanner. He prayed that once they arrived, Alex would be there.

* * *

Allie went to the cafeteria, while Carrie visited her grandmother. By the time she returned, Penelope had left and Carrie appeared to be resting comfortably.

"Any news, Allie?"

"Nothing so far. Remember, they say, no news is good news."

Carrie picked up the TV remote and started channel surfing. "I'm so sick of all this wall-to-wall news coverage. I got shot by a psychotic bitch, end of story. Can't people just leave it alone?" She switched channels, suddenly stunned by what she saw on the screen. "What the hell is she doing in the middle of this?"

A reporter was interviewing Louise Dickenson. Carrie turned up the volume. She couldn't believe what she was hearing. Louise had followed Maggie Andrews from the crime scene and had photographed her. Some of the photos appeared on the screen, as the reporter mentioned that the photos helped break the case. Louise was milking it for all it was worth. Carrie felt like throwing the remote at the television set.

"I don't believe it. That woman's been exploiting me since I was eight years old. After today, I thought I'd be rid of her for good, but now she's exploiting me again. What is she? A human cockroach?"

For the first time that afternoon, Allison laughed. "You might be onto something, Carrie. Seriously though, she did you a big favor by following Maggie and taking those photos."

"Trust me, Allie, she didn't do it for me. She did it for herself. Not once during that interview did she express any concern for me or the other victims. Alex had her pegged back when we were kids. It's all about Louise, period."

The nurse came back to take her vitals. "You seem to be doing much better. You're blood pressure is starting to go back down on it's own. Are you still having any pain?"

"A little, but not like before."

"That's encouraging and I think you're on the mend. I'll be back to check you later. With any luck, we'll be able to disconnect your IV sometime in the next few hours."

As she turned to leave, she noticed two people entering the room. They were a pretty middle-aged woman with long red hair, and a tall young man with dark hair and deep-set blue eyes.

"Sorry, visiting hours are almost over."

"It's okay, we're family," replied the woman as she approached Carrie's bedside and extended her hand. "I'm Julia Fields. I'm Jonathan's wife, so I guess that makes me your stepmother. This is our son, Daniel. He's your half brother."

"I see." Carrie wasn't sure what to say. She quickly introduced them to Allison.

"I know this must be awkward for you," said Julia. "We've always known about you, but you probably don't know a thing about us."

"Jonathan—I mean my father, told me a little the day he came to my office. He told me about being a recovering addict and he mentioned you and your son. He said you were his inspiration for staying clean and sober. He also asked me about my father. Not knowing who he really was, I gave him an earful."

"I remember it well," said Julia. "You told him you thought he'd abandoned you."

"And this is where it all gets so confusing. Why didn't he ever come looking for me?"

"He did. Once he arrived in Arizona, and saw you on a TV commercial, he flipped. He thought you were being exploited."

"He was right about that." Carrie looked at Allison. "I just didn't know it at the time."

"He managed to track you down, then you mother warned him that if he ever came anywhere near you, she'd go after him and he'd end up in jail. She was terrified of his former associates. She was afraid they'd come after you."

"I see. So where are they now?"

"Dead and buried, years ago, or so we've heard. As you've already been told, once he got off probation and changed his name, he never looked back. In fact, he now spends a lot of his time working with other addicts trying to go straight."

"Which leaves us as your typical, all-American dysfunctional family," added Danny with a grin.

"You two are definitely related," said Allison with a smile.

"Anyway, I'm here because your father's awake and he would like to see you. Are you ready?"

"I think so."

"Danny, would mind calling the nurse?"

Danny walked to the nurse's station, while Allison helped her with her robe and slippers. He returned a minute later with the nurse. They helped her out of bed, and she held her brother's arm, while Julia pushed her IV pole. She glanced back at Allison as they stepped out.

"I've got your phone right here," she said, holding it up. "You go visit your father. If I hear anything, I'll come get you."

Danny escorted Carrie into the next room. Jonathan looked up as she approached his bedside and embraced him. She started crying as the rest of the family stepped back. Finally, Jonathan told Danny to bring her a chair so she could sit next to him. Penelope handed both of them a tissue as Carrie sat down and took his hand.

"Are you all right, Cara Mia?"

"I'm fine, thanks to you. Are you all right?"

"I'm okay. I suppose if I still had my left kidney I'd have a problem, but someone relieved me of it the night I was stabbed in that parking lot. I'm told the bullet went through me and grazed you before hitting the building across the street. Luckily, no one inside was hurt."

"I can't believe you did what you did." Carrie squeezed his hand. "You saved my life."

"I did what any parent would do. I put your life ahead of my own."

"So why didn't you tell me who you were? That day last fall, at Alex's office, when we were first introduced, I said you looked familiar and I asked if we'd ever met. You said no."

"I know, and I'm sorry. It just wasn't the time or place. I was going to tell you that day at your office. Then that letter arrived, so I had to take care of you."

"I know, and my ranting about how I'd been abandoned by my father, and that he—you, were dead, probably didn't help either. I'm so sorry. I had no idea."

"It's not your fault, Cara Mia. What's done is done. I'm not blaming you, because right or wrong, your mother did what she did thinking she was protecting you. What matters now is where we go from here."

A nurse came in to check on Jonathan just as Allison stepped in to announce that Carrie's dinner had just arrived.

"We'll have to finish this conversation later, Kevin," said Penelope. "Right now, she needs to eat and then you both need to get some rest."

"I'll take her back, Grandma," volunteered Danny. He wrapped his arm around her shoulders and walked her back to her room, waiting until she was back in her bed before stepping away.

"Any word on Alex?"

"Nothing yet," replied Allison. "They haven't been gone long enough to have made it all the way to Tucson."

Carrie quietly ate her meal. After she finished, she settled into her bed. The day had finally caught up with her and she soon fell into an exhausted sleep.

⊱Forty-Six⊰

AFTER CARRIE WENT TO SLEEP, Allison began flipping through the channels, while she anxiously waited for Steve's call. Her heart skipped a beat when she finally heard her phone ring, but her excitement turned to disappointment when the caller ID indicated it was an out-of-state number.

"Hello?"

"Hello, Allison. This is Catherine Montoya. My husband and I just landed in Phoenix, but we're having trouble reaching Alex. Do you know where he is?"

"Sorry, I don't. Alex is missing, Mrs. Montoya."

"What do you mean he's missing? I just spoke to him a few hours ago. We heard about Carrie, so we told him we were on our way. He said to hurry up and get here because he needed us. Do you know if he's claimed the body?"

"I guess you haven't heard. The media got it wrong. Carrie wasn't killed. I'm with her at the hospital."

Allison could hear her talking to her husband. She waited for her to come back on the line.

"Thank goodness, but what happened?"

"She was shot, but fortunately, she wasn't seriously injured. They're keeping her here at the hospital for observation. She thinks she knows where Alex might have gone, so Steve and George McCormick are out looking for him."

Once again Allison waited while Alex's mother passed the information along.

"We're at the rental car counter right now. As soon as we're done, we'll come straight to the hospital, if that's okay. What hospital is she in?"

"Sonoran Southwest," replied Allison and gave them the room number. "There's a police officer guarding the door. Call me as soon as you get here. I'll come down to the lobby to get you."

"Thanks, Allison. At least it's not that far from the airport. We should be there in about twenty minutes or so."

* * *

George and Steve had exited the Interstate and were on the road leading to the Double-Diamond. It was after dark and so far they'd seen no sign of Alex. They were within a quarter mile of the resort entrance when Steve spotted a car off the side of the road.

"Look! It's a white Camaro."

George pulled over in front of the Camaro. Steve leapt out, racing to the driver's side door. The windows were tinted and he couldn't tell if anyone was inside. He peered through the windshield. The car appeared to be empty. He tried both doors, but the car was locked.

"Damn it! Where the hell could he be?"

"Wait a second," said George. "I'll get my lockout tool."

He stood by as George rushed back to his car. Quickly, he inserted the tool, carefully unlocking the driver's side door. He slowly opened it as Steve looked inside.

"Oh my God."

Alex was curled up in the backseat. His face was pale, his eyes were closed and he wasn't moving. Steve called out his name several times, but there was no response. His heart was in his throat as he pushed the seatback forward and felt along Alex's neck for a pulse.

"He's alive, but he's not responding." He began shaking Alex's shoulders. "Come on, buddy, say something. Please. C'mon Alex, talk to me." He heard Alex softly moaning. "That's it, that's it, c'mon, wake up and talk to me."

"Is he all right? Do you need me to call nine-one-one?"

"I don't know, George, maybe. He's hardly responding. What if he's overdosed on something?"

"Keep talking to him while I search inside the car."

Steve stepped aside as George thoroughly examined the inside of the car.

"They're dead," mumbled Alex. "They're dead. They're dead. They're dead."

"I don't see any empty pill containers or booze bottles," said George. "He's probably gone into shock, but it looks like he's trying to come out of it. Give him another minute or two. If he doesn't wake up, then we'll call the paramedics."

Alex slowly opened his eyes. It took him a moment to focus.

"Steve? What the hell are you doing here? Go away."

"I'm not leaving. Alex, listen to me. The news reports were wrong. Carrie's alive. She's at the hospital. Allie's there with her. Come on, I need you to get up."

"Keep talking to him," said George.

"Who's that with you? Whoever you are, get the hell away from me."

"Alex, it's me, George. We're here to take you back to Phoenix. Steve will drive you. There's a very anxious young lady waiting for you at the hospital."

"You're lying!"

"No, Alex, we're not lying," said Steve. "The media got it wrong. Carrie's alive. Come on, buddy, who else would have known you were here?" Steve reached for his phone. "Look, I'll call her, right now."

Alex blinked a few times. He appeared to be coming back to reality.

"So where the hell am I?" He slowly sat up, rubbing his face and looking around. "The Double-Diamond Resort? I remember driving in my car, but I had no idea I ended up here."

"You're in shock," said George, "but you'll be okay. Let me get you some water."

"No! I think I'm going to be sick."

George quickly pulled him out the car. Alex ran to the other side, barely getting there in time, while George stepped away, returning a moment later with a bottle of water. Steve was waiting, with a concerned look on his face.

"He'll be okay," said George. "I think his body's just reacting to the shock."

A disheveled Alex returned a short time later. George handed him the water and Alex began to eagerly drink it down.

"Whoa, buddy, slow down. Sip it, sip it."

"I'm putting this on speaker," announced Steve as he placed the call. Allison quickly answered.

"Did you find him?"

"Yeah, we did. He's right here and he's pretty shook. Can you put Carrie on?"

"Give me a minute. She's asleep. I'll have to wake her."

They could hear Allison waking Carrie up. Alex's ears perked up at the sound of her voice. She quickly put her on the line. Carrie sounded groggy.

"Steve? Is that you?"

"It's me, Carrie. How you feeling, kiddo?"

"All right, I guess. Did you find him yet?"

"Sure did. You were right. He was pulled off the side of the road in front of the Double-Diamond. Would you like to speak to him?"

"Are you kidding?" Carrie's voice suddenly sounded more alert. "Please, put him on. And Steve, thanks. I owe you one."

Steve took the phone off speaker and handed it to Alex. He immediately stepped away from the others.

"Carrie-Anne?" His voice was shaking.

"Alex, are you all right? I've been trying to reach you for hours."

It took Alex a moment to find his voice. "I'm sorry, Carrie-Anne. I guess I messed up. The building was in lockdown. Then Reggie showed me a news report on her tablet. They said you were dead. Everything gets kind of fuzzy after that. I know my mother called me. After that I somehow got out of the building and drove off somewhere. Next thing I know I'm in the backseat of my car and Steve is waking me up. Somehow I've ended up on the side of the road, outside the Double-Diamond Resort, just like Steve said."

"It's okay, Alex. As long as you're safe."

"What about you, Carrie-Anne? Are you all right?"

"I'm fine, Alex. I'm going to be okay. Jonathan Fields stepped in and took the bullet that was meant for me. I was only grazed. Jonathan's okay too. He'll make a full recovery."

"What about the baby?"

"The baby's fine, Alex. They checked me out thoroughly. I'm not going to miscarry, but they're keeping me here at the hospital for awhile, just to be sure." He was silent for a moment. "Alex, are you still there?"

"Yes," he replied, once he'd recomposed himself. "I'm so sorry I failed you, Carrie-Anne. You needed me and I wasn't there."

"It's not your fault. The courthouse was in lockdown. Steve and Allie were here with me, so I wasn't alone. And Alex, you're not going to believe this. It turns out Jonathan Fields is my father."

"What?"

"Jonathan Fields is my father. That's why he stepped in front of the shooter. He saved my life, and the baby's life too."

"I'm sorry, Carrie-Anne. I'm usually on top of things, but right now I'm totally discombobulated. I don't understand any of this."

"Whoops, there's another call coming in. Looks like it's your mother."

"I'm on my way. I love you, Carrie-Anne."

"I love you too, Alex. Take your time and I'll see you when you get here."

Alex disconnected the call and headed back to the car.

"You okay?" asked Steve.

"I don't know. I'm not all here right now. I just want to see Carrie."

"Then hop in the car and I'll take you to her. And by the way, I'm driving."

Alex didn't argue. He walked to the passenger side door and got inside. George said goodnight and Steve walked him to his car, thanking him again for helping. As soon as he drove away, Steve returned to the Camaro and slipped behind the wheel. The keys were still in the ignition. He fastened his seat belt and fired up the engine.

"Did they find the shooter?" asked Alex.

"They sure did. No surprise, it was Maggie Andrews." Steve put the car into gear and turned toward the Interstate.

"Do you know when she'll be arraigned?"

"I'm not sure. My best guess would be sometime tomorrow."

"Thanks." Alex reached for his phone. "I have a friend in the U.S. Attorney's office who owes me a favor. I want her charged with three counts of attempted murder instead of two. Carrie's pregnant and she tried to kill the baby along with her." Alex tried to power up his phone, but it wouldn't respond. "Damn, the battery must be dead. I keep forgetting to recharge my phone. No wonder none of you could reach me. Carrie's going to kick my butt."

"She might at that. Incidentally, that would either be four counts of attempted murder, or murder one, with three counts of attempted murder."

"You mean there's another victim?"

"Yep. She shot Scott along with Carrie and Jonathan. He's not expected to survive."

"Wow," said Alex, taking it all in. "I have no love for the man because of what he did to Carrie, but I wouldn't have wished this on him, especially since he has kids." He stopped for a moment to plug his phone into the car charger. "So what's this about Jonathan Fields being her father?"

"Apparently, it's true. George brought me up to speed on the way down here. It's a long, bizarre story."

"We seem to have some time, so why don't you fill me in?"

ᴥForty-Sevenᴥ

CARRIE HANDED THE phone back to Allison. The called ID indicated Alex's mother was calling.

"I have to go downstairs for a minute," she said as she disconnected the call. "Alex's parents are waiting in the lobby."

"I don't want to see them." Carrie's tone was blunt.

"What do you mean you do want to see them? They heard the news reports that you were killed so they caught the first flight here."

"Really? So did they sound disappointed, when you told them I'm still alive?"

"What? No! Carrie, what's gotten into you?"

"I haven't told anyone about this, because I'm still upset about it. It happened at your wedding reception, Allie, right after I caught your bouquet. Alex's father told him he didn't approve of our relationship, because of my past relationship with Scott and the photo shoot. He said I was a whore."

"What? No way."

"It's true, Allie. When I was young, I thought of him as my surrogate father. Guess I didn't really didn't know him after all."

"So that explains why the two of you left the reception in such a hurry. I'm going downstairs, then we're going to have a little talk."

"Allie, wait! Please, don't say anything."

"Sorry, but this needs to be addressed." Allison headed toward the door. "Would you like for me to get your brother?"

"No thanks, I'm fine."

Allison took the elevator down to the lobby. She spotted Alex's parents as soon as the doors opened. She marched up to Alex's dad.

"We need to talk, right now." She spoke to him in Spanish as she led him to a quiet corner. "So, what's this about you calling Carrie a whore?"

"I didn't say she was a whore. I just said she'd acted like one for doing that photo shoot and going out with a married man."

"Really? With all due respect, where were you? You weren't here, so let me start by telling you about the photo shoot. She was homeless at the time and you have no idea what she went through. None of us did. Steve and I offered her a place to stay, but she refused because she didn't want to impose. She thought she could handle it on her own, but then Louise Dickenson swooped down on her. She knew Carrie had no place to live, so she took advantage of her trust. She led her to believe she was helping her out, when in reality, she was using her in the worst possible way that anyone could be used."

"Couldn't she have stayed in some woman's shelter?"

"Those shelters are for women who are being battered by their boyfriends or spouses, Mr. Montoya. There are too many abused women out there and too few beds in the shelters. Do you honestly think Carrie would have taken up bed space if it meant turning away another woman whose life was in danger?"

"No, she wouldn't have done that."

"Of course she wouldn't have," continued Allison, still speaking Spanish. "So she camped out in her office, but had her landlord found out, she would have been evicted. If that had happened, she would have been out of business, so what choice did she have? She once told me that doing that photo shoot was one of the most humiliating experiences of her life. Why can't you understand this?"

Armando was silent. There was nothing he could say. Allison went on.

"Now, as for her getting involved with a married man, that's my fault, not hers. I'm the one who introduced her to

Scott. He was an acquaintance whom I'd known for years. I thought he was single, so when Carrie asked me, I told her yes, he was single. Come on Mr. Montoya, do you honestly believe that Carrie would have knowingly gone out with someone who was married?"

"No. She never struck me as that type. I know that's not the way she was raised."

"Of course she's not that type. Despite the fact that Scott lied to her, just like he lied to me, Carrie still feels a tremendous amount of guilt over this. But after today, I think it's safe to say she's paid the price for whatever sins she's committed, and she's paid with her own blood. Thankfully, her injuries weren't that serious, because she's also pregnant."

"I know she's pregnant. Alex just told us."

"That means she's carrying your grandchild, Mr. Montoya. She could have easily lost it today, but she didn't. She's strong, she's healthy, and she won't allow it happen, although under the circumstances, I wouldn't blame either Alex or Carrie if they decided to cut you out of your grandchild's life."

"She's right, Armando," said Catherine, speaking English. "I may not be totally fluent in Spanish, but I was able to follow most of what she said. We've made some false assumptions. Alex tried to tell us, but we wouldn't listen. I guess we're both guilty of thinking that no one is good enough for our son, but I don't want our pride to cause us to lose our grandchild."

"I don't either, Catherine." He looked back at Allison. "But I still have a problem with this."

"Then I don't know what else to tell you, sir" said Allison. "I guess it's just something you'll have to learn to live with. That's what she's had to do."

"What about Alex?" asked Catherine. "Is there any news on our son?"

"Yes. Steve called a short time ago. They've found Alex, safe and sound, and he's on his way here."

"Thank goodness, so where was he?"

"They found him just outside Tucson, near the Double-Diamond Resort. It's a special place for him and Carrie. That's how she knew where to find him. If not for her, Alex would still be missing."

Allison took them to the elevator. As they approached Carrie's room, they noticed several police officers gathered outside her door.

"What's going on?" asked Allison.

"Some paparazzi reporter just tried to sneak into her room," explained one of the officers. "He'd tried to disguise himself as a hospital worker, but he wasn't wearing a proper ID badge."

"Is Carrie all right?"

"She's fine. We stopped him before he got to her and he's been escorted out of the building. We've also informed him that if he tries to come back in we'll arrest him."

Allison introduced Alex's parents to the officers, saying they'd be allowed to visit. She brought them into Carrie's room. She was sitting up in bed. Danny was with her.

"I'm going back to our father's room," he told Allison. "If you need to go someplace, come get me, or another family member, and we'll stay with her until you get back. She's not to be left alone. Dad's orders."

"Got it, and I'm sorry this happened."

"It's okay." Danny told his sister goodbye as he left.

"Who was that?" asked Armando.

"Her half brother," replied Allison, while Carrie shot him a cold look.

"Come again?"

"It turns out Jonathan Fields is Carrie's father."

"You mean Jonathan Fields is really Kevin Daniels?"

"That's right," said Allison.

"Well, I'll be damned."

"So, how much do you know about my father?" They all heard the anger in Carrie's voice.

"Years ago," explained Armando, "when you were still a minor, your mother drew up some papers making Catherine and me your legal guardians in case anything ever happened to her. She told us who your father was, but she made it crystal clear that he was to never be anywhere near you. She told us the whole story. She said your father was a drug addict who—"

"I already know all about it," said Carrie. "He told me, and my grandmother told me. It all happened twenty-five years ago, and he's been clean ever since. He's now a respectable businessman, with a wife and a son, who you just saw."

"That's good, Carrie. I'm happy he got his life back and I sincerely hope it all works out for you. I'm just letting you know what your mother told us."

"Carrie, are you all right?" asked Catherine.

"I'm fine, all things considered. I was only grazed, because my father shielded me. Allie tells me you came because the media reported that I'd been killed. I have no idea how that rumor got started. I'm sorry if it scared you."

"It scared us alright. As soon as we heard, I called Alex. I've never ever heard that sound in his voice before. His entire world had been shattered. He told us to come, as soon as we could, because he needed us. He also said that you were pregnant."

"Did he say anything else?"

"No. The call suddenly dropped. I tried calling back, but something must have gone wrong with his phone. The calls kept going to voice mail, and he never called back."

"Alex is fine," said Carrie, matter-of-factly. "He was found a short time ago."

"Yes, we know," said Armando "Allie filled us in."

"So, let me guess your next question. You want to know if Alex is really the baby's father. Sorry to disappoint you, but the answer is yes. I know you think I'm a tramp, but trust me, your son's been the only man in my life for sometime now, although I'm sure we can arrange a paternity test if you'd like."

While Carrie was speaking, a nurse entered the room to check on her. The others silently stood by as she worked.

"Your blood pressure's starting to go back up," she said. "Not too much, but you need to calm down. You're not out of the woods yet." She looked at the others. "Sorry, but unless you're immediate family, I'm afraid I'm going to have to ask you all to leave. Visiting hours are over and she's had enough excitement for now. She needs her rest."

"But they've finally found Alex," pleaded Carrie. "He's my significant other and he's the baby's father. He's on his way and I haven't seen him since I got here. Please, I have to see him. I need him here with me."

"Alright, alright. Calm down. You can see him, but only for a little while. It's getting late and you need to get some rest."

"Thank you." They heard the relief in her voice.

"Her family doesn't want her left alone," explained Allison. "Some reporter just tried to sneak in, so I'd like to stay with her until Alex gets here. I promise I'll leave the minute he arrives."

"Alright, but I'll only allow one visitor at a time."

"My husband and I can wait in the lobby," said Catherine. "Good night, Carrie. We're glad you're okay."

As Alex's parents followed the nurse out, Carrie settled back into her bed. Penelope and Danny stepped in a short time later, letting her know the family was leaving, but would return the following morning. After they left, she went back to sleep. It was after nine o'clock and it had been a long, stressful day for everyone. Allison leaned back into her chair and began to doze off.

☙Forty-Eight☙

STEVE TURNED THE CAMARO into the main entrance at Sonoran Southwest Medical Center. Big news trucks with satellite dishes were stationed around the main building and the front lawn looked like a shrine. It was filling up with dozens upon dozens of flowers, balloons, stuffed animals, hand-painted signs and lighted candles while a steady stream of well wishers added more.

"What the hell is this?"

"The whole town's apparently gone nuts," explained Steve. "It's been like this for hours. I suppose it's because it's a high-profile case, and Carrie's still something of a public figure."

"Yeah, but the damn news vultures need to leave her alone. Looks like I'll need to have some security at the house once she's released."

"Wouldn't be a bad idea."

It was several minutes before a parking space finally opened up. Once the car was secured, they headed toward the entrance doors. The ten o'clock newscasts had just started and a few of the reporters recognized Alex.

"I have no comment," he repeated over and over as they pushed their way past the cameras and entered the building. Fortunately, there were police officers standing by the door, blocking the press from following them inside.

"Alex!"

Catherine waved as they stepped into the lobby. Alex rushed up to both his parents and held them tight. Steve stepped aside and called Allison.

"We're in the lobby. How's Carrie?"

"Asleep. She's finally resting comfortably. Overall she's doing better, but she got a little agitated when Alex's parents arrived."

"Really? Why was that?"

"Alex's dad has issues with her for doing the photo shoot and for going out with Scott. I tried explaining it to him, but he still has a problem with it."

"He's old school and from a foreign country." Steve looked over and watched Alex with his parents. "Although something tells me that whatever it is, they'll be able to work through it. Why don't you meet me down here? It's late and we need to head home. Once you're here, we'll send Alex up."

"On my way. I'll be there in a minute."

The elevator doors soon opened and Allison stepped into the lobby. She greeted Alex with a warm hug.

"I'm so relieved to finally see you, safe and sound. Carrie and I both were worried sick."

"I'm sorry that happened, Allie. I know I should have been there with her—"

"None of this is your fault, Alex," she said, quickly cutting him off. "What matters is you're here now, and she and the baby are okay. Visiting hours are over, but Carrie spoke to the nurse so they'll let you go up and see her. I also overheard them saying they plan to release her sometime tomorrow."

"We'll catch you later, buddy," said Steve, "and give her a big kiss for me."

Alex thanked Steve once again before he and Allison headed out the door. Once they left, he turned back to his parents.

"We'd like to crash in your guestroom, if that's okay," said Catherine.

"That's what I had in mind, Mom. Do you need me to take you to the house?"

"We're fine," said Armando. "We rented a car, but we'll wait here while you go see her. You look exhausted, and I think one of us should drive you home."

"Thanks, Dad. It's been a hell of a day. I won't be too long."

He stepped into the elevator and quickly headed to Carrie's room.

"I take it you're Alex," said the officer at her door, " but I'll still need to check your ID."

He produced his driver's license and the officer waved him through. He walked through the doorway, stopping abruptly as soon as he saw her. Carrie was sound asleep. He winced at the sight of the IV, but it didn't seem to be bothering her. He walked to her bedside and began stroking her hair. She began stirring. As soon as she saw him, her eyes opened wide as she let out a gasp. She shot up in her bed and they both immediately wrapped their arms tightly around each other, crying.

"Well, this must be a good thing." Dr. Arnold had just entered the room. "You must be Alex." He walked up and extended his hand.

"Yes, sir, I am."

"Have a seat." The doctor grabbed the box of tissues and offered it to both before pointing to a chair for Alex and turning back to Carrie. "I've reviewed the ultrasound and I've just gone over your latest blood work. Better get the nursery ready, because somewhere around September eighth, you two are going to be parents. "

"You mean that's my due date?"

"Yes, it'll be around that time. The nurse will come in a little while to disconnect your IV, however, I'm keeping you here until tomorrow, just to be sure there are no other complications. Once you're home, I want you on bed rest until your regular doctor says it's okay for you to resume your normal activity. You still have a gunshot wound and we have to watch out for infections, which is why I'll be prescribing some antibiotics. You'll need to stay on them until they're completely gone."

"I'm taking a few days off work and my parents are in town," said Alex. "Don't worry, there'll be someone around to look after her."

Dr. Arnold looked closely at Alex. "You know, at the moment, I'm honestly more concerned about you than I am about her. You don't look so good."

"It's been a bad day. I was in a secluded room in the courthouse, when the shooting happened. I didn't know about it until sometime later."

"Someone mentioned you'd heard the reports about her being killed. We set the media straight as soon as we found out about it."

"Unfortunately, I didn't hear that part. I recall sneaking out of the building and driving somewhere, then a couple hours ago my friends finally found me. I'd pulled the car off the side of the road just outside of Tucson."

"Sounds like you went into shock. I'd really like to have you checked out."

"I think I'm okay," argued Alex. "I probably just need some food. I think the last time I ate was just before noon, but it all came back up after my friends found me."

"No doubt you're dehydrated and your blood sugar's probably dropped. The cafeteria's closed, but I can have someone bring you a bottle of water and a sandwich."

"That sounds good," said Carrie. "Can you make it two?"

"My pleasure." Dr. Arnold turned back to Alex. "I've given her something for the nausea. She tells me she's lost a little weight since the pregnancy started. That's not uncommon during the first trimester, but now I want her to start gaining." He turned back to Carrie. "If he's not looking better after he eats, then please send him down to the ER."

"Will do," she replied.

Alex thanked the doctor before he stepped out. Their sandwiches arrived a short time later. As they ate Carrie noticed the color returning to his face.

"You know, Carrie-Anne, today was supposed to be a very special day for us. I'd made reservations for us tonight at The Saddleback."

"The Saddleback? That's the swankiest place in town."

"I know. We were going to celebrate Louise finally being out of your life, and I had another surprise planned for you as well."

He'd draped his coat over the back of a chair. He leaned forward to take something out of the pocket, but before he could say anything, the nurse came back in to check on Carrie and remove her IV. He dropped it into his pants pocket.

"You're doing much better, now that Alex is finally here," she said with a smile.

"I know." Her face was beaming. "He's the best medicine I could have."

As she was removing the IV, Carrie asked about her father.

"He's awake and doing remarkably well. Once I'm done, you can go tell him goodnight, but keep it short. After that, you'll need to send Alex home. He looks beat and he needs his rest too."

She left and Alex handed Carrie her robe and slippers. As soon as she was ready, he walked her to her father's room. Jonathan was propped up in bed, watching television.

"Daddy?"

"Come in, Cara Mia. I was just watching the ten o'clock news. They're still trying to save face over their earlier mistake about you, and Scott Andrews is still clinging to life. Hopefully he'll make it, for his kids' sake."

"Hopefully," she said as Alex pulled up a couple of chairs.

"And I see Alex has finally been found. Glad you're alright, but you look like hell."

"Thank you, sir," said Alex. "It's been one hell of a day. George McCormick told my friend Steve who you really are, and then Steve filled me in. I admit I'm completely blown away. I went through all of her mother's papers right after she passed away. We found a photo of you, along with some old court records, although part of the file was missing. We knew you'd been stabbed, but there was nothing indicating that you'd survived, so we both thought you were dead."

"As Mark Twain once said, 'Reports of my death are greatly exaggerated.' In point of fact, however, Linda knew all along that I was alive and well. I hunted her down right after I came to Tucson and started seeing Carrie on TV pitching Mercers Markets. I didn't approve of my daughter being used like that, but unfortunately, at the time I wasn't in the position I'm in now. I'd just gotten off probation and my jail sentence had just been dismissed."

"I understand," said Alex.

"Unfortunately, legal aid wasn't much help. Back then, I wasn't fully aware of what my rights were as a parent, nor did I have the resources to hire an attorney to fight for those rights. Linda had taken out a restraining order, and I knew if I forced the issue, I'd end up in jail. It would be a few years before I was finally able to hire an attorney, and by then, Carrie was a teenager. That's when Linda finally agreed to meet with the attorney and me."

Carrie let out a gasp. "What? When was this?"

"It was at the beginning of your freshman year of high school, Carrie, and yes, your mother and I met in person. I'd remarried by then, so your stepmother was there too. First, your mother assured us that you were doing well. She also said you believed I'd abandoned you and that you hated me. I said I wanted to see you so I could set the record straight. That's when she made the point, quite clearly, that if I ever tried to make contact with you she'd immediately take out another restraining order and flee the state. My attorney warned her that if she did she'd be charged with parental kidnapping but your mother didn't care. She said she was willing to risk going to jail if it meant keeping me away from you."

"I don't understand," said Carrie. "This doesn't sound like Mama. I was fifteen years old at the time. So why wouldn't she have told me and at least given me the chance to decide for myself if I wanted to see you or not?"

Jonathan let out a sigh. "We all have our darker sides, Cara Mia. I know her original intention was to protect you. That I understood. Let's face it. Off and on, for about a year or so, I was strung out on coke. It made me a lousy father and she didn't want to risk you being exposed to it again. Had the situation had been reversed, I might have done the same thing. But as the years passed, it had apparently grown into something more, and I didn't want your mother using you as a pawn for getting even me. So, rather than cause you any more pain and anguish, or having your mother end up in jail, I decided you'd be better off if I stayed out of your life. It was the most agonizing decision I've ever made. You know the rest of the story."

"So that explains why some of the records were missing," said Carrie. "Mama didn't want me going through her papers and finding out you were still alive. How could she do that to me?"

"Let's not dwell on it, okay Cara Mia? It's over and done with and we can't go back and change it. So, here we are. I've finally got my daughter back, just in time to learn she's in a family way."

"I'm so sorry Reggie inadvertently blurted it out. Neither one of us had a clue as to who you really were. No wonder the color drained from your face."

"You both thought I was the computer nerd who you'd never see again. Then, when the bullet struck me, I honestly thought I was about to die. That's why I called you Cara Mia, hoping you'd make the connection, which you immediately did. I didn't want to die knowing that you still hated me."

Carrie stood up to embrace him and they both quietly held

one another. Alex waited patiently until Carrie returned to her seat, dabbing her eyes with a tissue.

"The reason why I wanted to talk to you, sir," explained Alex, "is because I was raised by a Spanish immigrant father and I guess I still respect some of the old customs. I wanted to ask your permission for your daughter's hand in marriage."

Carrie let out a quiet gasp as she reached for another tissue.

"Carrie and I have known one another since we were children. We grew up together, but then we lost touch with one another after we started college. However, as the years went by, I came to realize that she was the only woman I'd ever truly love. Fate brought us back together, despite the peculiar circumstances, the same way it brought you and her back together."

Jonathan waited for a moment before giving his answer. "Well, all things considered, I guess I can't say no, can I?"

"I suppose not, but just so you know, this wasn't a planned pregnancy. We only learned about the baby a few days ago ourselves."

"Let me clue you in on something, son," said Jonathan, "they're usually not planned, trust me on that. But even if she wasn't expecting, I would have still given you my blessing. I'm not blind, you know. I watched the two of you that day in your office, and the day she got the threatening letter. You two are soul mates, just like her stepmother and me."

Alex reached into his pocket. "And just so you know, Carrie-Anne, I bought this for you last December, right after my birthday. Then I decided that rather than giving it to you for Christmas, I'd give it to you tonight at The Saddleback, but that didn't happen either. So, here goes…"

Alex opened box, revealing the diamond engagement ring inside. He reached over and slipped it on her finger.

"And if you don't say yes, sister, I'll marry him." Another nurse had just entered the room. She was short and heavy-set, with thick glasses and short, curly gray hair. "So, what's it gonna be? The doctor's on his way, and I don't have all night."

"Well, of course my answer is yes. Thank you for asking." There was a mock exasperation in her voice.

"Good answer, and while I hate to break up this special moment, you need your rest, your father needs his rest, and your fiancé here looks like he's about ready to drop, so I'm kicking him out of this hospital, right now. He needs to go home and get some shut eye."

"Can I at least walk him to the elevator?"

"Go ahead, but don't take too long."

"Goodnight Jonathan, and good luck with that one," said Alex. "I'll be back in the morning."

Carrie kissed her father goodnight and walked Alex to the elevator.

"That old battle axe is right, you know," said Carrie. "You look exhausted. Go home and get some rest. I'll be fine for the rest of the night."

"I will. Goodnight, Carrie-Anne. I'll be back in the morning."

"I'll be here."

They gave each other a long, lingering kiss while they waited for the elevator. After he left, Carrie headed back to her room, finding several nurses had gathered there.

"We just heard congratulations are in order," said one.

"So don't just stand there," said another. "Show us the ring."

Carrie held out her hand. Her face was beaming.

"Nice one."

"Get some rest," said another, helping her into her bed. "You're going to need it. He looks like a real stud muffin."

"He is."

They all had a laugh as Carrie settled in her bed, relieved that the worst was now behind her. The nurses left, and before long she drifted off into a deep, heavy sleep.

❧Forty-Nine❧

CARRIE WAS AWAKENED BY the sunlight streaming in through her window. She opened her eyes and looked around the room, trying to get her bearings. She spotted Catherine Montoya, reading a book as she sat in a nearby chair.

"Good morning, Carrie. How are you feeling?"

"A little disoriented. For a moment there I thought it had all been a bad dream. So what time is it?"

"A few minutes past nine." Catherine glanced at her watch. "Alex is at home. Still asleep, the last I heard."

Carrie looked down at her left hand. She smiled as she gazed at her diamond ring. It hadn't been a dream either.

"I know, I saw." At least Catherine had a smile. "Alex told us about it last night."

"Are you guys okay with this?"

"Of course we're okay with this, and we couldn't be happier. Honestly, Carrie, this whole thing has been blown way out of proportion. My husband can be an opinionated, cantankerous old curmudgeon when it suits him. Half the time he doesn't mean it, the rest of the time he gets over it. Over the years, I've learned not to take it too seriously. That said, he was really, truly shocked when he first learned about your recent past. We both were. He always thought of you like a daughter. He understands that Scott lied to both you and Allison, but he's still troubled knowing there are people out there looking at those photos and thinking of you in such a way. Deep down he feels guilty, because we weren't here when you were in such desperate need. We lost touch with Linda after you'd lost touch with Alex."

"So, how are we feeling today?" A nurse came into the room. "I see you're finally awake, and I heard there was some excitement around here last night. Let me see the ring."

Carrie extended her left hand. Her face was beaming.

"Very pretty." She started taking Carrie's pulse and blood pressure. They waited quietly while she worked. "Everything looks good, and the doctor plans on releasing you in a few hours."

"Thank goodness. I want to go home, but first I want to see my father."

"You can see him in a few minutes. The doctor's in there with him now."

"Is he okay?"

"He's doing very well. They're plan to release him this weekend, if not sooner. Meantime, how 'bout you? Any pain or nausea?"

"Actually, it's the first time in weeks I haven't woken up nauseous. Whatever he's given me for the morning sickness sure works."

"Good to hear. We'll bring you some breakfast in a little while."

"You know what I'd like instead? I'd really like a banana split. With extra caramel sauce."

"You're definitely pregnant," she said with a laugh. "With me it was pepperoni pizza with onions. Couldn't get enough of it."

"Chinese food here," added Catherine. "Sweet and sour pork, and it had to be on fried rice."

All three laughed, then Carrie asked the nurse if she could take a shower.

"Let's check your bandage." Carrie pulled up the side of her nightshirt, allowing the nurse to inspect it. "Looks like it's waterproof, but be careful and try to avoid getting it wet. We'll change it later on today and instruct you on how to take care of it once you're home."

The nurse stepped out and Carrie asked for her overnight bag. Catherine handed it to her and she eagerly rummaged through it. "Yes! Allie remembered my sweats, and a pair of tennis shoes."

She grabbed her gear and headed off to the bathroom. The shower felt invigorating. It was as if she were washing away all of the tragedy from the day before. She emerged in her sweats and began combing out her hair.

"Good morning." Julia and Danny walked into the room. "We just heard the news and we want to see the ring."

Carrie smiled and once again extended her left hand. As she was introducing Catherine to her brother and stepmother, the banana spilt arrived.

"Yuk." Danny winced as Carrie sat down on the bed and eagerly dove in.

"She's expecting, son, which means you're going to be an uncle."

"But I'm still trying to get used to being a brother," he said with a smile.

"Jonathan called me last night, after your son left," explained Julia to Catherine. "He told us about the baby, and about Alex asking her to marry him. He's still in the shock over becoming a grandfather. Is this your first grandchild?"

"Third. And don't worry, you get used to it. Times have changed. The image of gray-haired grandparents sitting in their rocking chairs on the front porch is definitely outdated. We still love rock and roll, and we spend most of our weekends on a Harley."

"Morning, Carrie-Anne." Alex and his father entered the room. He presented her with a bouquet of long-stemmed red roses.

"Alex, you shouldn't have."

"Only the best for you, future wife and mother of my child."

He bent over to give her a kiss before setting the roses next to her bed. Carrie noticed he was wearing blue jeans and a sweater instead of his usual business suit.

"And in case you're wondering, no, I'm not going to the office today. Reggie called a little while ago and told me to take the rest of the week off. She won't be going in today either, but she said to tell you she's coming to see you later. So, what exactly are you eating?"

"Breakfast," she smugly replied. "They gave me something

for the morning sickness, so I'm enjoying this banana split, especially now that it's getting all gooey and runny."

"Okay," said Julia. "Now that we're all here, I'd like for you all to come next door with me. Jonathan wants to have a little family discussion about the wedding."

Carrie grabbed what was left of her banana split. As she came into her father's room, she greeted him and Penelope with a hug and a kiss on the cheek before taking her seat. He too winced at what she was eating, while Alex quickly made the introductions.

"I know it's short notice," said Jonathan, "but under the circumstances, we need to get rolling on this wedding. Have the two of you thought about a date yet?"

"Actually," replied Alex. "I was thinking of waiting until after the baby's born. Carrie's been under a tremendous amount of stress with Louise's lawsuit, and what happened yesterday certainly didn't help. I just want to get her through this pregnancy without stressing her out over a wedding."

The room suddenly went silent. Everyone looked at Alex with an incredulous stare.

"Don't look now, counselor," muttered Carrie as she began scraping the bottom of her bowl, "but I think you've just failed to sway the jury."

"What?"

Jonathan finally broke the silence. "Sorry, son, but that was the wrong answer."

Alex turned to his own father.

"Don't look at me," said Armando, "I'm on his side. Look, Alex, no child wants to be born out of wedlock, and we're most certainly not going to allow it to happen to our grandchild."

Alex looked at Carrie. "So, what about you?"

"Honestly?"

"I wouldn't have it any other way."

"It's not that I don't love you Alex…"

"But you're siding with them, aren't you?" She shrugged her shoulders and nodded her head. Alex threw his hands in the air in mock despair. "Okay, you all win. I guess this means I've lost my case."

"Don't worry, Alex." Carrie patted him on the back. "It happens from time to time. You'll get over it."

"So, did the two of you have your hearts set on a big wedding with all the trimmings?" asked Jonathan.

"Not really," she replied. "I mean a big wedding's nice, if you have the time. We don't, and besides, they cost a lot of money."

"Don't worry about the cost, Carrie, I'm taking care of it."

"Thanks, Jonathan," said Alex, "I appreciate the thought, but we can handle it."

"You two might want to save your money for other things, like starting up a college fund. She's my daughter, so I'll take care of it. Since I wasn't there when she was younger, I need to do whatever I can to make things up to her now. I've already picked up the tab for her legal expenses, so—"

"That was you?" asked Carrie, amazed.

"Well off course it was me. Who'd you think it was?"

"Honestly, I had no idea, but of course, now it all makes sense." She walked up and kissed him. "Thank you, Daddy for being there. That was such a horrible nightmare."

"But as bad as it was, Cara Mia, it led me back to you, so now we're going to move forward, to much better days, okay?"

"Okay," she said as she gave him another hug and kiss.

"And since I'm the father of the bride, it's settled," said Jonathan. "So what we have to decide next is where and when, and the sooner, the better."

"I'm on bed rest for at least a week, Dad, and they won't be releasing you for a few more days. We both need some time to recuperate."

"I understand that, Cara Mia, but we need to get this done before you start showing."

"In that case we have some time. I'm only in my ninth week."

As they were talking, Billie Hughes stepped in. Carrie quickly introduced her to her father and the others.

"They're arraigning Maggie Andrews this afternoon at two o'clock," Billie explained. "I need to go over some things with you and Jonathan. So if the rest of you don't mind?"

"No problem," said Julia. "While you're doing that, I'll step into Carrie's room to make some phone calls." She looked at Alex. "The Double-Diamond is a special place for the two of you? Right?"

"Yes, very special," said Alex.

"They do weddings, and they're also one of our clients. I'll give them a call to find out what dates they have open, and see what they can do."

Julia stepped out, taking rest of the family, and Alex's parents, with her. Alex stayed behind with Carrie.

"Don't mind us," said Carrie to Billie, "we're just planning a little wedding."

"I understand, and congratulations." She stopped to admire the ring.

"What are the charges against Maggie so far?" asked Alex.

"Four counts of attempted first-degree murder."

"Good. So that means they're charging her for trying to kill the baby as well, and it sounds like Scott Andrews is still alive."

"He was, the last we checked. Apparently, it was touch and go for most of the night last night, but he rallied early this morning. Now they're saying he has a fifty-fifty chance. His fiancée arrived shortly after midnight. She tells me that once he's stable enough to travel she plans to take him, and the kids, back to Kansas City."

"You know, those kids really are the other victims," said Alex. "They've nearly lost their father and they'll most certainly lose their mother as well. Maggie will probably spend the rest of her life in prison. What was she thinking?"

"That she'd never get caught," said Billie. "Ken O'Dell said she was one of the most defiant criminals he's ever dealt with."

They got down to business, getting one last interview with both Jonathan and Carrie.

"That should do it." Billie dropped her notepad into her purse. "I'm heading back to the office, then I'll be going to the arraignment."

"I'll see you there," said Alex.

"You're going?" asked Carrie.

"I wouldn't miss it. I plan on being there each and every step of the way until she's carted off to prison. I intend to see that justice is served."

"As do I," added Jonathan. "Julia will be there as well."

A nurse came to check on Jonathan. Carrie kissed her father goodbye and Alex walked her to back her room where they found Julia, Catherine and Penelope busy going over notes on Julia's tablet while Danny and Armando stood off to the side. Penelope walked up to Carrie.

"Danny and I are heading back to Tucson," she said. "He needs to get back to school and I need to get back as well." She gave Carrie hug, holding the embrace. "You have no idea how happy I am to finally have my granddaughter back."

"Me too, Grandma. I've missed you, so much."

She gave her brother a goodbye hug before walking them to the door.

"You know, they're good people," said Armando after they'd stepped out. "I really think Linda should have allowed him to see Carrie. He's a good father."

"He is now," agreed Julia, "however Jonathan's admitted that there were many, many times when Linda came home from work to find Carrie hungry, crying and neglected, while he was so high on coke that he was completely unaware of anything being wrong."

"I can't even begin to imagine what that must have been like," said Catherine.

"I can't either," agreed Julia. "He's been an incredibly good father to Danny, but he still feels a tremendous amount of guilt over you, Carrie, so please, let him take care of the wedding for you. He needs to do this for himself as much as for you." She reached for her tablet. "The Double-Diamond has an opening for a wedding the first weekend in April. That's about eight weeks from now, which should be more than enough time for both of you to fully recover."

"That'll put me at four months. So if I am showing by then, it won't be very much."

"Then let's book it," said Alex, looking at his parents. "Will that work for you?"

"You tell us when and we'll be there," said Armando. "And as long as it's a weekend your brother can make it too."

"And I've already told Julia that I can help her," added Catherine. "So don't worry, you kids will have a nice wedding, even if it is on short notice."

Julia started making more notes while the nurse came back into the room.

"I need to change the bandages, and once I've finished with the rest of your paperwork you can go home."

"Thank goodness." Carrie laid back down on the bed. She pulled up her top just enough to expose the bandage.

"Oh my God," said Alex as the nurse removed it.

"Actually, it's healing quite nicely," she said reassuringly, "and there's no sign of any infection." As she put on fresh bandages, she noticed Alex looked a little green.

"I can help take care of it," said Catherine. "He's a bit squeamish."

"Better get used to it," said Julia. "You'd be amazed at all the cuts, scrapes, skinned knees and other things kids will get."

"I couldn't agree more," said another woman's voice.

They looked up to see Reggie entering the room with a bouquet of flowers, greeting Carrie with as hug as the nurse left.

"You have no idea how happy I am to see you safe and sound. I was standing near the exit yesterday when the shooting started. I saw both you, and Jonathan, going down. I tried to help, but the security guards were already blocking the exits and holding us back. Next thing I knew there were police cars and helicopters everywhere and everyone inside the atrium was watching live newsfeeds on their tablets. Then I started hearing people saying you'd been killed." She reached into her purse for a tissue. "Sorry guys, I'm still pretty shook."

"It's okay, Reggie," assured Carrie. "We're both fine now. They're even thinking that Scott Andrews might make it."

Reggie was brought up to date on Carrie's condition and told about Jonathan being her father. Like the others, the news took her by complete surprise. Carrie and Alex then showed her the diamond engagement ring.

"Well, it's about time, Alex. You still have some vacation time coming, so don't worry, you can have a honeymoon. Have you set the date yet?"

"First Saturday in April," he replied, "and the wedding's in Tucson, so anyone who wants to attend should be able to."

The nurse came back in to announce that Carrie had just been released. She took a few minutes to go over her discharge instructions.

"Someone will be bringing in a wheelchair shortly," she explained, "but with all the press hanging around we plan on taking her out the back. Problem is, there are reporters stationed at all the doors, even the service entrances. We can send some security guards with her, but be aware that you're still probably going to be hounded by the press."

"Wait a minute," said Armando, looking at Reggie. "Would you mind standing next to her?" Reggie walked over and stood next to Carrie. "See that? They're close to the same height and weight, and their hair looks similar too."

"I know where you're going, Dad, and I think it'll work." Alex turned to Carrie. "Would you mind if Reggie put on your robe and your slippers?"

"Not at all." Carrie began taking them out of her overnight bag.

"Are you okay with this, Reggie? We'll take you out first, load you into my car and take off. Then, as soon as the reporters leave, my parents can take Carrie home."

"Are you kidding? It sounds like fun. Besides, I'd just as soon share a ride with you to the arraignment. I'll even buy lunch, as long as you bring me back to my car later."

"Can I go with you?" asked Julia. "I'm planning on going to the arraignment as well, and afterwards I need to go pick up Jonathan's car. It was parked in one of the parking garages. Hopefully, it's still there."

Alex jotted down his cell phone number on the back of one of his business cards.

"Let me know if there's a problem with the car, Julia. I'll take care of it."

Reggie put on Carrie's robe and slippers while the nurse stepped away to get a second wheelchair.

"Your shoes are in my overnight bag." Carrie handed it to Reggie. "And I'll need you to take some of the flowers with you as well."

"We'll take care of the flowers," said Julia. "Just go tell your father goodbye."

Carrie stepped out, returning just in time for both wheelchairs to arrive. She grabbed her purse and the roses before taking her seat in one as Reggie sat down in the other. Both women put their sunglasses on and Reggie looked at Carrie.

"Ready?"

"Let's do it," replied Carrie.

Reggie placed the overnight bag in her lap. Julia gathered up the rest of the flowers while Alex kissed Carrie goodbye and headed out to the parking lot with his father. The rest of them took the service elevator to the back door where they nervously waited for Alex. A few minutes later, the white Camaro pulled up. Both women took a deep breath as the attendant opened the door and wheeled Reggie outside. The reporters and cameramen began to swarm around them. Julia quickly scrambled into the backseat, as Alex helped Reggie into the passenger seat. Once she was settled he hoped in and took off.

"Damn, that was scary," said Reggie as they pulled away. "One second thought, you're buying lunch today, Montoya."

"That can be arranged." Alex turned onto the main road. "Did they take the bait?"

"Hook, line and sinker," said Julia as she peered out the back window. "Don't look now, but we've got one, make that two, news trucks behind us."

"We've got some time before the arraignment, so I'll give

them the scenic tour, then I'll buy you two ladies lunch. Meantime, Reggie, would you mind calling Carrie? I need to make sure she got out all right."

Reggie pulled out her phone and placed the call. A few minutes later she turned back to Alex.

"She says they got out without any incident, and they're stopping at a drive thru on the way home."

ᚼ Fifty ᚼ

LOUISE DICKENSON PUT ON her robe and stepped outside to fetch the morning paper. She brought it in and dropped it on the kitchen table, unfolding it as she sipped her coffee. A big smile broke out across her face.

"Look Karl, they've published some of the photos I took yesterday on the front page, and the caption credits me as the photographer."

"That's nice."

"Of course it's nice. Look out Phoenix, Louise Dickenson is back."

She turned her attention back to the newspaper, noting the date. It was nearly a year to the day since her opening at Hanson Sister's Fine Art, and the year had not been a kind one. First, Hanson Sisters dropped her, and she'd had no luck finding another gallery to represent her. She tried reviving her commercial photography business, but many of her old clientele had either retired or moved away. Many more were working with Carrie Daniels and not interested in coming back. Louise had no choice. She had to put Carrie out of business with her copyright infringement claim. That too had backfired, until fate smiled and someone took a shot at Carrie.

"You know, Karl, I'm thinking of going back to being a free lance photojournalist."

"So where are you going to get the funds to get started? You've squandered away most of our cash on that ridiculous lawsuit, and now you've been ordered to pay for Scott and Carrie's court costs."

"Just because some judge ordered it doesn't mean I have to write her a check right now. I'm going to make them come after me. Meantime, I have to make a very important phone call. Caleb Wyman has wanted to buy the rights to the remaining photos of Carrie for sometime now, but I couldn't sell them because of the lawsuit. Now, all bets are off." She took a sip of her coffee. "You know, maybe it's all worked out for the best. After today, I'll be sitting pretty." She chuckled to herself as she took another sip of her coffee. "I'm going to the arraignment this afternoon. Would you like to come with me?"

"You go ahead. I think I'll pass."

* * *

A deputy escorted a shackled Maggie Andrews into the courtroom and sat her down on a bench. She looked at her attorney, who was from the public defender's office. Her thoughts turned to Scott, who needed to hurry up and die—the sooner the better. Once she had the life insurance money, she'd be able to get someone like Frederick Lancaster to represent her, and then she could buy her freedom.

Alex entered the courtroom, along with Reggie and Julia, and they took their seats in the gallery. It had been an emotional journey for both him and Reggie. Entering the glass atrium, barely twenty-four hours after the shooting, caused the events of the previous day to play back in their minds. Reggie reached into her purse for another tissue. Alex glanced around and noticed Louise Dickenson seated nearby. No doubt she'd come seeking more publicity for herself. He turned his attention to Maggie. Had it not been for the orange jail suit she was wearing, she could have easily passed for the president of her local PTA. How could such a typical, all-American looking woman have nearly destroyed his life?

The bailiff entered the courtroom and all were ordered to rise for the judge. She entered, and ordered everyone to be seated. When Maggie's case was called, her attorney waived arraignment and entered a not guilty plea on her behalf to all four counts of attempted murder. The judge ordered the case to go to trial. It was over in a matter of minutes. The deputy U.S. Marshalls whisked her away as they exited the courtroom. Out in the hallway, Louise approached Alex and Reggie.

"So, Alex, you may have won the battle, but I'll win the war."

"Whatever, Louise." They began to walk away.

"Hey, don't you go turning your back on me! Aren't you forgetting the fact that I still own the rights to all those photos of Carrie?"

All three stopped in their tracks, turning back to face Louise as she casually approached Alex a second time.

"I've been on the phone today with Caleb Wyman. Remember him? He's the publisher of *Gentry Magazine*."

"So what's your point, Louise?"

"My point is, dear Alex, that he and I have made a deal. He's sending me a big fat check, and I'm signing over the rights to all the photos. There are well over a hundred of them, so look for her to be featured in upcoming issues. Just so you know, this is business and nothing personal. Carrie knew I had the option to sell the rights. It was clearly stated in the contract. What's ironic is that I need the money, in part, to pay for her legal expenses. Now, if you'll excuse me, I have to get back to my office. I'm expecting an email with a very important attachment. It's our contact. I have to sign it and get it back to him right away. See ya."

As Louise stepped away, Alex's face flushed with anger.

"Damn it! It's déjà vu all over again. I need to file an emergency injunction. Louise's contract with Carrie stipulated that the photos were never to be published, and that she'd remain anonymous. I know I can win this thing."

"No, Alex, I'm her attorney now, remember? I'm on it and I'll have an injunction filed by the end of the day. You go take care of her."

They rushed to the elevators, getting out in the atrium just in time to see Louise stepping out of a different one.

"Good luck," she said, rubbing it into their faces before she headed out of the building. She had a bounce in her step as she walked to the parking garage. Once inside her car, she powered up her phone and placed a call to Wyman's office. His secretary informed her that the paperwork had just been emailed. She disconnected the call and drove out of the parking garage, heading for the freeway. The onramp fed directly into the Deck Park Tunnel beneath downtown Phoenix. She merged into the traffic, anxious to get home. She wanted the contract signed and sent back to Wyman before he left for the day.

"Damn it."

She'd just changed lanes when the semi in front of her abruptly slowed down. She quickly looked for an opening in another lane, but there was heavy traffic on both sides. She turned her attention back to the road, just in time to hear a loud pop. The semi had blown a tire off one of its eighteen wheels. A huge chuck of rubber suddenly came out from underneath the trailer. Louise automatically swerved to the left to avoid it. She heard the loud honking from the car in that lane. She quickly swerved back to the right, but she overcorrected, nearly colliding with the car on her right. She jerked back the left, overcorrecting again and hitting the tire debris with a thud as her car began weaving uncontrollably. She slammed on the brakes, causing it to roll. She could hear the sound of screeching tires and honking horns, along with the impact of other vehicles colliding with hers. The last thing Louise Dickenson would ever see was the tunnel wall, coming straight at her.

❧Fifty-One❧

ALEX PULLED INTO THE driveway and hit the remote. He let out a sigh as he waited for the garage door to roll up. Carrie had been through too many months of angst over Louise's lawsuit, and now he had to tell her that a new, even worse, nightmare might be about to unfold. He grabbed his phone and placed a call to Reggie.

"How's it going?"

"I'm almost done," she replied. "It's coming out of the printer as we speak, then Brenda will have someone run it over to the court. This will definitely put a crimp into Louise's plans."

"Thanks, Reggie, I appreciate it. I know we'll win this one, at least I hope we will. I just hate having to break the news to Carrie. Hasn't she been through enough already?"

"Yes, she has, but she's strong and she's resilient. She'll get through this too."

Alex disconnected the call and went inside the house. As he greeted his parents, he overheard a news bulletin on TV about a road closure in he Deck Park Tunnel due to a fatal crash. He quickly excused himself, heading off to the master bedroom where he found Carrie napping on top of the bed. He kicked his shoes off and laid down next to her. The stress and emotional trauma of the previous day had suddenly caught up with him and he felt both mentally and physically drained. He cuddled up next to her, wrapping his arm around her and falling into a deep sleep.

"Alex?"

He was in the middle of a dream, but he could hear her voice in the distance.

"Alex, wake up."

This time he heard the sound of a television set along with her voice. The dream faded away and he opened his eyes. The room was now dark, with the only light coming from the television. Carrie was sitting up, watching the evening news.

"What time is it?"

"A few minutes past six. Alex, you won't believe this. They're reporting on the evening news that Louise has been killed in a car accident."

"What? That can't be. I just saw her a few hours ago at the courthouse. She came to Maggie's arraignment too."

"They're saying it happened around two-thirty this afternoon. Apparently, she was heading east in the Deck Park Tunnel when she somehow lost control of her car. It rolled and crashed into the wall. She was killed instantly."

He sat up, focusing on the television screen. They were showing a headshot of Louise, followed by footage of her badly crumpled car. It wasn't much more than a big chunk of twisted metal. A few other vehicles were also involved, but fortunately, all the other people had escaped with only minor injuries. The accident itself, however, had caused a major backup on the freeway that was still affecting the evening commute.

"Well, I'll be damned," he finally said. "I guess a higher court has intervened."

"What do you mean?"

"I'll explain it to you later, Carrie-Anne. Meantime, are you all right?"

"I'm fine, Alex. I'm not feeling any sense of loss or grief over Louise. I'm sorry she's dead, but after all that has happened, I've learned she wasn't the person I thought she was. I feel bad for Karl, though. He's a decent man."

They turned their attention back to the television set. The media had also learned about Carrie's connection to Scott.

She watched in horror as once again, the photos from *Gentry Magazine*, with certain portions blurred out, appeared on the screen. Before either could say anything they heard a knock at the bedroom door. Alex hopped off the bed and answered. His father was on the other side.

"Can I come in?"

"Of course," he replied.

Alex switched on the light as Armando burst into the room. He snatched the remote from the nightstand and turned off the TV.

"I don't want you two watching anymore of this. They've been trashing her for the past hour or so. They're twisting everything around and making her out to be a home-wrecker. It's like they're trying to pin the blame on her, instead of Maggie Andrews. I just got off the phone with Jonathan. He's livid, and so and am I. Then, about an hour ago, while you two were still asleep, I went to go get something out of the car, and I got ambushed by a news reporter."

"What!" exclaimed Alex. "That shouldn't have happened. There's a security guard parked in front of the house. He's supposed to be keeping the press from coming onto the property."

"I looked around before I went outside," said Armando, "and I didn't see any news trucks. The man who approached me looked like someone from the neighborhood. He was wearing blue jeans and he was walking a dog. He must have had a hidden camera on him."

"So, what did you tell him?"

"Well son, I looked him straight in the eye, and I told him I was housesitting. I said you'd taken Carrie out of town, but I didn't know where, and I had no idea when you'd return."

"Did he buy it?"

"He seemed to." Armando reached into his pocket and handed Alex the reporter's business card. "He turned around and left. But just to be on the safe side, we've closed all the drapes. You two need to stay away from the windows and not venture outside until this all blows over."

"Thanks, Dad. You handled it perfectly."

"I wonder," Carrie mused, "if I should call a press conference so I can tell my side of the story."

"No," said Alex and his father at the same time.

"Don't worry," added Alex, " this will blow over, just give it some time."

Over the next few days the news headlines began shifting away from Carrie. Jonathan Fields was released from the hospital that weekend, while Scott Andrews would face a long and difficult road to recovery. Carrie spent the next few weeks bonding with her newfound family as plans were put in place for her upcoming wedding.

Danny was fascinated with his older sister. Along with his passion for golf, he too had an interest in photography. Julia, however, was a little more apprehensive. She didn't want to be perceived as trying to take Linda's place. Her fears soon faded once Carrie told her, and Jonathan, about Bernie Carson, explaining that she and Bernie had become friends as well. She even reminisced about the times Bernie had given her cooking lessons, and how she still missed him, along with her mother. Jonathan was relieved in knowing that Linda had moved on from their failed marriage, and had found some happiness in her life before her untimely death.

The week before the wedding, Carrie went to Tucson to spend some time with her family and to oversee the final preparations. The small wedding she and Alex originally had in mind had grown bigger than they'd planned with the addition of Jonathan's younger sister and her family coming in from Florida, as well as members of Alex's extended family and most of his coworkers. George and Betty McCormick were also planning to attend.

The day before the wedding Jonathan took Carrie on a short hike along one of the rocky creeks in nearby Sabino Canyon. As usual, she brought along her camera, shooting photos of her father, as well as the spectacular scenery.

"I used to come here, a lot, when I first came to Tucson," explained Jonathan. "I'd find a nice, tranquil spot, like this one, and I'd sit for hours, trying to figure out how I was going to put the pieces of my life back together without putting another spoon up my nose."

"I can't even imagine what that must have been like. I'll admit I tried smoking a little pot once at a party back in college, but I didn't really like it. All it did was give me a bad headache. I just wasn't into the drug scene."

"That's good to know, Cara Mia, and I certainly don't want drug addiction to become a family legacy. I've been honest and upfront with your brother about all of this, but he's at the age and stage where I'm really starting to worry. Fortunately, with his interest in sports, he's surrounding himself with a good group of kids. Peer pressure is a big factor too, you know. That's how I got mislead. I'd made some poor choices for friends."

"Unfortunately, Dad, I too succumbed to a so-called friend's influence, and as a result I now have my own checkered past that I have to live with."

"I know, and one of the reasons why I brought you here today is so we can talk about it. None of us can undo what happened, but Alex and I have been able to do some damage control."

"What do you mean?"

"Alex decided not to mention this you at the time, but the day she was killed, Louise Dickenson had told him that she planned to sell the rights to all your photos to *Gentry Magazine.*"

Carrie couldn't believe what she was hearing. Her biggest fear was coming to life.

"What! She couldn't do that. Please don't tell me this whole nightmare is starting up again."

"Relax, Cara Mia, it's okay." He reached over and patted her arm. "Reggie filed an emergency injunction that very day with the court. Later on, we found out Louise had died before she'd signed the contract, so none of the photos were ever sent to the magazine. The deal never went through."

"That's all well and good, but upon her death the rights would have automatically gone to Karl, since he's her heir. So what's to stop him from selling the rights?"

"He already has."

"What! I don't believe this."

"Calm down, Carrie. Please, let me explain. Apparently, Karl was more of a friend to you than you were aware. He says he never backed Louise on the lawsuit. In fact, he says he tried to convince her to drop it."

"I see." Carrie's tone indicated she was unconvinced.

"The day you came down here Karl called Alex. He said he's trying to settle Louise's estate. He plans to dispose of her computer and all of her photography equipment, and he wanted to know if you were interested."

"I know. Alex called me, but I told him I already have everything I need."

"And that's what Alex told Karl. Then he said he wanted to get rid of the photos of you. He says he wants Louise to be remembered for her commercial work, you know, things like the Mercer's Markets ads, and he felt those particular photos tarnished her image as well as yours, so he signed the rights over to Alex."

"What? You're joking. So why didn't Alex tell me this?"

"Because we both wanted it to be a surprise."

"Oh I'm surprised, alright." There was a hint of sarcasm in her voice.

"Now, don't be angry, Cara Mia, it's all worked out for the best. Alex took the paperwork over to Karl's house and signed it. He had a number of unsold prints leftover from that gallery in Scottsdale, so Alex took them." Jonathan stopped to clear his throat. "So, whatever happens to them now is up to the two of you, and I don't need to know."

"Thanks, Dad. I'm sure he and I will figure something out."

"Anyway, there's more to the story. The files were still on Louise's computer, and Karl wants to include the computer in the estate sale, so that's when Alex called me. Yesterday morning I drove up to Phoenix and I replaced the hard drive. While I was there, Karl gave me all of Louise's memory cards. He says he's deleted all of them, but he wanted you to have them as a token of his good will."

Jonathan reached into his backpack, handing her a small envelope. She opened it and inspected the contents.

"Thanks, Dad. Now these I can use. I can never have too many memory cards." She immediately stuffed the envelope into her pocket.

"Wait, there's more." Once again Jonathan reached into his backpack, this time removing a plastic bag. "Think of this as an early wedding present from me to you."

He opened the bag and removed Louise's hard drive. He reached back into his backpack, this time taking out a hammer.

"You understand, Carrie, that we can't go back and get the prints that have already been sold, but what I can guarantee is that once this hard drive is destroyed, no others can ever be printed, and all of the unused photos will remain unseen forever. So, would you like to do the honor?"

"With pleasure."

Jonathan handed her the hard drive and the hammer. She carefully placed it on top of a rock, lifted up the hammer, and smashed it with all her might. He quickly gathered up all the broken pieces and dropped them back into the bag.

"And with that, Cara Mia, it's all over. At least as much as it can be."

Carrie wrapped her arms around him and held him tight.

"I love you, Daddy."

"I love you too. Now let's get going. We need to go home and change before we head over to the rehearsal."

❧Fifty-Two❧

THE FOLLOWING DAY'S forecast called for partly cloudy skies and mild temperatures and the weatherman delivered. As soon as breakfast was over, Carrie packed her bags and headed off to the Double-Diamond Resort for her appointment at the spa and beauty salon. Allison would meet her there, and after a few hours of pampering, it would be time to go up to her suite to get ready for the wedding.

Allison had helped her find the perfect bridal gown. It was a simple yet elegant tea-length dress in ivory satin with lace trim and a loose-fitting bodice. Completing the ensemble was a pair of ivory-colored Mary Janes and a wide-brimmed matching hat trimmed with silk flowers and lace.

"Oh no, please don't tell me." Carrie was smoothing out the front of her dress as Allison zipped up the back.

"What's wrong?"

"I've got a baby bump."

"You sure do," said Allison, "but barely shows. You'll be holding your flowers in front of you, so I doubt anyone will see it, and even if they do, it's not like it's a big secret."

"I've noticed lately that all my clothes have been getting too tight on me, so a couple days ago Julia and I went shopping for maternity clothes. I just didn't expect to be wearing them on my honeymoon."

"Well, I wouldn't worry about it. From what I know about the two of you, neither one of you will have your clothes on for much of time anyway."

They both burst out laughing. Afterwards, Allison helped her with her hat and jewelry She was also loaning her an antique blue cameo necklace.

"Now you've got something old, borrowed and blue, all at the same time, which means you have everything you need to be a happy bride."

"Allie, I don't know what to say."

"Don't say anything. Just know that I love you, and I'm happy to see you finally marrying the man of your dreams. I knew, even back in high school, that you two were meant for one another, but I guess both of you had to go out and experience life's hard knocks in order to figure it out for yourselves."

"I'm so glad to have you here with me, and you look stunning too. You did a great job picking out your dress."

Allison glanced at her watch. "Whoops. The photographer is supposed to be here in five minutes."

They quickly finished putting on the final touches. Exactly five minutes later they heard a knock at the door. Allison looked through the peephole.

"It's your dad, Carrie, and the wedding photographer is with him."

She opened the door to let them in. Jonathan looked handsome in his tuxedo. Other than the glasses and the slightly graying hair, he looked much as he did in the old photo Alex had found in her mother's papers. A photo that was now framed and proudly displayed in their home. As she greeted her father with a kiss, the wedding photographer came in to shoot a few photos of the bridal party. Before long it was time to get in the elevator and head down.

"Are you ready, Cara Mia?"

"I'm ready, Dad. How 'bout you?"

"Let's do it."

Allison led the way. The wedding was being held at the pool terrace; the same place where Carrie and Alex had once danced under the stars. A wedding arch, decorated with flowers, had been set up. Alex was waiting in front of it, decked out in his tux, with Mark standing beside him. As Jonathan walked her up the aisle and handed her over to Alex his eyes opened wide.

"You've got a baby bump," he whispered under his breath.

"I know," she whispered back with wink and a smile.

The minister gave them both a look before clearing his throat and beginning the ceremony. Once it was over, and the pictures were taken, they walked into a nearby tent where the reception was being held. As their guest greeted them with applause, the deejay began playing "Unchained Melody."

"Would you like to have this dance, Mrs. Montoya?"

"I'd be honored, Mr. Montoya."

Alex escorted her to the dance floor. Steve and Allison joined them, along with Jonathan and Julia, and George and Betty McCormick. Before long most of the other guests were on the dance floor as well.

"So, are you happy, Carrie-Anne. Really happy?"

"Yes, Alex. This has been the happiest day of my life. And you? Any regrets?"

"None. Well, maybe one."

"And what's that?"

"That we ever allowed ourselves to lose touch with one another in the first place." She rested her head on his shoulder as he led her around the dance floor. "But you know what, Carrie-Anne? You're still my best friend."

"And you're my best friend too, Alex. Now and forever."

❧Fifty-Three❧

SCOTT ANDREWS SURVIVED, but he continued on a long, painful road to recovery. He remained hospitalized for several weeks, having to undergo additional surgery before finally being well enough to return to Kansas City. By then, all the charges against him had been dropped. While he was recuperating, he married Nancy in a civil ceremony. Sarah, Ben, and Nancy's adult son, were the witnesses.

Maggie remained in jail, held without bond and without the means to hire an attorney. She continued to be represented by an over-worked, under-paid public defender. The case against her was strong. Even without Louise Dickenson's testimony, her photos were more than incriminating enough to prove her guilt beyond a reasonable doubt. With no other options available to her, Maggie finally asked her attorney to negotiate a guilty plea, hoping the judge would show mercy and give her a lighter sentence. After following the proper protocol, a sentencing hearing was scheduled for the Wednesday after Labor Day.

Alex woke up that morning to the usual sound of his alarm, but when he turned over he found himself alone in bed. Carrie's due date was only days away, so he quickly got up to look for her. He found her sitting at the dining table, sipping a cup of chamomile tea.

"Are you alright, Carrie-Anne?"

"I don't know." She took another sip of her tea. "I've been up since four-thirty this morning. I woke up with a backache. I guess I must have slept crooked or something, and then the baby's been kicking up a storm. So, I decided that as long as I was up, I'd do a little housecleaning. I was just taking a break."

"Delores can do that, and she'll here soon. Do you feel up to going to the hearing?"

"I have to, Alex. She's the one who sent those photos to *Gentry Magazine*, and then she tried to kill me, and our baby. This is my one chance to confront her in a court of law. I don't care how lousy I feel, I have to have closure."

"I understand, Carrie-Anne, and I have to have closure too." He squeezed her hand and gave her pregnant belly a pat before going into the kitchen to make a pot of coffee. When he returned, he went over their plans for the day.

"As it turns out, I have to be back in court today myself. The hearing I had yesterday is taking longer than expected, so we have to finish up this morning. The judge agreed to hold off until after Maggie's hearing which, as you know, is at nine o'clock. It shouldn't be more than an hour at the most, and then I'm due back in the other courtroom at ten. I figured your father wouldn't mind giving you a ride home."

"No, he won't—" Carrie abruptly stopped. "Dang that smarts."

"What's wrong? You're not having contractions, are you?"

"No, just some really sore back muscles. I'm okay. I'm not due for a few more days, remember?"

"I know, but even so, let's take it easy."

"I'm fine, Alex." She was beginning to sound irritated. "I promise, once the hearing's over, I'll head straight home and lie down, so stop worrying. Meantime, could you do me one little favor?"

"What's is it?"

"Could you please help me out of this chair?"

Ninety minutes later he dropped her off in front of the Sandra Day O'Conner Courthouse, telling her to wait inside while he parked. He no longer had the Camaro. It had been sold and he'd purchased a new SUV. Carrie smiled as she stepped out, noticing that he'd put the baby's car seat in the back. As he pulled away, she turned and faced the plaza. She took a deep breath before she walked across. She entered the building and found her father and stepmother waiting in the atrium as soon as she went through security.

"I'll be right with you," she said, hurrying past. "But first, I need to get to the ladies' room."

She rushed inside, trying to take care of business as quickly as she could. Once she finished, she dashed out the door, accidentally bumping into a man passing by.

"Pardon me, I'm so sorry." She looked up, not believing who she was seeing. "Doug! What on earth are you doing here?"

"Looking for you. I tried calling your studio, but your phone was disconnected and your website had been taken down. Then I heard about the sentencing hearing on the news so I came, hoping to find you, because I wanted to talk to you. I blew it, Carrie, big time. Letting you go was the biggest mistake of my life." He looked down and noticed that she was very pregnant. He also saw the wedding set on her left hand. His face fell. "But it appears that I'm a little too late, aren't I?"

"Yes, you are. So I take it things didn't work out with Jennifer after all."

"No, I'm afraid not," he sheepishly replied. "Jennifer and I are no longer together. I caught her cheating on me—with another woman."

Carrie didn't know whether she should laugh or cry.

"Well, Doug, I'm sorry that happened, but as you can see, I've moved on. And just so you know, even if I was single and available, I still wouldn't have taken you back. You cheated on me. I would have never been able to trust you again."

"Believe me, I understand." She heard the disappointment in his voice. "So, who's the lucky guy?"

"You remember me telling you about Alex Montoya, don't you?" Doug nodded. "Well, after you and I went our separate ways, Alex and I found one another again. He's now my husband, and as you can see, we're getting ready to have our first baby."

"Carrie-Anne!"

Alex was motioning for her to come join him. Jonathan and Julia were with him.

"I have to go now, Doug."

"Take care, Carrie." He extended his hand. "I'm glad it all worked out for you."

They wished each other a good life as Carrie stepped away to join her husband and her father.

"So who was that?" asked Alex as they waited for the elevator.

"Doug Sanders." Her voice sounded incredulous. "I stopped just long enough to tell him goodbye."

"You'll have to fill me in later. Meantime how's the backache?"

"Still there. It seems to be getting worse, not better."

"What's that?" asked Jonathan.

"Nothing, Dad. I just woke up this morning with back spasms, that's all."

The elevator doors opened, revealing an empty car. They stepped in and Alex pushed the button for their floor.

"And you're still having them?"

"Yes, Dad, but I'm fine. It's just a backache."

Jonathan and Julia looked at one another. "I said I had a feeling," said Julia.

"You sure did," replied Jonathan with a nod. He chose his next words very carefully. "Okay guys, I don't want anyone to panic, but I've had two kids and I was there every step of the way through the labor and delivery with both of them. This is exactly how it started with your mother, Carrie. I'm pretty sure you've gone into labor."

"What!" The color suddenly drained from Alex's face.

"I'm fine, Dad. I've had a few contractions off and on the past few days, but they were no big deal, and I've not had any today. My due date is still a few days off. It's just a backache, that's all."

The elevator stopped at their floor. They got off and headed to the courtroom.

"The baby will come when it decides it's ready to come," said Jonathan, firmly. "Hopefully, we'll be okay for the next few hours, at least long enough to get through the hearing. Meantime, your stepmother had a feeling, so we brought our suitcases with us, just in case." He turned to Alex. "You said you have to be in another courtroom when we're done, right?"

"Yeah, but I'll see if I can get out of it."

"Okay, but if you can't, don't worry. She'll probably go for hours before she delivers. We'll take her home as soon as the hearing's over, and we'll stay with her until you get back. If you're still in court by the time she needs to go to the hospital, we can take her. If we do, I'll send you a text message."

"Thanks, Jonathan. I appreciate it."

They entered the courtroom. As they took their seats in the gallery, she noticed another man seated nearby, accompanied by two women. She was shocked once she realized it was Scott. He looked as if he'd aged ten years. His face was pale, he'd lost a good forty pounds, and his salt and pepper hair was nearly all gray. He, too, looked surprised when saw her and noticed she was pregnant. A few news reporters were also there, but so far they'd not approached them. Alex noticed them as well.

"Don't worry, Carrie-Anne," he whispered. "If they try to bother you I'll take care of it."

The doors opened, and three deputy U.S. Marshalls entered with Maggie Andrews, in shackles and dressed in a black and white striped jail suit. She was led to one of the two tables in front of the bench, where she was joined by her attorney.

"You've got to be kidding me," Carrie whispered to Alex. "That little snip of a woman is Maggie Andrews?"

"Hard to believe, isn't it?"

All were ordered to rise as the judge, Virginia Jarrett, entered the courtroom.

"Be seated," she said as she took her seat at the bench. The case was called, and she asked for the record if Maggie Andrews had agreed to change her plea to guilty.

"She has, Your Honor," replied her attorney.

The judge went on to explain that a sentencing hearing was less formal than a trial, and that each of the three victims would be allowed to speak freely before she handed down her sentence. Carrie was called first. As she approached the bench, she was asked to state her name for the court.

"My name is Caroline Daniels Montoya."

"Please go on, Mrs. Montoya."

"Thank you, Your Honor. About a year and half ago, before I was married, I met Scott Andrews at an art gallery opening. He presented himself to me as a single man, and yes, I did have a relationship with him. Then, once I began to suspect that he wasn't single after all, I immediately ceased all contact with him, and I deeply regret that I was an unwitting party to his infidelity." She turned to face Maggie. "However, that does not give you the right to do what you did to me. You stole my identity to make it appear as if I had plagiarized another photographer's work, and I admit that you did succeed, at least for a time, in turning my world upside down. In fact, you made my life a living hell, which was your intention all along, wasn't it? Then the truth came out, as it always does, and when it did, you attempted to kill me, along with child I'm carrying. You're idea of revenge is sick and twisted, and in the end, all your little plots have backfired. But don't you dare try to blame any of this on me. You're the one who did it to yourself. I want you to understand that I don't hate you, but I'm incredibly relieved knowing that you'll be behind bars for many, many years to come." She stopped and looked at the judge. "Thank you, Your Honor. That's all I have to say." She turned and went back to her seat.

"Bravo, Carrie-Anne," whispered Alex. "You just made me very proud."

"Thanks, Alex." She reached over and squeezed his hand.

Jonathan Fields was called next.

"It's kind of a strange story, Your Honor, of how I got to be here. Mrs. Montoya is my daughter." He stopped for a moment to give Scott Andrews a strong look. "I'm also the one who traced all the Internet activity on Scott's computer that day, Mrs. Andrews. No doubt you thought you were being clever, but in reality, you're a rank amateur. I knew, then and there, that it was only a matter of time before we got the goods on you. I was also in Carrie's office the day she got the threatening letter you sent her, and I don't take kindly to anyone who threatens one of my kids." He turned to face Scott again.

"And as for you... I've read each and every one of the emails that you sent to my daughter, you son of a—" Jonathan caught himself before he finished his sentence. He turned to face the judge. "I apologize, Your Honor, I guess I got carried away."

"The court understands, Mr. Fields. Please continue."

"Actually, I think I'm about done, Your Honor. That day, when we left this very courthouse, I saw her standing in the plaza. She just didn't look right, so my radar immediately went up. As soon as I saw her reach underneath her overcoat I knew what she was going to do, so I did the only thing I could do. I took the bullet for my daughter. That's why she and my grandchild are still here. If it was up to me, I'd send her to the gallows and I'd pull the lever myself. Thank you."

Jonathan returned to the gallery and Carrie stood and embraced him. As they took their seats, Judge Jarrett called Scott Andrews. He cautiously approached the bench.

"Thank you, Your Honor. In spite of being a victim myself, it seems I've also been made out to be one of the bad guys, and unfortunately, there's some validity to what they've said about me. Yes, I cheated on Maggie, and yes, I mislead Carrie into thinking I was single when I wasn't. Maggie had every right to be angry, but instead of venting her anger on me, she chose to vent it out on Carrie, in spite of the fact that I'd already left her my present wife." He turned to point out Nancy to the court, along with his sister.

"Now, I know what a big mistake I made. I was living a double life, and for a time there I really thought I had the best of both worlds. I'd chase after other women, and when I was through, I went home to my wife. The problem was, with the exception of Nancy, I didn't think of those other women as human beings. Her father's right. I was a callous son of a bitch. I have a daughter myself. She's going on seventeen, and if someone did something like that to her, I'd be furious, so father to father, I apologize to you, Mr. Fields."

"Whatever," mumbled Jonathan to himself.

"Anyway, I'm happy knowing that Carrie's now married and is about to start her own family. She's entitled to any happiness coming her way. That said, I've paid a high price for my infidelity. I was hauled off to jail for a crime I didn't commit. I lost my job, my dignity, and I nearly lost my life as well."

He was starting to become emotional. He stopped for a moment to compose himself.

"Don't get me wrong. Maggie did what she did of her own free will, and she knew what she was doing was wrong. That's why she tried to frame me for it. She most certainly deserves whatever punishment the court decides to hand down to her. I'm just saying that my own actions were, unfortunately, the catalyst for her to do the things she did, and for that I take full responsibility. Thank you, Your Honor."

"Thank you, Mr. Andrews." Judge Jarrett turned to Maggie. "Is there anything you wish to tell me, Mrs. Andrews, before I hand down your sentence?"

"Yes, Your Honor, I do."

"Then go ahead."

"Well, this has all been very touching, in a saccharine sort of way." Everyone could hear the venom in her voice. "So, Daddy's Little Girl gets to walk away free and happy and isn't that nice? Well, I did what I did to make a point. Scott always assumed that I was an imbecile. I wanted to prove to him that I wasn't, and what better way to do it than for me to bring down the Mercer's Markets girl."

The judge slammed down her gavel. Maggie ignored her and kept talking.

"I wanted the whole world to know that the innocent little girl from those old TV commercials grew up to become a whore."

Again the judge slammed down her gavel. Her attorney tried to speak, but Maggie cut him off.

"But hey, Carrie, it wasn't all bad. I arranged it so you'd get the prize money from the photo contest and you were getting five grand out of the deal."

The judge banged her gavel again. "Control your client, Counselor."

"I'm trying, Your Honor, but she won't listen."

Maggie began shouting over her attorney. "I figured as long as you were a whore you might as well be paid for being one, but no, you had to be a crybaby and go running off to the cops, didn't you? This is all your fault, Carrie. You can stop banging that gavel now, Judge, because I'm done."

The room went silent. Carrie cringed with another back spasm. Everyone could see she was in distress.

"Are you alright, Mrs. Montoya?"

"I'm not sure, Your Honor. I'm nine months pregnant, and I woke up this morning not feeling well."

"I understand." She turned to address Maggie. "Margaret Constance Andrews, you've plead guilty to all the charges against you, and you've shown no remorse for what you've done. In fact, you've done just the opposite. You've gone out of your way to demonstrate your contempt for the victims of your crimes. Therefore, I'm sentencing you to thirty years in the federal prison for each of the four counts of attempted first-degree murder, plus three years each for the counts of forgery and identity theft, and mailing a threatening communication."

She went over a few last-minute details before she banged her gavel and turned her attention to her clerk. As the other people in the gallery started to leave, the deputies hauled Maggie away.

"It's all over, Carrie-Anne." Alex stood up to leave. He bent to down kiss her on the cheek. "I have to go over to the superior court and take care of business, but I should done by lunchtime at the latest. Are you sure you're all right?"

"I'm fine, Alex. I'm still a little shaken by the things she was saying about me, so I'd like to stay here for a few minutes and pull myself back together, if that's okay."

"That's fine. As soon as you're ready your dad and stepmom will run you home. I'll call you as soon as I'm done."

Alex said goodbye and made his exit. A few minutes later she felt ready to leave, but as soon as she stood she doubled over. Jonathan and Julia helped her back into her seat.

"Holy Mother of God, make it stop!"

Judge Jarrett banged on her gavel. "Are you alright, Mrs. Montoya?"

"I think so," replied Carrie, trying to catch her breath. "For a moment there I thought I was dying. I'm so sorry. I didn't mean to disrupt the court."

"I was watching you during the hearing and I thought something might be happening. I think we need to get you to a hospital. Would you like to have my clerk call an ambulance?"

"No thank you, Your Honor. For the moment I'm okay and I'd rather have my father take me." A bad memory suddenly flashed across Carrie's mind. "What about Alex?"

"We'll take care of that," said Jonathan. "I'll send him a text message as soon as we get to the hospital."

He helped Carrie to her feet and began walking her out of the courtroom. When they reached the door Carrie turned back to face the judge.

"Thank you, Your Honor."

"Good luck, Mrs. Montoya, and have a happy, healthy baby."

☙Fifty-Four☙

JONATHAN PULLED THE white Camaro up to the plaza. Julia walked Carrie to the passenger door and helped her into the passenger seat. Once Carrie was inside, Jonathan briefly stepped out to help his wife into the backseat.

"She had another big one while you were gone," Julia remarked as they sped away.

"You know, I've really missed this car," said Carrie. "I'm glad it's still in the family."

"Yeah, but I'm having a hell of a time keeping your brother out of it."

"Here we go again." She started having another contraction.

"Breathe, Carrie," said Julia, reaching over the seat to hold her by the shoulders. "C'mon, deep breaths. There you go. That's right."

As the contraction eased, Carrie looked up and noticed the traffic light ahead was turning yellow.

"No! Don't change. Don't change."

"Carrie, calm down." Jonathan reached over and squeezed her hand. "I'll get you to the hospital in plenty of time and in one piece, I promise."

"Sorry, Dad." She reached into her purse and grabbed her phone. "I need to send a text message to Allison. She's my birthing coach."

The light changed while Carrie was texting. She knew Allison was in class and wouldn't be able to leave for a few hours. She sent a message to Alex as well. When he didn't reply, she knew it meant he was still in court. Ten minutes and another contraction later, Jonathan pulled up to the birthing center at Sonoran Southwest Medical Center. Julia exited the car on the driver's side, helping Jonathan get Carrie out. Each had their arm around her as they walked her inside.

"Our daughter's gone into labor," announced Jonathan as they approached the admissions clerk. She handed Carrie the usual paperwork to sign. By the time she finished, someone arrived with a wheelchair.

"Oh my God, it's happening again," she shouted as they began wheeling her down the hallway toward the elevators. "I don't think I can take this much longer."

"You'll be fine," assured Julia. "Tell them to give you a epidural."

"But I wanted natural childbirth. I want to be able to push."

"Carrie, it's the twenty-first century, and you don't need to impress us, okay. Take it from me, get the epi. You'll still be able to push."

The elevator arrived. Moments later they reached her floor and wheeled her into her room. It looked more like someone's bedroom at home instead of a hospital room. Here Carrie would have her labor and delivery, and the baby would stay in the room with her once it was born. Two nurses were waiting, explaining they would be with her throughout the whole process. One of them handed her a hospital gown. She took it into the bathroom to change. Julia went with her to help. She'd no sooner gotten into the gown when her water broke.

"Oh no! This is so embarrassing. Let me see if someone will bring me a mop so I can clean it up."

"Carrie, relax," said Julia with a smile. "You're about to give birth so don't worry about cleaning up the floor. They'll take care of it. You just saved them the trouble of having go in and break it for you."

When they opened the door, Carrie announced that her water had broken. The nurse stepped in the bathroom to take a look. She smiled, saying they'd take care of it.

"See, what did she tell you? You're fine."

Carrie glanced at the bed. It had been covered with plastic and disposable pads.

"If you ladies don't mind, I think I'll go hang out in the waiting room for awhile," said Jonathan. "I'll send Alex another text message. Come get me if you need anything."

Carrie walked up to her father and hugged him.

"Thanks, Dad. I love you."

"I love you too, Cara Mia. I'll be right outside if you need me."

"She'll be fine, Jonathan," added Julia. "I'll be right here with her."

He kissed them both goodbye and stepped out. After he left, Julia helped her onto the bed, holding her hand while the nurse examined her.

"Wow, five centimeters already. Good job."

Carrie looked at her stepmother. "I'm scared, Julia."

"It's okay." Julia reached over and smoothed Carrie's hair. "I know it's scary, but you're in the best of hands and you're going to be just fine. I'll be right here with you, I promise."

"Uh-oh!"

Carrie started having another contraction, this time she screamed in pain. Once it finally stopped and she caught her breath, she asked for the epidural. An anesthesiologist was summoned, and once it was administered she began to relax. Her pain was under control. She even joked about going out and getting her nails done. Julia sat by her side and held her hand. An hour later Jonathan stepped back in to check on her, and as soon as he left the nurse examined her again.

"Still five centimeters."

"You mean there's no change?"

"Not yet, but don't worry. We're watching the fetal monitor closely and everything's fine. This'll take awhile. It usually does."

Carrie groaned as she leaned back on the bed. A minute later she heard her phone beeping. Julia handed it to her.

"It's a text message from Alex."

They could hear the relief in her voice. She quickly responded to his message, asking him to bring her overnight bag. He arrived about an hour later to find Carrie sitting up on the edge of the bed.

"Carrie-Anne, are you alright? Is everything okay?"

"I'm fine, Alex."

"You're sure you're okay?"

"She's fine," said one of the nurses. "We've given her an epidural, so she's not feeling any pain or discomfort from the contractions."

"The epidural won't hurt the baby?"

"No," said the nurse, shaking her head. "It won't hurt the baby at all, and trust me, it makes things a whole lot easier on the mother."

Carrie started rolling her head around. "You know what would feel really good right now? A nice backrub. Right along my neck and shoulders."

"You got it," said the other nurse, who immediately started to work.

"We're helping her relax," added Julia. "She needs to save her energy for when the time comes to start pushing."

"When will that be?"

"Not for some time," said the nurse. "She's only dilated six centimeters."

"It's a waiting game," added Julia, "but as you can see, she's doing fine."

"So how long do these things usually take?"

One of the nurses started to respond, but Carrie cut her off. "Alex, why don't you go get my father, and you guys can go out and get a pizza, or go to a movie, or a ballgame, or whatever. I'm not on a time schedule. It's going to be awhile. You need to go take a chill pill, and let me do what I gotta do, okay. We'll call you when we're ready."

"Carrie-Anne?"

Julia walked up to him and gently pulled him aside.

"She's in labor, Alex, and even though they've given her something for the pain, she's still, understandably, feeling very anxious, so please, don't take it personally. It'll be sometime yet, so why don't you and Jonathan go grab some lunch? We'll call you as soon as she's ready."

Alex grudgingly stepped out. A few more hours passed with little progress. Allison finally arrived around four-thirty.

"Uh-oh, so what happened to you?" asked Julia.

"Steve and I got a suite at the Double-Diamond Resort the night of Carrie's wedding, and now the joke around his office is if you want to get knocked up, go to the Double-Diamond. At least my baby bump isn't that big yet."

"Hey guys, I think something's happening," exclaimed Carrie. "I'm starting to feel some pressure and the urge to push."

The nurse examined her again. "Finally. You're fully dilated and the baby's head is beginning to crown. Do you want to watch in the mirror?"

"No thanks, but would someone please go get Alex."

"You got it," said Julia. "What about your dad?"

"It's up to him. I could care less right now about who else wants to come in here. I just want to get this baby out."

Julia stepped out, returning a few minutes later with Alex. Someone handed him a surgical gown while she explained that Steve had just arrived, and Jonathan wanted to stay in the waiting room with him. As Alex was getting into the gown, the nurse midwife took her position at the foot of the bed and examined Carrie.

"It's show time," she announced. "When I say, 'push' I want you to lift her up by the shoulders. When she's done pushing, let her rest. Dad, you can stay up there with her, or come down here with me. It's up to you."

"I think I'll stay and help with the lifting, for now."

Alex took Carrie's hand, and as she started having the next contraction, she was told to push. They lifted her by the shoulders and afterwards they let her relax. They quickly fell into a routine. An hour later the midwife announced that the baby's head was visible.

"You may want to come down here, Dad. You really don't want to miss this."

Alex squeezed Carrie's hand and walked to the foot of the bed. "Whoa!"

He could see the top of a small head, covered with reddish hair, protruding out from between Carrie's legs. A moment later she pushed again, and more of the head began to appear. Alex watched in total awe. His child was coming into the world. As she continued pushing, one of the nurses began to suction the fluids out of the baby's nose and mouth.

"Just a few more, Carrie. We're almost done. Once the shoulders are out, I can ease the rest of the baby out."

"Come on, Carrie-Anne." Alex reached over and began stroking her leg. "One more ought to do it."

Carrie took a deep breath and gave one last, final push. The midwife pulled the rest of the baby out and she let out a loud squall. They quickly noted the time of birth. Alex stood in awe as the nurse handed her to him.

"Congratulations, Dad, you've got a beautiful baby girl. Did you want to cut the cord?"

The baby quieted down, opened her eyes and looked around the room. They were gray, just like her father's.

"You go ahead," said Alex. He was still in too much in awe. The cord was clamped and as soon as it was cut, he walked up and presented her to her mother. Carrie sat up and held her for a moment as the others looked on.

"You've finally got your family princess, Alex."

"I know, Carrie-Anne. I love you, more than you could possibly know."

After he leaned over and kissed her, one of the nurses tapped him on the shoulder.

"We need to get her cleaned up and checked out, and we have some final business to take care of with her mother, so why don't you come with me?"

"Go with her, Alex," said Carrie. "The baby clothes are in my bag. Could someone please get something for her to wear?"

"I've got it," replied Allison. She opened the bag, quickly picking out a little white outfit. The nurse told her to come and bring it along. He stopped to give Carrie another kiss before he took the baby and followed them out.

"I'll go tell the others," said Julia. She stepped out to the waiting room where she was met by two anxious faces.

"Well?" Jonathan finally asked.

"It's a girl." She walked up to embrace him. "I guess this means we're grandparents now."

Allison soon joined them, and a short time later Alex brought his newborn daughter into the room. She was dressed in her white outfit, with a little pink hat, and wrapped in a little pink blanket. His face was beaming.

"I'd like to introduce all of you to my daughter, Alexis Penelope Montoya. She came in at twenty inches long, seven pounds, three ounces, and no bullet burn."

Everyone gathered around to see the baby and to congratulate him as they took pictures with their cell phones. Alex handed the baby over to Jonathan to let him hold her while he got his phone and snapped a few photos. When he was finished he handed the phone to Julia. He stood next to Jonathan and they held the baby together as she snapped a few more photos. Afterwards, he handed the baby back to her grandfather while he sent the pictures to his parents and brother. Once he was done, he took the baby back so Steve would have a chance to see her. A few minutes later one of the nurses came into the room.

"Mom says to bring her back, right now, or else she's coming out to get her."

"I take it she's ready for visitors," said Alex.

"Ready and waiting."

Alex led the troupe into Carrie's room. She'd had a chance to freshen up and change into a pair of pajamas, and she was now comfortably relaxed in her bed. Her face was also beaming as she reached for the baby. Alex handed her over as he greeted her with a kiss and took a chair next to her.

"So, how are you feeling, Carrie?" asked Allison.

"Relieved." Everyone had a laugh. "And I'm looking forward to finally being able to see my feet again."

The nurses stepped out, giving Carrie and Alex some time to bond with their daughter and share the moment with their family and closest friends. Before long, Alex's phone started ringing. His parents and brother had just received their first pictures of Alexis and were calling to congratulate him. In a family with a propensity for having boys, a girl was a welcome surprise.

"Of course you know the next one will be a boy," he said to Carrie once he ended the calls.

"I know that, Alex, but let me recover from having this one before we start working on the next one, okay?" She watched as the baby yawned and fell asleep. Alex took her and gently laid her down in the bassinette.

"Well, I guess that's our cue," said Jonathan. "Come on everyone, dinner's on Grandpa."

"No, it's on Dad," argued Alex. He stopped to kiss Carrie goodbye, telling her he'd be back soon. The others stopped to give her a hug and a kiss as well. The two men were still arguing over who would pick up the dinner tab as they all began to exit.

"Julia, I really want to thank you for being here," said Carrie as she reached for her stepmother's hand. "Today's been one of those days when I've missed my mother terribly, and I'm so glad you're here with me."

"My pleasure, Carrie. You get some rest. We'll be back to check on you later." She bent down to kiss Carrie on the forehead before she stepped away.

The following morning Alex took his wife and daughter home. Julia would be staying with them for a few days, and Alex's parents would come the following week. Once Alexis was taken to the nursery, fed, changed and settled into her crib, Carrie went into the kitchen. She found a bottle of fruit juice in the refrigerator, and after she poured herself a glass she gazed out the kitchen window. A technician was installing an alarm on the pool fence while a landscaper was starting to work on the backyard. As she watched, she began to reminisce. It was a year to the day since she'd sat on the patio watching Alex as he took an evening swim. That was the time when she'd wondered who the future mother of his children would be, thinking the day would come when she'd have to step aside for her. She smiled to herself as she lifted her glass and took a drink, relieved in knowing that day would never come. She and Alex would be best friends forever.

THE END

❧Alex's Macaroni & Cheese❧

2 cups macaroni, cooked and drained
2 $^1/_2$ cups milk
1 cup sour cream
2 $^1/_2$cups grated Mexican cheese blend
(or 2 $^1/_2$ cups cheddar)
$^1/_2$ cup grated Parmesan cheese
4 tablespoons butter, divided
1 teaspoon salt
1 teaspoon dry mustard
$^1/_4$ teaspoon paprika
$^1/_3$ cup breadcrumbs.

Preheat oven to 350° and cook the macaroni in boiling water for 8 to 10 minutes. Drain. While pasta is cooking whisk milk and sour cream in a medium-sized mixing bowl and add seasonings. Set aside. Chop two tablespoons of butter into small pieces. Chill in refrigerator until needed. Melt remaining 2 tablespoons of butter in a small mixing bowl. Add breadcrumbs, blend thoroughly and set aside.

Layer half of the cooked and drained macaroni, chopped butter, and cheese into an 8 x 8 inch baking dish. Top with remaining macaroni, butter and cheese. Pour milk mixture over the top and sprinkle on the breadcrumb mixture. Bake for approximately 30 minutes, or until the top is crispy and brown.

If desired, ham or sausage may be added. Low-fat milk, sour cream and cheeses may also be used.

About the Author

Photo by Tombstone
Photo Studios
Tombstone, Arizona

Just like Gillian Matthews, the heroine in her debut romance novel, *The Reunion*, Marina Martindale began her career as a graphic designer and artist. After submitting a few articles to trade publications she discovered that writing was her true calling. Her life experiences, and those of the people around her, are the inspiration for her novels.

Marina Martindale is currently working on her third romance novel, *The Journey*. She resides in Tucson, Arizona, and in her spare time she enjoys traveling, photography, quilt making, and cooking.

For more information about Marina Martindale please visit her website at www.marinamartindale.com, or her blog at www.marinamartindale.net.

CPSIA information can be obtained at www.ICGtesting.com
Printed in the USA
BVOW08s1333260913

332119BV00001B/3/P